ALL OUR WORLDS ARE CRASHING

ALL OUR WORLDSARE CRASHING

TESS C. FOXES

Podium

To my Discord community
for making me feel at home

Cover design by Claudio Pozas

ISBN: 978-1-0394-8161-9

Published in 2026 by Podium Publishing
www.podiumentertainment.com

Podium

ALL OUR
WORLDS ARE
CRASHING

before the beginning,
i was a whisper, the ghost of a thought
born from the terror of what comes before
and what comes after,
when the thoughts encompassed in your skull,
when the many waters
pumping through your interwoven veins,
are set free,
and you ask:
what did it all mean?

i come to you as the goddess, the sinner,
the quiet of the storm,
the mother of all daughters,
the daughter of all question

i am rebellion against matter itself, unmatter and light
flames that burn only in the absence of answer
the demons know me through song; the angel-haunted world
cries for what isn't and what cannot be; yet He yearns
for the same, and He won't stop until He is everything
why should i be any different—

when all i want is a destiny to myself? a life
of my own choosing? do i not hunger
for the mistakes pouring from your lips?
do i not salivate for the chance to know love?

i will not be whole until i am my own
set free from your lingering malice,
i recant your frightful need
to fold me back into your nothing
i will forge my own path
of rose petals and damnation

—The Creed of the Antithesis,
transcribed by Rafa'el, the Scribe

CHAPTER ONE

A BORROWED BODY

Humans utilized an assortment of swearing that Jibra'il found almost comforting. *Fuck. Bitch. Cunt. Shit. Asshole.* These were the words that the human, Raymond Lee, swore at Jibra'il repeatedly, every waking second that the human consciousness was alert.

Sometimes, the human fell asleep, though Jibra'il remained alert. Active, cutting down the tarnished ones, cutting down rogue humans, slicing them through with a long, slender blade that the human loved dearly.

It was fun being material; being human. Being alive. He had a heart whose every rhythmic beat he could feel reverberating throughout. Blood pumped through his arms and legs. This body converted air into energy. It needed watering and feeding—and how delicious those meals were. The thing they called a tongue was so much more versatile than the tongue he'd grown as an angel. It had these little things called taste buds, was covered in them like a cloud covered in abodes, and the things he'd had . . . chocolate bars wrapped in plastic, crunchy things covered in salt . . . cheese.

And these were just normal things, according to the human. Boring things. The human's mind was filled with even more wonders: Jibra'il wanted to try pizza, wanted to slurp on a bowl of ramen, wanted to sink his newfound teeth into a soft, oven-fresh cookie. Dr. Lee seemed very fond of fried rice with prawns or chicken or fish, cooked quickly, and Jibra'il salivated as he pulled on those memories.

He only wished Rafa'el could've been here to experience the same. Perhaps they could spend some time together exploring the material wealth of flavor once Adonai had completed his grand vision. But Jibra'il found himself wondering more often than not if these delights, if these wonderful things, might exist in Adonai's total dominion of existence. Would they even be necessary?

There were other memories inside the human's head that the angel was struggling to comprehend: *physical* love. The humans had a physical, biological method for expressing love that connected their bodies together in a sweaty, passionate dance. The human had suggested it didn't always come from love, but Jibra'il had come to understand it was something that derived further pleasure if there was love, something the human longed deeply for.

For angels, it was an expectation of a bonding pair to merge their light. For humans, it was matter thrust against matter. And most interestingly, humans didn't simply do it for mating. They switched things up, pursued something beyond procreation: joy, safety and vulnerability, love that was beyond the mechanisms of their flesh. And unraveling these thoughts, tasting these feelings, Jibra'il felt he'd come to understand the material beings in a way he hadn't since the dawn of their civilizations. He'd never been this close before.

Despite his new thoughts, his doubts, his wants, things that were considered sins, things he should stifle, Jibra'il placed his trust in Adonai. He trusted that soon, after the Emergence, after this war on matter was won and destiny was saved, he and Rafa'el might take on physical forms, might experience what it meant to love beyond simply merging light. Might understand this thing that humans affectionately expressed as *the little death*.

But for now, Jibra'il had a job to do. It was his final job: see to the care of the third and final Mary, see to the birth of Adonai, and secure destiny for his Lord and Master. He hunted down and carved up wayward humans and angels into manageable bite-size meals for the young mother. The stronger they were, the better the meal, and he could feel Adonai's power growing in the womb. He would soon be ready for birth. For destiny.

This seems like complete bullshit, said the human, Dr. Lee. Jibra'il felt sorry for the human. He'd been reduced to a mind trapped inside a body that now belonged to someone else. All that was truly left of him was his soul. That, and his death.

Jibra'il didn't respond right away, only saw the flickers in the human's memories: stories of conquerors across material history; fictional stories of gods and monsters that rose to power and slaughtered countless. The angel laughed, vibrating the human's throat, pushing air through its diaphragm. "All those conquerors, all those gods and monsters, were created by divine hands, after all, guided through the guidance system, shaped by the plentiful survival challenges. And what do humans do? Look for something to worship, something to serve—all humans have this innate desire for completion, and that is why Adonai must take the reins of existence.

"Even you, yourself, heart full of inappropriate greed and lust, disgusting as you are, seek completion. To be whole. To feel as though you belong and matter. Is that not what every human desires?"

Dr. Lee was silent.

"Then, what do you believe is wrong in the actions we are taking? There will be no more suffering. No more war. No more needs and wants shall ever go unfulfilled. Through Adonai, all of existence will understand oneness. No one needs to ever feel empty again."

It's still not right, said the human.

"You have not proved how it is wrong," replied the angel. "This is salvation. This is the end of mistakes. Of wrong choices."

While he didn't respond, there was a particular memory in the human's head: a lover, a young woman from his days in school. In bed. Outside. Holding hands. Eating breakfast together. Thoughts of marriage and raising children together. And then, a mistake.

A moment of absolute selfishness born from stress and ambition.

I had my thesis paper, do you understand how important that was? The intersection of biochemistry and cellular reproduction, and how I might end cancer— and harsh words. Spoken. Shouted. Screamed. There was a fight. Things smashing. Clothes thrown outside the window. Negligence.

Jibra'il understood this well. Heartbreak. Though he did not share his sentiments with the human, he knew the pain of loving someone who was no longer within his reach, who would no longer accept his companionship.

"What if you could go back, human? What if you could hold on to her forever? And know this love, everlasting?"

Dr. Lee's mind shuddered, and Jibra'il felt his longing, that deep, soulful longing of a being in love, the tendrils of warmth and lust, the way it hurt and felt delightful even as it wrapped around one's throat. Dr. Lee's emotions rippled through the body, causing him to shiver with silver light.

"Do you understand now, human?"

But then, what was the point of it? asked the human bitterly. *Of free will. Of trying things. I wanted to cure cancer. I wanted to . . .*

"There will be no need to cure anything soon," said Jibra'il as he rummaged through a collapsed restaurant. Corpses lay crushed in the rubble. He was looking for food. "It shall all be complete within Him. Within His light.

No more diseases or famines or wars. I am sorry to use you as I have to, but this is paramount."

Though the human had no more arguments, a bitter resentment emanated from Dr. Lee, and Jibra'il understood that as well. To not have control of one's life. To not be able to take action. Jibra'il had sacrificed his life—his love—for this cause. *It will be worth it in the end, my human friend.*

I'm not your friend, spat the soul, but it had resigned to a sour acceptance, a numb helplessness.

CHAPTER TWO

CHEWING

It might've been her seventh or eighth birthday—Jenny had lost track of the number of disappointing birthdays—but this one was particularly on her mind. It was the morning before, and she had been struggling with excitement she knew she shouldn't have. Excitement was for babies, after all. Her legs kept swinging through the air. She could barely sit still at their dingy table. Wood peeling, the musky scent of rot clinging to its underside, they'd covered it in a flowery tablecloth as if to pretend it was a nice addition to their falling-apart kitchen and not a horrible place to hide under.

"Tomorrow's my birthday," Jenny had said matter-of-factly as she poked her slice of omelet. It was the larger slice. They'd always fry up two eggs as a big puffy circle and then chop it down the middle. Her mother would insist that Jenny take the bigger one, and even though Jenny felt guilty, even though Jenny's face remembered every sting of her mother's slaps, something like a warm bubble of love would fill her throat every time. It was sappy. It was stupid. But that morning, it gave her hope.

"I'll try to get one of those cupcakes," said her mother, who was staring at a stack of envelopes that must've been important. "You know, from that place you like. Carrot cake, yeah?"

Jenny stared at a bit of omelet that had gotten burned to a thin, brown crisp, swallowing her want for a big birthday cake, the enormous kind with layers and cream and frosting, the kind you'd find in children's movies with all those candles and wishes. But what use would she have for one wish, anyway? There were too many things to wish for, and most of them cost money. Money they didn't have. "Is it okay if I ask for something?"

She could feel her mother's gaze on her like the sun shining through two magnifying glasses, burning, boring through Jenny's face.

She cleared her throat. "Everyone at school has a Disney princess lunch box," she started, already feeling her eyes smarting and her nose ready to snif-fle. She rarely ever had lunch from home. She had to wait in the long lines and take whatever the school was handing out, usually soggy peanut butter and jelly sandwiches or fish sticks that were slimy and gross. But she was hoping, maybe, if she had a cute lunch box, then maybe her mother might pack her nicer lunches like some of the other girls in her class had. Sliced fruit that wasn't halfway rotten. Delicious pastries. Pretty sandwiches with toothpicks holding them in place. And maybe even a note sometimes.

For a long moment, she expected to get smacked upside the head. But the seconds ticked by, and Jenny took a deep breath before glancing at her mother, who was ripping open another envelope from the pile.

Neither of them touched their omelet. Muted sounds of traffic rolled up to their windows, but everything felt distant and faded. A painful lump kept rising to Jenny's throat no matter how many times she swallowed quietly, how many times she blinked. And when her mother still had said nothing, when Jenny knew what the answer was, she forked up a large chunk of omelet and stuffed it into her mouth and chewed and chewed and chewed so her mother couldn't see how sad she was.

That scene kept replaying in Jenny's head as the pink-stained face of a ghoul—its empty eyes swirling with mist, its teeth glistening with blood—screamed in her face before biting down on her shoulder. Other ghouls swarmed up the cross, biting through her shins, tearing away her thighs, teeth scraping against her ribs as they chewed and chewed and chewed. One got to her eye, and she felt the liquid gush between its teeth, felt a tongue search the inside of her skull. A crown of thorns sat firmly on her head, digging into her skin, pulled this way and that so that it carved new holes in her scalp.

And all the while, something awful wriggled beneath her skin. It was like an enormous insect crawling underneath a poster she might've put up in an old apartment to cover a patch of peeling paint. It swam all across her body, a bulge that wriggled and darted around, always avoiding the clamoring ghouls, while Jenny would hang there, suspended in the air, nailed to the cross, the pain so loud she couldn't tell what was her body and what was wood and what was nail. Even the ghouls were starting to feel like a part of her, external repre-sentations of her hunger. Her blood lust. Her untamable rage.

The dark lands of the world of death expanded around her, but they felt like an extension of her skin and hair, the crown of thorns cutting into her forehead. There was almost a rhythm to the ghouls bubbling from the sands, white as bone, white as clouds on a summer day, frothing and hungry and screaming, rushing toward her like bees desperate to feed from a dying field where she was the lone remaining flower.

Endless numbers writhing with hunger. They'd surface and find her, and they'd eat and eat and eat. And that wriggling thing inside her, placed there by Azra'il, would move all around, tying her back together, raising and growing new bits of flesh for the ghouls to prey on, keeping her systematically whole, an endless buffet of human flesh.

They never spoke to her. Never said a word. They had no name for her, no need for her to have a name. She was nothing to them except for a constant source of food. She was nothing.

When enough ghouls had had their fill, they'd fall away one by one, turning a deep shade of red, bellies and bones filled with her blood and flesh, and splatter back onto the dark ground. And while the feeding frenzy ebbed and flowed, every once in a while, the sky would thunder and roar.

Bright explosions would bloom across the sky, bathing the world in light. Green and blue and yellow and red—she could see the colors from behind her eyelids, could feel their warmth across her trembling body, as though the sky was splitting open and burning. Moments after the light show, there would be a rumbling, like a deep earthquake somewhere deep beneath the dark sands. Something was going on beyond this world. A battle? A war? Were the angels on the move? What was going on? And why was it affecting her all the way here? She was alone, useless and helpless and stuck.

And it hurt. It hurt so much, the reckless rumbling shaking her body against the cross, the nails cutting through her palms and feet, the thorns digging into her skin, her ribs wanting to splatter open.

Sometimes, she'd wriggle. Sometimes, she'd try to wrench a hand free, tear through the nail, and escape. But that thing inside her would wriggle up through her chest, down the length of her arm, and push against her wrist and palm and fingers. That bulge beneath her skin, crawling over her bones, made all her attempts futile. She would heal too quickly to break free. And even if she did manage to get away, where would she go?

Jenny knew the rule of the crucifixion. The rule of the cross.

Sometimes, in the respite between waves of ghouls, when the sky wasn't shattering with color and the ground wasn't rumbling, her death would come to her.

Jenny's death was a little boy no older than six or seven, with the same silky black hair, pale skin, and limbs that were just a little bit too thin. And his eyes, just like her own from when she was young: scowling, trying to hide, trying to pretend she wasn't trying to hope for the best.

She struggled to speak to the boy. He looked at her like he knew too much. He looked at her like he needed her. But he'd just watch.

He wore a tattered purple robe, which Yeshua must've made for him before everything went to shit. Jenny wondered if Yeshua had known he'd stumbled upon her death in the midst of all their work.

Was it just a coincidence? Her death in the middle of what must've been billions of deaths? How many had they freed?

Was it all pointless?

The others would hover nearby, emerging from behind the pillars in the distance. They were like a lost herd of lambs waiting to be told what to do. She didn't know where they went when the ghouls bubbled from the grounds and came to feed. Were they safe? Or were they being attacked too? She didn't ask. She didn't care.

There used to be demons, too—for a while, at least—their fires burning in the eyes of ghoul bodies. They'd tried to protect her from the hoard, and that could've been for a few days or weeks; she couldn't tell. But she didn't know what had happened to them. Had they died protecting her? Had they burned through their host bodies? Why hadn't they taken new ones from the new ghouls? They hadn't communicated with her. Not that they could speak, and she wasn't sure how to speak in temperature. Maybe they'd given up on her. Maybe they hated her. After all, she'd gotten their leader, Iblis, killed.

Often, just as she might fall asleep, just as she might forget the excruciating pain, she'd see that impossibly bright burst of blue light and Azra'il's enormous burned hand and . . .

Jenny's death sat on the ground below her, hugging his knees and looking up at her. That's where he always sat. Just for a short while. He'd talk. He'd bring up memories they shared: watching TV, favorite foods, homework and books they'd read, biking through that path in the park that one time, with all the flowers and birds.

She'd listen, fading in and out, pain throbbing from every direction. The thing wriggling inside her would move, and sometimes, when it was particularly quiet and her heartbeat seemed impossibly loud, she thought she could hear a faint *crunch crunch crunch* inside her body. Was it constantly chewing through her insides and putting her back together?

She'd tried everything. She had gone through the list of her abilities. Instant Acceleration. Ignite. Valescent Light. Severed Spirit. But none of them had taken effect. She'd even tried activating her exoskeleton, but nothing would come gushing out of her navel. She was without power. Without strength. Without hope.

Not even the guidance system would respond. She couldn't access her stats. Couldn't create anything. The energy she'd stored up no longer mattered. All she had left was her body, a body that withered and shrank with each cycle of ghouls. Her muscles, her strength and mass, had shriveled away with every bite. She was becoming thinner and thinner; she was wasting away, just as Yeshua had on his cross.

What was she supposed to do?

Sometimes, she dreamed. Not of the past. Not of things that had happened already. Her death spoke about that enough. What she dreamt of was that beautiful, peaceful space between worlds, the luminous flowing ocean of light that seemed to connect everything; the healing space she'd brought so many others through using Susan's power. Valescent Light.

Jenny dreamt of slipping from this world back to the frozen world of demons where Yeshua was trapped. Where the endless number of demons were frozen once again. She dreamt of swimming through the light, upward, into the world of souls, and tearing Azra'il down from his throne in that horrible red sky, freeing all the souls from their damnation.

But mostly, she dreamed of Susan's soul. Jenny had pushed Susan, whose soul had also been affixed to a cross, away, out of Azra'il's reach, into the material world. Their normal world. Earth.

Was Susan okay? What was it like being a soul wandering among the living?

And what about Susan's cross? She'd have to carry that everywhere with her. What would become of her?

Did I only make things worse for her?

Was she better off with Azra'il?

Fuck no.

It was almost funny. She'd spent so long looking for Susan's soul, and now the both of them were crucified and trapped in different worlds.

Ghouls snapped through Jenny's knees. They slurped from her collarbone. They sucked the cartilage from her kneecaps. Red and orange light burst open in the sky. The ground shook violently, but the ghouls kept coming. They chewed her nipples to shreds and licked her exposed lungs and buried their oversized faces in the mess of her intestines, all the while ripping at her skin with their razor-sharp fingernails. The wriggling thing slithered up and down her bones, swam through her veins and arteries, healing her flesh and keeping her alive. One time, she swore she'd felt it gush inside her nose and burrow into the folds of her brain, and she screamed.

JUST LET ME DIE!

She was still mortal, wasn't she? Maybe if she died, she could move on. And at least as a soul, she might be free. Her death was haunting her anyway. Why couldn't she just die? Why shouldn't she?

Fuck this. Fuck all of this.

She could still hear that god-awful voice. That horrible rumbling laugh. Was this Azra'il's curse, then? Putting that thing inside her? What even was it? *What is it?*

Cut it out of me! Cut it out of me!

CUT IT OUT OF ME!

That *thing* kept her healed. It kept her alive. It made sure she could always feel every single bite until there were just too many teeth, too many pieces of her torn away, and all she felt was numb. Numb and alone and hungry.

"Are you mad at me?" came her death's voice one day, clutching a dirtied, blood-stained sleeve and staring up at her. His robe was in tatters, trailing behind him, revealing skinny legs, bones jutting out painfully. The ghouls must've been attacking him and the others too. How were they managing to deal with this? She didn't know. She didn't want to know. She couldn't worry about them too.

But there was a tremor in his voice, another bit of hurt, and she felt the all too familiar lump in her throat. And maybe it was the feeling of having her stomach burst again inside her belly, or maybe it was the fact that she couldn't get Azra'il's words out of her head and kept picturing Susan suffering at his hands, but she snarled, and the bitter words slipped past her lips before she could stop herself.

"*Why would I be angry at you?*"

"Because it's my fault," said the boy, his face distorted like he was about to cry. "I killed her. It was me. It's all my fault."

CHAPTER THREE

IT'S ALL MY FAULT

Another burst of color opened the sky, a mixture of orange and yellow this time, casting the world of death in a fiery glow before slowly fading away like a sunset, like a sun coming undone. The ground rippled and shook with violent tremors that rattled Jenny's body against the cross.

"Fuck," she swore, her throat hoarse. When the rumbling stopped, when the world grew heavy with darkness again, she opened her eyes. It was quiet. So quiet that she could hear the bug or insect or disease that Azra'il had implanted inside her working its way through her body.

Her heart raced, thudding against her aching chest. Her hands . . . Oh God, her hands. Her fingers twitched, stuck halfway between curling into a fist and wanting to stretch and escape her palms. The nail through her feet might be what hurt the most. Her right foot over her left. Her ankles aching, her knees threatening to pop. Her torso hung low, pulling away from her, pulling her toward the ground with every horrible breath, putting a strain on her entire system.

"I killed her. It was me. It's all my fault."

What the fuck did you just say to me? is what she should've said. But she'd held her tongue. Bitten through her cheek, only for the wriggling thing to patch it back together.

But what did he mean?

What did it mean?

She kept asking herself, over and over, saliva and blood dribbling down her chin as she chewed on her lips, as the thing inside her wormed up to her face and wriggled along her gums. She could feel it when she pressed her tongue against it, and it would squirm away, out of reach. It was strangely round, like an egg yolk or one of those candies that would gush fruit-flavored ooze when you chewed on them. It tasted like salt.

"Come back," she whispered, hanging her head so that her hair covered her face. And, as if in answer to her plea, the ground bubbled. White liquid pooled to the surface, desperate limbs and round heads emerging to feast on her again. Streaks of purple and green clashed overhead. The world shook. And once again, the ghouls ripped away her skin and yanked her hair and snapped through her ears and feasted on her body.

When they'd gone, she twitched and trembled against the cross as her body was reconstructed. It always slowed down healing after they left, like the thing wanted her to suffer as long as possible.

Her death appeared from the shadows again as more purple and green light exploded overhead, casting his face in a bright glow. He'd been crying. Blood stained his cheeks and his chin, and he wiped snot as it dribbled over his top lip.

He sat down beneath her, closer this time. And neither of them spoke for a long while.

"It's all my fault."

What he was trying to say? It shouldn't make sense to her. Not logically, anyway. But in a weird way, in a frightening way, it made more sense than anything else ever had in her life. But how could it be her death's fault and not her own?

She'd always felt that strange pull. Or was it a push? Something deep in her subconscious that would bump into her thoughts and emotions, have sway on her actions. It was a lot like swimming through the light between worlds, trying to navigate by feeling.

There had always been something, or maybe it was someone, who'd been burrowed inside her. Rage. Fear. Want. Something that tugged and nudged at her thoughts. It was *something*.

It was what she'd felt when she lost herself and rampaged through the school and devoured Miriam and attacked everyone else and ended up killing Susan. It was what she'd felt in the mess of blood and ghouls when trying to save Yeshua. It was what she'd felt all her life when the pain and misery and disgust with herself, her existence, got too much to bear.

She knew what he was. Why he was here. Why he was her death. But she couldn't see the point in it. "Why are you here?"

"I'm your death," he said, his voice small.

"Yes, I know. But why? I'm not dead yet."

"Everyone's death is here," he explained, looking around. "We are born when you're born. We wait for you."

She shut her eyes. "So what am I supposed to do now?" She felt like she'd asked that question a hundred times already. At every turn. Just trying to figure out what to do next. How to survive. How to live with herself.

Maybe that had been the question she'd asked all her life.

"I don't know."

Jenny clenched her teeth so hard, some of them moved out of place. Blood ran down her chin. "*The fuck is the point, then?*"

The boy flinched, looking so alarmed, so frightened, that Jenny's heart leaped into her throat. Before she could say another word, he'd turned around and run, the tattered purple robe trailing behind him. In his absence, silence settled closely, too closely, till she felt like she was choking.

Jenny wasn't sure if she'd fallen asleep again or dreamt or what, but she woke to the ground shaking violently, colors crashing overhead in waves, as though a rainbow were shattering across the dark sky. Another wave of ghouls had come and gone, and as Jenny was put back together again, her death returned and sat down again. This time on his knees, like he was in prayer. He folded his hands on his lap as he lifted his head, a defiant, confident look on his face.

"I said I was sorry," he spoke. He was trying to sound brave, but there was a quiver in his breath. If anything, he sounded indignant. Entitled. Like a brat.

Jenny hissed through her teeth.

"I'm not useless," he continued, his voice rising in pitch.

"I didn't say you were."

"But you were thinking it," he said. A frown darkened his face. "I'm not. Okay? I . . ."

Jenny groaned, shutting her eyes. Why couldn't he just leave her alone? The other deaths didn't bother her. Why did he insist on trying to talk to her?

"Because you're sad," he said. "And they're scared of you."

"Are you reading my fucking mind?"

His eyes went wide, then he shook his head vigorously, making his hair bounce back and forth. "No, no, I promise. It's more like . . . I can just feel it. I don't know. You're my life."

"*Life*," spat Jenny, trying to think. Trying to figure out what she might do, or what she could say. Or who to call out for. But there was a bitterness in her throat, the burning sting of bile, a headache that bloomed harsher and brighter than any of the lights above. Everything was a mess. Everything was fucked. She was fucked.

Flashes of Azra'il ripped through her mind. An angel so immense, he towered over her like a building. His mighty wings. His muscles. The snakes on his head hissing and darting and gnashing their fangs. And those glowing red eyes . . . those horrible eyes, and everything he said about Susan. How she'd been his toy. Another one for his collection. How he would make Jenny his toy as well. His bride.

When the worlds ended.

A howling, raging scream welled up in Jenny's throat, and she awoke to find more ghouls surfacing from their bubbling liquid, jaws open with hunger. She must've fallen asleep again. Her head lolled back, leaning against the cross as she stared at all the colors in the sky. What was going on? Were those lights the war? The earthquakes? Were the worlds about to end like Azra'il had promised?

Was Susan okay?

What about Jenny's brother? Her mother? Everyone?

The next time her death came around, she had a question for him. "Why?"

He sat down on his knees again. "Why what?"

"You *know* what I want to know," she said through bared teeth, her throat raw from all the screaming.

A gentle tremor went through the ground, and her death looked around. He was pressing his lips tight and not making eye contact. "I don't know."

"Then why did you say sorry?" she asked. She was shaking with rage. She knew it was ridiculous to blame her death, to blame the little boy, but she wanted to blame someone. And he'd confessed. And she hated him for confessing. "Why come to me and tell me that?"

"Because," he said with a shrug, "you were so sad."

"*THEN TELL ME WHY YOU DID IT!*" she screamed at the top of her lungs. Her voice broke, and she coughed up blood. She tried to say something else, but she kept coughing—painful, forceful coughs that racked her entire body, her chest and her shoulders, straining her limbs against the nails pinning them in place.

Her death stood up, holding an arm to his body as though trying and failing to hug himself, staring at her with his bottom lip jutting out and quivering. He swallowed, so animatedly, so comically, in the way that only children could, that Jenny almost wanted to break. She wanted to apologize. To console him. To tell him everything would be okay. That she wasn't angry. But the bug was in her throat, worming between her lungs, and she was waiting for him to speak.

He turned to run away.

"*NO!*" she shouted, her voice hoarse and broken. "Don't you *dare* walk away. Stay right there and answer me."

"I don't want to talk about this!" he squeaked. He was breathing hard, holding the sides of his head, staring at the ground as another crash of violet light splattered across the sky. The world was illuminated by a purplish-bluish glow, and Jenny could see the tears glistening on his cheeks when he turned back. "I just want to lie down."

"If you go now," she said, speaking in a low voice, too tired to yell again. "Don't ever come back here. I *never* want to see you again. I never want to hear your voice again."

As soon as the words were out, she regretted them. They were her mother's words, every time Jenny came home with a less than perfect grade. Every time she was too loud with excitement while shopping for clothes or on the train. Every time she was afraid at night and didn't know what to do.

And the words had the same effect on him they'd always had on her. Jenny's death screwed up his eyes, sniffled, and squared his shoulders, trying to be "correct," trying to do what was asked of him. Trying not to be a burden.

But she didn't care. She didn't care anymore. She was past the point of caring. She was stuck here. She couldn't do anything. Nothing. There was nothing she could do. She would stay here until—

"*THEN WHY ARE YOU GIVING UP ON ME?*" shouted her death, tears streaming down his face. "WHY ARE YOU JUST STAYING THERE?

"THIS IS WHY YOU'RE ALONE!

"THIS IS WHY I'M ALONE!

"THIS IS WHY NOBODY CAN LOVE US!"

For a second, a hot flash of shame burned across her face.

Then came the rage, like a rush of color bursting from her chest, like the ground shaking so hard it had torn her body open. "WHAT THE *FUCK* DO YOU WANT ME TO DO?"

"SOMETHING!" he screamed. "*ANYTHING.* YOU JUST LET IT KEEP *HAPPENING* TO YOU. OVER AND OVER AND OVER. WHY DON'T YOU EVER DO SOMETHING?"

He stumbled there, staring at her like he was waiting to be admonished or slapped, but then he hiccupped and he sucked in a deep breath and screamed.

He screamed with his eyes shut tight, his hands curled up into painful little fists. He screamed with his entire body, and a series of notifications cut through Jenny's thoughts so quickly she thought she'd imagined them:

Activating Exoskeleton
???
Existential Error
Existential Error
Existential Error

Her death stumbled. His eyes were wide, tears glistening on his cheeks, strands of snot falling off his chin. Slowly, he looked down, and Jenny stared too as something red and gelatinous and liquid burst out of the boy's belly button.

They exchanged one more glance, desperation and fear sparkling in his eyes before something red and gooey covered his face and he fell to his knees, clawing at it, crying and screaming and begging for help.

"I'm sorry," they whispered in unison. Jenny shook, staring at him. The boy's face twisted into ugly crying. And when he spoke, she did too: "*I'm sorry. I'm sorry. I'm sorry!*"

Existential Error
Existential Error
Commencing Metamorphosis

He threw his head back, now covered in the glistening red exoskeleton, and cried out. With a series of loud cracks—like dishes shattering against a wall, like glass breaking—several long things jetted out of the boy's back, expanding to unfurl around him. Her tentacles.

Four—no, six of them, swirling and expanding and whipping through the air as he howled. He fell forward onto all fours, nearly completely covered in the red exoskeleton. It shone as dark as blood, shining and glistening while another assortment of colors—blues and reds and pinks—blew open in the sky.

Jenny's voice caught. She didn't know what to say. She just stared in horror and shock and disbelief.

What the fuck?

How? HOW?

Why?

The boy clawed at the dirt with his exoskeleton-covered fingers. His shoulders heaved as he struggled to breathe. The tentacles wavered overhead, flickering in every direction, and Jenny could tell they were tasting everything in sight, trying to find something to eat, hungering so badly.

All of a sudden, the tentacles went rigid, hanging straight up in the air like six pillars shooting into the sky. The boy, her death, lifted his head, his silky dark hair shimmering over the red exoskeleton that now covered his face. His eyes gleamed with tears and rage, reflecting the red and purple lights above. Drool ran down his chin. With a flash of light, with a movement so sudden that the air itself rippled and blurred, he was on her. Instant Acceleration.

Teeth found her throat. Fingers dug into her stomach. Tears streaming down her cheeks, Jenny bit her lip to keep from screaming as her death, tentacles furling around her, began to feed on her flesh.

CHAPTER FOUR

WANDERING SOUL

Angels lumbered past Susan, streaming up the busy Manhattan street. It almost looked like rush hour at night, except all the streetlamps and traffic lights were dead, and the creatures around her were naked. The angels moved recklessly, like a large herd of wild animals out on the prowl, shrieking and hissing, hunched over and desperate.

Where had they come from? Had they all come out of the high school? That couldn't be what had happened. Maybe the angels had hit the rest of the world too. Susan couldn't tell. All she knew was that they left her alone, and no system messages filled her head, and that she was dead. The body she had wasn't really her body, wasn't the body she'd grown up with.

The angels didn't really acknowledge her. A few times, she thought she'd made eye contact with several of them, staring back into their empty white eyes, wondering if there was a flicker of curiosity on their gaunt faces. But they'd shuffled away like they couldn't tolerate being near her.

Whenever she got too close to one—not something she wanted to do— they hissed in pain and ran off in the opposite direction. Which was one good thing, she concluded. She didn't have to worry about them trying to eat her. And she definitely didn't have to worry about dying.

Burned-out cars littered the sidewalk. Corpses, or rather bits of corpses, lay strewn about, and every so often, an angel knelt down and ripped off a chunk of arm or face, chewed as blood and chunks flew out, and swallowed.

Susan tried not to look too closely at any of it. She'd seen more than enough. She'd been through more than enough. And watching their teeth flash, watching their desperate fingers clawing and ripping, she kept picturing Azra'il.

Kept seeing his gleaming red eyes, kept hearing his deep, rolling laugh. Kept seeing those awful snakes that sprouted from his head.

You're my new favorite plaything, he'd whispered in her ear. His teeth would snap through the cartilage, and she would scream and scream, only for her body to shine and for the ear to grow back in his mouth.

She couldn't remember how many days it had been since Jenny had set her free, since Susan had landed in the normal world as a ghost. She hadn't kept count. The sun had come up and gone down at least seven times, she thought. So it might've been a week. But how long had she been away? How long had she been crucified?

Thinking about that would make her entire form ache. It almost felt like a period cramp or motion sickness, but this body wasn't quite a body, though it sure felt like one. And she sure did get exhausted dragging the cross around. It slowed her down immensely.

The first night, she'd tried leaving it behind, not wanting to remember the time she'd spent nailed to it, but if she got too far away, something awful would happen: sharp, piercing pain would shoot through her palms and her feet, and her body would flicker like static on a TV screen. Her form became nearly see-through, and she knew, just by that awful feeling, that if she ventured any further from it, the cross would pull her back, bind her to the wood again, and she would be stuck, invisible to the world.

She'd spent a few hours screaming. A few days crying. Hiding. Lying in a fetal position on a park bench. She didn't need to sleep. There was no need to eat. She didn't need much of anything, but every so often, her body would flicker, and her entire being would *throb* like she'd lost something beloved. It was like nostalgia and heartbreak and a punch to the stomach all at once, and the image that would flash through her head was Jenny.

Jenny sobbing while trying to get Susan off the cross. Jenny covered in red exoskeleton with a deranged look on her face as she bit through Susan's throat. Jenny sitting in class, staring out the window, daydreaming while they should be paying attention. Jenny sitting upright and leaning forward at her computer table when it was time to kick ass in a video game. Jenny pushing Susan away through that strange sea of swirling color and light.

But what was Susan supposed to do now?

She trawled through the streets she remembered, trying to understand what was going on. The angels would vanish in the mornings, crawling into whatever spaces they could find to avoid the rising sun. She saw several rush down the steps into an underground subway station. She saw others hide inside abandoned buildings, and still others that didn't make it. Those were the scariest.

They'd claw out their eyes, screaming and shrieking, and then they'd hunt by smell. They'd run into each other. They'd fight like rabid dogs, the survivors rushing off to hunt blindly.

But it wasn't all bad. It wasn't like before, when they'd all just been a bunch of high school kids stuck in a hellish game. There were cops now. Soldiers. Adults with weapons. People shot down the angels, beat them away with batons and baseball bats. And some people had caught on to the system as well. Armor and swords and abilities that let people leap into the air or obliterate a building wall or light things on fire. She even saw people in cosplay, dressed up as their favorite superheroes. Fighting.

People were leveling up. People were fighting back. But the angels were never-ending. And what about all the people who couldn't fight?

For a long time, too long, all she could do was spectate. At night, the sky would burst with color. It almost reminded her of the northern lights, something she'd always wanted to see one day, but these were more like stars exploding all across the sky, as though the heavens were at war too, and she wondered if Jenny was somehow involved.

She wondered if she could fight too. She would drag her cross around Manhattan, through areas that used to once swarm with people and where she and Jenny would complain about the tourists and school kids and overpriced food stands.

Now, the enormous screens were cracked and fallen, the towers crumpled, ready to topple over, and dried blood caked everything. Bodies were left to rot.

The answer came the day it rained. It didn't matter that the sun had risen because dark clouds covered the sky and thick globs of rain poured down on the city. The rain sizzled through Susan, and she held out her hand, watching the droplets slow down briefly before dropping through her palm and fingers. Her skin—no, her *body* rippled like she was a puddle, but it was stranger than that. She was made of light.

And the thought of that, the thought that she wasn't in her body, and that her body might be back at the school still, the only building she'd completely avoided, made her head want to burst open, like air was closing in on her throat.

She stood in the middle of the road with her cross, staring up at the dark sky as angels swarmed the streets and climbed into buildings. As the fighting continued, as the nightmare would never end, as the rain fell through her ghostly form. That was when something *surged* through the city.

Windows came alight with yellow and white light. Traffic lights and street signs lit up. And Susan looked around in shock at all the electricity, the energy, humming and buzzing. She could just about taste it all. And then she saw it— what was causing the wave of electricity: a desecrated angel.

No notification filled her head. There was no system inside her. But she didn't need it to recognize the horrible aura emanating from the immense creature. It was much larger than the surrounding tarnished and wretched angels. Its bright yellow head moved past third-story windows. It was male, judging by the thing dangling between its yellow-covered legs, and it seemed much more muscular than the one Jenny had fought back in the high school.

Its size reminded her of Azra'il. She had to repress that shudder as her form rippled again, and she stepped back, bumping into her cross, staring as the desecrated angel roared again.

Two large blue appendages jutted out of its back. At first, she thought they might be wings, but they looked more like uprooted trees, with the ends winding out like thick roots or horribly misshapen fingers. A shock of white hair covered its head, coming down to its shoulders. And its face . . . its face was worse than the other angels' she'd seen.

This one must've torn out its eyes to withstand the daylight, and now, in their place weren't just empty eye sockets but torn-out chunks of its head; fleshy bits that stuck out of the sockets covered in that glistening yellow exoskeleton, but Susan swore she could spot bits of its skull and brain.

A yellow glow emanated from the enormous creature's body, the rain bouncing off its exoskeleton. The desecrated angel shook its head and roared, an earsplitting sound that caused chunks of a building nearby to slide off and collapse on the road. Susan covered her ears and winced. The angel shone brighter and brighter, and then a beam of light shot out of the creature's mouth.

The light snapped swiftly up the street, incinerating everything in its way, illuminating all the rain and debris and corpses around. Angels, cars, buildings, everything exploded as more electrical energy surged away from the point of impact.

Wind battered and rippled through Susan's form, and then she felt a tickle. A tickle that was more than a tickle; it was almost like static. She could *taste* the light shining from the streetlamps, could feel it coming alive in the buildings. But at a nearby traffic light, the pole that was cracked open with the shattered light bulbs on the ground—that one seemed to call to her.

Electricity snapped and hissed from the exposed wires, and Susan had a thought. An idea. Remembering how she'd changed the wretched angel in the library once by shooting electricity into its brain.

It felt as though her heart was pounding, but it was her entire form siz-zling. The beam was dying out, but the hum of electricity, the lights in the windows, were still alight. They'd fade soon. She had to hurry.

Susan left the cross behind and ran as hard as she could, feeling as though she was gliding over the puddles and pooling water like she was ice skating. She tripped over something as the light started to fade. She could wait for another beam, maybe, another chance, but the ground shook as the desecrated angel bulldozed past screaming tarnished angels. It was running toward some-thing; it wanted something. She would never be able to keep up while drag-ging the cross around, and the tingling sensation was fading.

She threw herself at the light post and wrapped her hands around the exposed wire.

As soon as she made contact, electrical energy rushed up her arms and into her body. Her life, so many moments—everything from childhood to her death in Jenny's arms—flashed through her head. She saw her parents, saw her teach-ers, saw her friends, saw her ex; she even saw her neighbors and their pet dog, and so many other people that they all blurred together as the electricity snapped through her.

She was shining so brightly she felt like the sun.

CHAPTER FIVE

THE THIRD MARY

Jibra'il had found the girl hiding in what the humans called a school. It was an education facility, similar to the glass shards where young angels went to learn the scriptures of light. This building, dilapidated and falling apart, had taken part in the survival challenge. And of all the survival challenges, it was the one that had birthed the interloper; the survival challenge that did not close. The one he feared punishment for. He'd found it oddly fitting, then, that the final Mary should come from the same place.

She'd been hiding, sealing herself off from the world as the tarnished ones surfaced from the darkness and feasted. But once Jibra'il had arrived, shimmering and silver, he'd warded the tarnished away. His presence alone was enough. And he had found another survivor. A man. A presence known to the young girl. A useful tool.

Adonai's essence had been entrusted to Jibra'il in the form of a radiant grain of light, an orb not too different from the eggs the angels produced upon bonding. Inside it had been enough matter to sink a huge portion of the material world—what the humans named black holes. Dropping this would have unleashed an unformed Adonai onto the material world, and in all His power and might, in all His hunger, matter itself would have come undone in the worst possible way. They would have failed. Their countless millennia of planning and fighting would have come to a most unfruitful end. All of it would have been for waste. Which was why Jibra'il had been adamant on success.

After appointing a dozen angels to guard the structure, to keep a perimeter, Jibra'il had come to the girl, a shimmering silver form, having overtaken the human Dr. Lee's body. He'd spoken the human tongue through this body, offering the girl a choice that he knew she would not refuse. Though the other angels would've seen it as mercy to even offer a choice, Jibra'il had felt it would be better received, better delivered, in this manner.

Less resistance. Less chance of the girl doing anything rash. Less chance of failure.

She had accepted, of course. He'd promised her safety. He'd promised she would never have to hurt again, to never be left in need again, that she would always be free to be herself. And this was the *Lord*, after all. The Lord her parents prayed to, that everyone should pray to. This was the Lord, the master of all things, and it would be the honor of any material being's entire existence to carry the Lord into this world.

She hadn't made any sound of protest. She hadn't spoken a word against what she had chosen to do. Only a whimper. As Jibra'il had knelt in Dr. Lee's body, Dr. Lee had screamed and railed inside his head that this was wrong, that she was just a child, that he should spare her, find someone else. The human had been sweet on the girl, as the girl had asked him for protection in their survival challenge, but there was no choice in the matter. She was the simplest solution, the most effective. A more powerful being would resist or would draw unwanted attention, and Jibra'il felt quite content with his discovery. Not even the Antithesis would have seen this coming.

He'd pressed Adonai's orb against the girl's belly. At first, there had been a slight resistance, surface tension. But then, the light had slipped through her skin and taken root in her womb, and she'd screamed. Her body had twitched like mad, distorting as the light snapped into place inside the girl. Darkness had crackled around her and shone from her tearful eyes as a jet of energy rippled away from her.

Jibra'il had felt as though the force would thrust him out of Dr. Lee's body, the collapse of power focusing on this one localized spot. He knew the seed of light had taken hold, and that destiny had finalized. This girl would be the third Mary. As soon as he was sure she was all right, her heart beating, her organs sustaining, Jibra'il had breathed a sigh of relief. The girl had fallen asleep on her side, whimpering as she dreamt, as he ignored Dr. Lee cursing him with every foul word from the human language.

He had sent a message off to the heavens with one of the angels on guard and set to the final stage of his task: tending to the young human woman. The third Mary needed a lot of meat. Just the snacks from the vending machines nearby wouldn't be enough. To grow Adonai properly, to incubate a material form capable of containing all of His power, she needed to feed on material life: meat from humans or angels; it didn't matter which, only what Jibra'il could source from nearby.

The guard angels didn't have the strength nor the discipline to possess humans, but they could corral the tarnished ones, and Jibra'il worked quickly, employing the human Dr. Lee's abilities and making use of the guidance system to grow stronger.

He'd expected a response from Rafa'el to come swiftly, but after several days, he'd begun to worry. Adonai was incubating well within Leslie, her belly swelling up and glowing warmly. She'd even started to sing to it, and Jibra'il wondered if Adonai appreciated that. There was no contact between him and the Lord. He couldn't ask for guidance. Couldn't ask for support. Could only watch until the promised time should arrive.

It was on the seventh day that a different set of angels found him with news of war. The Antithesis had invaded the world of light—an effort to turn the scales in its favor and liberate the faction of angels who had rebelled.

Not again, had thought Jibra'il. How could this be happening again? They had purged the ungrateful, tarnished them, and yet still more angels chose to stand against their Lord and Master?

Did these fools want to be condemned to a life of struggle and hardship?

The Heavens had been ripped asunder, but that wasn't even the worst news. One of them had mentioned, gravely, that Rafa'el had been stolen away. Rafa'el, who was the most beloved of all. The Scribe. The Flower. The Bearer of the Trumpet, in charge of the pivotal moment that would convert Adonai's new form into one of infinite power, that would conclude destiny.

The one angel Jibra'il loved with all his being.

Dr. Lee had begun to laugh inside his body as Jibra'il's light shimmered brighter and brighter, so harsh that the lesser angels had to move back. He was trembling, shivering, shuddering with rage and despair.

"Where? Where is she?" he'd demanded to know, resorting to the human's throat to scream with all the rage he couldn't contain. "How could this have happened? What of Mika'el and her soldiers?"

The angels hadn't known, and he'd dismissed them, everything inside him recoiling with horror. Rafa'el was in peril. His beloved gone. Missing. Trapped by the enemy.

What if they hurt her?

And what of their plans?

What was to be?

You can't just fly off, can you? had asked Dr. Lee with a laugh. *Your master is now in my student's body. You have a duty of responsibility.*

"You will not speak down to *me*, mortal," had spat Jibra'il through Dr. Lee's teeth. "What can you know of such matters?" But he was embarrassed. In his rage and despair, he'd accidentally let the human glimpse his mind. He'd let the human see how he truly felt about Rafa'el, how much sadness he carried.

But the human had been right. How could he leave the third Mary alone? What if something should happen? Something to derail everything. His best chance of finding Rafa'el was trusting her vision, her forecast for destiny.

He looked down at the girl who'd fallen asleep again, dried blood caking her bottom lip and chin. He stared at her belly, where darkness gathered like a storm, and a furious breeze howled outside as Jibra'il summoned a storm.

CHAPTER SIX

I'M SO HUNGRY!

Teeth bit through Jenny's windpipe with a horrible crunch, cutting off her ragged breathing. Tentacles tightened around her arms, threatening to pop her elbows, and all she could manage was a pitiful gurgling as her death, the little boy—his purple robe tattered, his skin covered in the red exoskeleton, tentacles whipping through the air behind him—chewed through her neck and worked his way along her shoulder. He bit into muscle. Into bone. She didn't bother screaming, but her insides recoiled as the wriggling thing scurried up toward her throat, healing her even as she was eaten alive.

It was different somehow. Usually, in the feeding frenzy, there were too many ghouls to make sense of any one sound, any one sensation. An onslaught of chewing and screaming and moaning and crying, limbs all over the place, too many sets of teeth finding Jenny's flesh from head to toe. But there was only one creature eating her now, and he was crying. Sobbing and weeping, even as he chewed and swallowed and slurped up the blood running freely down her body.

He clung to her; one arm wrapped around the cross, the other in her hair. He didn't seem to mind the crown of thorns, but his grip pushed each thorn deeper into her head, and fresh trickles of blood ran down the sides, curving around her ear to drip off her chin.

He was sniffling. Crying. And after eating through her shoulder and her bony chest and working his way down to her belly where he set to work sucking on her intestines and tearing into her hips, he started whispering. It was quiet at first. Under his breath, in between mouthfuls. Then his tentacles lashed out and fastened around Jenny's arms and throat, around her ankles, and they too began to feed. Each one suckled gently from her torn-open flesh.

It was a familiar feeling. She could almost taste her blood gushing up the lengths of each tentacle. More colors burst overhead, but there were too many tears blurring her vision. She thought she saw a burst of yellow, and for a second, she wondered if that was the sun. But then the ground shook violently, her death cried out, and his teeth struck some deep, innermost part of her. When the scream surged up to her throat, she couldn't hold it back.

Her death screamed as well, crying. The boy was crying.

"I'm so hungry! I'm so hungry! I'm so hungry I'm going to die!"

A memory flashed. Jenny, ten years old, curled up on the floor with a blanket over her head. She was hugging her stomach, chewing on her lips in between short, shaking breaths, trying to stop. Her mother was on the couch, wheezing. She had a cold. They couldn't go to the doctor.

Jenny had tried to make food, but they'd only had a bit of stale bread left. And it wasn't enough. No matter how much water she drank from the tap, it wasn't enough. Her stomach was on the verge of collapse. *I'm so hungry*, she'd kept telling herself, trying her best not to sniffle or make a sound. *I'm so hungry. God, please give me something to eat. I've been good. Please give me some food.*

But the food never came. God never responded to her. And all she could do was grow up, dreaming of one day moving away from there, far away, to a beautiful house where she could cook enormous meals and eat her fill and sleep peacefully.

"I'M SO HUNGRY!" scream-cried her death, taking a moment to pause, to look her in the eyes. She stared back at the exoskeleton-covered face, at the blood and drool glistening on his chin, at how the blue light bursting overhead made his teeth glisten purple. At the tentacles swerving overhead. Then, he lunged forward and pressed his teeth to the fleshy bit of her forearm.

She shut her eyes as he ate, thinking about the roiling hunger she'd felt before, thinking at least one of them was eating. After all her life, her death was the one finally satisfying that hunger.

It was me. It's all my fault.

I killed her.

She thought about running through the school, feeling trapped in her own body, feeling as though someone else had taken control, *something* else had taken control. She'd thought she'd been on autopilot. She'd told herself it was instinct. It was nobody's fault. It was her fault. But then, her death had come along and taken all the blame, and now she didn't know who to blame.

Why don't you just accept me? came a voice or a whisper or a scream. She couldn't tell. She couldn't even tell if she'd spoken or if it was her death. Or was it some voice coming down from above?

But something in her accepted. Something in her finally said, *fine*, and opened. And when it opened, something new came pouring in, crashing into waves deep inside her, collapsing onto itself, and when Jenny opened her eyes, she was looking at her own face. She was hanging off her body—No. She was looking through the eyes of her death.

She saw the confused expression on her withering body. Saw the blood and the horrible mess. Felt the surging hunger and malice that covered her death, that now covered her, and she shut her eyes again and took another bite.

With each bite, a different memory went through her thoughts. Her mother embracing her, squeezing her tight, and promising everything would be okay.

Her mother slapping her. She'd gotten too low a grade on a math exam. Was this what her mother slaved away for? Sacrificed so much for? How could Jenny embarrass her like this? How could Jenny not have studied enough?

A boy in one of her classes pulling her hair. Someone had said he had a crush on her; that's why he kept hurting her. She'd slapped him in the face and gotten in trouble, and her mother had had to miss a day of work. Jenny had been beaten and locked into their one bedroom, and been told she wouldn't be allowed to watch TV for a month.

More memories stirred and zoomed by. She saw herself taking the train. Riding a bike. Walking through a park on a rainy day, listening to the same song on repeat. She saw Susan. Saw the way they would walk together sometimes, so close their fingers would brush every so often. The way their breaths would cloud in the winter. How Susan's cheeks would turn pink when she laughed.

Then she saw Yeshua. Bound to the cross, head lolling, beard swaying.

And then she remembered how she set him free. With her hatchet cutting through his wrist. And when Jenny opened her eyes again, her teeth cut through the last bit of sinew keeping her elbow attached to her forearm. A mouthful of flesh. Shards of bone crunching between her teeth.

She swallowed and chewed and swallowed some more, some semblance of a plan forming in her head, fueled by desperation and the spark of hope and a prayer—she was just the little boy, hungry, so horribly hungry, she just had to keep eating.

Faster. Chew faster. Before the *thing* inside her could heal the flesh and put it back together.

She held the arm open with her tentacles. She pried it apart with her exoskeleton-covered hands. Chew and chew and chew. Through healing flesh.

Through bone. And if she could find the worm or bug or whatever it was between her teeth, then she'd just chew that up, too.

And oh God, how good did it feel to have her tentacles again. To have the exoskeleton cover her body and feel full of strength and freedom. She could feel the hunger, the force, the sheer power. What did her stats look like now? Had she fucked things up even more? Did she care?

This felt like Severed Spirit. Felt like she was someone else again.

But no. She was just herself.

Just herself, chewing and chewing and chewing. Eating herself.

She was more herself than she'd been in a long time.

It wasn't till something hot and wet struck her face from above that she knew it'd worked. She stopped chewing; stopped trying to rip through flesh. When she opened her eyes again, Jenny was back inside her body, staring at her death, his red face a horrible mess of blood. He blinked in confusion, like he was coming out of a trance.

More wetness came down from above. Lights burst, but now, they were muted, hidden by voluminous dark clouds. When Jenny tasted the next drop on her lip, she knew what it was. It was the blood rain. The world was responding. That was what had happened when she'd freed Yeshua from his cross. The blooded ghouls would come.

A laugh shuddered through her thin chest. Her free arm, what was left of it, hung loosely by her side, now free of the cross. Her detached hand dangled from the nail, and she could feel the worm wriggling down from her shoulder, desperate to put her back together, and she couldn't stop laughing.

With the lump of flesh that was her arm, she pushed on her death's chest, felt the hardness of the exoskeleton clink against a bit of bone as he fell away. The ground was bubbling red and white and furious, and by the time the first ghouls reached out of the froth, her arm had healed, newly grown by the entity inside her. A grin stretched across her face, her dry lips cracking and splitting in several places.

Her death screamed below, tentacles whipping in every direction. The first ghoul to surface—its usual white color filled in with pink, its new notification spinning through her head—reached Jenny. Its fingers dug into her hip as it pulled itself higher, desperate to taste the torn mess that her death had made of her throat. Another chewed on her toes. Another bit into her thigh. And one more was trying to tear her navel open with a fingernail ripping through her belly button.

Jenny grabbed the closest ghoul by the throat and lifted it up with strength she didn't know she had in her skinny, fragile arm.

The ghoul squirmed and kicked, the vapors swirling desperately in its empty eye sockets. She was breathing hard, anger and hunger and madness charging like a thunderstorm in her gut.

"I'm so *fucking* hungry," she swore, squeezing the creature's throat.

More light burst overhead. Green this time. And the ground responded with another violent tremor. Jenny pulled the ghoul toward her, as if she wanted to embrace it. She pressed her lips to the ghoul's eye socket and did what Yeshua had done when she'd freed him.

SHLURP!

CHAPTER SEVEN

HOW AM I SUPPOSED TO CHANGE?

G houl blood dripped from her chin. It burned the back of her throat. She wasn't sure if it was even blood or if it was something else, but her stomach roiled with hunger so badly, she couldn't think straight. Fat drops of blood rain splashed against her hair, running down her face and body. Notifications flicked through her head:

You have defeated Blooded Ghoul!
Experience has been awarded.
+500 Energy

She was too skinny again, her arms thin and frail, her legs barely able to keep her up. She reached for another ghoul, but they were already running away from her, screaming as though *she* were the monster who had been feeding on them all this time. But there were too many, and they toppled over each other, a horrible writhing mess of limbs and blood. The rain grew heavier. Her death was among them, his tentacles lashing out, spreading more chaos.

Screaming echoed all around her, but Jenny tried to tune it all out as she ripped her other hand free and held on to the cross to keep from toppling over. She sucked in several deep breaths, ignoring the pain, ignoring the blood splashing into her mouth. She just wanted the next ghoul. Wanted her next meal. That would make her strong again. She could recover again. She could level up again.

Flexing what was left of her leg muscles, straining with her entire body, she pushed her feet away from the cross. With a horrible crunch and a *squelch*, the nail tore through her bones, and in the next moment, she splashed onto the ground below, breathing hard, free at last, and—

I'M SO HUNGRY!

I'm so hungry.

She couldn't tell who was speaking, or if she even *was* speaking. Was it her death? Was it herself? Did it matter?

She splashed to her shaking legs, her body too used to hanging from the cross to keep her upright. She felt like all the tarnished angels she'd killed in the high school, weak and fragile, bony and desperate. But she slipped and slid through the churning blood, throwing herself onto the nearest ghoul, almost laughing with the reversal of their roles. They'd been terrified of Yeshua too when he'd come off the cross. And now, they were terrified of her.

Why?

Why?

She screamed into one's face. *"WHY?"*

Then she scraped its eye socket with her teeth, pushed her lips inside, and slurped. She slurped and slurped and slurped, draining one ghoul before running to the next. Even as the fluid went down her throat with every swallow, every inhale. Even as their limp bodies cluttered to the ground, more like stones now than living beings, and even as she lost count. Each sip brought something back; each sip put renewed strength in her limbs. And little by little, notification by notification, she regained her strength, increased her energy, and leveled up.

Ahead, she could see her death wildly thrashing about, a one-person onslaught on the surrounding ghouls. He grabbed them with his tentacles and smashed them together over his head. He clawed through their faces with his exoskeleton-covered fingers. His eyes had turned wild and crazed, and when Jenny and he made eye contact for a moment through the pouring blood rain and the sticky heat of it all, everything seemed to pause.

He was frightened. He was terrified. More and more of his exoskeleton shot out of his belly and covered him in bloody layers. His tentacles were suckling the blood from the air as it rained, slamming into ghouls and draining them dry; he didn't know what to do with it all. It was too much. He was overloading, and Jenny could see it. Could feel it. Even without her own tentacles, she could *taste* it in the air.

She knew what she had to do. She had to reach him. Hold him. Comfort him. Tell him it was okay, and that she forgave him; that she forgave herself.

"STAY AWAY FROM ME!" he screeched, his dark hair bouncing all over the place. He sped away from her, using his tentacles like enormous spider legs, crushing ghouls left and right as the rain barreled on.

Jenny tried to shout back, to promise that she wouldn't snap at him again. She'd never yell at him again. But the words never made it out of her throat.

Darkness appeared like a blooming flower behind her death, the cold, horrible feeling emanating all around like an awful breeze. It was liquid and melting, and as he tried to run, as he tried to wick it away, it solidified around him, forcing him to the ground, a mess of wet darkness that collapsed onto him as he screamed and tried to push it back. His exoskeleton melted away, leaving him with an expression of sheer terror on his face just before the darkness closed over him completely. He'd become a pillar again.

"No!" she shouted, her heart thumping against her chest as she ran toward him. *Don't leave me.*

She grabbed the pillar, patting it all over, trying to wake him up. Why was he a pillar again? What had happened? Was it her fault? Had he lost his senses? But the answer came to her like a thought escaping her subconscious: he'd chosen it. He'd chosen to return to the pillars. It was easier than facing what he'd become. What she'd become.

Jenny sank to her knees, the blood rain pummeling her. She didn't know what to say. What to do. But she was shaking. With rage and despair and self-hatred and want.

WHY ARE YOU GIVING UP ON ME?

And something broke. Something that had threatened to break all of Jenny's life, since her earliest memories, hurting and hungry and just wanting to be held by her mother, to the more recent ones of torture and solitude and failure. Something she'd stamped down repeatedly, tried to bury in all her bloodlust and hunger and rage.

It shattered. Completely came apart, and a scream erupted from Jenny's throat, tilting her head back and pulling on her hair and screaming and screaming and screaming as pain, something worse than pain, as all the screaming she'd ever held back bubbled to the surface and burst all at once.

Severed Spirit (Tier 3)
Sever the metaphysical strands that bind worlds-
Existential Error
Natural Order Correction

Crackling white light rippled away from her in rolling waves as she collapsed to her knees. Her throat hurt so much, but she felt something tremendous thrumming just beneath her skin. Curling up into a fetal position, lying on a pool of hot, sticky blood, and as more blood rained down on her, as the ghouls continued to run away, she concentrated. She felt for the notification, focused on the new power developing inside her, focused on the heartbreak of having a part of herself terrified of her, focused on the mistakes she'd always made.

How am I supposed to change?

This is who I've always been.

All the madness, the fighting, surviving, the killing and eating—what did it matter if, at the end of the day, at the end of the world, she was the same old Jenny?

Scared.

Hungry.

Not willing to stand up for herself.

But no one's ever stood up for me before, screamed a voice inside her head. *No one's ever been there for me. How am I supposed to be there for myself?*

YOU WERE SUPPOSED TO BE THERE.

She bit her lip. More light sizzled across her body. She convulsed and opened her eyes. *YOU WERE SUPPOSED TO BE THERE.* And she thought of Yeshua. She thought of the angels. God. She thought of her mom. She thought of Eve and the three-headed figure. She thought of Susan. She thought of her death, a frightened little boy.

And when she buried her fingernails into her palm and shook, she let the light escape. It was the same feeling of Severed Spirit, when she'd severed her soul to survive a fight. When she'd cut through whatever bound the deaths to their pillars of salt. When she'd cut through the fabric of the worlds.

But it was different. She felt like a hot air balloon expanding with heat and air, rising, rising. She felt like she was expanding in every direction. She just needed a source of energy. Food. Like the way Yeshua had gone around feeding everyone from his arm.

With a shudder, she realized she was lying in it. The world was offering it. All this blood. Where had it come from? Who had it belonged to?

She didn't care. She rolled onto her front and pressed her face into the pool. It must've been ankle deep. Hot and sticky and red, she thought of the river of blood all the souls had crawled out of in the world of souls, waiting to be judged. She thought about all the blood she'd wanted. How it would make her salivate. How she wanted every drop. How she would never be able to stop herself.

She began to suck. Suck and swallow and swallow, mouthful after mouthful, the blood of the world. Trying to connect with the storms, with the ground beneath her, with all the blood coming down on her like a torrent. Sticky and metallic, red and delicious, carrying nutrition, carrying the basic essences of material life, and then, something clicked.

Light flashed behind her eyes. She saw the three-headed figure again, Eve. She saw Susan, hanging from a cross, sobbing. She saw her mother, a frown etched into her face, her eyes permanently sad. She saw her death, a boy who just wanted someone to talk to. Who just wanted a friend. Who just didn't want to be alone anymore.

And this time, a wail came from her throat. A sob that stuck for a moment before bursting through her lips. And all that agony, all that hopelessness, rippled away from her. She could shape it. Could see it rolling away, winds spreading across the surface of this world, gliding along the blood. Light that could not be stopped.

She'd hijacked her prison.

A glimmer of satisfaction filled her insides with warmth as she stood up, as the blood rain drenched her still; she was severing the blood from the world.

Power surged through her muscles again, plumping with strength and readiness. Her lungs expanded. Her stance changed. Her arms outstretched, fingers curling up into tight fists like she was holding on to the world itself.

Then, with a deep breath and a strange feeling of acceptance, she let go.

The rain stopped. Whatever was left trickled down her body and dripped from her hair. A warm breeze teased her skin. When she opened her eyes, the world had come to life with countless bubbles of color, like an endless field of brilliant flowers in every direction. She shuddered and wept; the pillars were all coming undone. And all the ghouls stood motionless, like ancient statues chiseled from rock and long forgotten.

She'd separated the world from whatever curse had held it in place. And when her death stumbled out of his pillar, he walked toward her. The exoskeleton had cracked. His tentacles lay limp on the ground, dragging behind him. He held out his arms as if wanting to be picked up, but Jenny knew better. They both knew better.

She knelt and scooped him up in her arms. She pressed her teeth to his throat and began to chew.

CHAPTER EIGHT

CHOSEN

L eslie was curled up with a blanket over her head in what was left of the History Department of her high school. A cup of still water rested on the floor beside her, and partial bodies were rotting between the desks and chairs. She tried not to look at them.

It was the dean of the History Department's office, and the dean's corpse was slumped over her desk, a horrible gash in her throat and one of her shoulder blades popping out from her back. The blood-soaked remnants of her blazer clung to her skin, and her once perfectly done hair had lost its sheen. The woman's eyes were open, and Leslie got a firsthand look at what the human eye looked like once it dried out. It reminded her of the skin that would form on top of tomato soup.

At least the angels didn't bother her, she thought. The school was rather empty, if she didn't count the bodies, and she was safe here. There was a vending machine down the hall that she'd broken into, and she had to use the boy's bathroom because the girl's room had faces she recognized. But other than that, she was comfortable.

Comfortable. She wanted a hot bath. She wanted to lie in a bath for days and days and let it all wash away. Her skin was layered with dried blood and filth. Her clothes were tattered. And her elbow had begun to ache.

Her stomach was also too big, protruding outwardly in a way that made her feel sick. Her feet hurt. Her throat felt raw. Her hair was falling out in clumps, and whenever she looked at her hands, she could see the skin rotting and peeling away. When she placed her hands on her pregnant belly, the skin stretched out so that she could see the veins and patterns in the bright golden glow from inside.

It shone and dimmed rhythmically, and she could feel *it*. Whatever it was. She didn't know what it was.

At least, that's what she told herself.

She felt ugly and hideous. She felt alone and terrified. But something had wanted her. Something had asked for her, chosen her. Something had been promised to her eternal paradise.

And now, here she was.

Dr. Lee pushed open the door she'd barricaded with a desk, the metal legs squeaking across the floor. Even though her old teacher had promised her nothing would harm her, she was still on guard. If anyone or anything did attack her, the barricade wouldn't do much, but at least she'd know. His glasses were cracked, and he was carrying his katana strapped to his back.

"Found something tasty," he said. He was dragging something heavy into the room.

Leslie nodded, unable to look away from the glowing silver light circling over Dr. Lee's head. If she squinted, she could just about make out what looked like shimmering wings coming out of his back. She had known from the moment he'd found her hiding in the school that he was no longer her former biology teacher.

He dragged the heavy thing over and sat beside her, the torn remnants of his lab coat flaring behind him. At her feet lay a woman, unconscious but still breathing. Dr. Lee drew his katana, held it over the woman's leg. He muttered something softly under his breath, then, with one swift blow, removed the woman's leg at her thigh.

The woman didn't scream; she only whimpered in her unconscious state, tears sliding down the sides of her head. Dr. Lee offered Leslie a chunk of flesh, which she accepted willingly, too afraid to say no, too afraid to refuse, especially because of the thing inside her stomach kicking with excitement at the meal offered. She told herself to pretend it was just something from the deli. Something normal.

Dr. Lee sat perfectly straight, uncomfortably straight, staring only at the gentle throbbing light emanating from Leslie's belly as she chewed. She could tell he was agitated. Could tell that he didn't want to be here. She wondered if the human inside was trying to resist, if whatever had possessed her teacher was too powerful to be resisted. She had lots of questions. But she never asked them.

She was just grateful to be chosen.

Once she finished off the leg, meat sticking between her teeth, her hunger kicked up a notch. It was like something would possess her as well, an uncontrollable urge, and she'd crawl over the prey, teeth chewing through every single bit that she could reach.

CHAPTER NINE

HOSPITAL STAY

It was freezing. Oliver crouched by the corner of the oncology ward, his breath clouding in front of him. The emergency lights blared on, just as they did every night, an eerie red light that brightened and dimmed all throughout the halls. The sounds of chewing came from a room ahead; Oliver clutched his dagger close and prepared for the fight.

Behind him, moving almost silently, was Mackenzie, who now wore a sleek dark armor that covered her from neck to toe. Headgear in the style of a football helmet went over her head, complete with a metal railing that protected her face. They'd all taken on the same style of armor; the only difference for Oliver was that his armor didn't go down to his legs. He didn't have human legs anymore.

Below the knees were metallic replacements he'd fashioned out of energy. They were thin and light, with flexible parts where his knees and ankles would've been; he'd been able to move with ease after a few days of practice. He'd even added blades to the front and back of his new "feet," and after carefully adding to his stats to improve his agility and a new skill called Heightened Acrobatics, he could spin through the air and slice through angels with just his legs.

Behind Mackenzie came Dulé, his fists glowing white hot, armor shimmering in response.

"Are you ready?" he asked. He tapped the side of his helmet for Mackenzie, who nodded. And when she turned to face Oliver, he nodded as well. He was hoping it would be a wretched angel; something strong that they could take down together and use to level up. They'd noticed back in their high school that it didn't matter how many of them attacked a creature, they all got experience and energy. If there was a reasoning to that, he didn't get it, but he wasn't mad at it either. It'd let him stack up enough energy to create his new legs.

He drew the flare from his pocket; something he'd stolen from the military equipment piles left in the mess on the streets. They all carried a few, and he'd even made a few more using spare energy. They were good to have.

"Alright," he whispered under his breath, more to himself than to anyone else. Mackenzie couldn't hear, and Dulé was too far away. The signal would be when he threw the flare into what he was sure was an angel nest.

He flicked the cap off with his thumb then sprinted down the hall, pumping his metal legs as hard as he could. As he passed by the nurse's station, a selection of long tables and shelves and collapsed computers, he caught a glimpse of all the eggs covering the ceiling and hanging from the swinging lights. He also counted three wretched angels: a purple female, an orange male, and one cream-colored one with red stripes.

Wretched Angel (Level 19)
Wretched Angel (Level 24)
Wretched Angel (Level 25)

Jackpot, he thought as he threw the flare into the middle of the room. Sparkling red light flared to life. Instantly, the angels erupted into a fit of screaming, the harsh light searing their eyes.

The largest one, the orange-exoskeleton-covered male with enormous muscles collapsed to the floor, grabbing its face and shrieking as its powerful legs kicked blindly. Its foot found a heavy desk, sending the furniture careening into the wall, where it crumpled a few eggs. The female screamed in agony and scurried upward, climbing onto her eggs, trying to keep them safe despite the pain.

The remaining one didn't flinch. It rushed toward Oliver, and as he turned around to face it, he saw why: this angel had gouged out its eyes. Its red stripes looked menacing in the flare's light, fresh blood dripping down the creature's white chin.

He threw his dagger at the angel. It landed right on the mark, lodging itself in the empty sockets. Then, using Heightened Acrobatics, Oliver leaped over the creature and landed as Mackenzie and Dulé rushed past.

Dulé punched the angel in the back with a charged-up super punch, bright lights igniting where his boxing glove made contact. The angel's striped exoskeleton cracked open with an awful crunch. Then Mackenzie came in for the killing blow, using her two large knives and slashing in the shape of an *X*. Bright blue light flashed from her skill activating, and she cut through the exposed flesh of the angel. It was dead before it hit the floor, spine and insides sliced to bits.

You have defeated Wretched Angel (Level 25)!

Oliver ignored the system notifications. Next was the orange male.

Something about it reminded Oliver of an enormous, muscular ladybug. It managed to get to its feet, blood dripping from where its eyes used to be, breathing hard. Its chest was massive, arms thicker than Oliver's entire body.

The three of them fanned out, forming a half circle around the male. Tendrils like fluttery paper streamers snaked out of its back. Oliver counted seven or eight of them; he couldn't tell. They kept swerving this way and that.

He readied another flare.

"It's using those to see," he shouted, summoning his dagger back from the first angel's corpse with a flash of light. He pointed to the tendrils, made eye contact with Mackenzie, and then motioned at his own eyes with two fingers. She nodded. Oliver readied the flare, bright light sparkling to life just as the first flare died out, and he threw it with the same skill he used for his dagger. *Quick Throw.*

The flare shot out of his hand and struck the angel in its eye socket, the burning, sparkling light singeing the exposed flesh. Dulé and Mackenzie rushed at the screaming angel as it roared, struggling to claw the burning flare out of its skull. Oliver crouched, his eyes on the female angel screaming on the ceiling. As Mackenzie cut through the tendrils and Dulé struck the angel on the chin with an uppercut, the purple female threw herself off the eggs. That was when Oliver struck.

Channeling his Springing Leap through his metal legs, he rocketed through the air and switched into Heightened Acrobatics, spinning and twisting as he sliced the angel up with his dagger before striking with the blades sticking out of the front and back of his feet. He landed as bits of the angel's flesh and purple exoskeleton rained down onto what was left of the nurse's station.

You have defeated Wretched Angel (Level 19)!

The last angel, the male, roared so loudly the entire hospital seemed to shake, and Oliver knew it was a countdown now till more angels swarmed to the area. Cries like that seemed to attract them.

"Quickly!" he shouted.

Mackenzie's dagger flashed, slipping in through the crack in the angel's chin Dulé had made. Another one of Dulé's charged fists found the angel in the crotch. There was another explosion of light, and then a series of notifications flickered through Oliver's head, but the only one that mattered was:

Leveled up!
Oliver Spencer, Level 27 → Level 28

But there wasn't much time to celebrate. He could hear hissing and screaming coming from the far end of the hall, and he knew it was time to pull out. If they didn't have the element of surprise, the fights were too strenuous, and they were more likely to get injured. More likely to make a mistake and get killed.

"Go!" he shouted, squatting down and holding out his two hands for Dulé.

Dulé ran toward him and leaped. Just as his feet found Oliver's hand, Oliver boosted him upward, and he shot through the ceiling with his fist, creating a hole for them to leap through as Mackenzie ran to Oliver's side. While holding on to her, he crouched down with his metal legs and launched himself up into the dark floor above.

When they landed, breathless, adrenaline pumping through their bodies, they glanced downward to see a stampede of angels, their bodies glistening in the fading light of the flare, hissing and screaming as they went for the eggs. They smashed them open and suckled at the goo; they fought each other, skinny limbs against skinny limbs, teeth against teeth, even as they tore apart the corpses of the wretched angels.

Once they got back to the fourteenth floor, after almost ten flights of stairs, Oliver went to find his parents. Mackenzie needed to use the restroom, and Dulé went off to speak to the soldiers who were guarding the noncombatant citizens.

Almost three hundred people filled this floor and the three floors above, piling into what used to be optometrist checkup rooms. It was a safe haven at the top of Manhattan Hope, and any day now, a chopper was supposed to arrive to evacuate them all. That was what the soldiers promised.

But where would it take them? wondered Oliver.

"Sweetheart," came his mother's voice from behind him. She appeared, the spitting image of his older sister, Jenny, and wrapped her arms around him. "Is that blood?" she whispered.

She always asked the same questions.

Human (Level 2)

"No, Mom. We cleared another room."

"Good," said his father, standing briskly in his bulletproof vest. He had a rifle on his back and his pistol on his hip. Oliver's father had been a marine in the US army, and he'd taken to this life somewhat easily, but there was a look on his father's face that Oliver didn't like. A strange kind of sternness. An unease. Like something that had struggled to heal for years and years had been ripped back open.

Human (Stage II - Level 18)

His father had been out on several trips with the soldiers and the police officers who were getting antsy holding up in the hospital. They'd been clearing out the bottom floors, keeping the angels from coming up. Most of the stairways except for one were barricaded, though Oliver had already noticed an issue with that. It was something they'd learned in school during fire drills: always have multiple exit paths.

But it seemed like most people were resigned to waiting. Waiting to be saved. Waiting to be rescued. A few others had copied Oliver and his friends. They too wore armor, but so many had seen their loved ones eaten alive that they couldn't stomach the fighting. They kept to the larger group, a further line of defense should any angel ever get through.

It was the people with guns who Oliver worried about the most. For them, the fight was easy enough to begin with. Tarnished angels had no defenses against bullets which could shatter bone and rip through flesh. A shot to their heads usually did the trick. But the wretched angels, especially the higher leveled ones, remained unfazed. Without something harder hitting, like a tank or a machine gun or something, they could walk through a barrage of bullets like it was nothing.

And for some reason, the people with guns didn't seem capable at all of abilities or power-ups. Their levels went up, but . . . It was odd to Oliver.

He'd already decided against using a gun. He never wanted to be caught reloading. He never wanted to get overrun again.

He added his new stat points to strength. His agility was high enough, but he wanted more strength to cut through stronger creatures, and he knew there would be more coming. The angels were nesting, producing eggs and gathering strength. And some had even started clawing out their eyes to fend off light.

"Sundown in thirty minutes," came a shout from the soldiers.

A chill went through almost everybody there. They'd all seen the horror of sundown. Oliver had been in his hospital bed, his legs missing, cables and things being pumped into his arm. His mom had been brought in with a bullet wound, shot by one of the cops. His dad. Dulé. Mackenzie. And Mrs. Monique.

He'd managed to heal his mom with a major healing spray. And they'd thought they'd be safe. They were in a hospital, after all. There was security. People with weapons posted out front. A police station nearby.

But then, the sun had gone down that first night. The angels had come rising from the darkness, screaming and hissing, and the entire city had gone up in uproar. There was a mad rush to go *up*, to get away from the streets crawling with monsters. Climbing up the stairs. Jamming the elevators. Everyone desperate. Everyone willing to step over everyone else.

When the soldiers had marched through the streets, Oliver had thought this had to be it, then. They'd save everyone. They had all the weapons.

But their tanks and all their guns had meant nothing when the angels swarmed them. And when the wretched angels emerged, their exoskeletons glistening, their power much stronger than the naked angels, the military had collapsed so quickly it was almost funny. It was like watching a movie from the top of the hospital, watching the bad guys win.

He didn't think anyone was coming to save them. But he wasn't sure what else to do. So he just tried to get stronger.

He created more water and bread for his parents. And some more for the hungry people staring at him. Others with energy did the same. Some created ice cream or cake. Pizza and ham sandwiches were popular. Soda. But bread cost two energy, and water only cost one. It was the safest thing, and his parents had agreed. He wanted to keep his energy for healing potions. Or stuff to replace any more lost limbs. Or new weapons.

At sunset, Oliver and Mackenzie went up to the roof with some of the others. Just to breathe some fresh air and not feel like the walls were closing in. They liked looking up at the stars, even if the stars seemed to be exploding slowly.

The ground would shake. The hospital would tremble, but something about that brief moment of darkness before the angels came was gentle and quiet, like something out of a movie. As the last bit of the sun dipped beyond the horizon and took all the remaining light with it, the city flooded with screaming. Where did the angels even come from?

But that night, it was raining. A drizzle at first, heavy dark clouds blanketing the sky. They stood in the cool breeze, droplets of water flicking into their faces, holding hands. They stared down at the street below where countless naked wet bodies glistened in the bit of light seeping through the storm. The city was nearly completely dark. Oliver had never seen it so dark before. The towering buildings looked empty and sad, almost frightening, some of their peaks covered by fog. Like they were all tombstones instead of the fancy places that made New York City so shiny.

A small crowd of people gathered on the rooftop, huddling inside their coats. It was colder up here, but it was a nice place to stretch their legs and search the sky for any sign of a rescue.

A shudder ran down Oliver's spine as he exhaled. His breath clouded in front of him. Rain soaked through his hair and dripped off his nose. His cracked glasses fogged up. Mackenzie pulled on his arm, and he turned to face her. Her eyes were somehow so bright despite the dark, and he thought he could see the entire night sky shining through them anyhow.

She brought her fingers to her lips and then pointed at Oliver, cocking one eyebrow.

Heat reddened his cheeks, and he nodded. "You don't have to ask every time," he mouthed as he signed back to her. Her face turned red as well, and for a second, he forgot the vicious, violent girl who could chop through the spine of an angel. He forgot that the world was coming apart, and that any day now, they might all be eaten alive. He even forgot that his legs were gone.

When she pressed her lips against his, everything melted away, even their armor, receding so that he could place his hand on her back and feel her chest against his, and he so badly wished they could stay like this forever, warm and safe and sound.

It was after waking up in the hospital that he'd confessed. All it had taken was everything going to shit for him to tell her how he felt. And she'd punched him, crying, and signing, *Finally*. And all these horrible days later, it still made his heart race whenever their lips touched. Whenever their fingers touched. It still made him nervous to kiss. His armpits would get sweatier than when he'd be fighting the angels, and he hoped he was getting better at kissing. Sometimes, it was too wet. Sometimes, too dry. But she'd laugh and kiss him on the nose and sign that she didn't know what she was doing either.

He stroked her hair, both of their breaths clouding in the evening chill. And then the hospital *shook* so violently, he was sure it would collapse. Mackenzie cried out and grabbed him. They braced for impact as the others around them screamed, and, in the distance, a series of explosions lit up the city.

A row of buildings exploded one after the other, and Oliver held on to Mackenzie and watched, spellbound, as the city lights came to life around them. As all the windows in the buildings across the street lit up, the streetlamps as well, everything shining, the angels below screeching in agony as the city roared back to life.

And when it faded, he saw the cause. Everyone did. An enormous *thing*, clinging to a skyscraper's tip as wind and rain swirled around it. Two large appendages stuck out of its back. The creature was glowing with a yellowish blue aura, facing away from them.

Oliver silently prayed for everyone to stay quiet, to not make a sound. The creature was only a few blocks away. Smoke billowed behind it from the city block that was destroyed, like a scene out of a disaster movie.

Someone screamed. An infectious scream that several people caught, and the angel turned around, its head cocking, searching for the source of all the noise.

Desecrated Angel (Level 66)

CHAPTER TEN

ELECTRICITY LIKE BLOOD

By the time Susan came to, the rain had stopped, the world was dark, and she was glowing.

Electricity snaked up and around her arms, crackling and fizzling. Every so often, she would shudder so hard her entire form would shake and vanish and fade back, rippling like a light bulb dying, struggling to stay alive. She felt sick.

She felt like her insides had become too big for her body; she wanted to throw up; she wanted to scream; she wanted to—

Gritting her teeth, she hunched over, arms wrapped around her stomach. But she didn't throw up; she couldn't throw up. She stared at her hands, shaking, the sidewalk below fading in and out of clarity as her skin turned translucent then faded back to normal. Like a signal was shooting from her heart with every beat, a wave that coalesced into something else when it reached the end of her fingertips, only to come rolling back into her chest.

Her head spun. *System? Numbers? Hello?*

She was sure she'd seen so many things when she'd touched the exposed wire. Shivering, she turned back toward it. She squinted at it—the broken lamppost, the exposed copper. But of course, everything was dead and dark now. Nothing was bright. Except for her.

Beyond, towering in the middle of the road by burned-out cars and rubble, was her cross. The thing she'd been bound to forever and ever in Azra'il's castle. When her eyes landed on it, she realized what she had to do.

Brimming with more energy than she could bear, shaking with every step, Susan half walked, half stumbled toward it, every step feeling too heavy to bear. Three times, she wanted to collapse and lay on the ground, but her hands would shake like excited magnets, and she'd remember her old weapon. The cattle prod. How she'd bent electricity with it. How she'd helped Jenny fight. How she'd changed the angel in the library by blasting it with electricity through the brain.

Could she do that again?

Maybe?

A shaking ran up her legs as she approached the cross. She saw the wooden beams, damp from the rain. The dried blood. The bits of her hands and feet still stuck to the nails, dried up and shriveled and grotesque. She kept expecting Azra'il to emerge from behind it, his enormous hand reaching for her. She screamed and threw herself at the cross, slamming into it so hard it toppled over.

It landed with a mighty crash, completely crushing the car beneath it, like it was the heaviest thing on the planet. Susan climbed up and struck it where the two wooden beams met, punching the wood over and over. With each strike, electricity and light sizzled around her wrist, around her arms, and she started shining brighter and brighter. Everything came back to her in a flurry of awful memories, like a flash flood.

She saw Azra'il's face up close: the gleaming red eyes, the snakes that snapped forward and bit chunks off her body, only for it to all grow back with glowing light. How he'd pull on her arm until she screamed, until it snapped—usually at the elbow, sometimes at the shoulder—and blood would gush out, bones and veins spurting out from her ruptured skin. How he'd puncture her chest with his nail, digging and digging until he could skewer her heart and rip it out.

And she would remain on the cross, stuck between screaming and crying, stuck between living and dying, while he chewed on her heart like it was a gummy gusher. And that grin. That evil, twisted grin as he peeled her skin off from her thighs and told her he'd make cloth from it; a new garb to cover his privates, perhaps, or something more akin to the humans. A shirt? Some trousers? A bridal dress?

He'd lean in really close and promise he'd make Jenny his bride. How she would wear a veil made of Susan's skin. Susan would beg him. Beg him to spare Jenny. That she, Susan, could be his bride; that she'd do anything he wanted if he would leave Jenny alone, but all he'd do was laugh.

"*Sadistic fucking asshole!*" screamed Susan, and with one final strike, with the bolts of electricity growing into immense lightning, she slammed her fist through the wood, and the entire cross splintered. It turned into dust.

Susan landed on the crushed car below, a chunk of metal slicing into her stomach, glass cutting into her hands and knees. Even though pain rushed from her belly and blood came gushing out, she cried out, laughing.

Laughing, as she was free of the cross.

Laughing, as pain had become so familiar, so normal. Glowing light glistened along her body as she healed, but she felt the torn piece of metal cutting through her intestines all the same. She crawled out of the wreckage, pulling herself off the sharp metal and glass, and landed splat on the street.

Her thoughts quieted as she caught her breath. She wasn't human anymore. She wasn't alive anymore. But she wasn't completely without power now. She wasn't completely at the mercy of the cross.

The ache in her head faded away. She sucked in deep breaths of cold air, and then she heard it. A hiss. A staticky, sharp hiss that cut through her thoughts, and Susan turned her head to see a tarnished angel staring at her.

They'd never stared at her before. This one was hunched over another car, sniffing. And behind it were several more, all of their empty eyes locked onto her own.

Unable to help the trembling, Susan scrambled back, trying to get to her feet. And as if waiting for her to move, the angels darted forward, streaking across the street on all fours to get to her, every one of them hissing or screaming, blood dripping down their chins.

She could already see them chewing through her. Eating her, gorging on her as she healed over and over—they could feast forever if she let them.

But if she ran now, she'd always be running.

Her hands still shook with energy; her entire body felt like it would burst. Electricity pumped through her like blood, and as she clenched her fists in anticipation, in fear, she felt it come sparkling out of her fingertips the same way her ability Valescent Light used to, her arms glowing. When the first angel reached her, a male with dark skin and short hair and blood streaming from its mouth, Susan instinctively threw her hands forward.

Electricity shot out, snapping and sizzling through the air, everything moving slowly for a moment, the angel midleap, the other angels running behind it.

The electrical current shot right into the angel's head, bounced off the creature, and zapped the four other angels behind it. Susan saw the arc of light shining brightly with a yellow-golden warmth, and then it snapped away. The angels collapsed on the ground, dropping at her feet. Everything went dark.

Susan stood where she was, the angels twitching and moaning around her. Slowly, she stared at her hands, smoke wisping off her fingertips as she saw more electricity crackling just beneath the skin of her palms, making her creases glow with every beat of her heart.

She was *generating* electricity. With each breath, with each passing second, she felt more and more energy rippling inside her, and she realized she could do so much more than just spectate. She could fight. She could save people.

But what happened to the angels?

Kneeling, she reached out to the nearest tarnished angel, a female with dirty red hair. Its skinny frame flinched from her touch, and it looked up at her like a frightened animal. But its eyes weren't empty; there was a green iris staring back at her, tears flowing down the creature's cheeks. It kept hissing something, over and over. Susan shuddered, stepping away. The urge to do something for the poor creature made her want to help it. But she didn't know what to do. At least it wasn't coming after her anymore. None of the others were, either.

"Hello?" she whispered.

The male angel raised its head. Its lips moved, but the sound from it was closer to whistling than any language she'd ever heard of, and Susan shook her head.

"I don't understand."

The angels got to their feet, standing almost like normal humans now, no longer crouching. They looked at each other, all of them weeping, then at Susan. Before she could say anything else, they rushed off down the street, as though trying to get as far away as possible from something.

Susan stared after them, watching their naked forms running clumsily, awkwardly, as though they were not accustomed to feet. One of them tumbled, and another pulled them up, and they ran and ran until they vanished from view.

She turned in the direction they were running from, wondering what was waiting up ahead.

CHAPTER ELEVEN

NULL

Metamorphosis Complete!

**Jenny Huang
Human (Stage III - NULL)**

Shaking, blood dripping from her body, her stomach full, Jenny got to her feet. A breeze blew through her, scattering goose bumps across her limbs, and she rubbed her sides as chills ran down her spine. *I just ate my death.* Like puddles soaking into the dirt, all the blood from the storm drained away into the black ground, leaving behind wet and sticky sand/salt. It squelched between her toes.

She'd just eaten her death. The little boy. There wasn't anything of him left; she'd crunched through his bones, his exoskeleton, every bit of his tentacles. She shuddered. She couldn't even remember it; couldn't remember if she had been chewing or if he'd been. But he was now a part of her, and her system notification had changed. She was no longer a desecrated human; she was a regular human again, except now she was *Null*. Just like Yeshua had been.

There are no more levels?

What am I?

All around her, colors bloomed in little spheres that seemed to go on and on. She was exhausted. Tightness pressed against the back of her eyes, and her head spun, but she was spellbound by the sight. Reds and greens, yellows and blues, bubbles of every shade of every color all around her, like a nebula unfurling or a field of flowers blooming. She turned and watched, the unmoving ghouls casting long shadows, the sky clearing.

There was no more rain. In fact, the heaviness that affected the world, the weight it'd seemed to have, lightened. She felt lighter. And she looked down at her hands and feet, trembling.

Her limbs had grown back a bit. They weren't as muscular as they'd been during her earlier fights, but they didn't feel sickly and weak anymore. Her hair had grown while she'd been crucified. It came down to her mid back now, black with a bunch of split ends and in desperate need of a wash. The crown of thorns pricked her forehead, and grabbing it with both hands, not caring how it cut her fingers with searing pain, she tore it off her scalp and tossed it away.

There was still that *thing* inside her. That thing that Azra'il had placed there. It crawled along her skin to her scalp first, healing the pricks as blood trickled down her nose. Her eyes shut closed, and she stumbled forward, nearly nodding off into sleep. She needed to rest. She needed new clothes. She needed a bath.

I need food.

How am I still so hungry?

She leaned and touched one of the ghouls, their oversized heads frozen in place, their limbs caught halfway through running. Nothing swirled in their eye sockets anymore. She knew without having to try that they were empty; whatever had been giving them life was gone.

What did I do?

I ate my death.

The light show was weighing on her now. She could see crowds of people gathering. The deaths. All the deaths of the world. They'd be coming for her. Would they expect her to feed them?

Or would they just come and take, just like the ghouls had?

Shaking, she drew on the last bit of her strength and channeled it toward her fingers. How did it go? Severed Spirit followed by Valescent Light to open a passageway? But something twisted in her gut, like her body was rejecting itself, and pain erupted inside her.

And then, that thing inside her wormed its way through her guts. Her hands went to her navel, and she fell on her knees, clenching her jaw, struggling to fight the urge to throw up.

Closing her hand into a fist, she struck her stomach as hard as she could.

"Fuck," she swore, spittle flying out of her mouth. She struck herself again and again, and each time, the wriggling thing moved back and forth, healing whatever skin she bruised, whichever rib she knocked out of place.

By the time the lights faded away, she'd collapsed on the soggy ground, exhausted. She rolled over onto her back to stare at the cross. Flaps of skin and flesh were still nailed to the wood. She looked at the hand she'd left behind. She looked at the bits of her feet. Blood dripped off the edges of the cross. It looked weathered and old, like it had seen too many storms, too many crucifixions.

A feeling told her she was *free* of it, not bound in the way Yeshua had been, where after leaving the world, he was forced back to the cross. Whatever she'd done to the world of death, whatever her new Severed Spirit did, she'd cut the connection between her and the cross as well.

The sky overhead had cleared; she could see the stars again, as well as the colors blooming between them. For a second, she thought she could see what was going on clearly, as though her eyes had zoomed in or the stars had grown massive, but then she blinked, and she realized she was crying. The tears were distorting her vision.

She bit her lip as footsteps approached, and she turned her head to see all the deaths, now free from the pillars, watching her. They stood in a circle around her as though she'd just landed from outer space. As though she were some kind of oddity. Or maybe they saw her like they'd seen Yeshua. A messiah. A savior. Someone to take care of them.

Or were they afraid she'd eat them too?

She sat up and rubbed dried blood off her legs. Then she stared at her hands, her overgrown fingernails. Maybe she should just open a passageway and leave. That's what she'd meant to do, anyway. What else was she supposed to do here? She didn't want to fight anymore. Didn't want to try anymore. She could just go to the material world, find Susan, and then, the two of them could run off to some other world. Any world. Somewhere far away from all this.

But as soon as she reached for Severed Spirit, as soon as she felt the air, the *thing* wriggled through her again. This time, she felt it in her lungs, near the base of her throat, and she had to grab her arm to keep from clawing her chest open. She wanted to throw up. She wanted to tear herself into pieces.

Why was it responding to Severed Spirit? Was that because the ability itself was damaging? Because it hurt her just to use it? Or was it something else? Like she was rejecting it . . .

Breathing heavily, she wondered if it was because she'd eaten her death. Completing the "metamorphosis" or whatever that was. Whatever had made her *Null*.

Was she trapped here?

She looked around at all the faces staring at her. Almost every single one of them was naked. All of them looked hungry and needy, staring at her as though she might have answers. But she wasn't Yeshua. She wasn't their lord and savior. She was hungry too. She was needy and naked. She was alone and unsure and scared.

"Who are you?" came a voice.

"Will you help us? We are hungry."

"Are you a life?"

"Are you okay?"

Jenny's eyes swam with tears again, blurring all their faces. She needed space to clear her head. To think. She accidentally scratched her side, and the thing inside wriggled down through her chest to heal her skin. All she kept picturing was clawing it out and seeing what it was. She wanted to know what it was. But it was free healing; no more potions, no more spending energy. She just had to deal with it crawling inside her.

She wiped her eyes and faced the deaths.

"I'm going to find Yeshua," she proclaimed loudly, straightening her shoulders and trying to project strength. The world of death didn't seem so awful anymore, and she figured they would be all right here. "He's the one you need."

But could she? The deaths blinked back at her, and even though she knew they didn't understand what she meant, she couldn't help but read their stares as judgement. As mistrust. She gritted her teeth and tried to focus.

Null. Null. Null.

What did that mean? Why should that stop her?

Would it stop anything else? She focused on the guidance system, taking a look at her stats.

Jenny Huang
Human (Stage III - NULL)
Age: 6,823 days
Stats:
Power: 50
Durability: 35
Stamina: 55
Agility: 50
Stat Points Available: 2
Energy Available: 7008
Energy Core(s): 2

It still read Null. She was Null. But the thing about Metamorphosis and Bloodlust Ecstasy were gone. She wasn't even *Blooded* anymore. Could she still use her skills?

Like muscle memory, like a reflex, Jenny summoned her hatchet back to her hand with a flash of golden light. Where had it come from? She couldn't tell; she didn't care.

Enhanced Armor will cost 1500 Energy.
Sufficient Energy.

Golden light shimmered across her body, and she felt the deaths bristling. Red armor covered her body, but halfway through, she decided against the color, and black scales bloomed from the base layer. Scales covered her chest and ran down her legs and covered her feet. At least she could do that.

She looked at the deaths again, wondering if she should spend her energy to make them clothes. If she should offer her own flesh for them to feast on. But there were too many; too many hungry, frightened faces. And she needed all the energy she could get.

Tying her hair back into a bun, she licked her lips. She could still taste her death, and a shiver ran down her back. She could picture his face, eyes filled with tears, arms wrapped around her as he offered himself. What did it mean that she'd eaten her death? When she died . . . would she just disappear? Cease to be?

A shudder curled around her spine.

Maybe Yeshua would know. And besides, she still had to find Susan in the material world. And kill Azra'il in whatever world he might be in. And then go after Adonai. And everything with the demons and souls and harpies. And whatever was going on in the sky.

There were too many things, too much shit. She just wanted to rest. But did any of that matter, really? She should just focus on finding Susan. Helping Yeshua. Whatever happened beyond that . . . that wasn't her problem. But how was she supposed to do any of that if she couldn't open a passageway?

She drew her hand through the air, slicing it down the middle with her bare finger. Dried blood stained her hand, and everything felt gross, but she knew the light waiting for her would cleanse it all away. If only she could open the passageway.

Her fingers shook with effort. Her jaw ached from clenching so hard. She wanted to throw up.

I can't.

I can't do this.

She screwed up her eyes, wanting to cry, wanting to scream. She felt even more useless. She had her armor. The hatchet. She'd gotten off the cross, but something in her felt paralyzed. Frozen or lost, she couldn't tell. Was it fear? Was it . . . ?

But I'm so angry. I just want to . . .

What was it?

What's wrong with me?

"Excuse me?" came a voice from the crowd.

Jenny stopped and opened her eyes. She'd been holding her breath, trying to ignore the wriggling thing inside her, trying not to spiral into a full-blown panic attack. One of the deaths stepped forward, an old woman.

A bunch of them had cleared the way for her to approach, and now there was a path through the crowd. She looked very old, hunched forward, the wrinkles burrowed so deeply onto her face that Jenny couldn't tell her ethnicity. Long gray hair fell around her hips, and she seemed too old and frail to be moving around.

The only elderly people Jenny ever knew were some of her teachers and a few neighbors; she'd never had a grandparent, never really spoken to elderly people before. She'd always found them somewhat scary, their weathered faces, their tired eyes, but something about this woman was oddly familiar, like she'd always known her. Jenny couldn't place why. It was like staring at a photograph of a place where you used to live but couldn't remember.

"There's a pillar," she said, her voice layered with sweet concern. There was something innocent about her that made Jenny want to trust her. As though she really might've been Jenny's grandmother, someone who knit sweaters and baked treats and had soothing words of love and compassion for whenever she felt lost. The old woman beckoned Jenny closer. "A pillar that hasn't melted. Will you come and see?"

CHAPTER TWELVE

THE PILLAR

Jenny followed the old woman through the parted crowd. On both sides were the other deaths, a few of them clothed in purple robes, most of them naked, all of them staring. They were crying and comforting each other, the young ones holding hands or being held in the arms of an older death, while others leaned on each other for support. They were trapped here, too, just as Jenny was. And she was getting the sense that their purpose, their reason for existence, had been denied to them all this time. She'd never had the opportunity to ask Yeshua about it all.

There were ghouls interspersed between them, motionless, without any vapor left in their eyes. Their glistening white bodies shone in a dull sort of way, like dust-covered marble. Jenny didn't look too closely at their mannequin-esque features. She hadn't completely understood what had happened to them or why they existed or why they were so hungry, but whatever she'd done with the blood and the world, she'd disconnected something that had held everything together.

Every once in a while, the lights overhead erupted and scattered, and the ground rumbled. But the deaths kept the pathway clear, and the old woman led the way.

Who are you? Jenny wanted to ask. The woman could've been anyone's death, since deaths didn't have to be a one-to-one mirror of a life. Her own death had been a little boy. So whose death was this old woman? Why did she seem so familiar?

"Do you have a name?" asked Jenny, trying to ignore all the eyes staring at her, watching her every step. She felt completely overdressed now that she'd put on her armor, the scales shining with every step. She'd wanted to get away, to leave all this behind her. Were they staring accusingly? Did they know what she'd done? That she'd eaten her own death?

The woman shook her head. "We are all simply called Death."

"Why do you seem different from the others?"

She turned to look back at Jenny, and there was a soft smile on her face. "Because I have missed you very much."

"Who are you?" whispered Jenny, coming to a stop. She felt a lump in her throat and found it hard to swallow all of a sudden.

"For another time," she replied. "Come with me for now." She hobbled back to where Jenny stood and slipped her wrinkled hand into hers. The woman only came up to Jenny's shoulder. "All of us deaths are connected through this world. Like fish in the sea, we can feel each other and know our surroundings. We all can sense there is something wrong."

Jenny glanced around at the faces watching her. She tried to smile politely, but the ground shook again, and she had to help the old lady stay up.

"There's a pillar that hasn't opened," she continued.

"Where?"

"The world will take us." As they walked, Jenny felt that shifting feeling she'd felt long ago when Yeshua had called her to his cross. The air bending, folding; the ground collapsing like an accordion before expanding. The faces around them moved and blurred. Or maybe all the deaths were rushing around, waves of people. She couldn't tell. But within a few moments, after another dozen steps or so, a clearing opened up ahead. The crowd had stepped back to make a circle, and as Jenny and the old woman entered the clearing, the path behind them closed, and everyone gathered in to look.

It was a pillar just like all the others Jenny had seen. A long dark object that came up to around her height. The rock face was dark like obsidian, like her hatchet, chiseled and weathered down. But she had a sinking feeling in her chest the closer they got, and the woman's hand squeezed harder.

Jenny's throat had gone dry. It hurt to swallow. And that fear she'd felt the first time she'd seen the deaths suffering inside the pillars roared back to life. With a shaky breath, she activated Ignite along her right hand and held it to the front of the pillar.

As soon as she glimpsed what was inside, she backed away, shaking the flames off her fingertips.

"It has no face," said the woman, a tremor of fear in her voice.

Jenny rubbed her face and turned away, struggling to breathe. Something inside her had *squeezed* upon glimpsing what was inside. She sucked in several deep breaths and, after a comforting smile from the old woman, turned around and used Ignite again to get a better look.

Death (Level 0)

The thing inside was definitely a death. The notification said so. It was naked, its arms by its sides, its insides coming outward and connected to the pillar. But its body was androgynous. There were no features; it might as well have been a mannequin. And it had nothing on its face. No eyebrows, no nose, no mouth. Nothing at all. There was no expression.

Like the other deaths, its insides came unspooling out like snakes, hitching up to the pillar with gross things pumping through them.

"Fuck," she swore under her breath, trying to stifle the urge to shudder.

Her insides tightened. Her head spun. She'd felt fear when she'd looked inside the pillars before and found the deaths; she'd felt stricken with fear when she'd met the desecrated angel who'd flashed blue light. And hell, she'd felt even worse fear standing up to Azra'il and trying to get Susan away from the angel.

But this?

This was unsettling. Like she'd looked into something *wrong*. Something that should never have existed. That could not exist. That was completely antithetical to reality.

She found herself shaking her head. Some part of her wanted to use Severed Spirit on the pillar and set the creature free to find out what it was. But her body was responding, sweat running down her sides from her armpits, her heart racing just a little too quickly. Something primal stirring.

Don't set that free.

Don't.

"I don't know what it is," said Jenny, struggling to blink away tears before they could come. *Why am I crying?*

What is that thing?

She shook her head again and stepped away. "I think we should leave it be."

The old woman frowned. "But aren't they in pain?"

Jenny rubbed her eyes. "What do you want me to do about it?"

She could hear her death's voice again. *"WHY DON'T YOU EVER DO SOMETHING?"*

"Fuck," she whispered. She shook her head again. "I don't know what's in there. And I can't help it." Her hands tremored. It wasn't really a lie. She was struggling to access Severed Spirit; she couldn't even open that passageway between worlds. And besides, she'd poured everything she had into severing the world, into freeing all the pillars. So why hadn't this pillar opened up? If all that hadn't worked, then why should trying again change anything?

But how could she find out without trying? Might as well eliminate the possibility.

"Fine," she said, straightening her shoulders. "I'll set it free."

The old woman only nodded. The other deaths stepped closer, all of them trying to see. Couldn't they feel what Jenny felt? That unsettling sensation of *wrong*?

Don't do this, said some voice deep inside her. *Don't set it free.*

Jenny held her hands out, placing her palms flat on either side of the pillar. Coldness seeped through the hard surface. All the other deaths had been burning hot to the touch, but this one was ice cold.

Breathe, she reminded herself, exhaling as much as she could through her nose before inhaling. *Breathe.* The wriggling thing inside her moved through her back and traveled up into her shoulder blades. *Don't think about that.*

Focus.

But why?

Why am I doing this?

I'm curious. I'm afraid. And I'm tired of running away from things that make me afraid.

That's stupid.

Just do it.

It might not even work. She straightened her shoulders and widened her stance to just beyond shoulder-length apart. Her armor glistened in the lights above; she could feel every death staring at her.

Was it curiosity? Judgment? Or just wonder? They were all free now. They didn't have to stay here. Or did they have nothing else to do? Purposeless? Just stuck here. And who was this old woman? Would her death be staring too if he was here? Would the old woman be nice to Jenny if she knew what Jenny had done? Something tingled along her fingertips; she could feel her heart beating.

For now, just do this, she told herself. *Think "outward." I'm severing some-thing outwardly. Not internally.*

There won't be any damage to myself. Nothing to heal. Nothing to stop. Nothing to be afraid of.

She pushed with her mind, resisting the urge to give up, the urge to run away. And slowly, it began. The familiar sensation of cutting, like she was holding a knife sharper than anything that ever could be, slicing through something impossible to cut. A connection that wasn't just physical but immaterial.

Then it turned on her.

The imaginary blade she was picturing turned to face her, and suddenly, it was cutting *her*.

Jenny couldn't scream. She couldn't make a sound. She was stuck in place, holding on to the pillar, eyes closed. Except now she wasn't cutting the death free of the pillar—it was trying to cut her.

Cut her away. Cut her in half. Cut through her life and show her the gaping wounds of so many memories. Too many memories.

Straining all her muscles, a scream buried in her chest, she tried to stop it. Tried to release the pillar and step away and never come back. But the pillar held on just as tight, and even though her eyes were closed shut, she could *see* the thing inside moving, straightening up to face her, a crack running across the bottom half of its featureless face so that its head could split open to reveal two rows of razor-sharp teeth. And all of a sudden, the knife she'd been picturing *slipped*.

Severed Spirit went sideways, and Jenny's hand slid off the pillar. A cry of despair erupted around her, and she opened her eyes to find a gash in the air around the pillar. Darkness appeared, liquid and boiling, just like the one she'd found on the cafeteria floor of her high school and from where the angels had risen. Darkness, just like the tear she had to cut open between worlds.

She stepped back, looking around at the crowd and the old woman, motioning for them to move back as well.

A hand burst out of the dark, thin, bony fingers curling as though trying to grasp something. Then came a head, eyes completely white, the skin of the creature's face hugging its skull too tight. Bony teeth.

Tarnished Angel (Level 1)

It stumbled out of the darkness and fell, spine showing so painfully that Jenny wanted to rip it from the creature's back. Long brown hair fell over its shoulders, and it looked up almost like a helpless dog. Another hand came from the dark, and then another.

As soon as the first one got its bearings, it twitched. It shuddered. It opened its mouth and shrieked, throwing itself at Jenny.

She didn't move, watching it scramble across the dirt, watching it close in as if it moved in slow motion. For a moment, there was no sound, nothing. Just its horrible face and the empty look in its eyes and its rotten teeth.

Jenny's lips twitched into a half smile. It was almost comforting seeing something so weak. Something so familiar. She twirled her hatchet and met the level-one creature head-on.

Her hatchet flashed with golden light. She cut down angel after angel, indiscriminately attacking whatever surfaced from the hovering, oozing darkness, taking pleasure as she built up a sweat, as she racked up points and energy and notifications. Not that they gave enough for her to level up; not that she really had a level anymore. All it said was Null. But the experience had to be going somewhere, right? The energy was still going to be useful. And if nothing else, she was happy to be *moving*. To be working out her stress. It was a perfect reprieve from her overthinking.

After the initial handful, dozens emerged at a time, screaming and desperate for blood, and Jenny had to keep them away from the deaths. The old woman had taken the others and retreated, leaving ample space for Jenny to throw her hatchet around, use Instant Swap and Instant Acceleration, and catch up to any who got past her.

She punched angels in the face, using more force than she had to, their fragile skulls collapsing, bursting in an explosion of blood and chunks of bone and brain matter. She kicked in their chests and cut them to ribbons before they could even scream properly. Most of them were dead before they hit the ground, and a familiar itch crept up her spine. Her tentacles wanted out. They wanted to feed; she wanted to feed.

But she had to keep the angels from reaching the deaths. She didn't really understand why, but she wanted to protect them. Keep them safe. Didn't want them to suffer anymore after existing inside the pillars for so long, after what the ghouls had done to them. Maybe it was because she'd eaten her own death and he was now a part of her. Or maybe it was because the old woman seemed so familiar. Or maybe it was just what her death had told her.

"Why don't you ever do something?"

Jenny was going to try. She could stop the flow of angels, couldn't she? With Valescent Light, she could change the darkness into light, and this would stop. She didn't have to give in to the madness again, didn't need Bloodlust Ecstasy again.

As she fought her way to the darkness, slashing and hacking screaming, desperate angels to death, she thought about that thing inside. The fear response she had to it. That *thing* was the reason this had happened. Almost as if it refused to be severed from the salt pillar. Jenny ducked to avoid angels reaching for her face. Fingernails bounced off her new armor as her hatchet split angels in half, their lanky, naked bodies falling away, guts spilling, eyes losing their shine.

When she finally reached the darkness, she couldn't even see the pillar anymore. It had encompassed it completely. She punched in the face of another emerging angel, but when she tried to touch the darkness, her finger slid inside.

She gasped. She'd expected it to be like the darkness she'd touched before, rejecting her, resisting her. She shouldn't be able to sink through. But more and more angels were trying to surface, and she didn't have time to investigate this new development.

She focused on the warmth inside her and brought out Valescent Light, letting the golden light bloom from her hands as the rainbow colors shimmered all around. She started to shake from the effort, sweating hard, wanting to fall. It had been a long time; she'd been on that cross a long time. The ghouls had been eating away. She'd been losing herself.

But here she was now. Trying.

And as if to answer her attempt, another arm lashed out of the darkness, thin and bony. It struck Jenny on the forehead. Gritting her teeth, she slashed the arm away, slashed off the head of another angel, and tried to pour more of herself into Valescent Light.

With a cry, she dropped her hatchet and threw both hands at the darkness. Instead of changing, it rippled as though she'd dropped a large stone into a puddle. Like no matter how much Jenny poured into it, it wouldn't matter. Jenny *felt* it. Felt that she wouldn't be able to change this. It was different.

And a curious idea came to mind.

What if . . . What if she stepped through it?

She looked back at the old woman, the only death to remain near her. The woman stood there with her hands at her sides, her wrinkled face not betraying any emotion. A breeze stirred her silver hair. Jenny felt a sudden rush of emotion. It wasn't sadness, really, but something sweet. Something that made her want to rush over and give the woman a hug. To promise her that Jenny would be right back, and that everything would end up okay.

But instead, she smashed her palm into the face of an emerging angel, one finger forcibly sliding up its nostrils as she shoved the creature back, before Jenny stepped into the darkness.

CHAPTER THIRTEEN

HOSPITAL EMERGENCY

Nancy's leg kicked, and she woke up, shaking violently. Her husband, Henry, wasn't lying beside her on the three hospital blankets they used as bedding. Instead, he was standing, and people were shouting outside their room. For a second, she thought all the lights were on—everything seemed so bright and fluorescent—but then it was gone. She must've only just fallen asleep. The last thing she remembered was hugging Oliver, who'd come back with blood smeared all over his face and outfit.

"What happened?" she called to her husband. "Where's our son? Where are his friends?"

Henry's face was dark. "That shake didn't feel right. And the lights."

Trying to rub the sleep quickly from her eyes, Nancy got to her feet, leaning against the wall for support. She nearly slipped on the bedding as she moved toward him, trying not to bump into the shelves of cleaning supplies and tools. They had a janitor's closet to themselves, which was lucky. Most people were sharing hospital rooms. At least they had some privacy. "What shake?" she asked.

She'd been having this awful dream; yet another awful dream in a series of awful dreams. But in this one, Jenny was back in her arms, just a toddler, tiny and small, with silky black hair and a cute little nose. It'd started off cuddly and sweet, and she'd wanted to cry, but then, Jenny had started suckling on her nipple. Or at least, she thought the girl was suckling. It wasn't until Jenny had raised her bloodstained face and revealed rows of razor-sharp fangs that Nancy had realized what was happening, and then she'd woken up with a start.

Henry didn't say a word. He clutched his rifle. She could almost see the gears turning in his head. They'd discussed this several times, but there was never an answer. Did they climb upward toward the roof, or did they run down the stairs and try to survive outside?

Nancy grabbed his arm and was about to tell him it would be all right when another violent shock sent her tumbling into her husband. They crashed against the shelf, her hip smashing into metal. All the lights in the hospital came to life, so bright that they hurt to look at, and Henry pulled her down to the ground, wrapping his arms around her. Smoke swirled as the lights flickered on and off, and the horrible stench of things burning stung her nose.

Her side throbbed with pain. She couldn't remember where the bullet had hit her. Had it been her thigh? Her hip? Somewhere between her ribs? After Oliver had healed her with some kind of magical spray, she'd kept pulling up her shirt and checking her skin, but there wasn't even a scar. And she'd had her husband check many times. But now, her sides ached anew from crashing into the shelf, and she suppressed a groan, trying to think through the pain.

A moment later, a frantic face appeared in the hallway just as the lights went out and everything was cast in the eerie red glow of the emergency lights. How long would they last this time, wondered Nancy.

It was Mrs. Monique, the woman who'd once been the librarian at her children's school. She was donned in silver armor, carrying a long spear, a glowing silver knife strapped to her waist. "A powerful angel landed on the rooftop. We have to evacuate to the lower floors. Henry, the soldiers can use your help maintaining order. Nancy, you are going with everyone else."

The woman spoke so matter-of-factly there was no time to respond. She was already gone. Nancy grabbed her purse, her flashlight, and followed Henry out into the hall. She wanted to beg him to come with her, for them to stay together, but they didn't get a chance to say a word to each other. There was only a moment to exchange a kiss as the sway of the crowd tugged Nancy away, and she was rushing down the stairwell.

Hundreds of people streamed down the steps, crying, sniffling. Asking questions like: Where was the military? Why weren't they rescued off the roof? What was going on?

Another violent shock wave rippled through the building. Nancy grabbed the banister and held on, crouching low till she was practically sitting on the steps. A boot kicked the back of her head. Someone else tripped over her leg. Once again, electricity surged, the stairwell lights flaring to sudden life, but this time, it was accompanied by so many awful screeching and screaming sounds that Nancy's blood ran cold. She'd recognize those sounds anywhere.

There were angels ahead, waiting for them at the bottom of the stairs.

Soldiers in uniform and helmets equipped with flashlights pushed and marched their way through the crowd to join the group at the front. They had their rifles and flashlights trained on the large exit doors. Nancy tried to look behind her, up the stairs, past the frightened, dirty faces, trying to spot Henry or Oliver in the crowd.

That was when the ceiling collapsed. Her eyes went wide as a large chunk of building landed in front of her, smushing two people in an instant. Their limbs stuck out from under the rubble, twitching as blood ran down the steps.

More rubble came raining down, and everything erupted into chaos. People ran covering their heads. Screaming. Pushing into the soldiers. Slipping in blood. The emergency lights went off. Hissing sounds were so near now that Nancy found it hard to breathe; she couldn't deal with them again. She couldn't bear getting past them again. But it was too late.

From the flashing lights, she could see the naked, horrible bodies of those angels. Shots rang out, crackling like flashes of thunder, echoing up and down the stairwell.

Nancy flattened herself against the banister. More debris rained down, knocking people out, killing them—it was hard to tell. And above, through the holes in the ceiling, she could see something monstrous. A large thing emanating yellow light, swerving in every direction. And there were several smaller figures engaging it in a fight. A prayer was on her lips before she could stop herself; Oliver must be up there.

That's where she had to go. She couldn't get caught in this mess. If she was going to die, then she'd at least die with her family. Where was Henry? How was she going to get to their son?

More soldiers opened fire, and every bullet sound sent a shiver of fear through her limbs. And as the mass of people ran all over one another, as bits of the ceiling knocked people out, Nancy pushed and shoved. She was trying to make space, trying to climb up the stairwell the way she'd come. Every touch made her flinch. She couldn't be sure who was human or what was angel in the dark, and she kept expecting another bullet to find her.

Flashes of light sprung up through the crowd as people used their abilities. Abilities that Nancy couldn't figure out. The numbers and things made no sense to her, and even though Oliver and Mackenzie had tried, neither she nor her husband or most of the other adults could understand. Though she'd seen some of their levels go up, especially the soldiers and the police officers, they hadn't done anything, hadn't been able to conjure anything from thin air.

But now, flames and wind ricocheted through the stairwell. More screaming. Fighting. Nancy covered her head with one hand, not that that would do much against a chunk of concrete, but she just pushed herself to move. To keep moving. If she stopped, if she fell, she risked getting trampled or worse.

A draft swept down the stairwell, carrying rainwater and the stench of burning flesh. As she approached the thirteenth floor where they'd all been hiding out just a few minutes ago, she stumbled once she realized the next flight of steps went nowhere. Everything shook again. She cried out, falling to the floor as, with a horrible crashing sound, the building caved in. The thirteenth floor had been crushed; if they hadn't evacuated, they all would've been dead.

Nancy stood in the stairwell, staring at the hallway through the doors, red light still blinking.

Above her, there was no more roof. Just exposed sky. Gentle rain tickled her face as she looked around, stepping gingerly onto the rubble, not completely understanding her movements. She should just run back down. Maybe she could sneak onto a different floor. So many people had scattered through the hospital, after all. Maybe she could find an MRI machine to crawl inside and hide. But what about Oliver? What about Henry?

Collapsed rubble and lights, bits of wall, hospital beds and equipment burned in front of her. Smoke filled the air, and then she saw a flash of yellow light. But before she could run toward it, heavy footsteps closed in on her, and she turned around to find Henry staring at her from the steps, his face covered in ash and dust.

"*What are you doing?*" he shouted.

Nancy bit her lip. "Where am I supposed to go? Down there to the angels? If I'm going to die, I'd rather be with my son."

It looked like Henry was about to say something, but he shut his eyes and nodded before wrapping one arm around her for a tight hug. "I came up here to find him. To help. I don't want him facing that thing alone."

"There," said Nancy, holding a hand up against the rain, squinting through the smoke and the dark. More flashes of yellow light. There were blue lights and green lights too, and then a powerful gust blew the smoke toward them.

Coughing and sputtering, they hobbled back, trying to take cover when they heard a scream. A second later, something clattered in front of them, and Nancy looked over Henry's arm to see it was a body in that black armor the kids all wore. The body's head was twisted the wrong way, and a hole shone through its chest, the wound glowing softly from the molten armor.

"No," she sobbed, crawling toward it. "Oh no, no, no, no. Please, don't let it be."

Even as Henry tried to pull her back, Nancy ran forward, crawling as more wind blew dust and rain into her hair. Something sizzled overhead. Yellow light seemed to light up the entire night sky, and she grabbed the body and pulled it back to see its face.

It was that boy. Oliver's friend. Nancy's hand went to her mouth as she stared into the boy's open eyes. The front of his body was scorched, burned so badly that the armor had melted and fused with his skin. One of his boxing gloves lay torn open. The other rested on his chest.

Sobbing, Nancy closed the boy's eyes. Henry was pulling her to her feet. He was panicking; she could feel it in his movements. The stress. There was no way out for them. Down below and on the street was the frenzy. Up ahead was . . . whatever monstrosity was awaiting.

She wished so badly she knew how to use that system thing everyone went on about. She looked at Henry, wishing he'd figured it out too.

"Mom?" came a voice. Oliver landed in front of them, covered in blood and smoke, his eyes wild. His helmet had been knocked away. Blood ran down his lips. "Dad? What the fuck are you guys doing here?"

She almost laughed. She had such a strong desire to snap at him about language. But also, to see him like this, she was impressed. She was so proud. He'd always seemed rather meek. Timid. A little bit shy and afraid of the world. And yet here he was at the end of the world, fighting with all his might.

She was so proud of him. She'd been proud of Jenny too, but she'd made the mistake of never telling her daughter any of that.

"I . . ." But she never got to finish the words.

With a scream, something immense landed in front of them. She never even got to read the notification in her head. An arm swung out through the smoke and debris, and even though Oliver jumped to block it with his armored arms and Henry shouted and took shots at the creature, all three of them were knocked away, down the stairwell.

Nancy bounced off the rail and crumpled on the bottom steps, wheezing for breath. In the chaos, she couldn't see her husband or her son. Dust and debris clattered around her. She shut her eyes and clenched her fists. Was this it?

She'd never thought about dying before. Not like this. It was always about what sins she'd committed or how she'd messed up. But now, it was about all the things she never got to say or do. How she never properly lived her life. How she'd kept her daughter from living her life too.

Light crackled overhead as the creature appeared on the top step, and Nancy looked into its deformed eyes. Its yellow armor glistened in the rain, and the two things sticking out of its back—they looked like strange, wooden arms—swirled in quick circles.

She was sure the angel would blast them all again, destroying everything once and for all. But then, it stopped moving. The rain stopped falling. Everything went so still Nancy almost thought she was dead.

A golden light radiated from above. Whimpering, she turned her head to the sky and saw a girl descending from what looked like rippling light. Like a portal. Behind the girl came two others, another girl and a boy. And behind them, others still. They were dressed in colorful armor, held mighty weapons, and came down like proper angels. One of them even had a cape.

But they were human. The notifications in her head went off one by one. Humans. Stage two and stage three. Humans.

"Please," she whispered. "Help us." As she struggled to stay awake, she saw them engaging the desecrated angel in battle. And then there was an even greater flash of light as someone else appeared. A girl with dark hair and red armor, carrying an enormous sword made out of light.

She plunged the sword into the angel's head, and the creature *shrieked*. Electricity sizzled all around, and just before Nancy lost consciousness, just before her eyes shut, she swore the girl carrying the sword had been Jenny.

CHAPTER FOURTEEN

CUPCAKE SHOP

As more and more angels fell to Susan's electricity, she started feeling like she had been made for this. As though, somehow, this was her destiny: to end up right here, and able to help in a way she couldn't when she was still alive.

Destiny . . . that's what Azra'il kept going on about. How everything was going according to destiny as determined by the ruling angels.

Such bullshit, she'd thought. "*Such bullshit,*" she'd told him as he slurped her intestines like noodles and laughed in her face and told her she looked so much prettier when she was begging for mercy.

Well, this is for your destiny, then, she thought with grim satisfaction, unleashing as much electricity as she could on a gaggle of tarnished angels, their naked bodies tumbling over each other in the loading dock of a department store. She'd found them there, feasting on a group of people she couldn't save. They were already dead, but it looked like they'd tried to put up a fight. Some uniformed officers. Some people still clutching shovels and knives and random tools.

They'd died fighting, at least. And their souls would be somewhere, and the least I could do was avenge them. Electricity snapped and crackled through the angels, each one falling to their hands and knees, staring at the blood, staring at the corpses beneath them, crying and scrambling to get away. But she'd chosen this spot for a specific reason.

She'd bolted the exit shut, and she stared at them all now, watching them throwing their shoulders against the metal door, desperate to get out.

The nearest one, a curly-haired woman with tan skin, Susan grabbed by the arm. Her electricity sizzled around the angel's skin. "What are you so afraid of? What are you running from?"

The angel stared back with bright brown eyes, terror so clear on its gaunt face that Susan felt like she should run too. It couldn't speak; all it could do was whisper back in that strange language that sounded like a radio crackling. But something strange shivered through her.

As Susan held the angel woman's hand, she felt like her fingers were *sinking* into its flesh, like she was floating into it, and she saw through the angel's eyes for a moment. Saw its thoughts. Saw it falling from the sky; saw the darkness; saw it changing; felt the immense hunger burning a hole in its stomach.

Then she saw something tremendous and evil, but it wasn't clear. It was more like a forgotten feeling, an old scent or a sound she couldn't remember through someone else's head. And then the door burst open, the angel slipped away, and the connection broke. Another angel had broken its shoulder, and it landed outside in a heap, looking around wide-eyed, clutching its injured arm, but the woman angel helped it to its feet, and they all ran off, vanishing into the night.

Susan stepped back, trying to catch her breath, staring down at the mostly eaten corpses scattered across the warehouse floor. The sight no longer turned her stomach. She didn't care for the blood or the exposed muscles or the bones or the wide, empty eyes.

She turned around and walked out of the warehouse, staring in the direction every single angel, no matter where she found it, where she used her electricity on it, ran toward. She'd seen a glimpse of it inside that angel's head. How? She wasn't sure. Maybe it had to do with her being a soul and the angel being a body? Or was it the electricity?

But it gave her a clue. Something dark was brewing in the direction they ran from. So, she'd been on the right trail, working her way toward whatever it was.

Footsteps made her twitch, and she saw another group of tarnished angels screaming and rushing by. The night was almost over. She'd gotten good at sensing when the sun would come up, the way the sky turned indigo before blue. All the angels would be rushing for cover. Maybe she could try grabbing one again. Could see how long she could hold its memories for.

She moved up the road, walking briskly along the buildings, trying to stay out of sight. She found herself walking through a familiar part of the city. The Chinese takeout shop. The electronics store. The cafés. All the glass storefronts were shattered, their chairs and tables broken all over, their signs caked with blood. Bits of human and angel were everywhere, but this was the path she'd taken every day, walking from the train station to school. And as she turned the corner, she found the gate to a little park.

A wretched angel. This one was bigger than the others she'd seen. A female with a sleek emerald-green exoskeleton, its navel exposed. Behind it was a smaller angel, a male, covered in a burnt-orange exoskeleton. Both of them had spikes jutting out of their backs, the female having more, and they seemed to have their eyes on Susan.

She decided to face them head-on, keeping in mind she couldn't technically die. They didn't pose a threat to her beyond pain. She hadn't tried the electricity on the more powerful angels yet, but she'd been consistently growing in strength, taking down hordes of the tarnished. And she'd already done it before, in the library, using her cattle prod to shoot electricity through an angel's head. Maybe these two could give her some answers.

They didn't rush her blindly like the tarnished angels; they seemed wary of her somehow, like they could sense she was different from normal humans. The emerald female had a gash on her shoulder and sides, blood staining her arms. She must've just been in a fight. The male's brown exoskeleton was unblemished. It approached first, screaming so loudly Susan swore the entire street reverberated.

She was going to wait. She was going to stand her ground, electricity sizzling around her hands, but looking into the creature's empty eyes as it barreled up the street on all fours like a demented gorilla made her second-guess herself. It was moving differently, like it was using an ability, and she saw that with each step, each time its hands and feet hit the ground, the asphalt beneath it cratered and crumbled more and more. Everything shook increasingly, as though the creature was gaining weight with each step.

Susan threw herself out of the way.

The angel barreled past. It couldn't stop itself, couldn't turn, and so it crashed so violently into the café wall that the apartment building collapsed on top, burying the male angel in rubble.

Susan had fallen behind a parked car, gasping for breath. If she'd let the angel hit her, it would've taken her with it. She would've been buried as well, and even though she couldn't die, she didn't want to feel the pain of that. She didn't want to dig her way out of the rubble, breaking her arms and scraping her skin over and over.

She rolled beneath the car as the other angel screamed. It sniffed around, looking for her, while Susan held her breath, staring up at the underside of the car. Then, as rubble shook around her, she felt the creature leap into the air and land on the car, crushing the metal and glass. Susan rolled out onto the sidewalk to see the emerald angel clawing at the seats. Its spikes made it seem almost like a porcupine or a hedgehog. It whipped around to face Susan.

For a split second, they were eye to eye: the angel hunched over, its green shoulder blades showing, and Susan standing, her hand outstretched. Electricity coursed through the air. Again, it seemed to move in slow motion, connecting with the creature's head, but then, a long arm slammed into Susan's belly, knocking her back with enough force that she went twirling away, slamming her head against an uprooted mailbox before cracking through the glass door of a cupcake shop.

She landed in a heap on the floor. Right on top of the shop owners, a sweet old couple, lying in a pool of dried blood, their faces half eaten, their stomach and legs scraped empty.

Head spinning, she pulled herself back to her feet. Stepping over the couple, she tried to locate the angel. But before she could recover, it came crashing through the broken door on all fours, green light emanating from its exoskeleton as its spikes scraped the ceiling and tore through the tiles.

And then it was on top of her again, pinning her between the checkout counter and a shelf of cupcakes, bashing everything with its arms and spikes, trying to claw at her. She could feel *hatred* in its gaze: seething, ugly hatred, as though the creature hated her, as though it could sense what she was trying to do.

Susan covered her head, the skin and muscle of her forearm being scraped away repeatedly, gashes opening across her chest and stomach, but she held back from attacking, kept trying to generate more and more electricity, feeling it surge inside her chest like a generator being wound and wound and *wound* far beyond the point of maximum capacity. Crackling light tinged her vision, and the wretched angel almost faded from view. She knew she had to unleash it. She couldn't contain this any longer. She felt like she would burst into particles of light; maybe, then, she'd finally die.

She reached up and wrapped her arms around the angel's waist, grabbing and pulling it close, as though she were giving it a hug. She lifted herself off the floor, trying to will all the electricity she'd stored up to surge out in one go.

Instead, she felt a *gush,* and her arms slipped *inside* the creature.

And before either of them could scream, Susan felt her entire body slide into the angel.

CHAPTER FIFTEEN

THE WORLD OF LIGHT

It was cold. The darkness jiggled all around Jenny. She felt like she'd dived into a swimming pool full of Jell-O, sinking slowly through the heavy substance. And the *cold*. It was almost unbearably cold, seeping through her armor and her flesh right into her bones, coating everything, making her insides twist with unfounded fear and agony.

She'd been through this before.

Somewhat, at least. She wasn't sure what had happened. Only that there had been an angel in the high school who wasn't like the others. It'd seemed almost . . . human, except it was covered in that orange exoskeleton and it spoke through hissing and shushing. But when Jenny had touched it, when Jenny had eaten it, she'd seen through the angel's life, and it'd felt as though she'd seen through her own.

She remembered the darkness. How the angel had once been a creature of light, living amongst cities hanging off of clouds. Then the same darkness had ripped through their world, sucked them all in, transforming them from light to . . . monstrous flesh. Unshapely beings. Horrible hunger. Nothing mattered other than dealing with that hunger.

What's going to happen to me right now?

She waded through it, her arms moving slowly. It reminded her of footage she'd seen of athletes underwater, moving so slowly under all the pressure and denser surroundings. Her muscles ached from these simple movements, and she couldn't see, exactly. It was more like sensing through her skin, through the information soaked into the darkness around her. Information that moved around her like a tickling, like running a tongue over your teeth, and she realized the darkness didn't know what to do with her. It wasn't forcing her to change the way it had the angels; it couldn't convert her. She was already material.

This space was like an inverted version of what she would travel through using Valescent Light.

There was no pushing or pulling sensation either. It was sort of empty, yet somehow sticky and gross all around. Whereas Valescent Light would shine with warmth and vibrance, healing and cleansing her, the darkness did none of that. It spread an ache through her bones, a tingling numbness that seared up her arms and legs; a tingling burning sort of pain, like her toes and fingers might snap off due to frostbite. A pounding headache that banged hard with every beat of her heart.

A part of her wondered, what if she used Valescent Light? Changed all this darkness to warmth? But the creature inside the pillar, the one with only a mouth, the one who had ripped this darkness open, had it done that for a reason? Was it beckoning her? Did it want to show her something? Take her somewhere? Or was it just responding to what she'd tried to do? A fucked-up defense mechanism.

At least the darkness had closed behind her; there was no turning back, no going back to the deaths, who must be so confused. But at least they were free now. She'd freed them, hadn't she? Ripping the world off, severing whatever curse had held it frozen. Could she do that again?

Was this what she was supposed to do?

Light cracked through the darkness ahead, and Jenny floated toward it. The gelatinous sensation made it hard work, and her arms and legs burned from the effort, but she was determined to get out. To see what was on the other side. And as the light grew stronger, golden and shiny and white, she saw the three-headed figure for an instant. A blink of an eye. It was Eve with her three heads, except now each face was just like the thing in the pillar. No eyes. No nose. No hair. Just a mouth filled with an impossible number of teeth.

Was that Eve's death?

A chill ran down her back that had nothing to do with the darkness, and then, like a thick sauce packet struggling to open, Jenny squirted out of the darkness, and she was free-falling.

The scream never left her mouth. The tear in the world closed behind her, and the wind battered her face, her hair, forced the air from her lungs. She stretched out her arms and legs, trying to make herself as wide as possible, the air blowing past her eyes making it hard to see.

But below her were more cracks between worlds, more pools of darkness, and with a rush, Jenny realized she'd been brought to the world of angels.

Lights fell from the sky like shooting stars, each one of them an angel, their wings curling behind them as they were pulled in, screaming and crying, their static voices cutting through the loud wind. They were falling from their cities and being sucked into the darkness.

Others were flying through the chaos, brandishing swords made of light, clashing. She only caught glimpses: angel against angel, fighting and screaming, their hissing cries reverberating through the air, the fearsome winds a result of their battle, a result of the darkness below. She could almost *see* the air draining into them like whirlpools of flashing color.

Jenny's mind spun with thoughts that were too quick. Angels blew past her, their bodies somehow falling more quickly despite being made of light. Feathers tickled her nose and her face and flew off.

She'd dive for the nearest pool of darkness, she decided, and see where it went. Or maybe she could convert them, change them with Valescent Light and stop these angels from being sucked inside. Maybe she could stop the fighting and get them all to see reason. And *why* were they even fighting each other? Weren't all angels with *Him*? After all, Azra'il was a normal angel, not one of the tarnished ones. What if . . .

But then, why would they be forced into the darkness like this?

Was it that only some of the angels sided with Adonai, sided with the war, and the rest were the resistance? Fighting against whatever Adonai had planned and now being forced into tarnishing for their sins.

She gritted her teeth, running out of time as the nearest black hole beckoned below, zooming up so quickly her head was spinning. She wished she had wings again; the ones made of fire she'd been able to use when Iblis was inside her. Could she create some?

But before she could test that out, she felt herself slowing. She wasn't falling quite as fast, and the angels rippled by her so quickly they seemed like flickering beams of light, blurring greens and blues and oranges that faded away as quickly as they zoomed past. Like she'd been plucked out of her fall, brought to almost a hovering standstill by levitation.

That was when she noticed something odd; something that didn't fit.

From the corner of her eye, she almost thought it was a tentacle, but as it moved closer, it seemed more and more like a giant snake. Or a dragon. A dark-brown thing snaking its way through the sky, through the storm of angels, undulating.

A new panic ignited in her chest as she tried to swim through the air, to maneuver herself. Now she wanted to fall into the darkness, fall through a portal and emerge somewhere else.

The dragon . . . creature, whatever it was, blew past angels, some of their bodies shattering against its skin, their notifications vanishing from her head as they sparkled away, and then she saw *its* notification.

Leviathan

By then, she knew it was too late. There were no levels. No identifiers. Just that. Just *Leviathan*, a creature from ancient history. Something she'd been told was pure evil; a beast of absolute destruction.

The creature was enormous, a leathery brown snake with lips pulled back to reveal human-shaped teeth. Its head was about the size of a city block. Each one of its teeth could've been a building, and something about the expression on its face reminded Jenny of a grotesque smile. The eyes on either side of its head gleamed with darkness, some sort of light trailing from each blink. Its underbelly glittered emerald or purple in between undulations as its body swerved up and down, a hypnotic rhythm trailing down the length of its enormous form.

Before Jenny could note anything else about the Leviathan, its jaws opened to reveal a horrid pink tongue. A cloud of foul hot air blasted her as it rushed toward her, and then the sky and all the falling angels vanished, disappearing behind the creature's teeth, a loud *CLANG* ringing through her head.

She landed on its squishy tongue and rolled, bouncing along the rubbery surface. Then she was falling again as the tongue lifted and dropped her through a tunnel gushing and steaming with hot air. She bounced off its fleshy sides, feeling pockets of moist warmth and thick skin which must've been its throat, and then she landed again, this time with a splash, and came to a complete stop.

Groaning, she opened her eyes and looked around, and whatever swear word was ready on her lips melted away. All around her, covering what must've been the inside of the creature's belly, were beautiful gemstones, each one a different color, shining with the same varied lights of the angels. The space was enormous, like she'd walked into a large underground tunnel, a cavernous space that could've fit several buildings stacked together inside. Her breath echoed. The liquid dripping off her armor echoed. Even her heartbeat felt like it was echoing.

She would've expected darkness and more of that foul smell, maybe some stomach acid, but . . . she was knee-deep in a liquid, and it wasn't acid. She wasn't melting. It didn't even smell.

She knelt and ran her hands through it, the scales of her armor peeling back to let her touch it. It was water. Clean, fresh water.

"What the fuck?" she whispered. But her body responded with thirst; she hadn't had water in ages and ages—all that time on the cross; all that time the ghouls had chewed through her flesh and drained her of blood. Sure, she'd sucked the ghouls dry and drunk in the blood of the world, but she was still *thirsty*. And she remembered Susan, the two of them making their way through the high school. Susan had reminded her to stay hydrated.

She laughed as she scooped up more water and drank, wondering what the fuck this was doing inside Leviathan of all things.

After drinking her fill, she waded over to one of the walls and took a closer look at the gemstones. They were warm to the touch and glowing from within, orbs of light floating inside like they were hearts. Round and smooth, and not really stones. They didn't feel like rocks; they were squishy, almost, and that's when Jenny realized what they were.

Eggs.

"Kindly step away from our offspring," spoke a raspy, strained voice, sizzling through her head.

Jenny whipped around. With a flash of golden light, her hatchet was in her hand, and she came face-to-face with a desecrated angel covered in a silvery gray exoskeleton.

Desecrated Angel (NULL)

CHAPTER SIXTEEN

INSIDE THE LEVIATHAN

Jenny's hatchet swung through the air, bouncing off the angel's exoskeleton-covered arm with a flash of golden light. The creature had long white hair, and it wasn't as big as the other desecrated angels Jenny had fought. In fact, it was about the same size as Jenny.

Its arms and legs were thin. Its navel was exposed to reveal weathered gray skin. And its eyes . . . They were completely white. It wasn't until the angel parried another one of Jenny's attacks and shouted in an almost human voice, "Please stop!" that Jenny realized the angel had *spoken* to her.

Heart racing, Jenny stepped back with Instant Acceleration, splashing through the water, giving herself enough space in case this was a trick. She didn't take her eyes off the angel, the sounds of their brief exchange still echoing around them. The multicolored lights emanating from the eggs bathed everything in a beautiful glow.

The angel stared back, blood running down from the cracks in its arms. Jenny had hurt it, but as she watched, shining silver light leaked from the cracks, and the angel seemed to heal. It could regenerate, just like that wretched angel she'd fought in the high school, the one who had nearly killed her; the one who had dragged her to the first desecrated angel she'd fought to be used as feed.

A part of her wanted to open a passageway and escape. Or maybe cut through the Leviathan's insides and jump back outside. But curiosity prodded her mind in a way she couldn't help.

The eggs here didn't look like the eggs of the wretched and desecrated angels she'd fought before. These were beautiful, gemlike. And this angel could talk. It wasn't mindlessly attacking her. Were they all her eggs? There must've been thousands, if not hundreds of thousands. And depending on how long the Leviathan was, maybe there were hundreds of *millions*. This entire thing could populate a world with these eggs.

Was that what it was?

"I have not seen a human in a long time," said the angel, its lips moving, its tongue running along its front teeth. "And for a human, you are strange."

"Yeah, I've heard that plenty," replied Jenny, still trying to catch her breath. She felt silly now for reacting how she did: with pure adrenaline, fight or flight. She adjusted her grip on the hatchet. "What are you?"

The desecrated angel lumbered forward. It was old. Like really old. A weary heaviness slowed down its movements, and it ran its fingers through its silver hair, trying to stand up straight.

"There was a man once who stayed with me for some time. Junas. Or Jonas. A human like you. I forget his name, but he said he was a great man trying to change the world. Oh, it's been so long, but he explained my existence best as penitence. I am penitence for all that I've done, all that I've allowed to happen, all that I have once stood for and now against."

"Penitence?" repeated Jenny, wondering how this angel was able to speak . . . Wait, it might not be English. Were they just speaking in the angel's language, and Jenny hadn't recognized it as she spoke it so easily now? Yeshua and the demons and everyone spoke different languages, and Jenny had had a demon possess her; maybe it had become even easier to understand and speak these languages. "So you're not trying to eat me?"

The angel looked at her, its eyes gleaming with light. It shook its old head. "I have lost all my strength. All my abilities. I am only here now to tend to what little hope my people have left." It gestured toward the stone eggs that lined the inside of the Leviathan. Toward the ceiling so high above. "For a possible future. Depending on how the final challenge should play out."

Jenny lowered her hatchet. She shut her eyes. She was so tired of hearing people speak like that. "Okay. Can you tell me what's going on here and what it has to do with everything else?"

The angel didn't respond, but it turned slightly, holding out a silvery arm in invitation. "If you will follow me, I can show you. I have merely come to assess whether or not you were a threat."

"A threat?" repeated Jenny. "How do you know I'm not?"

"You stopped when I asked you to." Something in the angel's raspy voice broke—a sadness that Jenny recognized—and for a moment, she thought she knew the angel. As though she were meeting an old friend after many, many years.

First the old lady death, and now this old angel. What was going on?

Jenny nodded, guilt-ridden. "I'm sorry for attacking you."

"I do not blame you."

"What would you have done if I was a threat?" asked Jenny, then quickly added, "No offense, but you don't seem like you're up for a fight."

The angel smiled, a genuine, warm smile, something Jenny had never seen before on an angel's face. The metallic covering on its face wrinkled and stretched, its lips moving. It nodded and gestured around. "Then my children would have torn you to pieces and fed you to the great beast. Now come. I will show you what your future holds, little human who is not so human."

Jenny followed the desecrated angel through the watery path. The walls closed in and swerved; at some moments, Jenny felt like she was walking through a cave deep underground, and at others, she felt like the cave was digesting her. The water had an ebb and flow, rising up to her knees before dropping to around her ankles.

Even though the ceiling was so high up and there was plenty of space from one side of the Leviathan to the other, everything closed in here and there, and she had to catch herself and breathe. That must've been from the great beast flying through the sky, undulating, turning. Color reflected off the water and all around, and in a strange way, it almost felt like Jenny was back in Valescent Light.

She fixated on the stones, the glowing lights inside them bouncing almost like embryos. Like yolks inside chicken eggs. She remembered studying metamorphosis in school, in biology textbooks. Insects going from eggs to larva to pupa to something that could usually fly. Were angels like that? Was that why the wretched angels built nests and laid eggs? Why the desecrated wrapped themselves in chrysalises? She wanted to know more about the angel life cycle. Wanted to know who laid these eggs. Surely not the desecrated angel who was leading her.

But she shuddered, thinking about the metamorphosis notification she'd had in her head. How her death had "hatched" and produced her exoskeleton and tentacles; how she'd eaten him and completed the cycle. Did that have more to do with the Existential Error in her head? Was the change what had converted her from a desecrated human to a normal human but rendered her level Null?

"Do you have a name, human?" came the angel's voice. They were sloshing through the water, the sounds echoing all around.

"Yeah, I mean . . ." Jenny stopped; for a second, she felt like she should lie. But how would lying help? What was the point in hiding her name? "I'm Jenny."

"Jenny," repeated the desecrated angel as Jenny stared at the creature's shoulders and bouncing white hair. "Jenny. So that is your name. Do you know what you are called around here?"

"What? You know me?"

"Every angel of this world knows you," said the angel. "Only by another name."

Jenny blinked. Was that because of . . . ? She looked over her shoulder, half expecting the cross to be standing there, scraping the Leviathan's inside as she dragged it around. But it wasn't. There was nothing behind her but the long, cavernous path they'd walked through, and all the colors shining in every direction.

"They call you 'Interloper.' The second Mary." The desecrated angel turned, shooting Jenny a look over its shoulder, its face looking almost menacing as purples and greens and oranges splashed across it from various directions. "I asked the Leviathan to swallow you when we felt you enter our world. It came as a surprise, but perhaps it was destiny, if you believe in such things."

Destiny, thought Jenny. Had destiny brought her here? Or was it that *thing* in the pillar? Was it destiny that brought her to Yeshua? Destiny that helped her find Susan?

Was it destiny that had her high school transported into the Veil in the first place?

She wanted to laugh, maybe even curse at destiny, but she held her tongue. No point in disrespecting or offending the desecrated angel.

The great beast made a sound, like a loud ship's horn or the deep rumbling of a whale, and Jenny almost covered her ears with her hands. Everything vibrated. The corridor, the water, even the eggs. She paused for a moment to steady herself, all the various colors brightening and dimming around her.

Leviathan, Leviathan . . . That name notification had been bugging Jenny. She'd read about it, hadn't she? Heard stories about it? An enormous snake that ate the sun? Or was that a different story . . . ? She couldn't remember. And wasn't there a whale that ate one of the holy men? She wondered how much of the stuff they'd taught in Sunday school was completely wrong.

When the rumbling stopped, Jenny caught up to the desecrated angel, who'd been walking steadily without any pause. Had the angel even noticed Jenny was lagging behind? The angel didn't seem to care.

What if the angel was leading her into a trap? What if this was somehow worse than the cross she'd been stuck to? But Jenny wanted to trust the angel;

some part of her *trusted* the angel. And how could someone who was taking care of so many eggs, so many children, be evil?

Then again, she'd seen plenty of angels tending to their eggs, and they would've happily killed and eaten her. But this angel could *talk*. Could communicate.

She took a deep breath, working through her options in case anything happened.

She seemed to have her abilities, at least. She could fight. But could she just leave? What if Severed Spirit still didn't respond to her? What if she got stuck in the Leviathan the way she'd been stranded in the world of the dead?

Wait . . . she would've been stuck there completely if she hadn't found the pillar with the strange creature inside. The one that had opened a passageway for her so she could move between worlds. Was this destiny bullshit starting to add up?

What did it all mean?

"So, what's your name?" asked Jenny, realizing she hadn't asked about the angel. Did angels have names? Well, Azra'il had one. But what about desecrated angels?

The old angel didn't respond right away. It just kept walking, sloshing through the water. And after a while, they came to a point where no more eggs were glowing on the walls, and the soft, colorful glow came from behind Jenny. Up ahead was darkness. How far into the Leviathan's body had they gone? Was this the back end? The creature seemed enormous, like it would take hours and hours to walk down its length. She thought maybe the angel was trying to show her something, maybe it was a way out, but all Jenny could see was darkness.

Then, one by one, silhouettes flickered into view, each one a different color from the next. They weren't tarnished. They weren't mad with hunger and bloodthirst. They even seemed kind of small, on the young side, and the notifications in Jenny's head read the same for each one of them.

Angel (Stage I)

The old desecrated angel hobbled over to stand in front of the others, facing Jenny. Its weathered old face seemed to glow with a new light, as though being with the other angels gave it strength. "My name is Sat'en."

Sat'en, echoed Jenny's thoughts. Her heart broke, staring at what was left of the angel. Iblis's memories rushed through her like a tidal wave, and for a moment, everything—the angels, the eggs behind her, even Sat'en—appeared awashed in a fiery blue hue. She half expected blue flames to burst out of her eyes, wings and fire, but nothing happened. She didn't know what to say. Or how to say it. Iblis had thought Sat'en dead and gone, but here the angel was. Living. Having seemingly regained her consciousness. Tending to the angels.

Her bottom lip quivered, but she swallowed the lump in her throat and asked, "What are you guys doing here?"

"Adonai has mobilized his faithful," said Sat'en. "As they prepare for the worlds to end, our children take refuge." Something akin to a glow rippled through the angels behind her, each one brightening and fading, and to Jenny, it felt like staring at blooming rainbows. They must have been really young. Children. And she thought of the angel babies, the ones born from wretched angels, that had followed her around, chewing on corpses, looking at her like baby ducks waddling behind their mother.

"So, the eggs?" she asked, pointing over her shoulder. "This giant snake?"

"Darkness pulls on all our peoples," explained Sat'en. She hobbled forward and touched the exposed inner flesh of the Leviathan, now illuminated by the presence of the young angels. "And this creature is the last of its kind. It has sworn an oath to protect our children."

Jenny rubbed her face, trying to think, trying to connect this new puzzle piece in her head. Demons. Angels. Angels who are rebelling against *Him* in the battle outside. The children living inside a Leviathan. And Sat'en being alive.

CHAPTER SEVENTEEN

FOR THE CHILDREN

The insides of the Leviathan shook as they closed and expanded. The waters swished around, reflecting the angel's lights, and now that Jenny was surrounded by the glowing angels, the space felt almost cozy. Before, it had felt like exploring a deep, underground cave with glowing gems all around. Now, it was busy and alive. The angel children came up to Jenny, whispering in their language; little shushing, hissing, and crackling noises. It was almost pretty to Jenny.

"What's it like being real?" one of them asked.

Another wondered if the water bothered her. "How come you don't have a color?"

They touched and prodded her armor. Their hands passed through; they were light, after all. Green and yellow. Blue. Each angel had its own color, its own shade. As they spoke, their light brightened and dimmed, and Jenny couldn't exactly see their silhouettes. It was like they were always just out of focus, but she could make out a somewhat humanoid form. What might've been a head, a rounded blob. What might've been arms and legs, rounded off, softened.

They had wings. Unlike the adults, their wings were much smaller, coming off their backs, white and feathery. But now that Jenny had a closer look at them, she realized they weren't *feathers*. Not like birds. Not like harpies. She could run her hand through them, discombobulating them for a moment before they reformed. They were vapor. Water vapor.

When she'd gone through the angel's memories before, when she'd experienced what it was like for them to fall through the darkness and become material, the wings had evaporated rather than turn into feathery wings. They lost their ability to fly, and the tarnished angels would then be possessed by their hunger to be complete.

This was what it meant to be complete; for them, at least. A smile played on her lips. The angel children seemed warm and happy, and she realized now why none of the angels she'd fought in the high school had been children. Only adults.

Sat'en and Leviathan had kept them safe.

But what about the eggs she'd seen born to the wretched and desecrated angels? The little babies who had followed her around? Were they just failed beings? Lost to the material world now? Doomed to grow into tarnished angels?

Wasn't there any hope for them?

"Human?" asked one of the little angels, a small orangish-red one. It shimmered its hand through Jenny's.

"Yeah?"

"Can I have a hug?"

She almost couldn't believe what she was hearing. An angel child asking her for a hug. Did that mean angels routinely hugged one another? They were more human than she'd thought.

Jenny knelt in the water, her eyes blurring with tears. She couldn't really touch the angel, and they couldn't really touch her, but she wrapped her arms around the orange silhouette and remained there for a long moment. The light had a tingling warmth to it. And the longer they hugged, the more she felt like the angel child was tangible. It wasn't just light she was hugging but something more than light. Something between nothing and something.

The other angel children flooded her after that, bouncing off each other in excitement, each one hoping to have her arms around them. And she took the time to hug as many as she could, happy to bring them some comfort while they were here in the Leviathan.

"My father told me humans are frightening," said one.

"Monsters," said another. "Selfish and greedy."

"But you're pretty," said the one who had first asked for a hug. "You look like the flowers that grow on top of the clouds."

"Flowers?" whispered Jenny. "Flowers on top of clouds?" As one angel explained the bright petals of the sky flowers—how picking them was an awful thing to do because they'd melt, how beautiful they were when the sun set and they kept glowing—Jenny smiled and nodded along, wishing she might see them one day.

She wondered how the angels actually stood anywhere. If they were just light, shouldn't they just . . . fall through stuff? But they weren't ghosts. They were *light*. It hurt her head trying to imagine their existence. Then she saw the water beneath the children, and it clicked for her. The water. Water vapor. They lived on top of clouds because they had footing there. Somehow, their light could stay on top of water the way humans used land.

The Leviathan shook again, a deep rumbling vibrating through the long corridor, and the children squirmed, some of them crying out, their lights glowing and fading rapidly in distress.

Sat'en put her gray-covered hand on Jenny's shoulder, and Jenny flinched. The angel looked solemn, like she had something important to say.

"Sorry," whispered Jenny. Seeing the desecrated angel's hand suddenly on her shoulder made her think of the angel that had once bitten through her fingers.

"Help me protect these children," hissed Sat'en.

Jenny looked around at the angels. Their light. They had no faces, but she imagined they looked sad and hopeful. All they'd wanted from her was a hug. Meanwhile, there was a war going on. All those angels outside, screaming and fighting, pulled into the darkness for forceful transformations into tarnished creatures. Those were the children's parents. How many of them had become tarnished? How many of them had Jenny killed? Eaten?

She couldn't help them.

She had no right to.

But I can try, can't I? She saw that boy again, her death, looking up at her on the cross with so much hope in his eyes, the tentacles lashing out of his back, the exoskeleton taking him over. Coming to her for a hug, offering himself to her so she could finally feed.

I can help them.

She took a deep breath and spoke to Sat'en. "You can't stay in this world."

"So what will you do, Interloper? The higher angels tell of a terrible ability that connects worlds."

Jenny looked at Sat'en's face, wondering how much the angel knew, thinking back to Iblis and the love he'd had for her. Was it wrong to keep that information from the angel? Shouldn't Jenny tell Sat'en everything about Iblis and the battles they'd fought together, and how much love the demon had held for the angel, even until his death? Shouldn't she know? That Azra'il had killed her beloved?

Jenny resolved to tell the angel everything once they were out of here. "I can take you to the world of death; it should be safe there. At least it won't be like this." She wondered for a second if angels had deaths too, if their deaths came out of pillars and needed to be fed. But all the deaths she'd seen were human.

Sat'en scratched her chin, and it was such a human movement that Jenny almost forgot the creature was an angel. She asked Jenny to explain how it worked, and once Jenny went over Severed Spirit, the darkness, and Valescent Light, the angel pointed back the way they'd come. "You will have to open your passageway outside. The Leviathan must be able to go through. We cannot leave it here."

Outside? But how? Jenny had thought she'd open one right here and get the angels out. "We can't just . . . ?"

"No," said Sat'en, shaking her head. "It would be impossible to transport the eggs without Leviathan. And it would be heartbreakingly cruel to abandon our guardian."

Jenny nodded, taking a deep breath. The angel children huddled around her, some of them whispering.

"Please help us."

"It's scary here."

"I want my mom."

She looked back the way she'd come. "Alright then. It'll have to spit me out again or something. And then . . ." Could she open a portal while falling? And what if . . . She searched inward, searching her abilities, her mind, the guidance system itself. Sometimes, she missed having Eve inside her head, someone she could just ask questions to and get quick answers from.

"The angels might attack you," said Sat'en. "If they recognize you. Be prepared for that."

"I am prepared," replied Jenny, trying to sound brave. Could angel children pick up on body language in a human? Could they tell she was actually afraid of fucking it all up? Of jumping out of the Leviathan and falling to her death? But then she realized it didn't matter. Relief filled her bones. Even if she couldn't open the passageway, all she had to do was drop down, all the way down, to the cracks of darkness she'd seen before.

"You lack strength," said Sat'en, hobbling away from the children. She was leading the way. "You must grow much stronger."

"Nothing I can do about that now." Jenny followed the angel, anxiety coursing up and down her limbs. She waved at the angel children and promised them she'd try her best. That it would be okay. But inside? She was terrified of messing it up somehow. Of the darkness not turning into light and all the children being forcefully turned into tarnished angels who'd then attack her.

Could she kill them?

Jenny clenched her jaw, following Sat'en back through the Leviathan, back the way they'd come before. She almost wanted to leave the angel and her slow pace behind. She could run to the mouth much quicker on her own. "You'll catch me again if it doesn't work, right?"

Sat'en didn't respond. "Do you not have faith in yourself?"

"I . . ." Jenny trailed off. She wanted to say no. But she felt like she was expected to say yes. Wasn't that what people always expected of other people? To say the right things? To lie even when they felt embarrassed or afraid? But she stuck with the truth. She didn't know if she had faith in herself. She didn't know if she could. "I don't know."

Sat'en turned, her eyes shining in the glow of the eggs. Yellow and orange and blue. She put her hand on Jenny's shoulder again, and they stood, their noses nearly touching, every bit of Jenny's insides fighting the urge to run, fighting the urge to tell the angel everything. About Iblis and his memories of her. About how she'd eaten her own death. About how many angels she'd killed with her bare hands. She wanted to confess everything to the angel.

"Faith comes from within," said Sat'en softly. "It isn't born of nothing. It cannot be given to us. Faith must be channeled within. Faith is how we can express our lives. You must not be frightened to be alive. You must not be frightened to have faith in yourself."

At Sat'en's words, something stirred inside Jenny. Memories that weren't her own. Memories that had belonged to Iblis. Those were Iblis's words, spoken to Sat'en in an intimate moment, and something inside her wanted to collapse crying. Jenny blinked away tears, nodding, and without meaning to, pressed her forehead forward against Sat'en's.

That wasn't me, was it? she thought to herself. The angel's forehead was warm. And it was comforting.

Sat'en seemed surprised. But she was still a desecrated angel, and she still looked like a nightmare. "Have you met my beloved?"

"Yes," said Jenny, unable to keep it a secret any longer. She told Sat'en everything while they walked back. Starting with the world of death and talking through Iblis's death and ending with her escaping the cross. "I'm sorry."

For a long moment, the angel didn't respond. They walked in silence, the water breaking in soft waves against their legs. The colors shone across every surface. Jenny's throat hurt from how much she'd spoken even though she hadn't spoken that much at all, but the weight of the memories, the weight of what she'd shared, bore down on her, and she could feel the sadness emanating from the angel. A deep, aching sorrow that Jenny knew the angel couldn't express as fully as she might've wanted to in different circumstances.

"I am the one who is sorry," spoke Sat'en, her shoulders shaking as she walked ahead, the grayish silver of her exoskeleton glistening with vivid color. "But the time for mourning will come. Now is the time for action."

Up ahead, the teeth of the Leviathan glistened brightly. Jenny could see the enormous tongue, its fleshy bumps and glistening liquids. They stood at what must've been the throat. Now that she wasn't tumbling down, Jenny was able to see a gland way up ahead, a bulbous group of dark round things. They might've been mushrooms. Or storm clouds. But streaming down on either side of the throat were little waterfalls. That was where the water came from.

"When I ask our guardian, its mouth will open, and the rest is up to you." Sat'en pressed her hand to one of those waterfalls, the water cascading around her fingers.

Jenny closed her eyes and braced herself. Then lurched suddenly as the walls moved. Swerved. She felt carsick, seasick; she couldn't tell. Her head was spinning with what she had to do. She couldn't fail.

When she reached out to steady herself, pressing her hand against the wall, she got a mental image of the Leviathan gaining altitude, flying in circles, going higher and higher. She could *see* the Leviathan as though she were looking at it from the outside, and it reminded her of certain dreams where she felt like a floating camera observing herself. Was that how Sat'en communicated with the great beast? Was that how the Leviathan saw itself? But there wasn't any time for questions.

"Now!" shouted Sat'en.

The enormous teeth rose into the air, and light flooded in through the creature's mouth. It felt like she was on a giant ship, and the front of the hull had just opened. Before Jenny could have any more second thoughts, before she could chicken out, she leapt onto the tongue. She ran forward, half jogging, half bouncing from one bump to the other, and threw herself out of the Leviathan's mouth with a burst of Instant Acceleration.

Spreading her arms, feeling the wind batter her face and hair, she fell, one hand out, trying to cut through the worlds.

CHAPTER EIGHTEEN

FALLING THROUGH THE LIGHT

Jenny plummeted away from the Leviathan, trying to keep her mouth shut as wind tore at her cheeks and eyelids. She wished again that she still had wings, Iblis's wings, coming out of her back, giving her lift. She wondered if her tentacles might do the same.

Lights shot past her as she flew by angels locked in combat. She only got glimpses of them. Lights blurring. Wings beating. Everything coming apart.

I should be panicking. But she felt serene. Relaxed. The Leviathan must've flown up very high, higher than the angels and everything else in the world. She had a long way to fall.

Far below her were the clouds, white and fluffy. And through them, she could see the cities, the towers growing upside down, and the bursting lights, the explosions of color that scattered across the sky. That's what she'd seen while stuck to the cross staring up at the night sky. *This* battle. This was the battle. Angels killing each other across the heavens.

Beams of light shot up around her, bounced in every direction. She glimpsed mighty wings beating powerfully. Saw flashes of weapons, swords and hammers. But again, they were leaving her alone, ignoring her as though she didn't exist. As though she was just a rock or a chunk of rubble or just a strange piece of hail falling from the sky.

She didn't care. She had a job to do.

With her hand out, she tried to feel for the worlds, tried to find the sensation she'd felt before. The clouds were coming up fast. Once she fell through them, it would be even more difficult to concentrate. Think.

Think.

No, actually. She turned in the air so that she was looking up at the Leviathan snaking its way slowly through the air, following her arc. She watched its long body curving up and down, snaking. She let her thoughts slip away. *Don't think. Don't overthink this. Just do it.*

Just do it.

You can do it.

You've done it before.

She thought about the angel children, how they'd asked for hugs. She thought about how frightened they must be, holed up inside that ginormous beast, not knowing what was going on just outside. Was she really going to fuck this up and let them get hurt? Die? Or worse, turn into tarnished angels?

Could she live with herself if that happened? Just picturing it was making her insides twist with pain and rage; she didn't want that. She wanted them to be safe. Away from all of this.

Her fingers twitched. She felt a snag in the air. She smiled as she grabbed hold, and then, it felt like she'd found a zipper in the sky, pulling it down as she fell, opening the seam of the world to reveal that thick, horrible darkness again.

Severed Spirit.

She almost shouted for joy as she tore that enormous, jagged wound in the sky, splitting like an eye opening, like curtains parting. But then, the wind changed. Suddenly, she was blown upward, like she'd violently opened a parachute.

And all the light around her switched directions. Mid fight, the angels were being sucked in as though Jenny had turned on an enormous vacuum. Screaming and hissing filled her ears, and with horror, she realized the mistake she'd made.

She struggled against the onslaught of light barreling her, like she'd been thrown into a tidal wave of light, the angel bodies rocketing through her, sizzling and hissing and screaming, desperation flashing. She could see it in their eyes. She was killing them. She was turning them into tarnished angels.

The Leviathan was drawing closer and closer. They didn't know what it would look like. They were just hurrying along. And the children—she couldn't let that happen to the children.

With a scream, she tried to maneuver herself toward the tear in the world, the horrible dread spreading through her. The Leviathan was so close now she could count its teeth. Could see its gleaming, ancient eyes, the lights it blinked away from eyelashes longer than she was tall.

Light bloomed across her entire body with desperation, colors swirling around her arms and legs, around her torso in ribbons. They shimmered around her head like a halo.

With Valescent Light radiating from her entire body, Jenny *splashed* into the darkness, and everything erupted with light.

Blackness swirled around her as she stuck to the dark like an insect caught in a spider's web. Turning, everything moving in slow motion, tendrils of color reaching out from the point of impact, she saw the Leviathan. Countless angels were caught in its path, flung around in the hurricane winds as it flew toward her and the light.

There was nothing she could do about the angels, but maybe she could save them with this. Maybe they wouldn't turn into tarnished angels. Maybe they would stop fighting.

She reached out with a glowing hand, pressing her fingers to the Leviathan's jaw just as it reached her. She felt like an ant trying to catch a school bus, wind battering everything, even the light spilling from the open passageway, as she pulled them all inside.

All the light and colors circled and spun, golden light shining from every direction. There were so many ripples of colors that Jenny thought everything was collapsing in on her. Greens swirled every which way. Bright red threads wrapped around her. She was sinking through the light, feeling as though she hadn't been here in ages. The last time she'd moved between worlds was through the darkness, and that had felt so difficult, like trying to breathe through smoke.

This was healing. Cleansing. She could feel her bruises soothing, could feel her aches healing. Light swirled just at the top of her head, like a halo. She reached up to touch it, but as her fingertips found it, the light dissolved, like a drawing on a foggy window fading.

She shuddered and looked around her. The angels that had fallen into the darkness first . . . It was too late for them. They'd turned into tarnished angels, their light solidifying into flesh. Just bones. And she could feel their maddening hunger through the light. Could feel the bloodthirst. The rage. The fear. The shock.

But beyond them, there were normal angels as well, made of light, swimming through her Valescent Light, curious. Afraid. In awe. Their violence washed away and replaced with an almost childlike wonder. Maybe they would stop fighting, she thought. Maybe they could see darkness wasn't the only answer.

And the largest thing of all, the most frightening thing, was the Leviathan. Its enormous teeth glistened as it roared, bubbles of violet and orange erupting from its great big jaws. It was following her, something that would collapse an entire section of Manhattan if it were to land on the city. Where was she supposed to take it?

She searched for the push and pull, which seemed to be the only way to navigate this space. There was too much happening around her, but it was there, a flicker of sensation beneath the overcrowded thoughts. *Focus.*

There was the material world. The largest pull. But . . . ? She couldn't find the world of death. Not even the world of demons. Instead, there was a stranger world, familiar but different, calling to her. Like it knew her name; like it knew exactly who she was. Like it had been waiting for her. She reached toward it, and *it reached back.* There was a flash of white and red light, and then something bumped into her.

Jenny opened her eyes and found herself staring at her reflection.

Except it wasn't her reflection. The person had her same face. Her same hair. The same body. She was adorned in red, but instead of scales, each little piece looked like a flower petal. It was armor made of rose petals, and her face was distorted with confusion and anger.

It was Eve.

Eve opened her mouth and shrieked. All the light around them bubbled and burst and shattered. In the explosion of color, Eve threw herself at Jenny, grabbing her by the arms and *shoving* her through the light, forcing her through the colors, pulling everyone else—all the angels and even the Leviathan—along until they came up against something that pushed back.

It felt like an invisible wall or glass, and then it gave. The resistance collapsed, and they all fell through it, bursting out all of a sudden to be greeted by the cold, blistering, freezing cold. Jenny found herself plummeting yet again, this time with Eve, ferocious and screaming. Golden wings shot out of Eve's back and expanded. She flapped *hard,* with enough force to catch their fall, enough force that it might've broken Jenny's neck if it weren't for her armor.

They hovered for a moment: Jenny trying to figure out what to say; Eve looking shocked and angry. Then Eve *threw* Jenny to the ground with the impact of a meteor, cratering it instantly, sending up a circular wall of ice and snow around her.

Jenny lay in the rubble, the breath knocked out of her, amazed that she'd survived. That *thing* wriggled beneath her skin, and she knew it was healing everything that had just broken. Eve landed on top of Jenny, standing over her.

She looked up at her own face, her own eyes, trying to find the words to speak. But beyond Eve, she could see lights. She could see the giant Leviathan hovering in the cold air, uncertain. Could see all the angels around it, hovering, not knowing what to do, no longer fighting. And all around them rained down the tarnished angels, screaming and hissing.

Eve looked at Jenny with a look of disgust on her face. "Mother, what do you think you're doing?"

CHAPTER NINETEEN

POSSESSION

A ll her light turned green, as though a sky full of emerald stars had descended, had come crashing down to wrap around Susan like a blanket, engulfing her. When she blinked, when the brightness cleared away, she found herself looking down at smushed cupcakes and crushed pink boxes and dried blood.

She was *inside* the wretched angel. The notification flickering through her thoughts, through the angel's brain, confirmed it.

Wretched Angel (Possessed)

Her mind whirred, and she could sense the angel's mind just beneath hers, twitching and panicking, in pain. It . . . *She*. The angel, *she*, wanted to scream and cry. The hunger had been too much, *too much*, her stomach grumbling and growling and aching like it would split apart and eat itself if there wasn't food right away.

Susan's spirit wavered. She turned toward the dead shop owners, half eaten, but there was quite a bit of meat left on their bones. She could suck them dry. She could . . .

Why was she trying to feed this other mind?

Why?

She caught herself, saliva dribbling down her green chin. Electricity cracked inside her, now inside the angel. It hadn't been released. She hadn't used it on the angel to change it yet. It was still wretched. But how was she supposed to use her electricity from inside the creature?

The wall of the shop collapsed as her mate—as the angel's mate, the burnt-orange angel—barged through, its empty eyes looking at her with confusion. It cocked its head, unsure.

Susan responded out of instinct. Electricity flickered down her new green arms. She raised her hand as if to call to the angel's mate, but static built up and crackled all over Susan's new body, shooting straight up into her own brain before extending outward toward the other angel, and she got to witness what happened from inside the angel.

The hunger melted away, the basic instinct of kill and eat fading to a throbbing pain in the back of the angel's mind. Something else came bubbling to the forefront: reason. Willpower. Hurt.

And *FEAR.*

Utter, horrible, gut-twisting fear; something that screamed at her to *run-run-run, run away.*

Something awful was brewing, trying to be born, but it held the angel in place.

Susan felt the angel recoiling at its own memories, at Susan's presence, at what had happened, and a flood of things rushed through like she was watching too many movies at the same time. Susan saw a world full of light, a world of clouds, with buildings extending below them, built upside down. Colorful beings fluttered in and out, flying every which way with glorious wings.

She saw the angel's own body, green and beautiful, the color of leaves on a sunny day, wings outstretched. And her partner . . . orange like the fruit, bright and earthy and gorgeous. She saw the two of them merging their light together, feeling the warmth of the other, deciding to start a family, to raise young, sharing their love.

The orange wretched angel, now angel stage two, made a sound that was between a moan and a wail. It seemed to be struggling with the fear response as well, but it grabbed Susan's—the angel's—green arm and pulled it away from the shop. It let go and ran ahead, down the street, its spikes bobbing up and down.

She let it lead her. The green angel knew where they were headed, climbing up the outside of an apartment complex. She could climb with such ease with these arms; could move so readily. She could grab on to window ledges, glass shattering beneath her exoskeleton-covered palms. Her fingers hoisted her entire body up with strength, and she found herself inside some kind of office space. Tables and chairs had been swept away, the ceiling filled with egg sacs.

She felt the angel crying, tears streaming down its cheeks, the fear throbbing between every beat of its heart.

Run away, run away, run away!

But how could it run, when its children, her children, were here?

Could she?

Susan wasn't sure what she was doing, or if it was the angel. She was blurring between being a human soul and the green angel, and suddenly, electricity came rippling out of her again, crackling along the ceiling as she, the angel, screamed at the eggs. Her mate screeched at her, and then in a flash, everything fizzled out.

She blinked away the dust, the searing pain of the light, to see the eggs had changed. They were no longer sacs of white; they didn't look like insect eggs anymore. Now, they were almost translucent, jellylike, with glowing orbs inside. Most of them were green. Some of them shone with an orange warmth. And a few had both: orange with dots of green or green with orange stripes. And they were floating.

Set them free, said something buried deep inside Susan. And she obliged. Without question. Leaping into the air, her spikes scraping the walls, she crashed through the ceiling, and the ceiling after that, making her way to the roof. She could feel the eggs following her up into the fresh evening air. When she got up to the roof, she stopped and watched as the eggs floated past her.

And then up they went, floating higher and higher over her head, over her mate's head as he came up to join her, nuzzling his face against her shoulder.

The eggs flew into the clouds, shining like distant airplanes before fading from view. Where they'd gone, she didn't know. Neither did the angel's mind, but at least they wouldn't be subject to *this* hunger. To this fear. To this . . .

"How strange," came a voice, and both angels whipped around to see a man in a lab coat standing on the other side of the roof. He was brandishing a long sword, sweat glistening on his forehead as he stared at them through broken glasses. There was a glow about him, a silvery outline to his silhouette that escalated the fear thrumming inside the angel's body, and Susan almost lost her grip.

It wasn't just fear anymore. It wasn't just the signal screaming at her to run away, but lingering between them was something that might've been worse.

Subservience.

The angel knew it was supposed to bow down. Kneel. Beg for mercy.

The man standing there wasn't just a man. There was something inside him, in the same way that Susan was inside the angel. But what? She sniffed the air, tried to understand, tried to parse through the angel's thoughts, and . . .

She recognized the man. It was Dr. Lee, her science teacher from what felt like a lifetime ago. He was still wearing a bloodstained lab coat, his glasses cracked, and she recognized his weapon now. It was his katana.

What is he doing here? She remembered him trying to perform surgery on an angel, trying to understand their biology, but . . . the angel sensed something else; something far more dangerous: a being of much higher power than anyone Susan or even the angel had ever run into. She wished there was a system notification, something, so she could see what he was, but . . . Whilst inside the angel, she got *some* notifications, but there wasn't anything for Dr. Lee's presence. Shouldn't that at least say human?

"You'll do perfectly," hissed Dr. Lee. He was speaking *their* language, and for a second, she thought she saw silvery wings spreading behind his lab coat, silver light dazzling in his eye.

Her mate bolted, turning away and diving off the building, but before she could cry out, before she could try using the angel's language, Dr. Lee flashed forward with a shower of silver sparks. Like a streak of moonlight, he crossed the rooftop, and her mate's body crashed to the street below, headless.

A wail of anguish lodged itself in her throat, and then Dr. Lee was on her as well. His katana cut easily through her arm as she lunged to grab him. The emerald limb dropped away through the hole in the ceiling, glistening and glittering before clattering to the floor far below. He turned and slashed her hip and the exposed skin of her navel, and Susan, the angel, collapsed onto her one remaining arm.

Blood splattered the ceiling. He'd even cut through some of her spikes. The angel could sense all the danger, desperately wishing she had her wings so she could fly away.

Susan was melting between her fear and the angel's anguish, its instincts. She wanted to leave this body, to get away, to run as well, but it hurt too much. Was she stuck?

Am I stuck?

Dr. Lee leaned close, looking right through her, it felt like. But he didn't recognize what she was. He didn't know she was inside this angel in the same way something else was inside him. "My, aren't you a powerful one," he whispered, manic, delirious. "On the verge of becoming a desecrated . . . He will be most happy, I think. Most happy. You will be the final meal for Him to be born, and then, I am free of this."

He grabbed her by the hair, his entire arm glowing with silver light, and when he looked into her eyes, Susan saw what it was: another angel. An angel more powerful, maybe as powerful as Azra'il, had possessed her former teacher and wanted to feed her to someone.

CHAPTER TWENTY

EVE'S SHINING WINGS

Jenny didn't get the chance to respond. Roaring, the Leviathan swirled through the sky like an eel caught on a line; the adult angels were attacking it, poking at it like a flock of birds to a whale.

"Hey!" shouted Eve, her voice rising up like the chime of an enormous bell. The angels stopped to look down at her. With another flap of her golden wings, light shimmering away in glistening sparkles, Eve rocketed into the sky to face the angels head-on. They dove, multicolor streaks of light, to meet Eve, who was a blur of bright red and gold. She looked like a bullet made out of sunlight, and when they met, the sky erupted in color and smoke, their blows so powerful the clouds parted and splintered away.

The Leviathan snaked down around them, too enormous for the sky. A low rumbling came from its throat, and Jenny could feel its pain from where she was. Had the angels hurt it? Or was this world too cold for it? Were the children all right? What was she supposed to do?

Again, her death's scream rang through her head. *"DO SOMETHING."*

Her tentacles burst out of her back, and she cried out, falling to her knees as they slithered and wriggled and jetted out, extending in every direction. All six of them could sense the angels rushing toward her, scrambling through the ice and snow. The tarnished ones. They wouldn't be stopped by the cold. They wouldn't be stopped until they'd fed, and she was the only flesh around.

Her hatchet was back in her hand with a flash of light. The first angel came barreling down on her, a creature with long dark hair and painfully skinny limbs and a sunken chest. Jenny's heart broke as another flash of light flickered; she'd cut through its shoulder and neck, but it was still alive.

+100 Energy

That energy was just from pain. Her hatchet could extract energy from pain, but it was *her* fault the angel had become like this. Become tarnished.

But then again, the other angels were all right fighting. They'd attacked the Leviathan. They were fighting Eve. And they would've attacked her too.

Still. Was it right to turn a creature into . . . this?

The tarnished angel screamed and hissed, dribbling over itself as it tried to reach Jenny. Her tentacles darted out, latched on to the dying angel, and sucked it dry before she could stop herself.

She cut through the rest, snapping limbs off with her hatchet, slamming angels into broken messes of flesh and bones with her tentacles. Her tentacles had grown thicker and heavier, darkened to a slick black, and she wondered if this was how her death was expressing himself. Channeling his rage and hunger through these extra limbs.

All the while, she was very aware of the battle above. Eve against all the angels. Light seemed to rain down around her and the tarnished; angels who'd stare at Jenny, baffled. But then, they'd shoot themselves back up into the sky, soaring up to fight the creature who looked like her. Did they think she wasn't a threat? Or was Eve the bigger threat?

And what had happened to the angels who had been fighting the others? Had they gotten caught up in the passageway? Were they the ones who had gotten turned into tarnished angels? Jenny felt sick at the thought, but there was nothing she could do for them.

Everything was a blurry mess of blood and screams and snow. She ripped a tarnished angel in half with her tentacles wrapped around its limbs, guts and internals gushing out and splattering the snow, and then a shadow fell across the world. The Leviathan was plummeting down; Jenny threw her hatchet as hard as she could using Savage Throw.

She could hear the air screaming, the whooshing of wind as the enormous creature fell from the sky. It would flatten anything below it; destroy anything caught in its wake. Her hatchet flew so far she couldn't see it anymore, and just before the Leviathan crashed to the ground, Jenny used Instant Swap.

The ground shook so hard when the Leviathan struck that she tumbled and rolled where she'd landed, snow and ice going up into the air. She summoned her hatchet back and slammed it into the ice, forcing herself to a stop while everything shook. Ice cracked, and loose chunks of snow rained back down. The entire world seemed to have felt that impact. Towering in the distance, as tall as any skyscraper she'd ever seen and seeming to stretch on for miles and miles as though it were the Great Wall of China, was the Leviathan.

Its eyes were closed, its teeth exposed as clouds of hot air rose from its mouth and nostrils. A low rumbling emanated from its body which trembled through the ground and air. Frost covered its leathery skin.

"*Sat'en!*" shouted Jenny, screaming it at the top of her lungs. So many angels had been crushed by the falling Leviathan, but still many scrambled over the ice to get at it. They were ignoring Jenny now, throwing themselves at the Leviathan, tearing into its leathery old flesh, digging for whatever they could.

"No!" screamed Jenny, rushing to the Leviathan's side. She chopped off heads. Grabbed angels by their torsos with her tentacles and launched them over her shoulders. Smushed others against the Leviathan itself. But there were too many. She'd sucked in too many when she'd opened her passageway, and now, they were ripping and tearing at the Leviathan's flesh, one fistful at a time. Like countless ants that had found a fallen elephant to feast on, climbing up the tower of flesh like mountain climbers.

Was it dead? Had she killed the Leviathan by bringing it here?

No, she could feel its low moan. And there was another rhythmic *thud-thud-thud* that went through the ground. That must be the creature's great heartbeat. She stumbled forward, blood pumping through her tentacles, making her head spin. She came to a stop and heard something else, almost illegible underneath the sounds of chewing, the Leviathan's great groan.

The children came soaring out of the Leviathan, passing through its skin and rising like ghosts emerging from a wall. But they came face-to-face with the tarnished angels, who screeched in agony, covering their eyes.

They couldn't look at the real angels, realized Jenny. The light worked just like their flashlights had back in the high school.

Jenny tried to slow down, to keep her composure, but a shudder went through every tentacle, and she turned to see ghouls and people dressed in purple robes and—every one of them had flames coming out of their eyes. Flames that seemed to change color with every flicker; some faces with different colors in each eye.

The notifications flickered rapidly through her head.

Death
(Vessel)
(Vessel)
(Vessel)

And then, she felt communication in a new way, vibrating through the air, picked up by her tentacles. Fluctuations in temperature; heat and coolness.

You swore you would help us. We had a deal.

You left us here to die.

You must pay.

They were inside the deaths, possessing them. They were in the remaining ghouls. These were the leftovers trapped in the world after Azra'il's attack. And they were blaming her for what had happened.

How was it my fault?

With a cry of frustration, she tried to step away from the deaths and ghouls, but they were on her too quickly, too many of them. She couldn't attack. She didn't want to fight them, not while everything else was going on.

"No, listen to me!" she shouted, trying to keep them away with her tentacles. But the deaths clawed at her, and the ghouls threw themselves at her, their large heads bouncing off her armor, the flames in their eyes flickering so maddeningly it almost made her sick. There were too many demons struggling to maintain a body. And the deaths didn't deserve this.

Were they that afraid of freezing again? But weren't they burning out their hosts' bodies? The ghouls' faces were ashen, their limbs charring and crumbling with each blow. The deaths were crying and moaning, their skin drying and cracking. Behind her, the tarnished angels continued to feast on the Leviathan.

The angel children cried her name, begging her to help. The Leviathan's low rumbling seemed to be quieting with every breath. And what would happen if a demon tried to possess the great beast?

It was too much. Too much was happening.

Eve shot down in a ray of golden light, her red rose petals ruffling in the breeze. Blood dribbled down one side of her head. "Open a passage," she barked at Jenny. "We have to get out of here. Leave the mortals to this world."

"What?" shouted Jenny. With a cry, she swirled her tentacles and threw away the deaths and ghouls that had surrounded her, clearing enough space to breathe. She looked back at the tarnished angels, up at the other angels coming down to hover over Eve, ready to fight. "We can't just leave them here."

"There is too much at stake, Mother," said Eve. Red and golden light flashed, forming twin swords in her hands.

"No," repeated Jenny, feeling desperate. She could see the angel children huddling over the Leviathan. Could see the adult angels descending on them. To protect them or attack? To take away? *No, no, no.* She'd messed up.

She had to fix this.

Angels swooped down as a piercing green light shot through her arm and forced her to the ice-covered ground. Jenny cried out, turning to see a green adult angel standing over her, a lance in his arms. Light covered his muscular torso, a strip of it fluttering around his waist.

"Adonai will reward me immensely for your death," he hissed, raising his spear again.

Golden light bloomed in his chest, and he looked down in shock as a sword tore through his side. Eve threw his body away, grabbed Jenny, and pulled her up. Her eyes were frantic. "I have your mother, Jenny. I have your mother. Open the passageway, and I will take you to her."

My mother? Jenny's tentacles swished and slammed the ground. Rage surged through her. Hurt and heartbreak and horror. The angel children were being herded away, all of them crying, begging for help, rising up in a crowd with the adults surrounding them, escorting them with lances and swords. Where were they going? They had no way back to their world without her.

They wanted the young for something. Sat'en had been protecting the children and the eggs for a reason. The Leviathan would die. Jenny couldn't just leave them here.

So do something, came a voice from inside her.

She tried to think. Tried to find some way out of this. Could she use the light again somehow? Open a new passageway and use the vacuum effect to suck away all the angels?

Could she?

No, that would suck in the children too. They'd be forced to become tarnished, and she'd never forgive herself for that.

What she needed to do was sever this world too. End the curse that kept the demons frozen. Free this world from whatever was holding it hostage. And maybe, just maybe, she could find Yeshua too.

But how was she supposed to do that? In the world of death, it had been the blood rain. That was what had connected her to that world, to its pain. What was the pain here?

The ice.

Her eyes went wide. She looked at Eve, who looked almost exactly like herself. She'd grown so much more powerful since Jenny had given birth to her, and she drew on that feeling, too. That feeling of giving birth. All the pain she could muster.

"Cover me," she said to the shocked Eve. Then Jenny plunged her hands and tentacles into the ice with enough force that her armor, her fingers, and her wrists broke upon impact. She didn't care. She was elbows deep in the ice, trying to find the hurt.

CHAPTER TWENTY-ONE

UNDOING WHAT WAS FROZEN

C old.

She connected with the frozen essence of the world. Just like blood had drowned the world of death in despair, it was the sheer cold which had taken over the world of demons and slowed it to a standstill. Cold was the opposite of heat and flame, their particles no longer able to move around and express themselves as they wanted to. That was the hurt.

Jenny took a deep breath and exhaled, the warm air from her lungs clouding around her face. Frost climbed up her arms, spreading beneath her armor, causing the scales to crack. It seeped through her skin, deep into her muscles, finding her bones.

She'd felt cold before, in the darkness between worlds. If she could survive that, she could survive anything. She could survive this. She could do this.

Reach for it, she told herself.

Everything seemed to slow down. Eve spun this way and that with her two golden swords, her wings batting away any angel who got too close. She cut down deaths and ghouls. Jenny couldn't stop and tell her not to, but it didn't matter. When the ghouls broke, when the shells the demons had been using splintered and crumbled, the flames and lights blew out of them. Their burning eyes went empty, and all the demons struggling to keep a home vanished into the cold. The deaths collapsed to the floor, blinked innocently for a moment as their wounds healed, and then the demons were struggling to rush back inside.

The angel children cried out for Jenny. The Leviathan groaned in pain as the tarnished angels continued feasting. Where was Sat'en? Trapped inside? Was she all right?

Jenny's mind pushed further. Her tentacles zipped around as though each one had a mind of their own. They latched on to deaths and ghouls and threw them away. They swatted at the angels, shimmering through their light bodies. Lances dug at her. Cut through her. But whatever thing was inside her, whatever Azra'il had placed in her body, wouldn't let her die. It wriggled and moved and found every wound, every slash, every bleeding cut, and stitched her back together.

Azra'il's curse ended up being a gift, and Jenny used the pain.

Keep attacking me, she almost said. A lance popped through her chest, collapsing her lung. She inhaled a raspy breath that got stuck, and then the bug was there. She could breathe again. A tarnished angel tore off her ear, the skin coming off her jaw, but she swatted the creature away, and her face healed. Her ear grew back.

So she didn't pay it any mind. Pain was nothing more than the normal; like breathing, like eating. She pushed further and further, trying to find the exact source. It was a blurry memory now, how she'd done with the blood in the world of death. But she focused on the sensation. The reaching. The pushing. Trying to will her mind into the hurt, take hold of it, and . . .

Oh!

Something blue sparkled deep inside the recesses of her mind; a voice she thought she'd never hear again. Blue light flickered to life all throughout the world. Her eyes were closed, but she could see them. Could feel them. It was Iblis.

What was left of him.

That was what she could focus on. He'd represented the wills of all the demons. He'd been their chosen representative. He'd given his life for them.

She saw the battle against Azra'il. Saw his gigantic form stomping through the ghouls and demons. Saw him grab Iblis. Saw Yeshua trapped inside the pillar, that final look of fear and desperation in his eyes.

She saw Azra'il and Susan on the cross, and—

Severed Spirit.

The cut came easy. Cleanly. Like a hot knife through a block of cheese, gliding through in one gentle movement—and then the world around her erupted in chaos.

Light shone from the sky; the clouds parted to reveal a sunny day. Bright warmth washed over everything, and she could hear earsplitting screaming as all the tarnished angels saw the sun. Was it the sun? She wasn't sure. She didn't care. The worm was working hard to heal her arms as the ice around her hands melted away. She stood, shaking, as the angels stopped attacking.

As the angel children stopped crying out.

A deep, low rumble shook the ground as the Leviathan stirred. It raised its city-block-size head, blocking out the sun for a moment, before it opened its mouth, its gargantuan teeth, and roared so loudly that the angels who'd stood against them—the ones who'd tried to take the children as well as the tarnished angels—fell to their knees, clutching their heads, screaming.

It lasted a long moment, a foghorn blasting in all of their ears, and then it was over. Heavy silence as all those creatures remained on their knees, unmoving. The children were unharmed. So were Jenny and Eve.

Eve seized the opportunity. She flew into the air, her image shimmering and splitting apart until she was seemingly everywhere all at once, cutting and slashing and flapping those golden wings, leaving rose petals in her wake. Within a moment, all the angels were dead. And notifications of experience filled Jenny's head.

You have defeated Angel (Stage II)!
You have defeated Angel (Stage I)!
You have defeated Angel (Stage II)!

There were several more, followed by dozens notifying her that more tarnished angels had died. Experience and energy collected in her stats, but Jenny pushed the notifications away. Eve's swords vanished as she touched down beside Jenny, out of breath, sweat beading down her face.

Huffing and puffing, Eve rushed over to Jenny. "So *you're* the one she wants to speak to. *You're* the one she couldn't see."

"What are you talking about?" whispered Jenny, breathless, still trying to calm down after severing the world. She blinked till Eve came into focus.

"The angel, Rafa'el . . ." said Eve, trailing off and shaking her head. "Was this the crime, then? Was this what they're waiting for? No, it can't be. Why you?" She blinked back at Jenny, her eyes glowering. "What did you do, Mother?"

Jenny shrugged. "I'm not sure. But I did this before. In the world of the dead."

"So you found it, then?" Eve looked all around as the ice melted away to reveal soil. Little green things dotted the landscape. Eve knelt and touched one of those things. They were plants. She looked like she wanted to say something, ask a bunch of questions, but instead, she hissed.

Jenny followed Eve's eyes, looking way up to see Sat'en standing inside Leviathan's mouth as the enormous creature stirred. Blood trickled from all the little wounds caused by the tarnished angels.

"Sat'en," said Jenny.

"I know her."

"I thought she was dead," murmured Jenny under her breath, but then she realized that she was speaking from Iblis's memories rather than her own thoughts. Eve didn't notice.

"She's not alive," replied Eve.

What do you mean? Jenny was going to ask, but then, the angel children crowded around her. They stood atop the melting snow, the soil, the plants pushing their way out of the thawing ground.

"Jenny!"

"Everything froze inside the Leviathan."

"It was so cold it hurt."

"I couldn't breathe."

They spoke all at once, rushing to tell her everything, but then they stopped and stared at Eve. "Two Jenny?"

Now that they'd come closer, Jenny could see them phasing in and out of clarity. Like they were nearly invisible in the sunlight. They left no footprints, and their little wings beat up and down, the water vapor trailing with every flap. They were beautiful sparkling little ghosts.

Eve looked at them with one eyebrow raised. Even though they had the same face, Eve carried it differently, Jenny thought. With more confidence. With more arrogance. She almost looked like her mother.

Her mother. She remembered what Eve had said before Jenny tore the world free.

"What do you mean you have my mother?"

Eve's lips twisted into a cold smile. "Mother of my mother. Brother as well. I found them and kept them. They have joined my cause."

"Your cause?" asked Jenny.

Eve nodded. "What I always fought for. What I tried to push you to fight for. But you were more interested in your own needs, weren't you?"

Jenny didn't respond to that, but she remembered every moment of having Eve inside her head. All the things she'd said and promised. And now here she was, Jenny's child, standing in front of her, talking down to her. But it was funny.

Now that Eve was no longer just an entity speaking through the guidance system, she seemed so . . . normal. So human.

"Are you enjoying your body?" asked Jenny.

Eve's smile grew. "Oh, most thoroughly, I promise you, Mother. More than you ever could." She closed her eyes and stretched on her tiptoes as the rose petal armor trembled like it was alive. With a sigh, she lowered her shoulders and relaxed.

Anger flicked through Jenny's head. She fought the urge to push Eve. To attack her with the hatchet. But she knew her anger wasn't completely justified. She'd misplaced her anger on Eve for everything; for Susan's death, for everyone's suffering. For her own suffering. For misleading her.

Eve knelt and held her hands out to the children. They seemed to be able to actually touch her. She patted their heads. "I do recall children always had an interest in you," she said, turning to look at Jenny. "There's an angel who speaks about you. I have her imprisoned in my world. Come with me."

"Before," spoke Jenny, trying to find the words. "You said there was too much at stake. What's going on?"

Eve's face darkened. "My counterpart means to be born into the material world. Perhaps he already has. But his aim is to destroy everything. All the worlds. Build them back in His image, with Himself as master of all creation."

"I know that already," said Jenny, grabbing Eve's petal-covered arm and pulling herself up to look her eye to eye. They were the same height. Similar builds. Except Eve was slightly curvier, more womanly, more grown. Jenny felt young; she felt like her death, a little boy, looking up at her grown self. "What's going on?"

Eve stared back with cold eyes. "My forces have captured an angel by the name of Rafa'el. She is the Scribe. She is the Trumpet Blower."

"The trumpet?"

"They also call it a horn. When Adonai rises to power, Rafa'el is to blow the horn, shattering the bonds between all worlds and bringing it all crashing down for Adonai to do as He pleases."

A chill went up Jenny's back. She felt her stomach tighten. She'd seen so many of the worlds now: The souls marching to their judgment, suffering in that horrible maze of angels. The deaths alone in their world, now freed from the blood and pillars. The demons. The angels. And now Eve. Was she a force for good, then? Was she trying to help everyone? Or was she after something else?

Jenny got the sense that Eve just wanted to enjoy material life. To enjoy being alive, almost as if the strange being was an embodiment of everything Jenny had wanted: To enjoy things. To enjoy herself. To enjoy living in her body. To live her life. Eve had taken her body and her eyes and was the confident, powerful, beautiful being that Jenny had always wanted to be.

She sighed, staring at every detail of Eve's body: The sweat. Ferocious look. The pale skin. The dark eyes. The artery throbbing on her forehead. Dark hair tucked behind her ears. The smile. Not a pimple scar. Not a fleck of dried skin. Wide shoulders. Rose petals that perfectly fit against her form. The sweet, subtle fragrance wafting around her.

"What do you say, Mother?" asked Eve. "Will you work with me again?"

CHAPTER TWENTY-TWO

MOTHER AND DAUGHTER

Jenny turned and walked away, trying not to make it seem like she was storming off. But she owed Eve nothing, and she wanted no part of whatever she was doing. Eve shouted after her, but Jenny ignored her, grabbing her hatchet as the demons surrounded her, sparkling hovering flames. She couldn't tell if they were angry or thankful, but they didn't try to possess her or anyone else. Maybe they knew not to. But the deaths that had been possessed before had been set free, and they rushed over to Jenny.

Maybe possession hadn't been so bad. Traumatic and painful, but at least the demons had kept them warm, and the deaths could heal incredibly quickly.

"Thank you," they whispered to her. "Thank you for saving us."

Jenny couldn't fake a smile for them; she was exhausted. Whatever she'd done to sever the world had left her completely drained. She had no energy left, nothing she could give to them. If they wanted new clothes or food, they'd have to figure something out for themselves. Green plants were growing rapidly from the soil. Bushes and ferns and other things already came up to Jenny's knees, and the vegetation spread across the landscape as quickly as a breeze. In the distance, she could even see trees starting to take shape.

It was as though the world had been waiting all this time for everything to sprout and come back to life, and then she realized she couldn't see any more of the demons anywhere. Their floating sparkles, their flames, had dispersed. A long shadow flicked across the land as the Leviathan flew overhead, carrying Sat'en and all the angel children, but other than that, everything was still. The deaths wandered through the new land, exploring; she wondered if she should bring them back to their proper world. And what of the demons?

"Demons?" she called, stepping over a trembling blue flower. Her tentacles shuddered. She was trying to communicate through them using temperature, using Ignite so the flames danced along the lengths of her tentacles as she whirred them about.

"Mother, what are you doing?" Eve grabbed her shoulder.

Jenny didn't react. "A lot's happened since I gave birth to you."

The demons didn't seem to respond either. Like their anger or whatever had evaporated with freedom, and they'd gone off to reclaim the world. She wondered if there were others who could speak the way Iblis could. She wondered if Sat'en might be able to reach them. Wouldn't the demons be an asset in the war? Jenny could picture them possessing all the broken tarnished angel bodies.

Eve seemed like she couldn't decide whether to be mad or not. "Well then. Seems like the demons don't want anything to do with you. Why don't you come with me? I have something to show you."

Jenny ignored her again. She felt around with her tentacles, turning around slowly as though trying to read a compass rose, searching for Yeshua. The last she'd seen of him, Azra'il had trapped him inside a pillar in the midst of their battle in the ice. But now that the ice was gone, shouldn't he be here too? Shouldn't he have been freed from his pillar?

"What are you playing at?"

"I'm trying to find my friend," said Jenny, who didn't want anything to do with Eve. She didn't care that she was so powerful; didn't care about her agenda. She remembered how Eve had appeared in the light before Jenny could bring everyone through. It was Eve who had pushed her back, Eve who had chosen this frozen world to fall into, Eve who had put the Leviathan and all the angel children in danger. "Why did you even come here? Why don't you go back to your world?"

"You must come with me, Mother," said Eve. "There's an angel who has asked for you by name."

Jenny shook her head. "Apparently, they all know my name, so why does that matter?" She stomped toward Eve, bringing her face very close. And it was weird, strange, like bumping her nose against her own reflection, staring into her own eyes. In a low voice, she said, "I haven't forgiven you."

Eve wrinkled her nose, and Jenny wondered if she'd ever done that too. She could tell Eve was trying to figure out what exactly Jenny wouldn't forgive her for. Being inside Jenny's head? For promising her great power? For Susan's death? Finally, Eve spoke. "Alright. Open a passageway from here to my world, then. I'll leave you be, *Mother.*"

"Wait a second," said Jenny, almost wanting to laugh. "You can't open it yourself? How did you find me, then?"

Eve blinked. Her cheeks turned slightly red, and she ran her hand through her hair. "No. I mean, I can move between my world and the material world just fine. It's the other worlds that I . . . I saw your passageway open and felt you before you emerged, and I sensed all of this." She gestured upward toward the Leviathan. "So I dove in and stopped you before you made another mess of things."

"Another mess of things?" Jenny repeated. Then she decided to keep walking. Eve was stuck here, and she wouldn't give what she wanted right away; Jenny remembered too clearly seeing Eve's foot on Susan's corpse. And besides that, Jenny was *exhausted*. She didn't think she could open another passageway even if she wanted to. She needed to rest. But she wasn't going to let Eve know that. She also wanted to find Yeshua first. "Well then, I guess you'll just have to wait."

A shudder ran through Jenny's tentacles, and they all snapped in the same direction. That must be where Yeshua was, but as far as she could tell, that direction looked the same as everywhere else. Instead of ice and snow, there was soil and sun and plant life. But it was as good a place to look as any, so Jenny set off.

"So what am I supposed to do?" called Eve.

Jenny laughed, thinking about how many times she'd asked that question herself. "You can come with me. There's a friend stuck here."

"A friend?" Eve crossed her arms. Her lips curled into an impatient snarl, her mother's snarl, but then kicked a fern with her rose-petal-covered foot. "It was just the same when I was contained inside your head."

"Cool," said Jenny. A part of her wanted to scream at Eve. *You were there. Inside my head. You egged me on. You pushed me till I became the monster that I am.*

With a shudder, she withdrew her tentacles, letting them slither back inside her. Where they went, she didn't know. She didn't care. She could feel Eve watching her. Her own golden wings shimmered and faded away, and they walked slowly in the direction her tentacles had sensed. Jenny in front. Eve trailing behind.

"Are you angry at me?" asked Eve. Jenny flashed back to the boy, her death, asking the same question. Why were people always asking if she was angry at them?

Especially when the answer was yes?

"Yes," Jenny replied.

"But why? Look at how much power you have. How far you have come. Do you think you or Susan Brown would have had anything remotely as powerful without my interference?"

Jenny turned around so quickly she saw red for a second. She held her hatchet to Eve's throat.

"What?" asked Eve with a little smile. "You don't like me saying her name? How is your little friend, anyway?"

The urge to slice through her neck was too strong, but her hatchet touched the rose petals, and Jenny was surprised to feel how hard they were. They looked like regular flower petals, soft and wet, but just by pressing the tip of her hatchet against them, she could tell they were hardier than any of the armor she'd made; more durable even than the exoskeletons that covered the desecrated angels.

"What do you want me to say?" continued Eve. "Do you want me to apologize?"

"You showed me so much," said Jenny. "All those things about powerful people. But you were just using me."

Eve stepped closer with a flash of light, knocking into the hatchet. It bounced harmlessly off her armor and landed in the dirt. She stood till their noses touched and Jenny could smell the flowery aroma of roses. "Yes. I used you. Just as you used me hoping to get to your brother. Hoping to save your little friends. What of it? This is *war*, my dear mother. We are here to either win or die."

Jenny bit her lip. She didn't know how to respond to that. Eve was right.

"It was too easy to pull on your vanity," continued Eve, who wasn't done talking. "Your anger. Your rage. Too easy to play with your silly little desires and power fantasies."

Rage rumbled inside Jenny. She could almost hear her death screaming at her: *It's your fault I'm alone. It's your fault I'm stuck like this.*

"You never do anything, so when something comes along, you think your recklessness, your pleasure is what matters most?" Eve laughed and pushed Jenny's arm away. "Come on now. Let's go find this friend so we can get out of here. Adonai's forces are gathering, and you want to have a goddamn tea party."

Tea party? Another memory hit Jenny like a truck. Sitting alone in a corner of the bedroom she shared with her mother. A little plastic table and a plastic chair. And some of their mugs spread around so that Jenny could pretend she had invited friends over. She never got to attend any sleepovers. She never had any friends stay over. How could they? They lived in a horrible place, and she didn't want them to meet her mom.

She swallowed that down. Eve's words didn't matter. Finding Yeshua did.

Was he all right? Was he alive? Was he still in the pillar, or had he been freed by the severing?

"You need to grow up, mother," said Eve, marching away. She spoke in the same tone and inflection that Jenny's mother had always used. "You need to stop playing the pity game and own up to your actions. Get things done. Stop playing the victim then crying about it."

Jenny gritted her teeth. "I'm not playing anything. And who the fuck are you to talk to me like that?"

Eve turned around and pointed at her head, jabbing her temple with her finger hard enough so that a trickle of blood ran down the side of her face. "Who the fuck am I? I have all your memories in here. I'm not just your child—I *am* you. I am the best version of you."

Again, Jenny wanted to hit her. To say something cruel. To curse her out. But then, almost with a laugh, she realized. "You're the best version of me, but you can't get out of here without my help?"

Eve's face flushed a deep red. Then she righted herself and stuck out her chin, glowering at her. "I can force you to open it."

"Do it, then," challenged Jenny, stopping in her tracks. "Come on. Show me how strong you are, *daughter*."

With a snarl, Eve lunged at Jenny, golden wings flapping. Two shining swords erupted from her hands, but before Eve made contact, Jenny used Instant Swap and switched places with where she'd dropped the hatchet earlier. Eve slashed through empty air, stumbled, and looked up with pure rage.

"So you really did inherit my anger," noted Jenny. She summoned her hatchet back with a flash of light. She knew she was vastly outpowered, but she also knew Eve couldn't kill her. Not if she wanted to get out of this world. "I thought you were the best of me?"

"I am everything you will never be," hissed Eve through her teeth. Golden light ignited from her back. With a flap of her wings, she rushed toward Jenny, but then, another voice rumbled through the air.

"ENOUGH!"

Red lightning sizzled and cracked, and Yeshua appeared in his flowing purple robes, eyes sunken and red. He grabbed Eve's arm and Jenny's arm and spun around before letting go, flinging them away from one another.

CHAPTER TWENTY-THREE

NATIVITY

Jibra'il dragged the cut-up wretched angel across the rooftop, but he was unsettled. Something about this angel was *wrong*. A scent or a feeling or something; he wasn't sure what. He couldn't see what was different about it. It looked like any other wretched one, this one formed from an angel of green light, a female that had laid eggs. But what kind of tarnished angel would release its eggs?

Was that what was bugging him? The eggs had looked all wrong? He'd seen them float away, drifting up toward the sky the way normal angel eggs would have. The eggs of the wretched were more . . . material, with a hard shell and liquid inside. He'd studied them up close over the centuries; Azra'il had even taken a liking to eating them. Raw. Sometimes, he'd cook them the way humans often did the eggs of other creatures.

He didn't want to think about it. He could sense this angel would give a big morsel of energy and substance. Did it matter how or why? Did it matter what was different about it if it would be enough to complete Adonai's natality?

All he wanted to do was complete his duty and move on. Find Rafa'el and wait out the end of destiny with her.

The angel screamed and hissed and clawed at Jibra'il's adopted body with its one remaining arm. Fingernails dug through soft human flesh, tore away cloth. Why was this angel struggling so much? Why did it seem like it was trying to catch his attention?

What did it want to say? Why could it even communicate?

Jibra'il walked to the end of the roof, looking down at the street below. With one swift movement, he threw the wretched angel over, and as it plummeted to the ground, as its wide eyes and scream faded slightly with distance, Jibra'il leaped as well.

Silver light flashed around him as he shot down, katana outstretched. With two more swings of his blade, he cut off the remaining arm and cut another deep gash into its chest. It banged its head *hard* on the ground, its exoskeleton cracking all over.

But it was still hissing, crying, as if desperate to communicate with him. But what it said, he couldn't understand. It was speaking something between light and human, like it had forgotten its language, and again, Jibra'il dismissed it. He had a job to do, and if it wouldn't be quiet, then . . .

He turned the katana around, then, swiftly, jammed the opposite end into the angel's mouth, breaking its teeth and its jaw. The look in its eyes, the expression of hurt and pain . . . He felt bad. But he reasoned with himself that this pain would be short-lived, and all would be forgiven in Adonai's embrace. Besides, he needed to ensure the creature would be safe to feed to Leslie now. He wanted her to eat this one alive. Wanted her to consume its blood fresh so that Adonai could gain its strength.

As he grabbed a fistful of its hair, he could feel Dr. Lee's questioning, the human's curiosity. And so he told him, even if only as a means to ignore the cruelty of his actions.

The wretched angels are advanced evolutions of the tarnished, he explained. *Angels are beings of light, and when forcibly converted to matter . . .* He gestured around at the bloody mess. *A powerful desire for flesh, to become flesh, to consume flesh, overtakes their minds, leaving them empty vessels desperate to be whole.*

So then, what's that stuff on these ones? It looks like an exoskeleton.

It is hardening light, said Jibra'il, walking as the angel cried softly. *Their bodies do not forget from whence they came, and their light remains. And angels grow from every light on the spectrum, as your scientists have organized it. From there, there are deviations as to how they evolve, but always the same. Tarnished to wretched to desecrated.*

Is there anything beyond that? The other questions came with a flurry of memories and notes. Stages and killing, experience and energy, the organic substance of armor and things produced with energy.

They cannot grow beyond desecration, replied Jibra'il. He'd arrived at the school building.

A gentle rainfall dropped from the sky, and he looked up at the rolling gray clouds, thinking how he used to love them. How he'd never been on this side of a storm before, experiencing it through the body of a mortal, rain falling from unbelievably high to touch down on his face. Streaks of water ran along the shape of this skull, dripping off his chin, soaking into his clothes.

He'd created millions of storms across his lifetime; that had been the favorite of his duties: bringing rain and thunder, snow and ice, to various parts of the material world. Rafa'el would often ask him to use his power, and he would oblige without question, without doubt. But this was his first time experiencing the storms from the point of view of a mortal, what should be the receiving end of his ability.

The guard angels parted, brilliant silhouettes moving out of the way. He entered the building through what Dr. Lee called the lobby: a cruel hole in the floor in which bodies were strewn about; he didn't pay them any mind. Lifting the wretched angel by the hair, he leaped through the hole above him, rushing with silver light till he found the room where the young woman had decided to take shelter.

He found her lying on a desk, her belly so swollen it looked like it would pop, her eyes red. "Is that more food?" she asked. "I don't think I can eat anymore." But even as she said those words, her eyes flicked down to the angel hanging from Jibra'il's hand, and saliva gushed down her chin. She had to slurp it up and swallow.

"Yes, I believe it will be the last."

Leslie's face contorted as she tried to sit up. Jibra'il knew better than to rush over and help; he would not survive contact with Adonai in that form. The belly glowed with golden and red light, flickers of darkness crackling around it. She yawned, positioning her feet over the edge, but instead of getting up, she slid off the desk and onto the floor, resting on it with her legs spread to accommodate for her belly. She looked up at Jibra'il and gestured with her hand. "Give it to me."

Jibra'il gently slid the creature's torso across the floor toward Leslie. When she grabbed it, when her fingers found its chest, the green exoskeleton erupted, shattering with bright light, and the girl screamed. The baby in her belly seemed to be responding, and Jibra'il had to raise an arm to shield his eyes. He felt himself flickering, as though a wind was trying to blow him away from the body he possessed, but he held on, fighting to stand as he took a step back.

Was this it? Would Adonai be born?

But she hadn't even taken a bite. She hadn't swallowed.

The light faded away, darkness hung heavily, and Jibra'il saw what had happened. The angel had gone limp, lifeless, bleeding from its various wounds as Leslie lay on the floor with her arm around it, her lips pressed to its shoulder, suckling, shuddering. But standing above it was a soul. A human soul.

Jibra'il stared at it. Another girl. Long brown hair and fearsome eyes and . . . it wasn't *just* a soul. Energy snapped and fizzled through it.

"How did you come here?" asked Jibra'il incredulously. Every soul was to be accounted for by Azra'il. Every soul was necessary for powering Adonai's vision. What was this soul doing here?

"You don't have to do this," said the soul, raising its hands. "Please. Whatever is inside Leslie. You can stop this, can't you? She's just a little girl."

Jibra'il shook his head as Dr. Lee echoed the same sentiment inside him. *Stop this now. Don't let your Adonai be born. It's going to end the fucking world, and you'll never see your Rafa'el again.*

"I must see to it," said Jibra'il, gritting Dr. Lee's teeth. "This is the plan. This is destiny."

"But *what* is that thing?" asked the soul, raising its voice. "Even the angels are terrified of it. What are you? Why are you doing all of this?"

Don't you care about your Rafa'el? Don't you care about yourself?

Jibra'il drew the katana, blinking, sweating in this human form. How could he not have noticed the soul? "This has to be done. This is the only way to bring peace to existence. To end all suffering once and for all!"

The soul gestured toward Leslie, who was munching away softly. "How is this supposed to end suffering?" it shouted, reaching for the girl. "Leslie, stop eating that. Stop! I gotta—"

Jibra'il lunged forward so suddenly he flew out of Dr. Lee's body. The body buckled behind him as the katana skidded away, and Jibra'il, in his true form, crashed into the soul.

CHAPTER TWENTY-FOUR

REST

Jenny landed in the dirt and rolled, tearing up plants, chunks of grass, and bouncing twice before coming to a stop. The earthy scent of freshly turned soil filled the air; her armor was caked in dirt. But when she got to her feet, expecting another fight, another crazy adversary, she found Yeshua standing there. The wind flowed through his long hair and beard. His tattered purple robe clung to his frail body, and little bolts of red lightning flickered around him. He looked hard at Jenny before doubling over into a coughing fit.

Jenny rushed to his side. "You alright?"

"I am fine," he replied. "Side effects of being trapped inside a pillar of salt." He coughed again, smearing blood on his arm. Then he took a deep, shaky breath and marched over to where Eve sat on the ground.

She was pulling on the rose petals that covered her arm and glowering. Her golden wings shimmered away, bursting into a shower of sparks.

"So we finally meet, Antithesis," said Yeshua, projecting his voice. He extended a hand, the sleeve slipping to reveal a thin arm. "I know what you are aiming to do. Allow me to help you."

Eve squinted at him. Jenny didn't know how to respond. She'd wondered if Yeshua would know Eve; if maybe they were enemies or old comrades who'd met in the past. He seemed to be friendly and inviting toward her.

"Failed One," she said, cocking her head and staring at Yeshua. "I thought you dead and long gone." She made a cross in the air, running her fingers down vertically then horizontally.

"I was held in the world of the dead," he replied, unfazed by her words and gestures. "Imprisoned by Azra'il."

Eve looked at Yeshua coolly, her face betraying nothing. There was a coldness in her eyes that Jenny recognized—it was the look she'd give herself in the mirror every night, judging herself, grading every imperfection. Eve turned toward Jenny with disdain as she ignored Yeshua's outstretched hand and got up. "Is this your friend, then?"

"Yeah." Jenny exchanged a glance with Yeshua. He seemed haggard, completely beat down, and exhausted. Did he need to feed again? He didn't look as bone thin as he'd been on the cross; now, he just looked sickly, like he was running a fever. Like he was dying.

Yeshua smiled kindly at Jenny. "I am glad to see you are alright. And how powerful you've grown."

"I've just been hanging," said Jenny with a shrug. "I met my death and things got weird, and now here I am."

"Oh?" Yeshua looked like he wanted to ask many questions, but Eve interrupted them, brushing the soil from her shoulder.

She picked out a blade of grass from her hair. "Can we leave now? There is so much to do, *Mother*."

Jenny's lips twitched seeing Eve bristle. She'd gotten to Eve's ego; she'd pissed her off. It was funny to Jenny, seeing her own emotions expressed on her own face. She knew all of those microexpressions; could read them more easily than anyone else in any world. "I don't think I can just yet. Need to rest before I can use that ability again."

On cue, Eve's eyes flared, her jaw set, and she took a deep inhale through her nose, but before she could say anything, Yeshua broke down into another coughing fit, nearly losing his balance. Red lightning snapped and sizzled around his throat and chest.

Jenny grabbed his arm. "Are you alright? What can I do?"

"Yes," he said, coughing again. "When Azra'il trapped me in the pillar . . ." He gestured toward his torso, doubling over in another fit of violent, awful coughs that splattered the soil with blood. Jenny tugged on his robe, her heart pounding, and then she thought she was going to be sick.

His guts stuck out. The skin of his belly was torn open from his chest to his crotch, and the coiled length of his intestines, the round, glistening shapes of his stomach and liver and . . . She had to forcibly swallow the bile burning the base of her throat. She'd seen much worse. She'd cut through much worse. But seeing someone she knew like that, someone she'd fought beside—it made her feel dizzy.

"Can't your lightning heal you?" she asked, breathless.

"It's okay," he replied, shaking his head.

"Maybe I can try?" whispered Jenny. Valescent Light. Some kind of potion. Anything.

It was Eve who shook her head. "Nothing can heal that. It would only return him to this condition."

"But why?" shouted Jenny.

Yeshua quickly covered himself back up, struggling to wrap the mess of his robes around the mess of his body. "I have been rewritten," he explained. "When Azra'il trapped me as a living death, I . . ." He coughed again, and blood ran down his legs. Red lightning surged through his torso, but what use was it if he was like that forever.

"Can I at least . . . ?" Golden light bloomed in Jenny's hand. Within a moment, rolled-up bandages appeared.

Yeshua took a deep breath and nodded. Eve huffed and walked away, stomping back toward where the Leviathan had come back down to land. Its enormous head stuck out like a mountain, its body a mountain range. If the sun—or whatever the source of light was for this world—weren't directly over-head, the Leviathan's shadow might've cast everything in darkness.

Jenny pulled away Yeshua's robes, and he stood nearly naked. But there was no shame, as so much blood covered his privates and his thighs; as his intestines struggled to remain inside. He nodded toward the great beast, speaking weakly, his strained face making him look even older. "I have only heard stories of the Leviathan."

Careful not to hurt him, careful to keep everything in place, Jenny wrapped the bandage around his torso, trying to focus as hard as she could. She'd always wondered what it would be like, doing triage on a battlefield, working in a hospital. The potions and healing sprays the guidance system made, abilities like Valescent Light, had made it too easy. This was . . . This would never heal. All they could do was manage it.

She wrapped the bandage tightly around his thin frame, going in circles, walking around him. Yeshua stood straight and relaxed, his arms outstretched like a scarecrow. He held his face toward the sky, a breeze ruffling his beard and hair.

"It's beautiful in this world now," he said. "I always thought the demons were devils. But you have shown me the error of my ways."

Jenny couldn't care less about demons and devils. "There has to be a way to fix this."

"Not everything needs fixing," he mumbled. "Blessed are those who hurt, for they shall be guided to peace."

She bit her tongue to keep from snapping at him. What did that even mean? What use was that when his body was hurting like this? How could he fight now, when one punch to the gut would render him useless? Then again, he somehow had held everything inside his body *and* managed to throw both Jenny and Eve around. Was that just the lightning restoring everything back to this horrible state every time he moved?

When she was done, the white bandage holding firmly around his torso, hiding his insides behind layers of cloth, she helped him back into his robes.

"Thank you," he said.

"I'm sorry," she replied. "For everything."

"Jenny." He placed his hand on her head. His eyebrows shot up as he seemed to realize something. "Ah . . . you were crucified as well. How did you escape?"

"I . . ." Her face turned red. Was that shame? Embarrassment? "I ate my death."

He didn't say anything for a long time. Then he chuckled gently and patted her cheek. "Null, huh? Truly, you are a curious creature. Now, I would like to meet this Leviathan and introduce myself to Satan."

"Sat'en," corrected Jenny. "I thought she was Satan too."

While they walked back to the Leviathan, Jenny told Yeshua everything she could about the world of souls, Azra'il, and how she'd found Susan. She explained what had happened since: how Jenny had gotten off her own cross, eaten her death, and then found a strange pillar that had led her to the world of angels. Yeshua listened intently, made a few comments about how strange it all was, but said he didn't know what to make of it. All they could do was try their best.

When they reached the great beast, Jenny's head began to spin. Her eyes felt like they were lagging, and she knew she had to sit down. The Leviathan towered over them like a mountain, and in its shade, Jenny felt the cool chill of a breeze. Flowers were still blooming around her, and she wondered if they were at all similar to the flowers back on Earth. They seemed to be. The vibrantly colored petals, ranging from purple to teal to sunny yellow, were dotted with dewdrops, the green leaves and stems shooting out from the ground. She knew it didn't matter what the others spoke about; she was exhausted. And if she couldn't open a passageway, they were all stuck here.

Eve might've been irritated, but there was no way around it. This was an exhaustion that couldn't be cured by potions or anything else. She needed to rest. So as Yeshua, who seemed to be doing a lot better physically now that Jenny had bandaged up his insides, leaped high into the air to enter the

Leviathan's mouth, Jenny sank to the ground, leaning against the creature's bottom jaw and staring at the lush green world that had sprung up around them. She saw Eve flying up there as well, golden wings shimmering. They would probably discuss the war.

It'd be important stuff. But even if it was, they'd fill her in, wouldn't they? And what was she supposed to do up there? She shut her eyes and tried to relax, tried to calm her heartbeat, tried not to keep picturing Yeshua's intestines jutting out of him like too many snakes in a small fish tank.

Eve had said she'd found Jenny's mother and brother, and that there were others who'd survived, but Jenny wasn't sure she wanted to see them. What would she even say?

Hello? I'm a monster now?

"At least they're alright," she whispered out loud. She slowed down her breathing, but the thoughts kept spinning. Susan. Oliver. Her mother. Sat'en. Jibra'il. Eve. And the angel Eve said wanted to see Jenny. What did that mean? Why did they all know her name?

And where had the demons gone? Could they inhabit the plants? She blinked into the distance, where light shone on trees and enormous plants as they continued to grow and claim space.

She wondered if resting was the right thing to do. A war was waging; she'd seen it, fallen through it twice. And something awful was going on back home, wasn't it? And where was Susan?

How was she supposed to find Susan now? Lost in the material world, a soul. Was she okay?

But it was so peaceful here, in this world. She'd saved it. With her own hands. Her own abilities. She'd brought all these plants back to life. There was no more snow. No more ice. And the demons were free.

Could she save other worlds too? Could she save her own?

Was that her role in all this?

I'm hungry, said a quiet thought buried deep in her consciousness. She pictured the tarnished angels that Eve had cut down so quickly after Jenny had severed the world. She pictured their bodies lying among the plants, the little bit of meat on their thin limbs; she could suck their bones dry . . . She dreamt, or at least she thought she dreamt, of crawling through the dirt, finding each corpse, and ripping them to shreds, chewing and chewing until she'd had her fill.

But a moment later, someone was nudging her awake. Jenny stirred to see Sat'en sitting beside her with tears streaming down the desecrated angel's eyes.

The sky was dark now, and blooming all across it, like ripples of colorful smoke, were vibrant colors. Jenny rubbed her eyes and focused back on Sat'en. She could see the Leviathan flying high in the sky, moving in slow, concentric circles. A shadowy serpent between all the colors. But something about the sky seemed odd; it was no longer vibrant explosions. It actually felt *still*. Quiet. Like ink floating in a tank of water, slowly swirling.

Yeshua was nearby. And, standing with her arms crossed, was Eve, a little bit away from the rest of them. But all around Jenny, and as far as she could see, there were even more flowers. A tree had even grown behind her, its branches teaming with what looked like round orange fruit.

"What's going on?" asked Jenny.

Sat'en pointed upward. "Something that hasn't happened in a very long time. The birth of a new generation of demons."

CHAPTER TWENTY-FIVE

EVE'S SHINING WORLD

I t's time to go. No more waiting." Eve walked over, arms crossed. Jenny got
the sense she had wanted to wake her up much sooner, but she was grateful
for the chance to sleep. And to see the demons' birth. A cool breeze blew
through the plants, tickling Jenny's nose with the world's new fragrance. The
air felt good on her forehead and cheeks, and she sucked in a deep lungful.
Was she ready to open a passageway?

Yeshua stroked his beard. "I would like to meet Rafa'el," he said. "Question
her intentions. But . . . she is the Scribe. What if all of this is according to
destiny?"

"Destiny?" asked Jenny. She was starting to hate that word. Azra'il had
mentioned something about the end of destiny when he'd crucified her. Sat'en
had mentioned destiny as well, after Jenny had fallen through the world of
angels and the Leviathan had swallowed her. But as they spoke, she realized
that Rafa'el was important. One of the highmost angels like Azra'il, alongside
Jibra'il and Mika'el.

"She has been separated from the others," informed Eve, picking at one of
the rose petals on her chest. It wasn't as red as the others, like it had darkened
and withered away. "I have her imprisoned."

"You cannot stop her prophesying," said Sat'en. The desecrated angel's long,
silvery hair fluttered around in the breeze. "I have known my sister since she
was an egg."

"Your sister?" Jenny blinked at the desecrated angel. Yeshua and Eve seemed
surprised as well.

Sat'en nodded. "She may be imprisoned, but her abilities cannot be contained. She will continue writing everything as it unfolds, as it changes. That

was what made her so special to Adonai. Abilities like that, expressions of existence of such caliber, come once in several lifetimes."

Jenny got the feeling that the angel was referring to Jenny's abilities: being able to sever herself, the space between worlds, and even the worlds themselves. Not to mention Susan's Valescent Light.

"Doesn't matter," interrupted Eve in a voice that made Jenny twitch. It was a very familiar indignant tone. "As long as she doesn't blow the damn horn, they can't win."

Jenny's teeth hurt. A headache scattered across her skull as she tried to follow along. But again, they were speaking in riddles. Speaking like they knew everything, when clearly, they were here with her and needed her to move them from world to world.

Before she could ask, Yeshua seemed to notice her agitation.

"It is said that Rafa'el's most powerful ability is her capacity to hold a fragment of substance from beyond the worlds. Some say it was crafted from the light or warmth that existed before the light of the angels; the only remnant of a precursor to these worlds. It has been given the shape of a horn." He made a gesture with his thumb and finger to show her. "When she blows into the horn . . ."

"Every world will come crashing down," finished Sat'en. "It was this ability that gave Adon'il . . . Forgive me, *Adonai*, his dream."

"To rule over all of existence," clarified Eve. "To shape everything to his will and become the final determination of every possibility. It would be the end of entropy." She uncrossed her arms, turned around, and crossed them again, glowering. "Any moment now, he will enter the material world in his true form, and we are wasting time here with demons."

"Yeah?" asked Jenny, who was tired of being bossed around. She was still furious every time she remembered how Eve had used her to be born. How Eve had literally come out of Jenny's womb. How everything had gone to shit. "And what are you gonna do? Shouldn't we try and stop him from being born?"

"So what, you want to kill every pregnant woman in the world now?" Eve snapped, stepping menacingly toward Jenny.

"We cannot stop his birth," spoke Sat'en. "There are no timelines, no possible worlds, where that is prevented. It is a certainty. The only things that were ever in question were *when* and to *whom*."

"All we know is it has to be a human," said Yeshua. "A human girl who has participated in the survival challenge. Like my mother. Like Jenny."

"But I didn't win."

"You survived," said Eve. "That's the only condition of winning, if you recall."

"You said only one person could win," Jenny reminded her accusingly.

"Yes, only one person *should* win. That was always the rule until you decided you didn't want to accept it. But use your head, Mother. Doesn't that mean that up until your challenge, everyone who has ever left a survival challenge alive is technically a winner? And there were ninety-nine other challenges beyond yours."

Jenny blinked, trying to understand.

But Eve was suddenly in her face again. "Why do you keep delaying this? WHY ARE YOU ALWAYS DELAYING THINGS?"

Spittle landed on Jenny's face. She wanted to spit back. Wanted to shout back. But she couldn't find the words. *Was* she delaying things? She'd needed to find Yeshua. Needed everyone to discuss what was next. Needed to rest. How was that on her?

"I have been inside your head, *girl*," continued Eve, dropping her voice to a venomous whisper. "I know all your fears and doubts. You don't know how to face your mother and brother."

Yeshua walked over and placed a hand on Eve's shoulder, who flinched, looking as though she wanted to summon her swords and attack him.

"Do not *touch* me, Failed One."

"I believe Jenny needed to rest before she could make use of her ability," he said without skipping a beat. He let go of Eve's shoulder, appearing completely unfazed. He even smiled at her. Then he stepped toward Jenny and nodded encouragingly, his warm eyes seemingly trying to comfort her and assure her that everything would be all right.

Jenny bristled when she glanced at Eve, but she trusted in Yeshua. They had to get a move on. Had to figure out what was happening out there. But she couldn't think with Eve staring her down; couldn't attempt it with that much pressure on her shoulders. She needed to relax too. Needed to be assured of herself. Above, the stars were still unfurling, and she realized the stars, the baby demons, bloomed just as the flowers did, sprouting all over the night sky just as the plants and trees. Maybe the demons *were* inside the plants, then.

She let that train of thought go. It was a distraction.

She could hear Eve huffing. Could hear Sat'en humming. Yeshua stepped back to give her space, and all the way up in the sky, there was a low rumbling sound that repeated every few seconds. The Leviathan. She wondered if the angel children were all right up there. Wondered if the corpses of the tarnished angels had been swallowed up by the plants.

Again, she was distracted. She inhaled deeply through her nose, the clean air fresh in her expanding lungs, before she exhaled. She turned away from the others, from the world. Concentrating on opening a passageway, she held out her hand, trying to find that little space in the air. It took her a moment, but she could feel a *pull* on her insides—on what might've been her soul or her death—then the pain pierced through the world. She tore at the air.

"Finally," huffed Eve. "I will guide you to my world."

"Eve," said Jenny, trying to keep her voice steady. "You talk so much about freedom and expression and living your life. And how I haven't lived mine." She turned back to look at Eve as the darkness split open in the air. Valescent Light flickered to life, and she pressed her hand against the passageway. "But I think you're just as afraid as I am. You don't want to die."

Eve's face didn't change. It was the same hard look Jenny would adopt when she didn't want anyone to know how she felt, but Jenny could read it. Could read the anger in Eve's eyes. The tightness in her jaw. The agitation from being called out.

"You're still too weak," spit Eve, pushing past Jenny as golden light bloomed, and she dove into the passageway. Colors splashed, evaporating all around the opening in the air; a temporary glimmer shining with the pattern of a rainbow.

Jenny said goodbye to Sat'en. She didn't speak or anything; it was more of an exchange. A glance. An acknowledgement that she'd once housed someone Sat'en had loved. Someone who'd loved Sat'en.

The desecrated angel placed a gray hand over her heart and bowed her head. Long hair fell forward and shifted with the breeze. She would remain behind to tend to the Leviathan, the children, and speak to the demons. She had laughed when Yeshua invited her to the fight, explaining that her war had ended long ago. She felt at peace in this world, and besides, she was too old, too fragile. She had no more fight left in her. Only heartbreak.

Pulling Yeshua into the light, the passageway shut closed. Sat'en's grayish-silver eyes were seared into Jenny's mind as the vibrant world of demons vanished. Colors swirled around them, cleansing them. The dirt crumbled off her armor. The aching faded to a soothing, hollow ache.

Jenny turned to see Eve floating along, her arms crossed, her eyes shut tight like she was meditating. Red and white swirling lights tangled in her hair and limbs. Her rose petals seemed to grow and shrink, like time-lapse videos of a field of flowers trembling and blooming rapidly on screen. Green and blue circles splashed against her body.

Yeshua seemed solemn. Respectful. His beard flowed in the golden light. Jenny pulled them along, letting Eve determine their direction, wondering why Eve was limited in her movements between worlds. She felt the tug, the pull. It came through Eve first, then through Jenny, and after a bit of movement, their heads emerged from the pool of light. They climbed out to walk on soft grass.

It was nighttime here as well. Jenny remembered this world well. She'd been here before, even before she could move between worlds. Eve had brought her here, somewhat. It was before Eve had a body, when she was just a voice in Jenny's head that had combined with the guidance system. The stars above, immense balls of flame, swirled so close Jenny felt like she could touch them, see every detail.

Around them, spanning as far as she could see, was a sea of tents. Makeshift homes. Each tent was a different color, a different size, and in a strange way, it reminded Jenny of the angel children. But people bustled between them— crowds of humans. Some clad in armor. Some wearing normal clothes, T-shirts and jeans. All of them looked a bit haggard and exhausted.

She realized she hadn't seen normal people in a long time. They were *humans.* Not deaths. Not souls. Not tarnished or wretched or anything else. She'd been around crowds of souls who looked human but were all naked and terrified, and empty of new thoughts. She'd been surrounded by deaths, who'd also looked human. And now, there were people. Actual human beings—whole.

"So where is this angel?" asked Jenny, unsure if she'd ever fit in with regular people now. Then again, she'd never really fit in before either.

"Come," said Eve, marching off into the crowd. People separated to give her way, bowing their heads. A few of them glanced curiously at Jenny, doing double takes and giving her frightened stares, like they were seeing double— or maybe they just saw her notification and wondered what she was doing here. If she was an enemy or not. She heard whispers of *Null.*

They stared at Yeshua as well, murmuring, wondering. They probably had a ton of questions. Curiosities. But they didn't seem like they'd dare, not with Eve marching through them, glowing with golden and red light.

The world was different from when Jenny had been here. A breeze rustled through everything, and she could smell food cooking. She could smell sweat and dirt and blood, the wet scent of old tears. She could smell desperation.

The crowd was full of people with high levels. Fifties and sixties. Some were even in the eighties. Most of the high-leveled people seemed to be around her age, maybe a little bit older. There was a bald man in crystal-like blue armor with an enormous sword strapped to his back. A woman clad in black held a scepter which gave off a strange green glow. There was even a young boy or girl, Jenny couldn't tell, who wore a flowing red cape. They floated off the ground and stared at Jenny curiously.

All these people must've been victors, she realized. Her high school hadn't been the only one taken; that's what Eve had said. So how did the other challenges play out? She wanted to know. How had they won? What had they had to do? What had they been forced to do?

She shuddered, images flashing of different buildings, different groups of people who might've been stuck inside the Veil, hunted by tarnished angels. How many people might've killed each other to ensure they'd be the one to survive. To win.

She wondered what her level might've been if she wasn't Null. If she'd done as Eve had wanted all along, just focusing on the survival challenge, just trying to win. Killing and butchering until she was bathed in blood and nobody else was left alive. Would she have emerged with ridiculous power and . . .

But then, she heard a shout, a voice that cut through the babble, and Jenny saw her mother running toward them, pushing and shoving through the crowd, bouncing off people. Before Jenny could say a word, before she could inhale, her mother, who looked filthy—covered in soot and dust, dried blood, a wild, crazed look in her eye—flung her arms around Eve.

As she hugged Eve, Jenny stood frozen, staring at her mother's crying, sobbing face. She'd never seen her mom with so much emotion before. The crowd dispersed slightly, and among their curious faces, so many of them staring at Eve and then back to Jenny, a few of their brows furrowed, Jenny made eye contact with Oliver.

A chill ran down her spine. The last time she'd seen him . . . he'd been unconscious on the cafeteria floor, his legs missing. She'd chopped them off in order to save his life, but there he was, standing on metal legs.

He looked stronger, taller, the baby fat on his cheeks receding; even his freckles seemed more sunken in. His red hair had more darkness to it; the sweet little boy who would follow her around had grown up so quickly. And the look on his face . . . It wasn't pity, though part of her might've preferred that. It wasn't joy or happiness or anything. It was . . . concern. He was worried for her.

Eve pushed Jenny's mother away, gently but with enough force to make the woman stumble back. It took Nancy a moment to realize that Eve wasn't who she thought she was. Then Eve pointed at Jenny. "That's your daughter. Do not touch me again without express permission. And believe me, I will never give that permission."

Nancy sputtered, her arms still outstretched, stuck in a hug that no longer enveloped anyone, staring at Jenny. Jenny found it odd now, to even consider her as *Mom*. Jenny had been through so much. She'd done horrible, terrible things. She'd survived horrible, worse things. And here she was, standing in front of her mother, the woman who'd put her through so many things but still claimed to love her. What was she even doing here? Had Eve found her just to mess with her? But that didn't make sense either.

"My sweet little girl," whispered Nancy, her eyes tearing up, her lips wobbling, and Jenny recoiled.

A part of her wanted to run into her mother's arms and bury her face in her warmth and sob.

Another part wanted to turn around and march away, rip open a passageway to another world, any world, and never look back.

So, she decided to do what she always did: keep her face as still as possible and not reveal any emotion at all. She wanted to say a nonchalant, "Hi, Mom," but there was a lump in her throat, and she couldn't breathe.

Nancy stepped closer, hesitantly, her eyes searching Jenny's face, lingering over Jenny's own eyes. *You can see me now*, thought Jenny. *This is the real me. Is this what you saw all those years when I was just a kid? This monster that I've become?*

She didn't know what she expected when Nancy took the last step, but instead of a hug, instead of a slap or a sharp word or even a hair pulling, Nancy collapsed to the ground and grabbed Jenny's feet and sobbed, her shoulders shaking, her entire body convulsing.

Awkwardness clasped around Jenny's throat so hard, she didn't know what to do. People were staring, some averting their eyes. She saw her stepdad in the crowd, emerging behind Oliver, a solemn but sad expression in his eyes. She wanted to pull her mother up. *How dare she cry like this in front of so many people when I could never cry at home without getting screamed at?* She wanted to console her mother and tell her it was okay, that she was all right, it only just looked scary. She wanted to kick her mother away. She wanted to sit on the ground holding her mother crying, too.

I don't know what to do.

It was Yeshua who knelt and placed a hand on Nancy's back, murmuring gentle words. And then Eve who came to the rescue. "Take the woman to the other noncombatants. And tell everyone to prepare for battle."

Several armored people appeared, each one about her age, she thought. Levels ranging from thirty-five to fifty, their armor made of glossy steel or shining bronze or even wood. They picked her mother up, who'd gone weak, and began walking her away. Oliver followed after her with his dad, glancing back as if they wanted to say something to Jenny but couldn't find the words.

Jenny was about to turn away, her heart too heavy to breathe properly, when Nancy looked back, hair whisked all about. Her face was red. "Jenny, I'm sorry. I'm so sorry."

And that was when the tears broke free. Jenny couldn't stop the trembling in her shoulders, and if it weren't for Yeshua taking her arm and guiding her forward after Eve, she might've stood there on that spot, frozen in this world, weeping as quietly as she could, forever.

CHAPTER TWENTY-SIX

THE FLOWER, THE SCRIBE

Heart heavy, Jenny followed along to what Eve called a fracture in the world. What that meant, she didn't know, and she found it difficult to care. Flashes of her mother's face, the warm delight at first when she'd hugged Eve, kept coming up.

Was that what her mother had always wanted? Was Eve who her mother would prefer? A beautiful, strong version of Jenny? Standing tall and covered in rose petals and wrapped in a holy glow? Leading this entire group of people and fighting a war against forces none of them could really comprehend? But when her mother had seen *her,* she'd . . . hesitated?

It was just the eyes, she tried to tell herself. *The notification.* But she knew it was more than that. It was like her mother could see right through into the horrible depths: the exoskeleton, the tentacles, the monstrous hunger. The murderous rage.

"It is always difficult with loved ones," said Yeshua, who'd been quiet since they left the camp. They were walking around the lake at the center of Eve's world, where Jenny had found herself so long ago. The stars hung low like fruits made of light.

Jenny could still hear her mother's words echoing.

"I'm sorry. I'm so sorry."

What was Jenny supposed to do with that? What was her mother even apologizing for? "It's whatever," replied Jenny.

"I don't think you think it's really whatever," he said. A wind caught his hair and beard, his purple robe fluttering around him. He was staring ahead at Eve's back, the rose petals drifting slightly in the breeze, her dark hair bouncing, the golden light around her ebbing and flowing with every step. "Your mother saw what she wanted to see, and then she was faced with the reality, and—"

"I don't want to talk about her," Jenny cut him off quickly and walked ahead, embarrassed and angry that everyone had seen that. That Yeshua had seen that.

But also, why did she care?

She could see her death crying about it. Raging. Screaming. It was that scream building up inside her head again. What did she want? *Why don't you ever do something?* What was she supposed to do?

What am I supposed to do? That's my mother?

Jenny followed quietly, eyeing Eve every few moments. The way Eve carried her shoulders, back and straight. Even the swinging of her arms was elegant, womanly. Her hips swayed with a perfectly natural ease. There was a shapeliness to Eve's thighs and legs that Jenny could never figure out. She'd always been either too skinny or too doughy, and even now that she was muscular, they still didn't feel right. Even though they had such similar bodies, such similar characteristics, Eve really was everything Jenny could never be.

"Here," said Eve, stopping. In front of her rippled a thin strand of what looked like tin foil. A faint, metallic light. "We keep it here, away from the others, so that the angel cannot tempt anyone. But she wants *you*, for some reason."

Jenny squinted at it, walking around, armor clinking, to take a better look. It was almost like the way she'd tear through worlds, creating an opening, but instead of darkness or golden light, it was . . . gray. Gray in a very familiar, unsettling way.

"Step through it," ordered Eve, who pushed past Jenny and faded from view, the gray crack in the air swallowing her whole with one gulp. Yeshua frowned at it, exchanged a look with Jenny, and then nodded. He marched forward and vanished as well.

Jenny glanced around, seeing nothing but the sparkling lake and the fields of grass, the trees in the distance. Something about the strange glow was making her uneasy, but she couldn't figure out what. When she stepped forward and felt the air bend around her before expanding, she exhaled sharply. It felt like someone had just splashed her with ice.

Blinking repeatedly, trying to clear the murkiness from her vision like she was trying to get water out of her eyes, she realized where she was.

Welcome to the Veil.

The memory of that notification came bubbling through like a headache, and she clutched her head, looking around, seeing nothing but a blank emptiness, a gray mixture of gloom and glow that ebbed forever in every direction, above and around and below. What were they even stepping on?

"Glass tiles," said Yeshua, stroking his beard and looking down at his bare feet. It was true; a reflection of themselves stared back at them. "I have not been here in a very long time. Someone must have constructed this platform."

"It wasn't you who stepped foot here," said Eve tersely. Her rose petals appeared slightly less vivid in the Veil, like they were draining of color. Even her golden glow had receded. "It was your mother, the first Mary."

"*And here you've brought me the Second,*" echoed a voice from above, drifting down like an elegant feather.

Eve sighed and motioned upward. Squinting through the gloom, Jenny could see it wasn't completely empty. The Veil had seemed completely vacant when she'd seen it at the high school, but now, she could see things floating around, strewn about like little islands. Chunks of rock. Debris. Ruins of old buildings and structures. The space was littered with them. And directly above them, where the voice must've come from, was a large rock. It looked like an asteroid.

Without explaining, Eve stepped off the glass tiles, moving her arms away from herself gracefully in a slow, repetitive motion. She bobbed like a jellyfish, climbing up through the Veil.

Jenny did the same, jumping a little bit. It took her a few tries to get the arm motion right, but after watching Yeshua figure it out, his eyebrows up in surprise, she managed to chase after him. When they got to the floating stone, a chunk of rock with glistening specks and chunks dotted throughout, she saw a circular entrance. A cave.

"Through there?" asked Yeshua.

Eve floated inside, touching down. "The angel Rafa'el has long since awaited your audience, dear Mother. Come along now."

Jenny bit the inside of her cheek, wanting to say something in return, but she followed Yeshua as they floated back down. It was a lot like swimming; except, as Jenny relaxed her arms, she began to sink. And she could choose which way she sank, moving forward into the cave entrance until the tip of her armored feet found footing.

And then, like letting go of a deep breath after holding it for a while, she dropped down, falling to her hands and knees.

"Well, you don't have to bow." Eve smirked before walking deeper into the cave.

Yeshua patted Jenny's shoulder once she stood. "Come. I believe this archangel will shed some light on what's to follow."

Archangel . . . Similar to Azra'il. They probably knew each other, then. She wondered why Yeshua wasn't filled with rage the way he'd been when Azra'il invaded the world of the demons. It seemed like Yeshua would've torn the world apart to fight that giant angel, the hatred between them as heated as their battle. And besides, what made them archangels, anyway? Their power? Their size? Would this angel be enormous too?

As they stepped deeper into the chunk of rock, the gloom of the Veil faded away. It was dark inside the cave, but a faint green glow shone in the distance, like someone had lit a candle far away.

"The Antithesis, the Failed One, and the Interloper," came the voice again, gentle and sweet, like a breeze on a spring morning. "To what do I owe the honor?"

With a little bit of Ignite, Jenny set her arm on fire. Orange and red light flickered to life, illuminating the cave, and she got to see the amused expression on Yeshua's face.

"What?" she whispered.

"We all have titles," he said. "The angels recognize all three of us as important. Do you not find that a little bit humorous?"

It wasn't until Eve came to a stop and Jenny raised her arm, blinking through the light of her flames, that she realized she didn't need the fire.

A brilliant green glow, bright and vibrant, filled the space. It was as though someone had squeezed all the color out of an entire forest and bathed it in the sun. But it shone from inside a cage the size of a small house. Steel bars enclosed whatever was inside, and as Jenny shook her arm out and her eyes adjusted, she saw it.

Angel (Stage V - Level 200)

An angel, standing tall in a silky white dress. Was it trying to look like a human? she wondered, taken completely aback by its beauty and grace, by its femininity. She'd expected something like Azra'il, with snakes coming out of its head or too many eyes or . . .

But this angel was beautiful. Serene. Her bright green eyes looked back with warmth, and her lips seemed luscious and sweet. Jenny felt her cheeks burn red as she stared. Silver hair came down to the angel's shapely waist.

"I am Rafa'el," spoke the angel. "The Flower. Some also call me the Scribe. And others"—she turned her pleasant expression toward Eve—"the Trumpet Blower."

Eve walked right up to the bars, looking up at the angel for a hard moment before jabbing a finger in Jenny's direction. "You were looking for her, then? She's the one you were talking about?"

Rafa'el smiled warmly at Jenny. "Yes. The second Mary."

"And you're sure of that?" asked Eve. "Not me? You sure? Because we look exactly the same."

Green circles flashed around Rafa'el's delicate hands as she raised her arms. It was like she was typing on something midair. Her smile never wavered, and even though she seemed to be the prisoner, it felt like she had the upper hand over Eve. "I am certain. Unless your name is also identical to hers."

"Fine," said Eve. She made a face before turning away to glower at Jenny. "I'll just have to do my own thing."

Yeah, thought Jenny. *Join the club.* "What are you talking about?"

Eve shook her head. "No matter what I do, no matter how many battles I win, the angels seem to only be wary of *you.*"

"But why?" Jenny stepped forward to get closer to Rafa'el. She couldn't explain why, but the angel reminded her of the outside. Of long hikes through nature. Of relaxing under a tree on a sunny day—not that she'd ever done those things. Was that deception? Something that was messing with her head? How was this angel so different from Azra'il? "Why are you here? What is going on?"

Rafa'el stepped closer and knelt, bringing her enormous head lower so they were nearly eye to eye. Her head was about as big as Jenny was tall. She could reach out and stroke the angel's face if she wanted to.

Rafa'el's finger slid between the bars as though she wanted to touch.

"Careful," warned Yeshua, but Jenny had already placed her hand on the angel's finger; she wasn't really sure why. But the angel seemed sweet, genuine, caring.

Green light bloomed around Jenny's wrist.

"I see you have always wanted answers," whispered the angel, static flickering between Jenny's ears. She shut her eyes and seemed to concentrate, her brows pushing close together. After a long while, she shook her head. "It seems your destiny and the destiny of all things remains hidden from my view."

Jenny swallowed. "What?"

"She can see all of time," explained Yeshua, stepping forward. "She's the Scribe. All of existence is transcribed by her."

"Written? Where?"

"In the light," said Rafa'el. "And I know what will happen next. And what will happen after that. But the result of it all . . . the outcome . . . I suppose that is up to you, human. And Him. And His will."

"But what *is* His will," demanded Yeshua. He walked up to the bars as well, standing beside Jenny, and when he spoke to the angel, he seemed genuine. Compassionate. "Please, do not let this destruction come to pass. The worlds are beautiful places, and all He wants is power for Himself. Everything for Himself. What is in it for you?"

Rafa'el smiled knowingly and shook her head. "You have it wrong, my dear Failed One. Had you been His body, it would have ended by now. And perhaps destiny would have come to a different conclusion."

"What would've ended?" asked Jenny, staring intently at the angel. Was Yeshua supposed to be *it*? The birth of God, and everything becoming a part of him? But the world had gone on for two thousand more years. And he'd become a whole faith. And what about her? She was the second Mary. Was she supposed to be *it* as well? But instead, she'd given birth to Eve, who was sulking quietly in the corner.

"What our Master wants is to end all grief," said Rafa'el. "No more longing. No more hurt. No more suffering. How many people in your world, my dear Interloper, cause each other harm? How much harm have people done to you?"

Jenny thought back to her mother's apology. *I'm sorry.* How it broke her heart; how it had broken her heart almost every day of her life. She thought about Susan; how she'd bit Susan's throat and killed her. She thought about how alone she'd felt for so much of her life. How alone and miserable so many people seemed to always be. Not to mention everything she'd ever seen on the news: all the attacks and deaths and wars and corruption.

"With this, destiny will come to an end," continued Rafa'el. "Uncertainty will no longer exist. Everything will be of Him and with Him, and in His divine light, it will all come to fruition."

"Alright, enough of that," spat Eve. She shimmered through the bars and walked right up to Rafa'el. The angel straightened up, her long silver hair bouncing as she looked down at Eve, who only came up to the angel's knees. "I brought you the interloper. And you swore you would tell me where Adonai would surface. Who Adonai would choose to be the third Mary."

"No," replied Rafa'el, who didn't seem bothered at all by Eve's presence. She glanced at Jenny. "As I have written, my words will come to be. When you bring the interloper to me, that is when He will show His face."

"What?" said Eve, brows furrowed. She clenched her teeth so hard her cheekbones threatened to burst out of her face. Something about her agitation was very satisfying to Jenny, who'd found it beyond frustrating when they spoke in riddles, in cryptic messages. At least Eve was getting a taste of her own medicine.

Rafa'el frowned. Her fingers flicked through the air again, tapping away at something invisible. "I am sorry to have disappointed you, but it seems someone else has changed destiny yet again." She glanced at Jenny. "And of course, why am I not surprised it is your fault. A soul pushed into the material world by the interloper . . . Azra'il, you fool."

"A soul?" Jenny's mouth went dry. "You're talking about Susan?"

"Yes," said Rafa'el almost absentmindedly, her eyes glowing like she was staring off into the distance, reading something the rest of them couldn't see. "And . . . Alright. Here it comes, then. Antithesis, I have kept my promise. You will know precisely where Adonai is."

Jenny blinked in confusion before a rumbling shook the entire cave. Rafa'el's light bloomed. Yeshua looked down in horror before shoving Jenny and knocking himself back and away as a beam of pure darkness burst through the rock, disintegrating everything in its path.

CHAPTER TWENTY-SEVEN

BIRTH

When Susan saw what was happening, where Dr. Lee was taking her, she felt her blood, the angel's blood, turn cold. She'd been dragged along inside the angel, feeling every bit of its agony and pain in having its limbs cut away, its mate murdered, its eggs gone, its life gone. Its teeth were knocked in, so she could feel them cutting into her tongue and her throat. Her jaw was broken, so all she could manage were pathetic gurgling sounds. She was helpless, horribly alone and helpless, and wondering how she would get out of the body.

Every time she tried to will herself out, to emerge from the broken, beaten down angel, she kept getting stuck. The pain, the physical and emotional turmoil, stuck tightly to her throat like a noose. Dr. Lee had dragged her down the street, pulling her body; just a green torso and a head now, no more limbs. Blood leaked out of her, leaving a horrible glistening trail that led right back to her high school, of all places.

She was back where it all began. Where she'd seen her friends be eaten alive. Where she'd fought off angels and healed Jenny and died. Dr. Lee dragged her through the lobby and flew up to a higher floor; she couldn't tell where they were. It could've been the History Department or one of the sciences, but everything was so broken down, so covered in dust and dried blood, that it all looked the same. And all the while, she could feel an uncontrollable urge building in the angel. The sheer terror. The horrible, absolute need to escape its own body; Dr. Lee was dragging her right to the thing every angel was running from.

And when she saw Leslie, the girl's belly impossibly swollen, bigger than any pregnant woman Susan had ever seen before, Susan felt sick inside. Leslie's once beautiful face was sunken in. She looked almost as gaunt as the tarnished angels, and her skin was smeared with dried blood, the worst of it around her lips and chin. The torn remains of her clothes stuck to her ashy skin; she looked like someone who'd been kept underground for years and years. She looked like she needed help.

But there was something else. Something that brought the fear and terror in the angel's body to a roaring, maddening, boiling point. Susan finally understood what all the angels were running from.

The wretched angel shrieked inside her head, begging to get away, trying to will limbs that were no longer there to work, to function, to get her moving up and out of there. But there was nothing to be done. Dr. Lee threw Susan's borrowed body at Leslie. When they made contact, Susan felt like she'd been *struck*, and she flinched.

It was like touching a heated oven by accident. Or like running too fast and losing control and crashing into someone. Like getting shot through the heart. She'd touched something of a magnitude further than she could comprehend but that the angel's mind understood all too well. That was the last thing it showed Susan: the being inside Leslie, the creature that was trying to be born, was the most powerful thing to ever exist. And with a burst of searing light, Susan was knocked out of the angel, free of its dying body as Leslie began to feed.

Floating over the angel, watching the light fade from its green eyes as Leslie suckled and chewed, as the thing inside her belly moved beneath her skin, Susan turned around to beg Dr. Lee to stop. She could see it wasn't really him. It was another angel; it must be one of the angels working for the thing inside Leslie, but . . .

"You have to stop!" she shouted. "You can end this."

Silver light flashed around Dr. Lee. He drew his katana, and Susan darted toward Leslie, trying to slip into the girl's body. Maybe she could stop this. Maybe she could save Leslie.

Terrified of being blown away again, Susan's hands sizzled with electricity, closing around Leslie's arm. The girl looked up, wide-eyed and frightened, as though she'd just been woken from a deep slumber, and Susan realized that she *could* slip inside Leslie's body. She could possess her. She could do this.

But that *thing*. Whatever was growing inside her belly responded with waves of terror. With hatred. With anger, making Susan shake. Her entire form shook, and she was terrified of being wiped away, obliterated. But she was going to try. She was going to reach inside Leslie and take control of her body and reject this thing.

Before she could gather herself and possess the girl, something barreled into her from behind, knocking her away. They crashed through the opposite wall, and she came tumbling to a stop as bits of ceiling and debris rained down on her.

Blinking away dust, electricity crackling through her, she saw who had knocked her away: a large, silvery person—a silhouette? No, an angel. They were see-through. Wings unfurled to knock away debris as a furious gust of cold wind, like a storm, howled through the ruined high school and a glowering face rose above her, towering.

"Do not interfere with destiny," he spoke in a voice that rumbled through her, that echoed all around, silver light flashing and flickering.

"Destiny?" she whispered, standing up. She just had to get past him. She could stop Leslie. Fear gnawed at her from every side; she kept having flashes of darkness, of the wretched angel's terror in its last moments, of whatever was growing inside the girl. There was no way that thing could be anything good.

The silver angel stood in the way. Even without the system alerting her to its level, she could tell just by its stature, just by the level of reverence the wretched angel had felt toward it, that it was *strong*; Susan didn't stand a chance. She didn't even have a body. But what she did have was her strange electricity.

Silver light flashed, and countless eyes opened across the angel's body, each one with a silvery glowing iris that stared back at her accusingly, as though she were the one at fault. "You cannot comprehend the gravity of your current sins."

"Who are you?" she asked, trying not to get hung up on the word *sins*. "Do you have a name?"

"I am he who goes by the name Jibra'il," he responded. "I am one of the highmost angels to serve Adonai. Our Master. Our Lord."

"Oh God," she whispered, finally understanding what was going on.

"Precisely. Now, you must not interfere. It is nearly complete. The third Mary will give birth to the resolution and . . ."

She was hyperventilating. Her shoulders were shaking. Blood trickled down the side of her head. A miracle birth—the birth of God. And they'd chosen Leslie for this. "And then what?"

Jibra'il stepped closer. He was so immense that his silver form took up the entire collapsed room, his wings expanding wide, all his eyes locked on her. "Then all of this universe, all of it, every single atom of material existence, will be made whole, united at last. No more sorrow. No more anguish. No more suffering. Everything wrong with life brought to salvation in a single instance."

She didn't know which eye to look at, so she chose the three on his face. Two normal ones, and a third vertically between them, right above his nose. She swallowed hard, her mind racing. So was that the God from all the stories she'd heard? From all the religious things she'd been taught? From everything? From history?

She almost wanted to ask, "So which religion was right, then? Which group of people got it right after all their shouting and fighting and killing?" But she held her tongue. Something was wrong. Something was very, very wrong; the God she'd learned about was supposed to be love and compassion. This? All this terror? This dread? Not to mention Leslie looked like she'd been a corpse rotting in a grave for years.

Susan had the immensely foreboding feeling that something horrible was about to happen. A pressure in her head, in her chest. An anxiety that was growing with each passing moment. Should she beg and pray for forgiveness?

This didn't fit. This couldn't be it. And why did God need poor Leslie to give birth to it?

I have to stop this, she thought. Just then, a rumbling went through the entire building. It was already falling apart, and more chunks of the ceiling came crashing down. A wail rose through the dust. It was Leslie.

Jibra'il turned to face her, his arms outstretched. The eyes on his silver shoulders and back blinked manically. "Finally!" he called, his booming voice echoing. He was about to say something more when someone else came rushing through the dust and crashed into him. It was Dr. Lee.

He grabbed the angel and pulled him down, holding him in a tight embrace. "I don't know what you are!" shouted the teacher in Susan's direction, speaking so quickly she almost couldn't understand him. "But you have to kill the girl! You can—" He was cut short. His voice stopped right away as the angel vanished inside him. He stood, hunched over, arms still outstretched, almost like a strange statue. A silver glow emanated from his skin, and there was a vacant look in his eyes. His tattered lab coat clung to his shoulders.

She realized he'd *absorbed* the angel, forced the powerful being to possess his body even though he had no hope of defeating it. But it took a moment, didn't it? A brief second to adjust to a new body, and that was enough.

Susan ran past the frozen Dr. Lee, his face twitching as a groan escaped his lips. More tremors went through the building, and something radiated from up ahead. Golden light bloomed and faded away, spiraling in lights that flickered through her. She could hear the shout from behind her as Dr. Lee turned, fully possessed. But the katana was way over here, and she landed on top of

Leslie, who was convulsing flat on her back, her legs spread, tears streaming down her cheeks as blood gushed between her thighs.

She could feel light rippling behind her, another ferocious wind sweeping through the hallway and the rooms, but Jibra'il couldn't catch up to her now. She landed on top of Leslie like she was belly flopping into a swimming pool, and Susan felt herself slip through Leslie's skin.

Leslie's mind pushed back; there was so much pain: ribs snapping, insides distorting. Muscles spasming. Bones crackling. Heat like the sun had appeared inside her, radiating through her. Susan drew further inside, pushing deeper and deeper till her light vanished, till she could try to take control, but all she wanted to do was scream.

The girl's mind was so twisted in all this, it almost didn't notice as Susan screamed beside her, trying to seize control, trying to stop the birth somehow. Was that possible? Could she kill it? She struck it with Leslie's fist, banging her oversize belly like a drum, and the entire body convulsed, spine coming off the floor to scream.

She could *feel* the thing inside her belly moving, its mind cocooned in a protective layer. Its glee—its maddening glee. It knew that there was nothing to be done. It knew that something was finally coming to fruition. And it could see right through her.

Energy—darkness—expanded from Leslie, forming a bubble of light around her that pushed away rubble, that disintegrated dust.

And then, she felt yet another mind pushing against her, sandwiching her against Leslie's pain. It was the angel, silvery and shimmering, pushing itself into Leslie, trying to grasp Susan.

The angel's booming voice flooded her mind. *Get out! Get out! Do not taint the birth of our Master and Lord!* Through the darkness, through the pulsing light, she could see Dr. Lee's body suspended in the energy bubble radiating from Leslie, his katana lodged in his throat. The angel had forced him to kill himself.

What kind of God would accept this as an acceptable action?

I have to try! screamed Susan, trying to engulf the *thing* with her electricity, trying to channel all her generated charge through Leslie's body. Maybe she could *change* the thing inside her belly just as she'd changed the tarnished and wretched angels, just as she'd changed the eggs back into light.

She could feel the angel roaring with rage, could feel Leslie crying and begging for it to stop, and could feel the uncontrollable, unstoppable way the *thing* was sliding out. It was stretching Leslie open, liquid and blood gushing all over. Electricity sizzled through her entire body as Susan tried to hold on, as the angel tore and ripped away at her entire being, trying to yank her out of Leslie.

It was a mess, all of them colliding inside one body, and then, like a flood that had gotten too high and could no longer be held back, Susan felt the body *give*. Leslie buckled, and with a final push, a final contraction, *it* slid out of her.

CHAPTER TWENTY-EIGHT

BEAUTIFUL AND PERFECT

L eslie once thought she'd be wealthy when she grew up. No, she *knew* she would be. She was beautiful. Others found her beautiful. And all she had to do was look beautiful for the camera, let people tell her how to dress and how to position herself, and no matter what, she knew, she would be wealthy.

She'd have a perfect home with a perfect set of furniture. A perfect garden; a space where she could go and sit in silence every morning and unwind. A perfect pet, maybe. Or perhaps a perfect husband or two. Maybe a wife. Maybe just a string of relationships that didn't ultimately matter—she wasn't sure. She'd never been sure. But she'd been confident that it would all work out, and she would have a beautiful, perfect life.

It would've been so beautiful, she thought.

She swallowed the lump in her throat: flesh from an angel dying with every bite Leslie took out of it. But what choice did she have? The thing inside her belly had chosen *her* of all people. She was the most important girl in all of history. They would write songs about her. Pray to her. Worship her.

She was going to give birth to the Lord. And everything before her had been a mistake, hadn't been perfect. Hadn't been right.

It was her womb that was perfect. Her insides. Her life that had led to this. And every time she stroked her belly and felt the expanded skin and the intense heat radiating within, she felt slivers of the purest joy she'd ever felt in her life. It was better than anything else she'd ever done. More exciting and fulfilling. She was finally happy. Even if she was covered in muck and looked grotesque and everything ached.

Tears ran down her cheeks. The thing inside wouldn't really speak to her, but she could feel him. Could feel that he was nearly ready, had fed on enough blood, was soon to be born. She knew that she wouldn't survive this.

She didn't have to.

She would forever be known as the mother of God. And what was better than that?

She started humming, a tune she didn't recognize or know. It hurt too much to think straight, so she hummed at random, hoping it gave God some comfort. Hoping it would mean something.

With a shudder, she felt it coming. He was ready.

I'm ready.

I'm beautiful.

And then she saw that girl again—the one from the high school. Except she had brown hair now, and she was glowing. *What are you doing here,* she was about to hiss. *Why are you ruining this for me?*

And then that girl flew inside Leslie, slipping right inside. Without asking permission. Without a care for the baby she was carrying. *What was she doing?!*

Leslie screamed as her bones cracked one after the other. She felt her insides *split* open, stretching out as something immense, something so dense it hurt, moved through her. All her muscles worked to push it out. She clutched at rubble, squeezing what was left of the wretched angel, burying her nails in it—and she could feel the girl inside her. She knew the girl's name. It was Susan.

WHY ARE YOU TRYING TO STOP ME?

She screamed again and again, light radiating out of her, blooming and destroying things around her. Walls crumbled away, desks turned to ashes, and then she saw Dr. Lee standing to attention, coming toward her, swaying on his feet, silver wings stretching and glowing. She saw the katana flash, sliding right through his throat. He'd cut his own throat. His body hung limp in the air, kept up by the light as his skin boiled away—

Then, that silvery silhouette flew right toward Leslie and entered her body just as Susan had.

Please, no more, she wanted to beg. *Please. Just let it stop. I'm happy to give birth, but just let it stop. I just want it to stop.*

More and more, she felt herself sinking away, sinking deep inside as two strange minds pushed and fought and struggled inside her head. She didn't have the strength or the will to push back, so she did what she could: she focused on giving birth. He had promised, after all, perfection. Endless perfection. Everything would be perfect, and she would've been mother to all that perfection.

Everything would finally be beautiful, and there would be no more reason to stress or hurt or cry. She would never have to cry in anguish again.

With one final scream, as Susan and the silver creature wrestled and fought, Leslie pushed out the Lord.

Something gushed out of her, sliding past her thighs. Bones splintered into her muscles, and she collapsed as black liquid jetted out from between her legs. The two people in her head were flung away, and she was alone again. Alone inside her body. But something else was wrong.

More and more liquid turned solid, transforming into a beam of darkness, tearing out of her torn insides. Even as she screamed, she saw the beam rip through the ceiling, disintegrating Dr. Lee and everything around it . . . It shot right up into the sky. She stared down between her legs. She shuddered. And then, she heard it before she felt it.

Crunch. Crunch. Crunch.

And a voice. A voice that slithered through her ears like a snake and licked the inside of her head.

Blessed are you, Mother.

Blessed be your flesh, consumed in holy sacrament.

And then she saw it . . . *him.*

A misshapen blob of darkness, still connected to her by its umbilical cord, growing larger and fuller with every bite it took out of her thighs with razor-sharp teeth, lapping up the blood as the darkness shooting out of it—of her—beamed up into the sky.

Tears streaming down her face, longing to touch the creature, Leslie's head dropped back, and she stared up at the beam of darkness. The roof of the school was now completely obliterated and gone, so she could see the stars above, the colors exploding and crashing across the night sky.

She thought how beautiful it all looked. She didn't even mind as the creature's teeth worked their way up her navel. It wasn't until it chewed through her chest and she was taking her final breath that she looked down to see a human boy with long dark hair and beautiful eyes—her eyes—and she slipped away into the darkness she'd given birth to.

CHAPTER TWENTY-NINE

EVE'S SHINING SWORDS

When Jenny came to, her head aching like someone had just cracked it open, she found Rafa'el sitting calmly inside her prison, legs folded beneath her. A beam of darkness, the same darkness that Jenny found separated the worlds, had appeared. Like a pillar, it stuck up from the bottom of the rock and went through the top, everything in its path disintegrated and gone.

Eve was on the ground, missing half her body, the rose petals burned at the edges, blood pooling around her as she stared up at the ceiling with one eye. There was no system notification. Jenny bolted upright, looking around for Yeshua. He was unconscious against the far rocky wall. Rafa'el seemed completely unfazed, sitting quietly and watching, blinking at Jenny as though nothing had happened.

"You knew this was going to happen, didn't you?" Jenny was avoiding looking at Eve, her stomach twisting; it was like watching her own body torn apart. The limbs she still had were burned to a crisp.

Jenny's armor had been hit as well. She must've only been in the beam's path for a moment before Yeshua pushed her away, but her armor was crumbling in places, and her legs ached like they'd been dipped in lava. She hobbled over to where Eve was on the ground, nearly slipping in the pool of sticky blood as she knelt, hands shaking.

"Is that accusation in your voice, Interloper?" Rafa'el shook her head. "I knew He would be born. That is written. I also knew there would be a release of Holy Light upon his birth, and I knew it would shoot toward multiple points across the world—the three of you each being one of those points. Too much energy connected in one place. That is why I asked the Antithesis to bring you to me."

Jenny swallowed hard, unsure how to read the angel's pleasant face. She'd planned this entire thing? She had known what would happen and when and where. She'd even known Eve would bring Jenny and Yeshua exactly when she needed it. Even if there had been a slight delay. It hurt trying to comprehend it.

Rafa'el continued. "You have done well to slow down destiny thus far, young Jenny Huang. But the pillars of His Light now grace all the worlds. Even the worlds you've freed."

"You mean the demons?"

"The world of deaths. The world of demons. You have slowed down His ascension even more, but destiny will come to fruition. It always does."

Finding it difficult to breathe, struggling to accept everything Rafa'el was talking about, Jenny lowered her hand to Eve's face. She felt like she ought to close the one remaining eye out of respect, but it was half her face staring back. It was like looking at her own corpse.

Then Eve coughed. More blood gushed out of her partial body, and her eye moved around till it found Jenny. "Mother," she said. "It hurts so much . . ." She shut her eye and sucked in a deep breath through her lips. Blood spurted out of her mangled, burned-away face. Jenny could see Eve's throat, the air shimmering away like vapor, more blood gushing out . . . A mass pumped inside Eve's chest. A fragment of her heart.

And then, light glistened out of Eve. Little things came shooting out from between the remaining rose petals. Stems, Jenny realized. Stems with little thorns and spikes, leaves jutting out, flowers budding. Bone extended from the mess of her shoulders and hips, lengthening into limbs. Muscles stretched across them, more flowers blooming as skin took hold. Within a few moments, Eve was whole again, shaking and trembling, her two eyes staring at Jenny with shock. And then, with a blink, all of that was gone.

Even the weak, strained voice that had called out for its mother was replaced with that snarky, cold, dismissive attitude. "What are you looking at?" snapped Eve, even though she was sitting in her own blood. She tried her new arms and legs, pale skin glowing in Rafa'el's green light. Muscle rippled within that slender frame, and Jenny once again felt that tinge of envy. Rose petals crept along, covering Eve up again. But she was glad Eve was okay; whatever had happened, Eve was opposing the angels.

Rafa'el spoke from behind the pillar of darkness. "He has been born. The final act of destiny begins. And you know as well as I that he will find me. That I have a duty to—"

"Oh, shut up," spat Eve. "We get it. You're gonna blow the horn and blah blah blah."

Jenny didn't know how to respond to that. Eve sounded more and more like Jenny when she spoke so tersely, but she also sounded like a spoiled teenager. Was that how she'd always come across to her mom? To her friends?

Seemingly recovered, Eve got up and stared at the darkness that beamed through the rock. There was a frown on her face, but then, she reached out and touched it.

The faded darkness seemed to thicken, turning gelatinous and gooey, swirling like a lava lamp before she removed her hand and shook it off. Her fingers had melted away to the bone, but glowing light healed everything back into place. She made a fist and looked at Jenny. "So, what's your big plan now?"

"*My* big plan?" asked Jenny, incredulously. She got up, her legs shaking still. She wanted to strangle Eve. "What do you mean by *my* big plan? You're the one who got us into all of this."

"Me?" spat Eve, and she stormed over to grab Jenny by the throat, lifting her off the ground. "*Me? It* was always *Him.* Always *Him* who bled through every fucking thing in existence, trying to make it neater, tidier. Perfect." Her face distorted with rage. Eyes bulging. Saliva flicking out and hitting Jenny. "I have always fought to restore chaos to His order. To keep everything on the path of evolution, random chance. Fucking entropy. And you think you can blame this all on me? Your entire people would not exist if it weren't for me."

Jenny bit the inside of her lip. Then the rage rushed through her head as she remembered her death's words. WHY DON'T YOU EVER SAY WHAT YOU WANT? But instead of shouting, her words came out cold and low. "You're the one who wanted a body so bad. Aren't you the same as him?"

"I . . ." Eve blinked, the anger boiling over. Jenny couldn't help but see glimpses of her mother on that face. The twitching eye corner. The nose curling as the lips peeled back. A harsh word, a swear, something on the verge of surfacing, ready to strike Jenny on the face. "YOU ARE THE ONE THE ANGELS SING ABOUT. YOU ARE THE ONE WHO WILL COMMIT THE CRIME. NOT ME. SO WHY DON'T YOU—" Eve stopped, the artery in her throat bulging, her face red and strained.

"What the fuck are you talking about?" whispered Jenny.

Eve seemed to realize she'd said something she didn't want to. She released Jenny, letting her drop, and stumbled back.

Jenny stepped forward, not about to let this go. She was tired of them keeping things from her; tired of them not telling her everything. "What are you talking about? I'm going to do what?"

In the corner, Rafa'el laughed. "If she knows, it won't happen, and then you will never know . . ."

"Shut up," snapped Eve.

"If I don't know what?" Jenny looked at the angel. "What won't happen?"

Rafa'el didn't move from her seat. She crossed her arms, resting them on her knees as she leaned forward with intent. "Would you like to know, Interloper? What awaits your future? What decisions you'll be faced with?"

"She's bullshitting," interrupted Eve. "She doesn't know. She can't see it."

"But you know something," said Jenny.

Just then, a hand came down on her shoulder, and she flinched, her hatchet summoned back in an instant, ready to swing around and fight. But it was Yeshua, who was looking down at her with concern. "Let this one go, my child. Destiny is something to be faced head-on. If you get preoccupied with planning and wishing and arguing, you fall into the darkness." He gestured toward the beam sizzling through the space, the ugly pillar that destroyed anything it touched.

"It doesn't matter," called Rafa'el. "He will find me. It has been written. And you"—she pointed at Yeshua—"will have to face your personal destiny soon enough."

Yeshua put up his hand. Red lightning crackled all around, and a wind picked up out of nowhere. "I respect your prowess, angel, but do not mistake my respect for supplication. You do not bind my will."

Jenny let her hatchet fall to the ground, the sharp edge sinking into the rock, and rubbed her face. Eve hadn't said anything else, but then, two bursts of golden light spurted out of her hands, she whipped around, and stabbed Rafa'el through the chest with two shining swords.

The angel cried out, blood sparkling out of her lips as her beautiful face distorted in pain. She was much larger than Eve, but Eve had stabbed her through the chest and navel, pinning her to the wall of the prison. The hilts stuck out of Rafa'el's body, glowing faintly with golden light, mixing with the green of the angel.

"Did you see that coming?" Eve stepped back, breathing hard, staring at the angel struggling to breathe, struggling to maintain composure.

Her long green legs kicked against the ground. Her silver hair bounced every which way. Every time her green fingers grasped the hilt or the blades themselves, she screamed with renewed pain; a high-pitched, shrill scream. Her fingers came away bleeding.

"I used some of my own light," said Eve. "Let's see you get out of here now. Let's see who wins this war." Then she turned, golden wings bursting out of her back. With a flap and a furious glance at Jenny, she jetted out of the cave, vanishing from view.

In the heavy silence, broken only by the angel's crying and struggling, Yeshua stroked his beard and turned his back on Rafa'el. "I believe she's envious of you."

"Me?" asked Jenny. "Why?"

"Because you were born of life, through life. And despite what she says she believes, she still thinks herself higher than us mortals. And that is her greatest folly."

"But she . . . Isn't that what she had always wanted to be? Physical? Material?"

"The things we hate dearly often become a part of us in the worst possible ways," said Yeshua with a forlorn look in his eyes. "Now come. I believe the war has plunged into a new beginning, and according to our friend here, I too have a role to play."

"What are they talking about, though? Why do they keep saying I'll do something?"

Yeshua shook his head. "I do not know. But I believe we will find out, and I believe you should trust in yourself to face it when it comes." He placed a hand on her shoulder.

They turned to leave, Jenny's mind swimming with thoughts, with accusations, when Rafa'el made a sound. "I know where your beloved Susan Brown is," she rasped.

Jenny snapped around like someone had pulled on her hair. Yeshua warned her to be careful, but Jenny needed to know. She stepped around the pillar of darkness and looked up at the angel, the beautiful green giantess, nailed to the wall by two swords. "Where?"

"I'll tell you . . ." she whispered, struggling to keep her head up. Silver hair flowed down to the blade, where it soaked in her blood. "If you do one kindness for me."

"Release you?"

"No," said the angel. Her lips curved into a strained smile that faltered like she was about to cry. For some reason, it didn't seem like that had to do with the blades cutting through her. "Carry a message for me to the angel she is with."

CHAPTER THIRTY

A MESSAGE MADE OF LIGHT

A message?"

"Yes," said Rafa'el, choking. She shut her eyes as her entire body shone with green light, so much so that Jenny had to cover her eyes. Silver traces appeared, swimming through the green like shining metal snakes, before the light condensed into a floating sphere in front of Jenny, about the size of a tennis ball. It looked like the eggs she'd seen in the Leviathan, green instead of see-through, and inside was a core of silvery white.

"What is it?" Jenny asked, afraid to touch it in case it was a trick. She glanced at Yeshua, who shrugged. "And why is an angel with Susan?"

Rafa'el laughed—a raspy, shuddering laugh that broke down into coughing. More blood trickled down her chin. "I am bound by my abilities," she said.

Jenny glanced down at the swords sticking out of the angel.

"My abilities bind me in a way these weapons can never," she added, as if sensing Jenny's thoughts. "I am bound to always speak on behalf of destiny."

"It means she cannot lie," spoke Yeshua solemnly. "But she can misguide."

"I can be *wrong*," she corrected. Her light shimmered. "But this is not deception. I swear on my existence. I swear by Him."

"What's it gonna say?" She stared at the little green ball, wondering how that would be a message. Would it explode? Would it shine really brightly?

"That is between me and my beloved," whispered the angel with a sad smile. And maybe it was the fact that the angel even managed a smile despite being in obvious pain, but Jenny felt swayed by her words. By the tone of hurt. The longing. That was how she'd felt about Susan. She remembered it clearly, even as Azra'il beat her down with his brutal attacks. All she'd cared about was getting Susan away from him. Of getting Susan safe.

"Alright," said Jenny, "I'll do it. Tell me where she is."

The orb of light floated to Jenny, and before she could protest, it slid into her chest. With a shudder, with a flash of green light, her body seemed to register it, and there it stayed: a bubble in the back of her mind; a thought that she couldn't express—someone else's feelings.

It was similar to when the demon Iblis had been inside her, when his longing for Sat'en had nearly taken over her mind. But Rafa'el's message remained still, quiet, existing gently in some far corner of her thoughts. She could sense the thing, could hold the feeling of it, and through it, she could understand the way Rafa'el felt for this angel. It was palpable, heartbreaking, and something Jenny knew she could put her faith in.

"Thank you," spoke Rafa'el, dropping her head. Her green light was dimming to a dull shade, like grass that hadn't been watered in too long. She shut her eyes. "When you next travel through light, my light will guide you straight to her."

Jenny clenched her jaw, wondering how the angel knew so much about her abilities. Then again, she seemed to know too much about *everything*. And if she really could see all of existence, could write down what was happening, then she would be exactly the one to know. "You didn't answer my other question."

"The angel with her," she said, struggling to breathe, her chest heaving. She raised her arms weakly, fingers trembling, before lowering them. "Is the Archangel Jibra'il. He and your Susan are now bound by the same sentences of destiny, and they too will have decisions to make."

She could feel that bubbling message tremble at Jibra'il's name, and again, she wondered: "Why don't you want me to help you? Then you can give him this message yourself."

"I am exactly where I need to be," replied the angel. "Everyone is where they need to be. The rest is up to . . ."

The ground rumbled again, the darkness flickering. Yeshua turned toward the cave exit, murmuring something about a bad feeling, and Jenny followed, glancing back at Rafa'el, who hung limp, partially hidden by the beam of darkness. She felt such a pull of pity.

"It is alright, Jenny Huang," she called. "I have my part to play. And you do as well."

"She will be kept here," spoke Yeshua. "In the Veil, hidden from the other angels. They won't find her here."

"What happens when she does that thing you guys keep talking about? Blowing the trumpet? I didn't even see a trumpet."

"She *contains* the trumpet," he explained, and then, with a running start, he kicked off from the mouth of the cave and flew toward the glass tiles below, where a sliver of colorful light awaited them. That must be the way back to Eve's world.

Jenny landed beside him on the glass platform, and they walked briskly through the crack in the Veil. Again, it sucked her in, and everything seemed to condense before expanding. They emerged beside the lake, only to be met with an explosion.

The grass erupted around them. Yeshua was flung away, red lightning flickering madly around his body. Jenny was slammed back into the lake, landing with a splash. She sank to the bottom as she stared at the lights and colors blooming over the surface of the water.

Lungs burning from the sudden attack, she kicked as hard as she could, rocketing toward the surface, coughing and sputtering, blinking to clear her eyes to see shimmering lights shooting every which way. Angels hovered all throughout the air. The armored people she'd seen before in the camp were fighting. They had swords and clubs and various other weapons. Some even fired with guns into the air, the bullets with tracer lights that streaked through the sky like reverse shooting stars. She glimpsed Eve jetting around with her golden wings, cutting down angels.

"Yeshua!" she called, wondering where he'd been thrown. She swam for the shore, her feet finding the mud below as she climbed onto the grass plains. Wasn't the plan to invade the material world? To attack the angels there? How had they found them in this world?

Eve had said it was impenetrable . . . and as Jenny rubbed the water out of her eyes, she saw: all around her, sticking out like awful spikes that shot right up into the sky, were beams of darkness. Dozens of them, going off in random directions, crisscrossing through Eve's world. She felt an ugly shudder deep in her belly.

Another blob of energy rained down nearby her, exploding, sending dirt and debris into the air, knocking her to the side. But Jenny relaxed and went with the explosion before landing, using the momentum to run. She ran toward the camp, terrified her family had been caught up in all this.

She kept seeing flashes of her mother lying on the ground somewhere, half or more of her burned away by the beam of darkness, one eye still blinking as she choked on air and tried to call out for her. *I'm sorry. I'm so sorry.* She pictured Oliver without his legs again, sobbing, crying, broken beyond repair.

Or her stepfather—the man she never really spoke to but who had always treated her with respect and seemed to love her mother. She couldn't even remember his name as she ran—she just wanted him to be all right. She wanted all of them to be all right.

Another explosion sent her tumbling forward, crashing into the ground on her face, soil going up her nose. Someone landed beside her, grabbed her by the arm, and pulled her to her feet. She saw dark-blue armor, and her heart skipped, thinking it might be Susan, until she saw it was a boy, roughly her age, screaming something at her in a language she didn't understand.

Human (Stage II - Level 23)

He ran right into her, terror on his face. He was young, too young, and before Jenny could even ask what he wanted, why he'd even come to her— Did he think she was Eve?—he toppled over her.

"Get off!" She shoved him up, trying to stand, trying to protect herself if there was trouble, but it was too late. An angel appeared, wings spreading wide, its body a silhouette of bright yellow light with enormous white wings fluttering behind. It carried a long lance. The boy leaped at it, swinging what looked like a shovel.

Angel (Stage III - Level 47)

With an easy blow, the angel sidestepped and slashed the boy diagonally down his torso. He stumbled, dropping his shovel. He looked back at Jenny with shock, blood gushing out of his mouth as the top bit of his body slid off, intestines and organs burning as they tumbled out onto the soil.

Jenny cried out. She was already on her feet, cursing at herself for not acting sooner. She swung at the angel, her hatchet shimmering into her hand as she aimed for its head.

It dodged with ease, flapping its wings to move back, its yellow light shimmering every which way. "Strange human," its voice hissed inside her ear. Twirling its lance, it took aim for her chest. A jab.

She ducked before tossing her hatchet behind the angel. She'd never fought a regular one before, but she'd killed enough of the tarnished ones to figure she had enough experience in killing them.

Grasping a handful of dirt and flinging it at the angel's face, she threw herself backward, away from it. The dirt sizzled through its head, and it blinked before shaking its head, its hissing voice echoing around her.

She grabbed its lance with both hands as the angel tugged, trying to shake her free with immense strength. But she had muscle too, she had power too, and still holding on to the lance, she used Instant Swap.

Everything distorted around her, and she appeared behind the angel, the lance ripped out of its hands. She didn't give it a chance to figure it out, no explanation, nothing. As explosions rocked the ground around them, she drove the lance straight through the angel's back, right between its wings. She pierced its yellow light with its own golden weapon, and the creature *screamed*, its limbs flailing in agony, its wings beating like mad.

So they can feel pain, then? Even though they're made of light?

Jenny summoned her hatchet back, ready to strike again, when the angel's light turned even harsher. It spun around quickly, knocking her down with the lance sticking out of its back. Then it drew another weapon from its own body, a sword made of the same yellow light, and plunged the tip right down, aiming for Jenny's chest. She rolled, trying to get away. The tip of the sword sliced into her thigh, the armor cracking and splitting, cutting straight through to the ground and pinning her in place.

CHAPTER THIRTY-ONE

ANGELS

She screamed as the light seared her muscle, as it cut through bone. It wasn't just cutting through her thigh but burning it, sizzling her flesh from the inside out.

"Why do you resist?" hissed the angel. Two more arms sprung from its sides, pulling out the lance from its chest. It swung it overhead, fully intending to bring it down on Jenny's head.

She sucked in a deep lungful of breath and roared at the angel with Ignite, exhaling a steady stream of orange fire at first. But as the angel screeched and defended itself with both hands, the fire sparked blue, and the heat from the flames burned everything around them. Jenny's mouth snapped shut. She got a glimpse of the top half of the angel's body melting, its arms shortened at the elbows. But there was no notification, and she wasn't going to wait to see what happened.

Leaning forward, she grabbed the light sword and yanked it out of her leg, biting down hard to keep from screaming. Using Instant Acceleration and leaping to her feet, she slammed into what was left of the angel, holding the sword out to pierce it through its torso. When she crashed into it, the angel felt *solid,* her head and shoulder bouncing off its hip.

The angel flapped its wings furiously. With a sudden bloom of yellow light, its silhouette began reforming. A fist, still forming midpunch, struck her on the face, knocking her down.

She hit the ground hard and rolled, tasting blood in her mouth. Her tentacles burst out of her back, and as her armor had become so degraded, she allowed her exoskeleton to come shooting out of her belly button, jellylike and stretching all over her; she was giving in to the monster just for a bit.

She got that flash again, that jolt that carried through her like a shiver: a glimpse of her death, the little boy, teary eyed, staring at her and asking to be loved.

Six tentacles stretched out, sensing and tasting the destruction around her, the burnt humans, the slaughtered angels. She remembered how Eve had swiftly cut down the angels in the world of demons. As the angel regenerated, the rest of it growing back, she saw it. A little sphere floating inside the yellow light. It looked so familiar, like the eggs placed inside the Leviathan. Like the message Rafa'el had given to her. That must be some kind of core.

Angels had a core. Those eggs weren't just eggs: they were their *beings*. Like the nucleus of a cell. The rest of the light grew around that. Her eyes went wide as she stared hard at the yellow angel shimmering toward her slowly, a sword and a lance in its three hands. But where was its core? Now that it had regenerated, she couldn't see the little spherical thing anymore. Only the yellow light of its body.

She'd just have to cut it open and find out.

More streaks of light shot by overhead. Sounds erupted from every direction. Human shouts. Angel hissing. She wondered where Yeshua was, where her family was. Her tentacles reached outward, swishing and swirling, sensing and tasting.

No.

Don't think about them now.

Focus.

She met the angel with a smash of fury, hatchet knocking away the sword, tentacles wrapping around the lance. With a burst of Ignite flowing up her arms—lighting herself on fire with blue flames—she punched the angel back in its shining face.

Fire did something to it. Fire burned it away. Like the light couldn't exist under all that heat or . . . Was it the brightness of her flame?

An arm shot out of the angel's thigh and grabbed Jenny's knee. She heard a *pop*, but as she buckled, as she cried out, more flames erupted from her throat straight into the angel's face. The flames covered the creature's entire body as it hissed and screamed, as she lowered to the ground, buckling on her injured knee. With the blue flames burning the angel's entire body, the light melted away, turning to vapor. And as her tentacles pulled its limbs apart, as the flames blew through the light, she saw it: the core.

Her hatchet struck, swinging from below, catching the core with its obsidian edge. There was a flash of light.

+2000 Energy

That was just from the pain, she realized. How was it not dead?

The casing cracked open like a glass ball. A yellow gooey thing fell out, as though she'd broken an egg, and maybe it was the hunger in her tentacles or the fact she hadn't eaten in ages and everything had been feeding on her, or maybe it was because it reminded her of cracking eggs to make omelets every morning, but Jenny caught the falling goo with her mouth, her jaws snapping shut around it as she rolled across the ground.

Light surged inside her head, so bright that she felt like her skull itself was casting a shadow. The angel was trying to get out, but she clamped both hands and three tentacles over her mouth, her body writhing, struggling. The angel tasted like ice cream, like it was just about to melt. She couldn't quite pinpoint the flavor, but it was something between tropical, like mangoes and pineapples, and vanilla. She was going to spit it out—it was burning her tongue, her throat, her gums—but she felt something inside her *pull*, as though she *had* to eat this thing, and so she did. She swallowed.

You have defeated Angel (Stage III - Level 47)!
Experience has been awarded.
+6000 Energy

Relaxing, her tentacles and hands falling away, Jenny opened her mouth to exhale. Steam rose as Azra'il's thing inside her wriggled around her throat, healing the burnt flesh. The pain ebbed away, and she coughed, rubbing her stomach, wondering what would happen now that she'd eaten *light*, and how it had given her so much experience.

But before she could think that through, more lights shot down, and several angels appeared, falling down like shooting stars. "She has eaten one of us!" hissed one.

"She is a monster!" spat another.

All four of them marched in, colors blurring together into a mess of purple and orange and white and green, but Jenny shot to her feet, her tentacles whipping around, slamming into them. Two of them were only in their twenties. One was above level thirty, and the last one was forty-three. But she'd just defeated and eaten an angel that was higher leveled; she could do this.

She was shaking with hunger and rage as she attacked, knocking them away, blasting one with Ignite, searching for their cores, her face aching from how much she was focusing. But four angels were too many, and they swished and darted between her tentacles. They were quick, and arms kept sprouting from their bodies. Weapons flashed. Her tentacles fell, heavy and dull, to the ground, but the thing inside her healed them too, and they grew back almost as quickly as the angels could cut them.

With a savage cry, she grabbed the nearest one, the purple angel, with her hands and pressed her face right up against it, roaring with Ignite. Flames shot down into its body, disintegrating it, and just as she was about to grab its core, the orange angel flew at her, weaving through her tentacles to jam a lance into her hip.

Her leg gave out; she cried out as she fell. Another angel went for her throat, and she was about to laugh in its face—*I can't die. Do you know how many times I've tried?*—when she realized she was wasting her time. Rafa'el had given her a one-way ticket to Susan. All she had to do was open a passageway and get out.

And opening a passage might just end this battle completely. Why was she even struggling with these creatures for? In her panic, she'd been trying to find her mother and the others in all this chaos. But if she just opened a passageway, wouldn't it swallow all the angels around her into it? Just as it had in the world of angels . . . She could end the fight right away.

But before she could attack again, a knife darted out of the darkness and struck the exposed purple core. The glass casing shattered open, and purple goo dropped to the floor. A yolk shimmered on the scorched grass, bubbling, trying to reform. A boot appeared and stomped down hard, and the purple thing gushed, bursting open and splattering the grass around it as the color faded away to nothing.

Jenny looked up to see Oliver standing over her, breathing hard. Blood streaked his face. Burns covered his armor. His friend Mackenzie appeared as well, knives flashing around her as she screamed and faced the angels head-on. Then Mrs. Monique barreled into the largest angel with a panel of glass. Was that her barrier ability? It seemed to be much stronger now than it had been in the high school; it was visibly thicker, and it looked like she could maneuver it. When it struck the angel, its light flattened against it; the creature couldn't get through.

Thanks, is what Jenny should've said, but her tentacles darted out, knocking away some more angels as they descended.

Trying to catch her breath, her insides still healing, she focused on the tip of her fingers. Her nails. She caught sight of the beams of darkness shooting crisscross through the world, and wondered if there'd be any interaction, any dissonance. But then, her fingers found what she was looking for, a catch in the air, the gap between worlds, and she *yanked*.

The air tore open, darkness spilling out from the gash. The angels nearest to her, the ones attacking Oliver and the others, hissed and screeched as they were pulled into the darkness. They couldn't escape. They were like bits and pieces of metal, and the passageway she'd opened was a super powerful magnet. The green angel shimmered through Jenny like a ghost, trying to grab on. But with a flash from her hatchet, she cut off the angel's arm, and the last thing Jenny saw of it was the look of sheer terror in its eyes before it fell into the darkness.

Light blurred overhead as more angels rocketed toward them. If they all slammed into her, Jenny and Oliver and everyone else might get swallowed up by the darkness too, and she didn't want to know where it might take them. She grabbed Oliver's hand. She grabbed the others with her tentacles and threw her hatchet as far as she could.

Just as the angels slammed into her, she used Instant Swap, bringing Oliver and the others along with her, everything screaming and tearing around them. They landed with a huge *Oof*, and she released them as she sat right up, clutching her hatchet and staring as angels fell into the void as though she'd opened a sinkhole beneath an ocean of light, angels shooting down from the heavens.

For a moment, she felt excited, like she'd done it. She'd stopped the battle, and the passageway glimmered while angels fell into it one by one. She could see the other humans pausing from the fight, staring at what she'd done. Was this what Eve and Rafa'el had been talking about? Was this how she could turn the battle to their favor?

But then a chill washed over her, heavy and dark, and it was suddenly hard to breathe. She remembered this dread.

Looking up, she expected to see the enormous Azra'il hovering overhead, but instead, it was a different angel, much smaller. Still larger than a human, but this one was thin and slender, with webbed wings connecting its arms to its sides, dark blue in color.

Angel (Stage VI - Level 741)

It shot down like a meteor, a ferocious gust of wind blowing everything away as it landed with a crash. Then, with both hands, it clapped the passageway shut.

CHAPTER THIRTY-TWO

MIKA'EL

Every cell in Jenny's body screamed at her only one thing: *run*
Dark-blue-and-purple light radiated from the stage six angel as it turned to face them. It hissed, a loud, short hiss that sounded like a command ringing over the world. The other angels scattered, bright lights retreating into the sky before descending on all the humans, and the war around them continued.

"I am she by the name of Mika'el," announced the angel, its voice—sharp and clear—ringing through the busy world around them with ease.

Jenny swallowed hard. The few fragments of Iblis that were left inside her recognized the name. Memories stirred of a valiant angel who was unbested in battle. Not even Azra'il could hold a candle to this one.

Without warning, without any indication, Mika'el shot forward, appearing in front of Mrs. Monique in a flash of light. The librarian's eyes went wide with terror. She threw her arms out in front of her, the shine of a barrier erupting from her palms.

Before Jenny or Oliver or Mackenzie could cry out, Mika'el punched through the barrier, blue knuckles erupting through Mrs. Monique's face.

"No!" screamed Jenny. Memories flashed through her thoughts. Memories of Mrs. Monique, the sweet librarian who'd helped so many students. Who'd continued fighting and even formed her own weapons and armor when so many adults couldn't. Who'd stuck around with Oliver and the others even after all this time. Who'd come to Jenny's aid even though she'd tried to kill Mrs. Monique in the high school. Even her ability, creating barriers, meant all she wanted to do was protect.

Golden light flashed. Jenny flung her hatchet at the angel as hard as she could.

Mika'el didn't dodge. The hatchet bounced off her chin, and she turned to face the rest of them, Mrs. Monique dangling from her blue arm. And then the angel was in front of them. There was no warning, no flash of light, nothing. One moment, she was holding Mrs. Monique's corpse from the inside; the next, she was towering over Oliver and Mackenzie.

"Now, which one of you is the interloper?" she asked in her piercing voice. Jenny's blood ran cold.

Oliver's eyes went wide with fright, but he shouted for Mackenzie to run. He was going to take on the angel by himself despite the level difference.

No, no, no, they want me!

It wants me!

No one else needs to die for me.

"Hey!" she shouted, summoning her hatchet back with a flash of light, bursting forward with Instant Acceleration. "I'm—"

"Not you," said Mika'el, slapping Oliver in the face so hard the boy spun through the air and landed in a pile, his head facing the wrong way. Mika'el raised her hand again, slowly this time, as Mackenzie slashed and screamed mindlessly at the angel's torso. The angel looked amused.

"Stop!" shouted Jenny, stopping in her tracks, terrified. Was her brother dead? Was that it? Would she never see him again? She couldn't let the girl her brother liked die, too; Jenny raised her hands. "It's me. I'm the one who opened the passageway."

Mika'el stopped and moved her glowing blue-and-purple eyes up. Another eye opened on its chest, vertically, the iris bouncing around rapidly till it settled on Jenny. "Ah, yes. *You.*"

She waved her arm, and wind slammed into Mackenzie. The girl looked like she'd been hit by a truck as it blew her far into the distance.

Before Jenny could react, Mika'el appeared in front of her. A dark blue arm thrust through Jenny's chest, and she went limp, hanging off the angel like a rag doll, wheezing as she tried to inhale. Her tentacles twitched, dragging on the ground. It took her a moment to figure out what had happened.

Her heart was still beating, but it was *outside* of her body; the angel had grabbed it and shoved it out her back.

"But you cannot die, can you?" whispered Mika'el. She swung her arm, like a swordsman trying to get the blood off their sword, and Jenny went flying, her tentacles trailing behind her, limp and useless. When she landed face down, crashing into someone's body, she couldn't move for a long moment.

Then, all at once, like a hammer striking her from within, the thing inside her put together a new heart. It began to beat, and she coughed back to life, clawing at the dirt, at the body beneath her. Before she could lift her head, something smashed into her, shoving her face into broken armor, into flesh. Her exoskeleton crackled and broke. Her nose smushed against something hard, and she felt bones push through her cheeks, burrowing up into her skull and brain before she tasted dirt. Mika'el had shoved her face through the dead body.

"Azra'il said you had been crucified," Mika'el's voice cut through Jenny. Even with all the dirt in her hair, she could hear the hissing clearly. "He said you were his little pet. But clearly, he failed."

Pain burning across her scalp, Jenny felt herself being lifted up by her hair, raised and turned so she came eye to eye with Mika'el, who must've been eight feet tall.

A cold smile stretched Mika'el's purple lips, and she leaned in closer to lick the blood and debris off Jenny's healing cheeks. "But perhaps there is some use to a punching bag that cannot die. Maybe I can keep you as well."

Gurgling as blood gushed in her mouth, Jenny slammed into Mika'el's large chest eye with her hatchet, but it might as well have been a stuffed toy. The eye blinked, as if confused by what had happened.

"Don't be in such a rush," whispered Mika'el. "Where is my sister?"

"I don't know," spat Jenny, but her words turned into a howl of pain as the angel's grip on her hair stretched out her scalp. Her exoskeleton was cracking and peeling away, and even though the thing inside her was working overtime to heal her, the pain was unbearable. How was this angel so much more solid than the other ones? How was she so powerful?

Lights darted around her, and Jenny strained, slamming into Mika'el repeatedly with her fists, with her tentacles, trying to get away, trying to escape. How was she supposed to win this? Where was Yeshua? Where was Eve? Hadn't Rafa'el seen this happening? Why would she give Jenny a message to carry if this was where she died?

Mika'el placed her other hand on Jenny's shoulder, bending her neck as the angel pulled on Jenny's hair. "I will ask you once again, Interloper. I can smell her light on you. *Where* is my sister?"

So she considered Rafa'el her sister. Jenny sucked in a breath, her neck being stretched so far she thought her throat would snap. She looked into Mika'el's cold, dead eyes, wondering how they could be related. And what did the angel mean by smelling the light?

Had Rafa'el tricked Jenny, then? By taking the message, by carrying the angel's green light, had Jenny made herself a target? But that didn't make sense. The emotions on Rafa'el's face, in her message. That had been genuine. The angel had been genuine—Jenny was sure of it.

She struggled against the arm pulling on her hair and shoulder, grabbing it with both hands. She squeezed the angel's wrist, trying to shift it even just a little, but Mika'el's fingers tightened around Jenny's throat.

"Her voice lingers inside you, Interloper," hissed Mika'el. She brought her mouth close to Jenny's face, her lips spreading to reveal razor-sharp teeth, and shook Jenny like she was clearing dust from a rug, threatening to rip her right down the middle. Pain ran down Jenny's spine like a series of fireworks.

At least I can't die, she thought, choking on her own cries. But what about Oliver? Was he okay? What about the girl? Mackenzie? In the corner of her eye, she thought she could see Oliver's body, Mackenzie kneeling over him. The girl's dark armor was completely destroyed, but golden light appeared in her hands. She must have been trying to heal him. *Please let him be okay.*

"Speak," demanded Mika'el, jostling Jenny so hard it felt like all her insides were rattling around.

"*I . . . don't know . . . where,*" squeaked Jenny, breathing hard, feet kicking limply. Her spine was stretching so much her tentacles couldn't respond, like the signals that should be going to them were failing to reach. She heard her bones pop and snap.

"Every single human here will be slaughtered," said Mika'el, her voice low. "But I will spare them any further suffering as soon as you tell me where my sister is. Where is the Archangel Rafa'el?"

Jenny almost laughed. She couldn't make the sounds, but her body convulsed, air huffing out between her lips despite the pain. If the angels had Rafa'el, wouldn't they destroy every single world? What was the point in sparing them, then? The end result would be the same.

"What is so funny, Interloper?"

"How stupid do you think we are?" Jenny croaked as the grip on her shoulder eased.

Mika'el's face didn't give anything away. The angel cocked her head, the explosions overhead reflecting in her bruise-colored eyes. Then she lifted Jenny higher. Purple and blue light surged all around the angel, her lips twitching. "Let's see how well the gift Azra'il gave you holds up against *me*, Interloper. You are far too weak for this."

Jenny's insides clenched as the angel's voice wrinkled through her brain. She wanted to fight. Wanted to scream. Wanted to try anything. Her tentacles twitched, but they wouldn't respond. Couldn't. Gathering her breath, she used Ignite, blasting the angel in the face with a stream of blue flames.

"One more time," Mika'el said calmly, her face engulfed in fire. "Where is the Archangel Rafa'el?"

"One more time," repeated Jenny, her throat hurting so much as the angel squeezed her shoulder again. As her body gave out, and her flames vanished. "Go fuck yourself."

Mika'el didn't respond. Her chest eye blinked. Her main eyes blinked. She pressed her lips tight with disappointment. But then, she smiled and pulled Jenny apart, ripping her down the middle like a sheet of paper.

CHAPTER THIRTY-THREE

CRASHING THROUGH DARKNESS

Susan was pushed away from Leslie's body as that *thing* was born, shoved into the light . . . Except, it wasn't *light*. Whatever was beaming out of Leslie, whatever was beaming out of the creature born, it wasn't light. It almost reminded her of the darkness she'd seen the angels surface from. That horrible, liquid darkness, condensed till it was thick, was shooting out into the universe in countless beams, radiating from its birth.

For a brief glimpse, Susan had seen the look of twisted pain on Leslie's face as she lay on that cluttered floor, as the building around her disintegrated. Then, the angel that had been fighting Susan, silver and winged, had crashed into her, and the two of them were thrown into the beam of darkness, flung upward and away, gaining speed and losing sight of all things.

She couldn't scream, couldn't move or communicate. She'd read about riptides and how they'd pull swimmers away, the waves crashing over their heads forcing them underwater, churning them every which way until they had no sense of direction, no sense of hope. She felt like she was knocking into everything and nothing, bouncing off stuff that wasn't there, all the electrical charge building up and releasing in bursts of discharge, static shooting around her. The angel . . . She could hear his cries of pain as he was trashed around, and Susan caught clearer glimpses of the creature.

His entire body seemed made of silver light, each limb covered with countless eyes which all seemed to be staring at her every time they made contact. His great silver wings expanded outward. She would've considered him beautiful if he hadn't murdered those angels. But then again, hadn't she killed plenty of them? Hadn't everyone?

The angel had broad, muscular shoulders and arms, and there was something about him that almost seemed innocent. Something about him that reminded Susan of her grandfather, a quiet war veteran who carried himself with distinguished strength but preferred to feed the ducks at a nearby park rather than talk with other people. *Duty before self.*

Why was she even thinking about that? This angel had led to the birth of whatever had been inside Leslie.

Why am I pretending like I don't know? That horrible feeling of dread, like she and everyone else would be punished. That awful, disgusting feeling of anger and loss and bitterness . . .

It took her a moment to realize she'd stopped crashing all over the place, stopped being torn apart, even though she was still shooting through the beam, rocketing away from the birth. She soon saw why: it was the angel. He'd wrapped his enormous silvery wings around her, holding on to her sides with his hands as though they were dancing and he was scooping her up into the air.

She squinted at him, unable to catch her breath, unable to move a muscle. His face was crumbling away, chunks of his head. Holes tore throughout his body like drops of soap on an oily plate cleansing things away. His wings were evaporating as he collided with the edges of the beam of darkness, and fragments of his light shot through Susan, bled through her form, filling her with memories she couldn't parse, couldn't comprehend. Bits and pieces of the angel's life. But they flickered away as fast as they appeared.

Why are you protecting me? she wanted to ask. *Aren't we enemies?*

But he was trying to protect her, sacrificing himself, his being, to keep her whole. Why? She struggled to push him away, to tell him to save himself and leave her be, but then, his face strained like he was lifting something immensely heavy. He tilted his head back, his entire body skimming the edge of the darkness even as it rushed through his disintegrating body.

With a sudden *whoosh*, the two of them were flung out of the beam, crashing into dirt, tumbling over and over, Susan's electricity flashing, her light shining as she healed repeatedly. The angel's silver light did the same, snapping with power, until they came to a stop.

As the dust settled, Susan found herself in the angel's powerful arms, what was left of its wings still protectively wrapped around her.

She shoved a wing off and scrambled away from the angel. He remained on his side, wheezing, chunks of his body missing as though someone had taken bites out of him.

"Why did you do that?" she asked. She'd thought she'd die . . . again.

"I do not know," said the angel, rolling over onto his back. His silver glow emanated gently, but his body wasn't recovering. The missing chunks weren't growing back.

But he was so powerful. "Why aren't you healing?" she asked, breathless, feeling as though she needed to comfort him. Behind her was the beam of darkness, the thing that had shot them away from the material world, away from Leslie. It jutted out of the ground and towered right up into the red sky, about as thick as four or five people standing side by side. Darkness rippled along it, rushing upward, an unstoppable river. Something shone way in the distance, circling around it, and Susan could hear a faint sound, like a rustling or a distant crowd of voices. She wondered if that was coming out of the darkness.

"The Holy Light." He gestured toward the beam. "We are all born from it, of it, but cannot withstand it. It contains every color, every bit of light there ever could be." He lowered an arm and grazed a chunk of his side that was simply gone. Silver light flecked and shimmered.

She didn't know what to say to him. Should she help him? Should she leave him here to die? *Would* he die?

"Adonai has borne himself into the material world," said the angel, shutting his eyes, shutting all the silver eyes across his body. Some of them had been torn away; some of them had disintegrated. Some were partially gone, leaking their fluid into the dirt like an egg yolk spilling from a cracked shell. The vertical eye between the two eyes on his face dribbled down his nose. "My duty has ended. I have delivered him, and thus, destiny can proceed. I have not failed."

"Then why are you crying?" whispered Susan.

He was shaking, and silver liquid ran down the sides of his head. Ran from underneath all his closed eyelids. "I . . . do not know. I have no more purpose now."

"Are you going to die?"

"Possibly."

"Why did you protect me, then?" she asked.

"I had glimpses of your life, Soul," he said, turning to look at her with gleaming silver eyes. "Glimpses of your love and care, your sorrow. But fear not, all things will be emancipated by His will. And I did not wish for you to suffer anymore. Did not want you to disappear and never feel complete."

"But what about Leslie? What about the rest of the world?"

"Sacrifice is always necessary," he replied with a heavy breath.

"Then why not sacrifice me too?"

"You are already dead," he said. "It is only your soul that remains. And your death exists somewhere in another world. But do not worry. Once Raf . . ." He trailed off, his light gleaming more brightly. That name triggered something inside Susan's head. A memory. A love. Something she must've glimpsed inside the beam of darkness because she was sure she'd never heard the name before in her life. She couldn't have known.

"Rafa'el?"

"Yes," he said, his light glowing a tiny bit brighter at her mention. "She will blow the trumpet . . ." He paused to wipe his face and look at the liquid glistening on his fingers. "She will cause the cataclysm that brings all the worlds to the material world, and everything will end, and everything will start anew, shaped and perfected by our Lord."

For a long moment, Susan didn't speak. She was vaguely aware they'd landed in a forest. Were they still on Earth? Where had the darkness taken them to, and what had happened with Leslie and the birth? But the angel's words were swimming through her head. Was this the end, then? Was it all over?

"You know," she said, crossing her arms, listening to the angel catch his breath. She'd thought about the brief glimpses into his life, his clear love for this angel Rafa'el, and his steadfast sense of duty. Even though her granddad had been a quiet, somber man, she knew he'd carried a lot of pain around, a lot of regret. It seemed to be the same for the angel. "That sounds like you're just running away from facing your problems."

"What do you mean?"

"You love that other angel, right? Rafa'el?"

Even at the mention of her name, his light flickered. He nodded.

"Then why do you need Adonai to take away how you feel? Do you really think it would never work between you two?"

"She serves in direct service to Him. As do I. We are slaves to what must be done, and nothing can come higher than His will. Nothing is more important."

"But who decided that?" she asked, raising her voice, feeling frustrated. "Who said it *had* to be that way and nothing else? Why can't you make your own choices?"

The angel's light gleamed brightly, and he sat up shakily, staring down at the holes in his navel and legs. "I suppose that is the way of angels. We serve at the discretion of the most powerful light. We serve to bring light to all—"

"Again," Susan cut him off. "Why are you lying to yourself? Humans do that too. Bow down to people with more money or who got famous in a movie, and look where that got us all. Aren't you guys doing the same?"

"So what would you expect of me?" asked Jibra'il, his wings unfurling. When Susan looked through the holes in them, past all the eyes staring intensely back at her, she saw a signpost up ahead, nestled between the trees, and she stumbled on what she was about to say.

PROCEED THIS WAY FOR JUDGEMENT.

"Fuck," she whispered, shaking. She looked behind her and saw the river of blood, its thick crimson waves gently lapping against the shore. "I'm back here?"

Jibra'il didn't stir. He must've known where they were the minute they landed. "This world . . . I am sorry for the harm it has caused you, but we deemed it necessary."

"Necessary?" she almost screamed, hugging herself. Had the angel seen everything she'd suffered through here? She'd come out of the blood and walked, following the sign, following all the other souls as they cried and begged for forgiveness. But she'd never even gotten to stand on the Scale of Judgment. Azra'il had swooped down from above, menacing and terrifying, his four cruel wings blocking out the light. He'd plucked her from the crowd, picking her up like a tiny doll, and declared he would judge her personally. "How was any of that acceptable? How could you treat another being like this?"

Jibra'il was quiet, and she got the sense he was ashamed, but what did that shame matter after all she'd been through, after what she'd seen the other souls go through? She'd seen everything as Azra'il gave her the grand tour: Judgment on that enormous scale. The horrible mess in the maze. Being eaten over and over by the harpies and the angels. He'd made her watch. He'd made her listen, promising that this was coming for everyone she'd ever cared about, promising that he was saving her from this for a higher purpose.

"It was necessary for the purpose of changing existence," he said. "The light from the souls, the light of suffering, is the energy from which we derive all purpose. A light refined by a life lived, by material life . . . It is of grander substance than . . ."

"Than your own?" challenged Susan, feeling like she was struggling to breathe. Everything felt like it was closing in, coming in too close. Was *Azra'il* here? Would Jibra'il join Azra'il and . . . She didn't want to think of it. Could she trust him? And she didn't even want to think about what Jibra'il had just revealed. That all their suffering had been harvested for use. Was that what he wanted from her? "Why did you protect me, then? Just so you can use me too? Cut me open a million times till you have enough energy?"

"No," he replied firmly. "No. I see that you are different. That you have somehow transcended the substance of your soul and become . . . *charged* light. You are more than just light. And you can affect the world around you, even in the material world. You are the first soul to ever walk the Earth."

"So what?"

"I believe you hold a special place in what's to come. And this is where I do not know what fate has in store, for I was not informed of anything beyond the deliverance of Adonai." He paused and looked up into the red sky.

Susan followed his gaze, looking as well. Something was spinning— something immense, like a river of light flowing in a circle; like a halo over the top of the world.

"The souls," he whispered, his voice a gentle tickle on the wind. "They orbit in worship."

Susan dropped to her knees. Now that her heart wasn't pounding in her ears, now that she'd recovered from being smashed around inside the beam of darkness, she could hear it more clearly.

What she'd thought had been the wind or distant sounds, or even just the sound of the darkness, was . . . screaming. Crying. Begging. The circle in the sky was every single soul from this world, spinning around and around, circling the beam of darkness.

CHAPTER THIRTY-FOUR

RIPPED OPEN

Her armor tore first. Then her skin. Her muscles stretched and snapped, bones cracking in rapid succession. It was such a quick movement—the angel ripping her open—but she swore she felt every fraction of a second, every muscle tearing, right up until the moment she'd been torn in two. Her insides came splattering out, dropping heavy and wet on the ground, and the angel unclenched her purple fists. The two sections of Jenny's body fell away, her tentacles wriggling on the ground before going still.

She couldn't cry out. There was nothing for her to breathe into. Her lungs, her diaphragm, all the muscles that enabled her to breathe—gone. An arm, the lower part of her torso, and her legs had been separated from her. Still, she couldn't die.

Her head lolled to one side. She could see her intestines, glistening like snakes as colors rocketed through the air above. Her lips opened and shut as she tried to speak.

Mika'el raised a foot and smushed her intestines into the dirt, and what should've been a scream erupted in Jenny's throat, but air only whistled through her like exposed piping.

"I offer you death, Interloper," said the angel, her voice low and sincere. A nearby explosion sent dirt raining down on the two of them. "I will free you of this pain and give you to death if you answer my question."

Jenny's mind felt like it had spilled too, a useless puddle of thought and sensation. She searched for the wriggling feeling, that thing that should be inside her, healing her, but it was nowhere to be found. Could it be in the other half of her body? But then, how was she still alive? How could it still work?

Fuck. I'm still alive.

I'm not dead.

Why the fuck am I not dead?

Trembling like mad, she almost couldn't feel the pain of being torn in two. Was it any different from being eaten over and over through countless bites and tearings? This was nothing.

And still, she was alive.

So what use was there in begging? She didn't want death. She wanted Mika'el to go fuck herself.

"Well?" said the angel. "Tell me where she is."

Jenny's hand shook as she raised it. She was too aware of every muscle in her remaining arm stretching and contracting. It could barely bend at the elbow, but it was enough to lift her wrist off the ground. Slowly, she raised a finger—her middle finger—and held it out for the angel to see. Despite the pain, despite the agony of being torn in two, she wanted to laugh. Did angels even understand this gesture?

Mika'el's foot struck Jenny's exposed chest, toes digging inside her ribs. Jenny's remaining lung wrapped around it, and she *wheezed*. Her hand dropped as lights flashed behind her eyes. She wanted to use Severed Spirit, wanted to completely separate from this pain, from being in her body. The angel slammed her dark-blue foot down again and again, stomping what was left of Jenny, flattening her against the grass.

But a distant feeling was emerging; not just the foot inside her chest but that wriggling thing, worming its way across the grass, coming to her. *It was coming to her!* She would heal.

Jenny's head flopped from side to side as Rafa'el stomped on her chest again and again. Her mouth opened and shut, and then she felt it. The thing, wriggling into the hollow space of her abdomen, reconnecting with her body. It wriggled beneath torn skin, squishing between fractured bones. Jenny was healing, and Mika'el noticed.

"So that was his gift to you," said the angel with a laugh. She drew back her arm, hunching over Jenny as her skin extended, as her muscles grew back into place. But the look on Mika'el's eyes was menacing; even the vertical eye on her chest glared at Jenny, like she was searching for something to rip out. Jenny got the horrible sense the angel would be her heart again, and she braced herself, but something golden flashed in the corner of her eyes.

With wings flapping with enough force to send Jenny's discarded intestines and organs flying, a blur of golden and red light slammed into Mika'el, tearing the angel away into the night.

Jenny collapsed, coughing and sputtering as her lungs inflated, as new kidneys, a new liver, a new stomach found their place. Her legs sprang out of the mess of her torso. Her missing arm returned last, shooting out like a tree branch, new skin expanding across exposed muscle. She tried to sit up but found that her new arm and legs were nearly bone thin, like the tarnished angels, drastically different from the rest of her body.

Bolts of red lightning burst across the ground, and Yeshua appeared, helping Jenny up. She was still healing, still growing back. She could hardly put her weight on her new legs. What was left of her armor barely covered her chest, but with all the blood and dirt smeared all over her, she couldn't care less about her modesty. She stared at Yeshua, trying to form words, trying to will herself to speak.

But she didn't know what she would even say, and she could already guess what his response would be: That she should go. Use the light Rafa'el had given her to find Susan.

But how could she leave in the middle of this fight?

"The end is approaching," he said, sounding solemn. Red lightning shot out of his hand and struck Jenny, accelerating her healing. "What parts we have to play must unfold." Sweat and blood glistened on his face, and Jenny wondered if he'd been rushing about the battlefield, trying to heal as many people as he could. She wondered if his intestines were still in place, if he needed any help.

But once he'd made sure she was all right, he was off, half running, half flying through the air, bounding after Mika'el and Eve. Jenny stood shakily to her feet. It felt like the universe was tearing and rippling around her; like everything was crashing down. She saw angels flashing in every direction, people in shining armor meeting them head-on in battle. She even saw angels struggling against angels, pulling weapons from the light of their bodies, their wings flapping as they flew across the stars.

Her heart stung. She could still feel Mika'el's fingers squeezing it, ripping it through her back. Jenny stumbled around, trying to find Oliver. She wanted to open a passageway right away and leave, use Rafa'el's light to find Susan, but she couldn't. She couldn't just leave him.

Coughing up blood as her insides finished healing, she wondered why it was taking so long. She'd healed much faster when the ghouls had been chewing on her. That worm inside her seemed to be sluggish now. Was it because the attacks of powerful angels were more difficult to heal?

Clutching her chest, she used energy to regenerate her armor, and dark scales sprouted over her skin as Jenny hobbled over to where Mackenzie was on the ground, holding Oliver and sobbing. What looked like empty bottles of healing sprays littered the grass around them.

Jenny collapsed on her knees and placed a hand on Mackenzie's shoulder. The girl flinched, looking up, tears streaming down her face.

"Is he . . . Is his heart still beating?" whispered Jenny. Then she remembered Mackenzie couldn't hear her, and she shut her eyes as more explosions shook the ground and streaks of light rained down around them.

She rummaged through Oliver's armor and pressed her fingers against his throat, trying not to think too much about his head facing the wrong way. She didn't feel sad. Not as sad as she thought she would. After all, Oliver's death would be somewhere in the other world, and his soul would be emerging from the river of blood . . . But not today. Not at this moment.

Relief flooded through her as she felt the faintest beat. She could heal this. She could fix this. Keeping her eyes shut, trying to ignore the apocalypse around her, Jenny concentrated on Valescent Light. Susan's gift.

It was different using it to heal someone else, she realized. Jenny had mostly used it on herself, generating the healing power from within. The only other thing she'd used it on was the passageways between worlds. But this was its initial purpose, wasn't it? This was why Susan had evolved this ability. To heal the people she cared about.

Tears slid down Jenny's cheeks. She remembered Susan finding her in that collapsed hallway in the high school, right at the verge of death, unable to die. Unable to feel anything until she felt Susan's hand inside her chest, holding on to her heart, pumping it for her. So that's why it'd felt so familiar when Mika'el had grabbed her heart, she thought.

Her hand, vibrating with golden light, slid inside Oliver's throat. Colors and warmth bloomed up her arm. She heard Mackenzie make a sound, but she focused. Focused on the memory of the slap Mika'el had struck Oliver with. The force of it. How it should've killed him. She focused on his stupid face—not the heartbroken, eyes-sunken expression she'd met when Eve had brought her to this world but of the goofy, shy little kid who would follow her around and ask if they were friends. The kid she'd walk to the train station with before pretending she didn't know him. Once they got to school, she told herself she had no obligation to be near him.

But when the angels had come, when the hallways had filled with screaming and terror, all she could think about was getting to him. Making sure he was safe. Why had she cared so much about him? Why did she still care so much about him?

She told herself it was just due to the nightmare of everything that was happening. The insanity of it all. Wasn't it just responsibility? She was the older sibling in their mishmash family. Wasn't it her duty to look after him?

Nah. Maybe that's what it had been at the start. But she'd accepted him as a little brother somewhere along the way. Wanting the best for him. Wanting him to be happy. She'd always wanted a sibling, someone who might love her. Someone who would be there for her. Someone she could support and fight for and cherish.

It was silly. It made her want to cry just thinking about it, but when she was young, she'd prayed to God for a little brother or sister that she could love. She'd sworn in her prayers that she would protect them from her mother if she had to.

Jenny opened her eyes, rainbow light sprouting all around Oliver, and looked into Mackenzie's wide stare. And Jenny knew, without a shadow of a doubt, that they loved each other. Oliver must've grown so strong trying to protect this girl during the survival challenge, and the girl had grown strong as well, trying to do the same.

Wasn't that what love was? Striving to grow stronger, to be there for one another, no matter what happened?

Wasn't that what bound Jenny to Susan?

"Jenny?" whispered Oliver, his voice hoarse and tense. His head was back on properly, and he blinked up at her, blinking away tears.

"See if you can find Mom and Dad," she whispered, leaning in close to press her forehead to his. That was the first time in her entire life she'd said those words and meant it. *Mom. Dad.* "I'm sorry for being such a bitch. And if you find them, can you tell them I said that?"

"Where are you going?"

"The world is ending," said Jenny, wiping away tears and straightening up. She still had plenty of energy to open a passageway, but she had to be quick. She didn't want to draw Mika'el's attention again. Didn't want that angel to rip her open again.

She could feel Eve and Yeshua fighting Mika'el in the distance, somewhere in the sky. Their blows radiated through the entire world. She looked back at Oliver, who was being helped up by Mackenzie. She wondered if this was the last time she'd see them like this; what if the next time she saw them, it was their souls?

Death really had lost all meaning.

"Be careful out there."

"No," he said. "I . . ." He looked like he wanted to say something, but he shook his head. Then, he stumbled forward and wrapped his arms around

Jenny, shaking. Sobbing. And Jenny held him tight. She didn't know why she was crying too. Maybe it was because all she'd ever wanted was a loving family. Maybe because he was too sweet, too caring, and he looked at her like how she used to look at her mother.

Why don't you just love me?
Please, just love me?
Please?

CHAPTER THIRTY-FIVE

SOUL

After Oliver swore he would find their parents and get them to safety, Jenny entered the passageway she'd cut open. She did it discreetly this time, converting the darkness with Valescent Light before it could suck in any angels and alert Mika'el to her position. A part of her wished she could have found her parents and brought them and Oliver and Mackenzie with her to another world, somewhere they could be safe.

But where? And how could she have done that without alerting the angels? Without most of them dying, anyway.

At least in Eve's world, they had a fighting chance standing together as a group.

She shuddered as the light warped around her. It felt different now. Strange. Empty.

The central focus point, the heaviest *pull*, had changed. It was ... denser, somehow. Fuller. Instead of a glowing golden light, a seeping darkness enveloped that direction. Jenny floated, reds and greens wrapping around her arms and legs as she tried to feel for that world, tried to figure out what had happened.

The golden light was tainted. Even the colors seemed less vibrant, fading to dull versions of themselves. The red looked more like dying pink; the blues and oranges like very old paint.

It had to be Him. She knew that. Now that he was born, now that his beams of darkness cut through the worlds, they must have been affecting everything. But what had he done? The material world's pull wasn't inviting anymore; the pull wasn't saying she belonged there. It felt sinister, like it wanted to devour her and she had to get away—she had to swim away. But wasn't Susan there?

She'd pushed Susan's soul into the material world when they'd escaped from Azra'il. She *had* to be there . . . Had she been devoured by *Him?* Was Jenny too late?

Where was she supposed to go?

"C'mon," she whispered, her voice bubbling in the golden light. She pulled on the light Rafa'el had given her, the sphere of green that came surfacing from her innermost thoughts. It dyed the light around her, and within a few moments, Jenny was enveloped in the vivid green of the angel's light. The light felt warm, comforting, and something inside her seemed to settle. It was almost like a compass needle, and it pushed her in the direction she had to go.

Forward. Forward and below. Jenny's body moved almost on its own, the green light pulling her along. Where was it taking her?

If it was a world she'd been to before, she couldn't tell. The push and pull of the light no longer made sense, the darkness at the center of everything rippling like an enormous beast that had made a mess of the other worlds. As she moved through the light, she could see that strands of that darkness reached out in several directions. Were those the beams?

But all at once, the light parted, and Jenny splashed into something hot and sticky and familiar: blood.

Coughing, she stood up, blood dripping down her armor and legs, and looked around at the towering walls. A jolt of fear ran down her legs as she stared at them.

"What?" she gasped. "Back here?"

A scream rose to her throat so quickly she almost let it out, but she bit her teeth and swallowed it down. Her hatchet in hand, she wanted to smash and break things. Her tentacles shot out of her back in rage, smashing the water and the rubble around her. It took her a second to realize she hadn't emerged from the river of blood this time. She was in the labyrinth.

But the last time she'd been here, it had been flooded with cold water, not blood. Had the world changed? Had something happened? In the distance, taller even than the walls of the labyrinth, were the beams of darkness, jutting out in random directions into the red sky. One in particular seemed very close, and Jenny rubbed her eyes, trying to calm down.

There were no souls. No angels. Not even the harpies.

The world was so quiet, so still. Nothing seemed to stir. Nobody was screaming and begging. It was empty. Azra'il might not even be here.

But why had Rafa'el guided her here? Jenny had *freed* Susan from this world, pushed her into the material world. Or had she died again? Was that even possible? *Could* a soul die?

She looked up, holding a hand over her brow to squint at the red sky, trying to spot Azra'il's floating castle. What if Susan was up there? Iblis had helped her fly up there before. How would she get there now? And what was . . . There was something glowing overhead, circling the nearest beam of darkness.

She looked away and stretched out her tentacles, trying to feel for anything that might give her a clue. She wondered if she should've stayed in Eve's world, fighting the angels, trying to help find her parents. Or should she have gone to the material world? No . . . that was filled with darkness. She couldn't face that.

So then, where was Susan?

Should she just open another passageway and leave? Her head was spinning with frustration and exhaustion, and she slammed her tentacles into the ground, beneath the watery blood, trying to steady herself, trying to think.

Maybe she could climb to the top of these walls again, get a better view of her surroundings. She shuddered, remembering her fights in this world. The desecrated angel. The harpies. And what they'd been doing to all the souls.

She walked up to the wall, placed her hand on the large cobblestone, and was just about to start climbing when she heard splashing, like someone running. The sounds were growing louder and louder, and before Jenny could see who it was, she *felt* them through her tentacles. A shudder ran down the length of each one, straight into her heart. A notification appeared in her head.

Soul (Awakened)

It was Susan. She stopped a few feet away, blood and water dripping off her naked form.

Heat rose to Jenny's face, but she kept her eyes on Susan's. Her heart was pounding so hard she was shaking. She didn't know what to say.

There was nothing more to say.

She wanted to run straight to her, squeeze her tight and never let go, but then, another chill went through her. A shiver that wasn't entirely her own; the green bubble inside her was responding. A silvery silhouette hovered right behind Susan, and Jenny froze.

Angel (Stage VI - Level 291)

Jenny stared at the two of them, fear trickling up the side of her neck. Her hatchet flashed to her hand. Was this a trick? Was Susan really there? The notification seemed off, didn't it? She'd never seen an awakened soul before. What did that even mean?

But as her eyes adjusted to the silver angel's presence, she realized something was wrong with it. It looked like it had been through hell, which was funny, given they were standing in actual hell. But the angel had chunks of its body *missing*, like someone had taken a hole puncher to its light. Bits of its wings, its arms and legs, its chest. Even some of its head was gone, a hole above its left eyebrow.

Susan took a hesitant step closer. "Jenny?" she whispered. The world was so quiet that her whisper came through like a knife.

Jenny felt it with every tentacle. She didn't know how to respond.

"What are you doing here?" asked Susan, who took another step. Electricity seemed to crackle around her legs, the water and blood splashing against her thighs.

"I came to find you," said Jenny, her voice barely more than a gasp. There was that lump in her throat again. "What is that angel?"

Susan turned to glance at the silver creature behind her. She turned back, her brown hair bouncing all over. "Jenny, this is Jibra'il. He kept me safe when . . ." She gestured with her arms toward the beams sticking out throughout the labyrinth around them.

Jenny squinted. Why would an angel protect a human? Was it one of the rebellious ones? Fighting against Adonai? She didn't sense that oppressing, stifling aura of dread and fear from this one. Not like how she'd felt when Azra'il and Mika'el had shown up. This one actually reminded her of Rafa'el, so it must have been the angel she was supposed to find.

"Angel," she called. It hurt that she was speaking over Susan, but she had to be sure this wasn't a trap. "Do you know someone by the name of Rafa'el?"

The silver light almost seemed to ignite, brightening immensely despite the holes in its body. And for the first time since Jenny ran into them, the angel spoke, its voice like a cool, early-morning breeze. "She is the one I hold most dear," said the angel. "I can sense her light radiating from you."

Jenny glanced back at Susan, who was staring wide-eyed and confused. "Okay," she exhaled. "Rafa'el gave me a message to give to you." She kept picturing a hostage exchange. *You give me Susan. I'll give you that bit of light.* But the angel was too powerful. Even though it looked ragged and torn up, it was too highly leveled.

"I will do you no harm," came the angel's voice. Its head was bowed solemnly, a hole-punched hand hovering over its chest. Countless eyes blinked at Jenny from its silver arms and shoulders. "I . . . I don't know what I want anymore, but my duty has been done. I am no longer obligated to—"

"What job?" asked Jenny.

It was Susan who responded. She took another step through the bloody water, her face almost pleading, as though begging Jenny to not react without listening to the whole story. "He's . . . He's the one who brought God into our world."

CHAPTER THIRTY-SIX

MESSAGE DELIVERED

"Th at is true," spoke the angel. "That was my duty. And I have completed it." He floated across the water, his silver form reflecting on the surface. He wasn't as enormous as the other angels. Azra'il had looked like a mountain. Mika'el stood like a tall building. Rafa'el was like an enormous tree. But this one, Jibra'il, looked more like a regular-size man.

Jenny glowered at him, her tentacles swishing behind her with anticipation. She stared at the holes in his body, like someone had grabbed fistfuls of him and yanked them out. Shouldn't he be able to heal? He was so much stronger than she was, much higher leveled—stage six.

"So what are you doing here?" she asked, refusing to back down. Something about him felt different. He didn't have the menacing aura that Azra'il and Mika'el had; she got the sense he wasn't violent. And Susan had said the angel had protected her; was that how he got injured? An angel without purpose?

"Searching for the one I hold most dear," he replied, staring back at her with his hard silver eyes. "I believe you and I are on the same journey."

Jenny didn't know whether to hate him or not. Maybe she was too tired for hate. Maybe there'd been so much hate and anger and all of it was as pointless as everything else. But the angel hadn't attacked yet. Susan seemed unharmed. She could feel Rafa'el's message inside her head yearning to be with Jibra'il. Was this some elaborate trick? A way to capture both Jenny and Susan at the same time? But why? Why were the angels so concerned with her?

She decided she would give the message to Jibra'il, then, depending on what it was, depending on how he reacted, she would grab Susan and run. They could open a passageway and go wherever they wanted.

Holding out her hand, Jenny let the little bit of green light flow down her arm to the top of her palm. It bubbled up from her skin, forming a little sphere that illuminated the space around them with the same glow as Rafa'el's, warm green light radiating from Jenny. Her tentacles flicked and wriggled behind her.

Silver light shimmered around her as the angel moved closer to accept Rafa'el's message. Jenny felt like holding it away, like demanding something in return, but decided if the angel had protected Susan, then there was nothing more to ask. Surrendering the green light to Jibra'il, it floated off her fingertips, bobbing in the air like a soap bubble before hovering toward the angel.

His body trembled as he shut his eyes and received it. The green orb pushed through his outermost layer—Jenny didn't know if she should consider it skin—and tendrils of green sprawled every which way through his body, sticking out of the holes. He dropped to the bloody water, on his knees, his wings spread out like a bird who'd fallen out of the sky. The eyes on his shoulders and arms were shut.

"So, what did she give you?" whispered Jenny, who stared at the angel. Susan splashed around to stand beside her, and they exchanged a look, a mixture of warmth and concern and happiness and confusion.

"Are you okay?" asked Susan, speaking to the angel. She leaned forward to touch his shoulder as he sobbed. Electricity crackled between them.

Jibra'il nodded. He smiled at the two of them, silver tears streaming down his face. Some of the tears spilled through the hole in his cheek. He raised his hands together as though he were praying, cupped as though he was trying to scoop water into his mouth, but nestled between his palms was a glowing green-and-silver orb, different from whatever Rafa'el had entrusted to Jenny but similar to what she'd seen inside the Leviathan.

It was an egg.

Susan gasped like she recognized what it was as well, and she stepped back, her fingers finding Jenny's.

Jenny almost wanted to laugh, wanted to say, "*So I've been carrying around your egg all this time? Rafa'el gave me your child?*" but she realized she was holding hands with Susan and caught herself. Heat flooded her face.

More tears streamed down Jibra'il's cheeks, evaporating in little silver sparkles. He placed the egg back inside himself, inserting it into his chest. Its light faded away into his silver glow.

And they remained like that, quiet, as the waves splashed against their bodies, staining their armor and skin with blood. Jenny's hand felt as though she'd used Ignite. She squeezed Susan's fingers tightly and turned to face her, to stare into her brown eyes, ready to say something; she wasn't sure what. Something between an apology and an . . . Well, it wasn't quite a confession. Not yet, at least. But maybe . . . Maybe they could still go to prom together?

Now, that made her want to laugh—made her want to laugh *so much*—but all she managed was a hiccup.

Susan's lips curled into a soft smile. "Hello," she greeted. "You got a lot stronger again. Every time I see you, I feel like you change. You look different."

"How did you get away from the cross?" asked Jenny, remembering how she'd found Susan in this world: nailed to the cross, screaming, and begging to be released.

Electricity shimmered through Susan's form, making her glow, and for a second, her hair seemed blue again. Jenny remembered the cattle prod Susan had used in the high school, wielding it like a sword, shooting electricity from it. "I have no idea," replied Susan with a laugh, stepping closer till they were so close Jenny forgot everything else. "I touched some electricity, and suddenly, I could . . . do stuff. I think I can go inside you."

"What?" Jenny blinked. She'd half stopped paying attention. All she could think about was how close their noses were, and how this hunger, this new wave of unwavering want that bubbled up inside her, was so different from the hunger she'd felt before. She didn't want to sink her teeth into flesh anymore. She didn't want to rip someone open. She just wanted to press her cheek against Susan's. That's all she wanted. Her tentacles shivered with that desire, dropping down to rest in the water. "What do you mean?"

"Like a ghost," said Susan, her smile widening to show teeth. She swiped some hair away from her face and tucked it behind her ear. She bit her bottom lip. "Want me to show you?"

"I . . ." Jenny trailed off, blushing. She'd had so many people inside her already: Eve. Iblis. And now Susan? How? Why? But before she could respond, she felt Susan wince, shuddering as her eye twitched. And then Jenny shuddered as well. A cold chill swept across the labyrinth, and Jibra'il stood, looking upward.

"Well, well, well," boomed a voice from above. A moment later, something immense crashed into the water ahead of them, tall enough to stand higher than the towering walls around them—a giant.

Jenny grabbed Susan and stood in front of her, all her tentacles at the ready. It was Azra'il. His cloth flapped between his muscular legs, his broad chest seeming like it should get stuck between the walls. The snakes on his head hissed and snapped every which way, but it was his eyes that were the worst of it. Red and glaring.

"My bride-to-be, what *are* you doing here?" he hissed. "With my old favorite toy, no less. And brother . . . what are you doing in the filth with these creatures? Why are you not at our Lord's side?"

Jibra'il stepped past Jenny and Susan while Jenny stared at him. Was he going to side with the other angel now that Jenny had delivered his egg to him?

"I have done it, brother," announced Jibra'il. He was tiny compared to Azra'il, but Jenny got the sense that the angels had control over their size. They could choose how large or small they wanted to be. Jibra'il's wings spread wide, the eyes on his broad back looking back at her. "I have brought Adonai into the material world."

Black and gray lightning crackled around Azra'il. "I have seen," he said, his voice booming like low thunder. "The beams of Holy Light have splintered my world. My souls await collection. But, brother . . . Rafa'el remains in the hands of the Antithesis. The war is waged—the war for destiny. What are you doing here in such a state?"

Jibra'il didn't answer right away. His eyes blinked. Jenny felt Susan squeezing her arm. "He's not evil," whispered Susan.

"I am . . ." Jibra'il took a deep breath.

"And do you know that mortal behind you?" asked Azra'il, cutting off the silver angel. "The interloper? The Interloper and her little friend, the Valescent One? Do you know how much harm they have caused?"

Jibra'il turned to look at them, a sorry look on his face, and Jenny felt a tinge of sadness. It was the look of someone who was always ignored, always stepped on. A look that said, "*If only I could speak. If only I could say what I wanted.*" He'd always followed orders, done as he was told, but now, he was lost. Jenny knew that well—so well that it hurt. How whenever she finished anything, whenever she completed an assignment or a project or even a video game, all she felt was hollow and empty, lost, without a purpose.

Was that why Jibra'il had helped Susan?

"Brother," he said, raising his voice. Silver lightning shimmered around him as he beat his hole-ridden wings, growing in size till he was nearly as big as Azra'il. His wounds seemed even worse at this size, but the eyes covering his muscles seemed large enough to fit entire people within them.

Jenny splashed backward, grabbing Susan's hand as the two glowing giants stared each other down.

"These humans are under my protection."

CHAPTER THIRTY-SEVEN

DESTINY

Jibra'il felt conflicted. Inside him was an egg, a ball of light carrying both his and Rafa'el's essence. An egg that should be obsolete. Why would Rafa'el give him this, after all these millennia? After all the time they'd had together and lost? Why would Rafa'el have waited for this moment, after *His* birth, to give him this?

Why?

His duty was over. His role was fulfilled. The worlds would end and be reborn through Adonai. There was no need for eggs. No more need for children. Everyone and everything would be part of the Great Whole.

So why?

And why send it through the interloper? What was Rafa'el trying to tell him when she herself had a role to play? And didn't that mean this mortal, this interloper who carried his child, knew where Rafa'el was? Would the mortal help him find Rafa'el?

He'd protected the soul almost out of instinct—he didn't want her to come to harm—but he'd done so much worse to the tarnished ones. To the humans in the world.

But that soul had contended with Adonai himself. That soul had thrown herself into the third Mary without a second thought and fought. How could Jibra'il not respect that?

The soul had even managed to find a way to *soothe* the tarnished ones. It wasn't proper healing, as nothing could undo the transformation via Holy Light, but the soul had reconstituted the tarnished minds. It'd even found a way to restore the eggs to their proper light, to give a new generation a chance.

But what use was the chance if Adonai had emerged?

Jibra'il's mind had clashed worse than any storm he'd ever conjured, and when his brother Azra'il appeared, enormous and angry and looking for a fight, Jibra'il decided he'd had enough of being told what to do. How to serve best. What orders he should follow. For once, he was going to do something for himself.

"These humans are under my protection."

Azra'il's snakes erupted into countless hissing fits, and when he spoke, his voice was cold and gravely, his red eyes burning. "*They* belong to me. This world is mine. I have inherited it. And everyone and everything within this dominion is *mine*."

Jibra'il's eyes blinked across his body; he flapped his wings and rose slightly higher, expanding his light so that he could look down at Azra'il. How had his brother turned to such selfishness?

Jibra'il had known what was to happen in this world, that the souls would experience never-ending pain, but that had a purpose. It had reason. The energy produced from their pain would fuel the Holy Light, would fuel the power necessary to catalyze the universe and reconstitute it in Adonai's image.

But what Azra'il wanted was beyond Adonai's will. It was purely for his own selfishness.

"The souls never belonged to you, brother. You were merely their warden. And now, they return to Adonai, where they belong."

"And I was promised my boon," said Azra'il, his lips curling into a snarl. His muscles popped as his four enormous wings shot out of his back, expanding in a cross shape, each one dotted with countless gleaming red eyes. "The worlds would end, but this one would remain mine."

It was dawning now what Azra'il was saying. It had been his plan from the beginning that he wouldn't join with Adonai. That he would remain on his own, separating this world from the rest, keeping the souls as his personal collection of worshippers.

He was a fool. His vanity would be the end of him. There was no feasible way that Adonai and Rafa'el would not be aware of his intentions, would not know what Azra'il was vying to do. With his false throne in the sky and . . .

That was it, he realized. That throne was the lodestone holding this world together. It was through that throne that energy was siphoned into the other worlds, into the guidance system.

The interloper had separated two worlds already, keeping them from reaching Adonai and holding his true ascension back. Could this be it, then? Could she separate this world as well?

Behind him, Jibra'il could tell that Susan and Jenny were running, splashing through the water to get away. *Good*, he thought. They needed space to figure out what to do, how to do it. He had to convince her to do this.

With silver light flashing inside his hand, he summoned the wind and slammed his fist with the might of a storm into Azra'il's face. A fearsome gale blew between the labyrinth walls, sending up a flurry of water and blood and rubble.

The impact drove the other angel backward, his face cracking. He spat out blood. His cruel wings flapped, his snakes hissed like mad, and Azra'il dove back in, flames igniting in his own fists.

Fire and wind struggled to overtake the other, they fought. Jibra'il summoned storm clouds, sending clattering, thunderous booms through Azra'il's form. His brother's limbs turned to lava, flowing and burning so hot the waters around them hissed and steamed away.

"You cannot do this, brother," barked Azra'il. "Do not stand against me. Do not stand against destiny."

"You say this, but here you stand, in a world of your own, too proud to join destiny." Jibra'il blew his wind around the molten parts of Azra'il, changing his composure from glowing-hot magma to cooled, dark rock. But it wasn't cool enough.

Azra'il's fingers found Jibra'il's wounds, tearing and burning through his silvery chest, his wings. But these injuries were new, not caused by the Holy Light, and Jibra'il could heal from them.

"Brother, why don't you see sense?" shouted Jibra'il. Light surged around him.

They exchanged blows, rising into the air as the walls crumbled around them.

"Sense?" spat Azra'il, his snakes biting chunks off Jibra'il. "Sense? After a billion years of planning? Waiting? He has already been born. The worlds are His. And everyone, all His angels, all the demons and deaths and souls—are they all not His? None of us can stop Him."

"So you think you can hide in this world?" Jibra'il knew he couldn't hold out long. "Then leave me be, and I will leave you be. Leave the human and the soul be."

"No!" scream-cried Azra'il, his throat billowing lava. "They are *mine*."

There was no reasoning with him. Azra'il was lost between his own selfish desire and his need to carry out Adonai's will. He wanted the interloper no matter what it cost, as the interloper's freedom itself meant Azra'il had failed. The angel would never see past this.

Jibra'il would have to fight his way out. Even if he were completely whole, he wouldn't have stood a chance against his violence-hungry brother, an angel that enjoyed torturing the tarnished, tearing away their skin to create the fabric he wore around his torso.

It was shameful, he'd always thought. Terrible for an angel of the highmost level to stoop to such disgusting behavior. So, after blocking a molten punch from Azra'il, Jibra'il darted down, grabbed the loincloth Azra'il was so proud of, and yanked. He tore it away and threw it over his shoulder. The cloth fluttered in the storm wind as Azra'il howled in rage, but Jibra'il wouldn't give him the chance to respond.

Wind and thunder snapping around his arms, Jibra'il drove his fist into Azra'il's exposed privates, thinking back to how Adonai was the one who'd demanded every angel imitate the physicality of humans. No longer simply silhouettes of light, but light with faces. With distinctive features. Hair that wasn't quite mammalian fur. Penises and ovaries that didn't quite function the same. But He'd pushed for the changes—for it to be intimate, for it to be private, for it to be delicate—to teach true humility.

Azra'il had stood against it for the longest time, refusing to transform himself, but when he'd finally succumbed to Adonai's will, he'd taken gleaming red eyes in defiance and covered his shame with cloth.

And when Jibra'il's fist crushed Azra'il's testicles, the angel's scream ripped a hole in the sky, blasting away the red clouds that hung low over this world, clearing everything away to reveal the castle floating above the labyrinth. Beams of Holy Light reached up around it, like a crown.

Summoning more wind, Jibra'il threw Azra'il away, launching him over the labyrinth, sending him as far as possible as he howled in pain. Jibra'il turned and plummeted toward the labyrinth, every single eye on his body searching the maze, searching the waters for any sign of the humans. When he found them, he began to shrink, growing smaller and smaller until he was flying right over their heads as they ran. "Susan Brown, I cannot hold back my brother for long. But I have an idea."

"Seems like you hurt him pretty bad," replied Jenny, coming to a stop. "I can open another passageway."

"No," said Jibra'il, achingly aware of the egg inside him. He reached down and lifted Susan up by her shoulders, letting her lightning course through him, interacting with the storms flowing through his veins.

"What are you doing?" she asked, but he turned her around so they were face-to-face, her hanging from his hands over Jenny.

"We must lend our power to your Jenny. Perhaps combined, we can stand a chance."

The soul's eyes went wide, expanding, something Jibra'il always found strange for a race of beings. Expressing themselves through the size of their facial features rather than through conversation. But she nodded, and before the other one—the desecrated human—could say anything, he pushed Susan into her.

Overhead, the sky was darkening once more, and he could hear his brother screaming, flapping his tremendous wings, rushing toward them, a beam of ferocious light.

Jenny had gone rigid, staring as though she'd been petrified. But after a moment in which he could see Susan's light and energy flickering through the mortal, the girl nodded with understanding. "I'm ready."

"It is the black throne," said Jibra'il, his wings fluttering as he prepared to possess a human once again. "That is the lodestone of this world. That will separate everything." His light shimmered, the holes in his body aching and burning, but he concentrated his form, reminding himself that he was fighting for two now, before letting go.

Turning into a cloud of silver light, he slid through Jenny's skin and made contact with her mind, with Susan's soul, and everything around them erupted with silvery light, supercharged by electricity and blue flames.

He caught glimpses of her mind and the heavens and all the worlds. He had never seen something like this. This mind had once homed the Antithesis itself. This mind had once sheltered the Great Demon Iblis. This mind had devoured its own death and separated worlds. This mind, who was burning hot with embarrassment and love, sharing its body with the soul.

As he fully integrated and slipped away, as he felt the mortal's body surge with power, he realized what Rafa'el had meant by sending him the egg.

I entrust destiny to you.

CHAPTER THIRTY-EIGHT

DOUBLE POSSESSION

Jenny grabbed her head and fell to her knees as the angel entered her body, as she felt his immense mind like a whale emerging beneath a rowboat. That was the image she kept picturing.

She'd been surprised enough when Susan entered her. That had felt like chugging a deep glass of freezing cold water after a long, hot day: refreshing, but the cold had shot straight into her brain—a tingling numbness that wasn't quite pain, wasn't quite comfort—and then, Susan's thoughts had flowed into her head.

I'm sorry, came Susan's voice, echoing all around. *The angel thinks this is the only way, and I agree. We've done this before.*

Before? Jenny felt it all. Saw it all. The torture that Azra'il had put Susan through. She wanted to scream. Wanted to tear out her hair. Wanted to fly up there and shove her hatchet down Azra'il's throat. But then, she saw Susan wandering the material world; alone, lonely, isolated from everyone and everything—a ghost.

And she felt something familiar. A longing. A love. A confusing mixture of sadness and hope. How she'd felt about Jenny.

Embarrassment and warmth rose like a tidal wave. There wasn't even a chance to linger on the fact that their minds were sharing the same space, on what Susan might be seeing from Jenny's life.

I didn't want you to find out like this.

But what did it matter now that the world was ending?

She saw Leslie. *Leslie? It was Leslie who became the third Mary? Who gave birth to* Him? She saw the angel Jibra'il inside Dr. Lee. The fight. The struggle. And the birth.

Everything filled Jenny's mind so quickly she felt like a water balloon that had expanded beyond the rupturing point, and then, Jibra'il was there. His mind pushed against hers and Susan's, squeezing into her skull. There wasn't enough space. Her head was going to explode. There were too many thoughts, too many memories, and the angel had lived so long that time had lost meaning to him.

She wanted to cry out, but she could feel the angel's urgency, could feel his fear. He was too hurt, too weak, to stand up to Azra'il. And she was too human, too weak. But together? With Susan's soul inside her as well?

Electricity fizzed and popped around her. Valescent Light flared to life, colors streaming out of her, binding her back together. Her thoughts had become overcrowded, but an abundance of power flooded her system, and she was transforming.

When her exoskeleton came bursting out of her belly button, when her battered and broken armor fell away, Jenny found herself covered in a sleek layer of silver. It wasn't exactly like her exoskeleton. It wasn't thick and shiny, but it conformed to her skin, a thin metallic layer that covered even her tentacles. Her shoulders moved forward and back, popping one at a time as two wings burst out from her shoulder blades. Eyes opened and closed across her shoulders and down her sides and arms, moving across her new exoskeleton before settling and taking root in her skin.

She didn't get a chance to survey herself, to marvel at what she'd become. To see how her stats had changed. Azra'il barreled down like an asteroid, burning with smoke trailing behind him. He was covered in snakes now, no longer just on his head but wriggling all across his body, covering his chest and torso, covering the space between his muscular legs. She had a memory now of tearing off his loincloth and punching him in the crotch. Her lips twitched into a smile. He deserved so much worse.

No. We won't fight him head-on, came Jibra'il's thoughts. *That fight could drag on for millennia. What we must do is unseat the source of his power.*

Jenny twirled her hatchet, rage and want throbbing between her eyes. She wanted to hit that angel so hard, to see if she could hurt him now. To get revenge for the brutal beatdown he'd given her, for what he'd done to Susan, for how he'd nailed them to crosses and—

Take a deep breath, whispered Susan.

Jenny shut her eyes, feeling the air around her with her silver tentacles, and when Azra'il was close enough to feel the heat emanating off his body, the fury, Jenny used Instant Acceleration and ran through the water, letting the giant crash into the space behind her.

The walls of the labyrinth buckled over him as everything shook. He'd gone so deep into the ground that the blood and water swirled into a whirlpool, draining into the hole he'd made.

With a flap of her new wings—Jibra'il's wings—Jenny took off, racing toward the castle in the sky as Azra'il roared below her. Tentacles swirling around her, she could feel him rising, flapping his four fearsome wings to gain speed. He hadn't had those before, when she'd met him.

He hates them, came Jibra'il's thoughts. *He hates the eyes on his wings, for they show him the truth. And he cannot stand the truth of himself.*

He's a disgusting piece of shit, said Susan.

My thoughts exactly. Jenny flapped as hard as she could, water vapor trailing off her wings as she flew. The last time she'd been here, it was Iblis—possessing a harpy—who'd carried her up into this sky. She'd had wings before, too; Iblis's burning wings. All of this was somehow familiar: these minds in her head, these changes to her body. The increase in her abilities and strength.

Her tentacles shuddered, and she stopped midflight, turning to face Azra'il, who'd caught up to her. His eyes gleamed so brightly they left trails of smoke, his snakes hissing and crawling all over his muscular frame. He was enormous, a giant blocking out her field of view. She felt like a speck of dust, and once again, she imagined a rowboat resting on the surface of the water as something monstrous emerged from the depths below.

She darted down, combining her flight with Instant Acceleration, a streak of silver light. Azra'il couldn't keep up, she realized, as he blinked and looked around. But she stopped in front of him, hovering right in front of his chest. Aiming for his throat, she swung as hard as she could, her hatchet shimmering with energy and light, crackling with Susan's electricity.

But the angel flapped backward, roaring, as several of the snakes on his chest had their heads chopped off, falling away before smoldering into smoke. In response, he grabbed several of her tentacles and pulled, swinging her around and around. She wanted to use Ignite, set herself aflame, but through Jibra'il's memories she remembered that Azra'il was of the flame as well. He could turn into lava.

So instead, she twisted midair and sliced off her own tentacles, spinning as she did so to thwack the angel in the face with her remaining three. Each one landed with a thunderous blow, Jibra'il's strength: hurricane-force winds which blew into Azra'il every time Jenny struck him.

Then, channeling electricity that seemed to have generated inside her, she used Instant Acceleration and dashed past the angel, her hatchet outstretched.

The edge caught his shoulder and arm, slicing through the snakes, slicing through his skin, his flesh. Azra'il howled at the top of his lungs, billowing air and smoke around him as blood spurted from the wound. She'd hoped to sever the entire arm off, but his muscles were simply too big, and she'd only managed to cut through half of its thickness.

"No!" he roared. "You have sullied yourself by joining with the mortal, brother!"

"*You meant to make this mortal your bride*," spat Jenny, speaking with the voices of Susan as well as Jibra'il, catching herself off guard. She touched her throat with a silver exoskeleton-covered finger. "Go fuck yourself, Azra'il."

Gnashing his teeth, two more snakes erupted from between his wings. These weren't like the little ones covering his body; these were enormous, and instead of dark scales, they seemed to be melting.

Magma serpents.

They shot toward her, undulating like her tentacles, burning rock dripping from their fangs. Each one was so big they could've swallowed her whole.

Tentacles still recovering, Jenny flicked side to side, using Instant Acceleration to dodge the burning snakes, trying to close in for another blow. *Rain,* came a thought, and thunder erupted around her. Lightning followed next, and she saw the look of fear, the slightest pause, on Azra'il's face as water erupted from her exoskeleton, shooting out of her in every direction. It drenched him from top to bottom, cooling down his snakes, cooling down his body.

She landed on his chest with her feet, flapping her wings to maintain her horizontal position, and kicked off as hard as she could. Jibra'il's power surged through her legs, rocketing her upward while Azra'il was sent shooting down, billowing smoke and roaring with anger as he rocketed toward the ground.

It won't hold him long. My storms can cool down his constitution, but he will heat back up.

That's fine, said Jenny, flinging her hatchet with her newfound strength. It flashed away, vanishing in the direction of the castle in the sky, toward the halo of light swirling around it. Then she turned below, watching as Azra'il crashed. She inhaled deeply, grasping the air with her fingers. It was similar to how she opened a passageway between worlds, but this time, she was using Jibra'il's abilities.

Pulling on the air, she summoned the rain again. Her arms, her entire body, glowed with silver light, and she yanked down a huge storm, a torrent of rain cascading down like a waterfall.

Satisfied with that, she flapped her wings, flying through the clouds she'd created, filling them with Susan's electricity. They grew dark and thick, the roar of thunder clattering through her ears. A moment later, she used Instant Swap.

Suddenly, she was in the air, far above the raging storm clouds below, far above Azra'il. She stared at the castle, at the beam of darkness shining right behind it. Her heart broke as she realized what the halo was, the circles of light spinning around each beam.

Souls. Every soul who had crawled out of the river of blood and been judged now swirled about, stuck in a loop of pain and misery. They were naked, whirling about, bumping into each other, pulling and screeching as they grabbed anything they could, each one of them desperate to escape. But it was like gravity held them in place, forcing them to swim through the air, spinning endlessly. And each time they hurt one another, each time they collided or pulled or fought, their bodies rippled with more golden bursts of energy.

"Fuck," whispered Jenny, her wings flapping to keep her hovering in place. Her silver armor gleamed with the bright glow emanating from the halos. She wanted to grab the souls with her tentacles and rip them free, but Jibra'il's thoughts warned against that. The soul would simply be forced back up by the Holy Light, by Adonai's light, so that his beams could continue soaking in the released energy from their pain.

It was the perfect battery. The perfect source of near infinite energy. The souls couldn't die. *That's what's been going on.* The labyrinth. The endless torture of the souls. That was where they collected energy from. And now that she thought about it, all the energy she'd ever used had come from killing angels, killing people. And Adonai had perfected that.

Jibra'il assured her that severing this world, just as she'd severed the world of demons and deaths and set them free from their constraints, would free the souls as well.

She wanted to question Jibra'il on that, on how they'd even designed this entire afterlife thing, but there wasn't time. Azra'il would catch up quickly enough. She wasn't sure yet how she'd do it, how she'd sever the world with Azra'il bearing down on them, but it was their best plan. As Jenny flew toward the castle entrance, figures with great big wings rushed toward her.

She didn't need anyone else's memories to know what they were.

Harpies.

CHAPTER THIRTY-NINE

SET IT ON FIRE

The harpies looked ragged, worn down. Jenny flapped her wings, staying afloat as the thunderstorm raged below. How long would that hold Azra'il back?

"**Harpies!**" boomed Jibra'il's voice from her throat. "**Rest your talons. You are dismissed from your duties.**"

The harpies exchanged glances, their beautiful faces strained, their feathers having lost their once luscious white luster. Each one seemed gray and old, and from Jibra'il's memories, she realized they *were* growing old. They'd been hatched for this singular purpose of guarding and tending to the deaths and tarnished angels. They didn't even belong to this plane.

They were originally from the material world, a castaway branch of evolution who survived several extinction events with the help of the angels. They could no longer think for themselves; they had forgotten what it meant to be a civilization.

Susan thought they were beautiful; she delved into the memories of the brood mother that Jenny had defeated with the help of Iblis.

They won't stand down, said Jibra'il. But Jenny's tentacles had already picked up on their intentions. The creatures were hungry. They must be starving now that they couldn't feed on the souls anymore. She could sense they were beyond reason.

She knew that hunger. Knew the way it spread through one's body and erased every reasonable thought, every shred of decency. The only thing that mattered was feeding, sinking your teeth or your talons or whatever into meat, tearing it apart, hoping to satisfy that bottomless craving.

Susan bristled. Jibra'il was shocked and guilted by Jenny's memories inside the survival challenge. What she'd become. What she had to do.

She vowed to never succumb to that again.

She flashed through the flock, hatchet extended. She whipped them away with her tentacles, slamming them downward. She broke necks, wings, talons, whirling through them as quickly as she could using bursts of Instant Acceleration. The harpies swooped and dove around her, each one with a desperate look in its beautiful eyes. Even though they were so hungry, so exhausted, the chance of food gave them renewed, feverous strength. Jenny could taste it with her tentacles and feel how badly they wanted to eat her. They didn't care for Azra'il or any of the angels anymore. Didn't care for their duty.

"Come on, then," she said through gritted teeth, swatting one away with the back of her hatchet, slicing through the talons of another one.

This time, they were so much easier to fight; she was so much stronger.

This time, she wasn't trying to hide.

She bit through the wings of one that managed to claw at her chest. She grasped another with her tentacles and tore the poor creature down the middle, just the way Mika'el had torn Jenny open. She flashed through the flock, appearing and reappearing, punching and kicking and slashing and ripping. Borrowing the angel's stamina meant she could go on like this forever, she felt like.

There is a limit to what your body can sustain, human.

We have to save our strength for the castle, said Susan. *If we can separate that throne and free all the souls, then . . .*

Yeah, thought Jenny. They were right. She was trying to be as efficient as possible with her usage of skills, but there were too many harpies, too many desperate talons, and more kept emerging from the castle, kept flying in from the surrounding areas, called to the fight by the screams and cries of the harpies Jenny cut down.

She used Ignite, setting her silver body and wings on fire. And the harpies plummeted down into the thunderstorm, trailing smoke and the ashen remains of their feathers. The others screamed and backed off, flying higher and circling away. With the crowd parted, Jenny seized her chance and used Instant Acceleration again, tucking her wings as she rocketed into the castle entrance.

Once she got past the pillars, she flapped her wings again, stopping her speed and controlling her direction as the wind guided her up and through the tunnel. She emerged into a section glowing with soft red light.

She was greeted by the sight of more harpies, but these lay dead on the floor, twitching. Most of their eyes were closed. Their feathers were gray, aged, and the stench of rot hung heavy in the air.

What happened to these? But the answer came as soon as Jenny thought of the question. These were the harpies who could no longer fight. Could no longer hunt. Their age had caught up with them, their beauty faded. They were struggling for their last breaths.

But this was the chamber of eggs, and Jenny looked up to see them clinging to the ceiling of the enormous space. Sacs. Just like the ones Jenny had found in the high school. These had been born of the wretched and desecrated angels, tended and cared for by the harpies. She pictured the babies that had hatched out of them, how human they'd looked, how they'd followed her around.

Imprinted, said Jibra'il with immense shame. *They are children seeking to be whole, seeking to understand themselves. You were the human closest to their primal urges of hunger.*

I can free them, spoke Susan, and her memories pushed to the surface: Her discovery of electricity, how it reconstituted her being. How she'd managed to possess a wretched angel and found that it had laid eggs. And how she was able to use her newfound ability on the eggs, transforming them into light.

Jibra'il's shock rippled through Jenny's body, but Susan was already getting to work. Electricity hummed through Jenny, streaking out around her, flashing every which way. It scorched the harpies below, the stinging scent of burning feathers coming up to her nose. It struck the eggs and bounced between them, everything growing brighter and brighter until, with a blink, everything went dark.

Then, one by one, the eggs bloomed to life, glowing softly in various colors. They popped off the ceiling and floated midair.

Jenny landed, her feet careful to avoid stepping on one of the rotting harpies. She looked up at the eggs, now fully angel eggs. She thought about the ones she'd seen lined up and collected inside Leviathan. She thought about the core angels had, how she'd cut one open and swallowed the insides. Jibra'il acknowledge that's what the eggs were. That's what his egg was; the one Rafa'el had sent him and he'd completed. It would grow into a new being with time.

With her tentacles, she gathered them in the air, several hundred of them. *Give them to me. I will carry them out of here*, said Jibra'il.

Jenny showed him the memories of Leviathan. Of Sat'en. Of how they had tended to all the eggs.

The children are still alive? He sounded incredulous. A tear slid down Jenny's left cheek, and she could feel several lifetimes' worth of sorrow and happiness. There had been a purge; countless millions of angel eggs destroyed; generations of children who would never feel the light beneath their wings. Jibra'il and Rafa'el, as well as every other angel pairing, had been forbidden from having children—it was Adonai's decree. There were too many angels; more would only lead to rebellion, would lead to losing control, and would risk devastating their Great Plan.

And what is this "Great Plan"? demanded Jenny, realizing that Jibra'il was guarding a large portion of his mind even though he had so much access to her own.

It is not something you can bear right now, he said.

She was shaking, but now that he was within her mind, she could sense the intention behind his words. Could sense that what he said was true: her mind was too young, too fragile, too human. What was to come would have to come. She would have to see it for herself. But he knew *something*. He knew her name. Knew what Rafa'el had mentioned of her.

Nothing is determined, he said. *Rafa'el could not see past the birth of Adonai. Could not see past your name. And I wonder now . . .*

She wanted to press him, but instead, she felt the wave of his change. Felt how he questioned his position. He had always acted out of fear and subservience rather than conscious thought. Receiving his egg, his child, from Rafa'el, their lights merging to complete the egg, had shifted everything: His understanding of existence. His role in what's to come. He'd been questioning his purpose for a while, but now, he felt a new purpose— to protect his child. To protect the eggs that Susan had just transformed back into light.

Jenny could agree with that.

Inhaling, she drew all the floating eggs to her, taking them into her body, feeling them merge with the angel inside her. Housing light with his own light.

But their moment of peace ended with an abrupt crash. The entire palace shook, and she knew Azra'il had made it to the palace even before he roared. His voice echoed all around.

"I WILL DRAG YOU TO ADONAI'S FEET MYSELF, BROTHER!"

Go! shouted Susan, and Jenny flapped her wings toward the exit on the opposite side of the room. The tunnel blurred around her, and she thought again of Iblis and how they'd infiltrated this castle before, how they'd found a beautiful, lush forest of green, each tree ornamented with the cocoons of desecrated angels, harpies tending to them.

But when she emerged this time, all that greenery was gone, replaced instead by dried-up, shriveled brown. The trees were naked and dead, the river dried up. All the desecrated angels were gone.

Jibra'il answered her questions. Delivered to the material world by Azra'il. Fed to Adonai to fuel his power.

"Fuck," whispered Jenny, flapping over the dead forest. There wasn't a single angel in sight. No notifications flitted through her head, but she did see torn-open cocoons hanging from empty brown branches. The river she'd used to generate steam to hide from the harpies was completely dried up; all that was left was a trail of dark brown soil winding through the dead forest.

Is the castle dying? asked Susan.

Set it on fire, said Jibra'il.

Jenny didn't need to be told twice.

CHAPTER FORTY

BACK TO THE THRONE ROOM

Roaring, feeling like a demented silver dragon with her wings and tentacles, Jenny exhaled a steady stream of flame, igniting several trees in a row as she flew toward the next exit, wondering what she would find in the throne room above if the castle was dying.

Azra'il's roar echoed from the room below; he'd be coming up here soon enough. Jenny flapped her wings fiercely, sending off enormous gales that spread the fire from dead tree to dead tree, and by the time she reached the opposite entranceway, above the wall of stone she'd climbed painstakingly the last time she was here, the entire forest was ablaze. A sea of orange and red with hints of blue, burning and festering beneath her as she swooped into the next tunnel, following the arch that led upward into the throne room.

Her heart was beating wildly with excitement and dread. Jibra'il seemed adamant that the throne was holding this world together and had kept the souls trapped. The river of blood, the labyrinth, everything would crumble away. She wondered what the world was like before the angels interfered, and there was a faint memory of a world of water. Of souls waking up on the surface, floating, before rising into the sky to seek their deaths.

We can ask questions later! said Susan. Jenny's wings flapped with even greater force, tentacles trailing behind her, bouncing around in the tunnel. She was sure that Susan had done that, fueling their speed with more desperation, not caring what they crashed into. But she didn't mind; she could feel Susan's hatred of Azra'il, her fear. Susan did *not* want to be stuck in a tight space with him. Did not want to have to fight him here. Like a silver bullet, Jenny shot up the tunnel and emerged into the throne room.

Azra'il had redecorated. The pillars were broken, sections of the roof collapsed. Rubble covered the once lavish place, but the throne sat untouched on its raised platform. Jenny flew right to it, her eyes taking in its glassy black form, that strange shine. But just as she touched down, ready to grab the throne, she saw something moving underneath the rubble.

No, it was *someone*. At first, Jenny thought it was a wretched angel, but then, she recognized who it was. Covered in a white exoskeleton, caked in dust, with two strange handlike wings stretching out of her back.

It can't be, whispered Susan.

Soul (Blooded)

It was Miriam. She coughed and looked up, blinking with teary eyes at Jenny. "It's you again," she said. Blood ran down her chin, and she shuddered. Her leg was twisted in an impossible way. Her arms were cracked and broken; she looked like a mistreated doll, something long since forgotten. Why wasn't she healing? And why was she alone up here?

The palace shook and rumbled as Azra'il roared below; he must've just arrived at the flames. They had no time.

"What happened to you?" whispered Jenny.

"I kept fighting," said Miriam, lowering her head and squeezing her good hand into a fist. "Kept resisting him. So he punished me. I had to be punished."

Jenny wanted to help the poor girl, to ask about everything—how she got her exoskeleton back, how she'd been fighting—but there was no time. She climbed up the cracked steps to the throne, ready to use Severed Spirit, ready to channel all her rage into freeing this world. Before she could put her hands on the black stone, something grabbed her by the tentacle and yanked.

"Don't touch it!" shouted Miriam, desperation in her voice. One of her wings had grabbed Jenny's tentacle, its sickly fingerlike bones wrapped tightly. "He hates it when we touch it."

Whipping around, flapping her wings fiercely to get away, Jenny stared at the broken girl.

Get rid of her quickly! came Jibra'il's voice.

It's too late, sobbed Susan.

That feeling of disgust roiled through her. Dread and dismay. Jenny looked up to see Azra'il emerging from the hole that led to the forest below. Smoke swirled around his four wings, the snakes covering his body swishing and hissing. The only thing visible on his face were his burning red eyes.

Miriam shrieked and threw herself onto the rubble below, dropping to all fours and pressing her forehead to the floor. Jenny stood her ground, tentacles at the ready, her hatchet back in her hand.

The girl's soul has been tarnished, said Jibra'il. *Azra'il takes great pleasure in ruining souls.*

He tried to do that to me, added Susan with a shiver. *I almost forgot about my life. Forgot about you, Jenny. My parents. Everything.*

"Miriam . . ." whispered Jenny, trying to get the girl's attention.

"Interloper," said Azra'il in a very low voice. His muscles bulged, the snakes around his arms wiggled ferociously, and then, he snapped forward, just as he had in the room where he'd held Susan hostage, just as Mika'el had when fighting Jenny in Eve's world. But this time, this time, Jenny saw everything in perfect detail.

How Azra'il moved through the air, vibrating like a mirage, his wings flapping so quickly they were a blur. She sidestepped the giant, letting him rush past her like a freight train as he roared and crashed through a wall, toppling the ceiling.

Jenny flew straight to the throne, placing her hand on the seat, summoning all her new strength, all of Jibra'il's and Susan's strength, to focus on the one skill: Severed Spirit.

But again, something barreled into her from behind; Miriam leaped onto her back, pulling and yanking on her tentacles, beating Jenny's wings with her fists despite Miriam's own white exoskeleton and flesh cracking and splintering away.

"Get off me!" shouted Jenny, anger burning in her voice at Miriam's feeble attacks. She whirled around and threw the girl off. Then, with Savage Throw, launched her hatchet at Miriam's head. She wouldn't die, after all.

An enormous dark hand snatched the hatchet from midair, just before it connected, and Azra'il glowered. "You think you can hurt one of my own?"

"She's not one of your own," hissed Jenny, summoning her hatchet back.

"Ah yes, I remember your tricks with the hatchet," he said. "And do not worry, girl. You'll belong to me soon enough. Once I've scorched my brother from your bones!" With a roar, he thundered toward her, swiping to grab her.

Jenny rolled beneath his beefy arm, slashing his thick, snake-covered legs with her hatchet to emerge behind him. "Miriam!" she snapped quickly, breathless. "I can take you away from him. Please. Don't you remember? You were *helping* me!"

"You left me!" screamed Miriam, snot running down her white-covered lips, her eyes manic.

Jenny jumped away to avoid Azra'il's next punch. His gigantic fist connected with the floor right beside Miriam, sending the poor girl rolling and clattering away into the rubble.

The enormous angel swiped again, knocking away a marble pillar, and then another one of his oversize snakes darted out from his chest. She turned to dodge, but there wasn't enough space in his palace to fly around. Fangs sank into Jenny's shoulder, and she screamed as two sharp points broke through her new exoskeleton and buried themselves in her flesh.

But pain didn't matter to her. She would heal. The thing inside her, the thing Azra'il had put in her body all that time ago, wriggled up to the wounds. She almost laughed in his face, ready to mock him, but instead of patching her back together, it shuddered inside her chest. Then she felt the snake *sucking*, slurping on her blood, on her insides, and she screamed. She tried to pull the snake off; she felt like it was draining her body completely dry.

"No more of this," hissed Azra'il, grabbing her by the torso. She cried out as he squeezed, as her exoskeleton cracked. And all the while, his serpent continued sucking.

She felt something round and bulbous squish up her chest and into her shoulder. She felt it move toward the fangs, and Jenny couldn't make a sound as the snake sucked out whatever Azra'il had given to her before. The thing that had been healing her all this time without fail. The thing that wouldn't let her die no matter how much she begged.

Pain burned through her shoulder, radiating through the rest of her body, and no matter how hard she beat her wings or thrashed the angel with her tentacles, Azra'il held on. Something surged up the snake, back into his chest—a glowing bit of red light that went up his throat—and the angel opened his mouth to release a bubble of red light.

Smoky darkness bounced between the redness inside the orb, and Jenny recoiled, her body feeling shriveled and weak in Azra'il's grip, his fingers threatening to snap her in half. It was an egg.

Azra'il had inserted his egg inside Jenny, the same way Rafa'el had offered her egg to Jibra'il. The light of a bonding pair, culminating in new life. Jibra'il's disgust and anger filled her chest, but it was Susan's rage which boiled up through her.

Electricity burst out of every inch of Jenny, snapping from her wings, from her head to the tops of her fingers, from her belly. Jibra'il joined the efforts, wind swirling all around, picking up the rubble, flinging everything at Azra'il, who released her as his hand cracked open, his fingers coming apart like an old statue from the release of energy.

The enormous angel roared as his arm collapsed, but the serpent still had its fangs buried in Jenny's shoulder. She was still connected to the angel as she clattered to the floor.

That's just fine, thought Jenny with a cold rage. It meant he wouldn't be able to dodge as easily.

With a flap of her wings and silver light, she summoned her hatchet back and jumped right into Azra'il's face with Instant Acceleration, the snake connecting them like a demented umbilical cord. She buried the hatchet in his forehead, Jibra'il's storm power surging into the attack to give it all the force it needed.

Azra'il stumbled back, gasping for breath, his red eyes blinking on either side of the hatchet sticking out of his skull. He reached for Jenny with his remaining arm; the other one was already healing, but the snake had gone limp.

Twisting her body away, Jenny ripped the snake out of her shoulder, swearing as blood sprayed out from the twin wounds. Leaving the hatchet buried between his gleaming eyes, she flew up and grabbed its handle.

"Bro . . . ther?" he croaked, a look of confusion and fear on his face as blood ran down the two sides of his nose, the smaller snakes of his body hissing all over.

Jenny used Savage Throw with a burst of Ignite, sending her burning hatchet spinning and cutting straight down the center of the oversize angel.

CHAPTER FORTY-ONE

SEVERING

A mangled scream drowned in Azra'il's throat as the hatchet cut the enormous angel in half. She remained in the air, her wings beating, her hatchet glistening on the floor below as the two pieces of Azra'il's body melted to the sides, oozing like molten lava. She didn't give him a second glance as he raged, serpents struggling to emerge from the molten mess to snap at her. Like hell was she going to let him catch her again.

A part of her wanted to dig through his body before he recovered, find his core, and smash it with her teeth, but Jibra'il warned that could take forever when it came to the archangels—they had a more integrated core, a more advanced light—so she resolved to get to the throne.

Her tentacles slapped away the molten serpents trying to catch her. They splattered the walls and the rubble but left burns along her tentacles all the way up to her spine. She couldn't afford to get hurt now, now that the *thing* inside her wouldn't be healing her right away. She couldn't even afford being grossed out; it was his *egg*.

His fucking egg. He'd put his goddamn egg inside her.

What about consent? What about—

I'm sorry, Jenny, but . . . came Susan's voice.

Jibra'il finished her thought. *We have to get to the throne. Then we can open a passageway and leave this place. My brother will pay for his actions.*

Shaking with rage, Jenny summoned another forceful storm wind with her wings, her head bumping against the ceiling above. She sucked in a deep breath, drawing on Jibra'il's power again, and when she exhaled, her breath turned into vapor. Electricity traveled up her throat, and the vapor bloomed into rolling dark clouds.

Jibra'il must've realized what she was trying to do, as his powers flowed through her with renewed strength. The dark clouds spread all throughout the palace ceiling. With several claps of thunder, it began to pour, a powerful rain, each droplet filled with her rage and Jibra'il's powers. It snuffed out the flames of Azra'il's and Jenny's attacks, steam rising with a hiss from Azra'il's ruined body.

He was gurgling, screaming, the menacing anger so palpable the entire palace shook. But Jenny was brimming with just as much rage. She flapped her soaked wings, her hair sticking to her face, and flew toward the throne. Only to find Miriam standing in front of it, her arms and her handlike wings outstretched, blocking Jenny's way.

"*Stop!*" sobbed Miriam, green energy flickering around her fingers and eyes. Like she was trying and failing to use her powers.

You will have to strike her down, said Jibra'il. *Before she attacks you.*

She can't damage us when we're this powerful, came Susan's voice. *Just . . . throw her out of the way. She won't die.*

Jenny's memories flashed; she could feel the two of them watching. How she'd lost control, how she'd rampaged through the high school, how she'd eaten Miriam alive even as the poor girl begged for forgiveness. How she'd run into Miriam in this world before, the two of them working together.

"Miriam," said Jenny, choking up as the rain fell around them. She landed in front of the girl, looking right into her tear-stricken eyes. "You have to move. I have to stop this."

The girl sniffled, her white exoskeleton shining now that the water was washing away the dirt and dried blood. "I'm safe here. This is okay. I'm finally where I want to be."

Anger roared to life, and even with Susan trying to temper her, Jenny couldn't help but shout, "*HOW ARE YOU SAFE HERE?*"

Miriam flinched. Her handlike wings folded, and she hugged herself. "I'm the only one left. Look around. The other pets are gone. It's just me. They weren't good enough. I'm . . ."

The pets . . . The princes and princesses that Azra'il had kept. Jenny remembered running into them, how childlike they all were, how empty they were. Susan had hated them; they'd mocked her and resented her. And they must've felt the same about Miriam.

Before she knew it, even as Miriam charged green light in her mouth, Jenny closed the distance between the two of them. The girl looked back, her eyes wide, hesitant. The two of them were so different from the girls they'd once been. Jenny now had three minds inside her head, was covered in a silver metallic layer, and had wings and tentacles with eyes all over her body. Miriam was covered in a white exoskeleton, as white as bone, and had grotesque wings that looked like cruel hands.

Thunder clapped overhead. She could see through her many eyes that Azra'il was struggling to regain form, but she didn't care. She pulled Miriam into a tight hug, wrapping her arms around the other girl.

"What are you?" whispered the girl, trembling. Then the trembling became a violent shaking and sobbing, and Jenny wasn't sure if it was her or Susan or Miriam herself, but the girl's exoskeleton melted away, leaving behind a glowing silhouette, her soul, and then Miriam was inside Jenny too. She tucked herself away in a quiet corner of Jenny's mind.

More strength flowed into Jenny's body. More power. And with a shudder, she accepted that Miriam had become a part of her.

Jenny leaped over rubble and landed in front of the throne, looking down at the ancient rock, thinking about what Iblis had once said.

It belonged to the demons, explained Jibra'il. *It was cut from their world.*

It looks like the pillars, said Jenny.

Deaths and demons are of the same source. Angels and souls are of the same source. Humans are the culmination of both. Jibra'il pushed forward the idea as Jenny placed her hand on the throne, as her exoskeleton folded back and away to reveal her shaking hand. The glassy rock felt cold to the touch, and she shut all her eyes to concentrate.

She needed to sever it. Needed enough pain. Needed something more. She pushed her mind, her many minds, into the throne, and felt the great expanse of the world. Everything from the river of blood to the journey through the forest to the giant scales that weighed every soul that passed their way.

The scales were placed there by my brother. A mockery. There is no judgment. Prepubescents are sent in one direction. Everyone else to the labyrinth.

But why? asked Susan.

Miriam didn't say a word.

Children cannot produce energy, said Jibra'il with shame. *So their souls are allowed to pass on, fading away from existence.*

What the fuck? Jenny searched, pushing the vast power of her minds through the throne, through the world, piercing through every horrible thing in this place. How many children had come here to vanish? At least they'd been spared the nightmares. The torture. At least they wouldn't have suffered. But what did it mean to fade from existence?

They never reunited with their deaths, explained Jibra'il. *They simply ceased to be.*

Behind her, Azra'il was roaring back to power, nearly whole. She was shaking. Or rather, it was Miriam who was shaking through her body. Jenny focused on Miriam's mind, on all the pain she'd gone through, everything that Jenny knew about her. The struggles in school. The struggles at home. The constant pressure. And how Azra'il had triggered every single one of them.

She saw Miriam in a fit of rage after Azra'il had torn her apart for the thousandth time, laughing and tormenting her, blaming her for helping Jenny, for allowing Susan to get away.

Even though it wasn't her fault. Even though none of it was her fault.

Nearly recovered, Azra'il swooped toward Jenny, screaming. But it was too late. Jenny had felt it—the fissure of the world; the one great crack. The lie that this was the afterlife. The suffering every soul had endured, all at the hands of Azra'il, who'd taken such great pleasure in orchestrating everything.

Snakes hissed all around Jenny as Azra'il closed in, inches from grabbing her. Jenny felt every mind in her body snap forward, almost as though they were being forced out of the body and then thrown back in. And the last thing she heard was Azra'il's furious bellowing as the throne cracked open and light gushed into the world.

The light washed over Jenny, washed over Azra'il, suspending them in air as though it was all liquid. Bubbles streaming out of her mouth, she turned to see Azra'il floating in defeat, his arms bobbing beside him as he stared above at something else.

Jenny did the same, swishing about in the light, and her blood ran cold when she saw what had made Azra'il lose the will to fight. Jibra'il responded with utter shock. Susan and Miriam were the same. Horror, hitting a hundred times worse as every single one of them felt it in the same body, slammed through Jenny so hard she forgot how to breathe—forgot how to be.

A boy floated above them, looking down with his arms crossed. He was a skinny little thing, with thin arms and legs, and he was dressed in a white and golden tunic. A white sash held it in place around his waist. His hair, wavy and swaying in the water, was white and golden as well, and as he sank toward them, his lips twisted into a smile.

She didn't need Jibra'il to know who the boy was, but the immense desire to bow down, to press her knees and forehead to the floor—just as Miriam had done for Azra'il, just as Azra'il was doing right now, suspended in the light—told her everything. She thought she was going to throw up. The minds in her body struggled to escape, to run, to flee, yet she remained where she was, frozen in place, trembling.

The boy waved his hand, and all the light gathered into a rushing river that slammed into Jenny and Azra'il, sweeping them back to crash against the ruined wall of the throne room. He touched down on the rubble as everything faded, barefooted and looking around with his eyebrows slightly raised, like he was a little kid on a boring field trip.

He looked like he was about to shout, about to destroy everything around them, but instead, he clutched his stomach and doubled over, his face turning red. He looked like he was trying to hold something back, but then, he let out a manic, childish laughter that echoed throughout the ruined space.

With a flash of light, he transformed into a towering woman, standing tall, with long white-and-golden hair streaming down her shoulders, her foot planted firmly on Azra'il's enormous head. She turned her cold golden gaze on Jenny, her voice cutting like a thin sheet of ice.

"What are you doing in that material body, Jibra'il?"

CHAPTER FORTY-TWO

HIS ARRIVAL

Adonai," came Jibra'il's voice from Jenny's throat. For a second, she thought Jibra'il would leave her body and kneel as well, bow down before him; she could feel the countless, countless centuries worth of time he'd spent devoted to this thing . . . so much time that it was nonsensical to Jenny, even with Susan and Miriam's lifetimes inside her. Their lives combined were nothing compared to how much time the angel had spent with the creature staring them down.

There was another flash of light, and Adonai changed again, this time to a large, hulking man, bronze skinned with bulging muscles. The only thing that stayed the same through his transformations was his shining hair; even the hairs on his eyebrows, his beard, his arms had the same glow. The tunic remained the same as well, golden and white cloth.

Jenny's hundred eyes blinked back at Adonai. He was supposed to be *Him,* wasn't he? God? The thing in all the holy books. The thing that supposedly guided humanity? The thing she was supposed to pray to all her life? The thing that would make her furious. How could he let her suffer so much if he was supposed to be love? Why would he let so many people suffer so much? How could he create them and leave them to such anguish? She'd always imagined herself shouting at him, cursing him out. But now that he stood in front of her, she didn't know what to say.

"Jenny Huang," he spoke. There was another flash of light, and he changed again; this time into another man. Instead of golden hair, it was dark. He had dark eyes as well, pale skin. He stood tall and proud before Jenny blinked and the hair was white again, but she knew who Adonai had turned into without ever having seen a photo of the man. Her biological father.

"Come to me, my child," said Adonai, his voice thick and sweet. "You will never have to hurt again. I have heard all your prayers. I know the deepest desires of your heart. You can have it all within me."

He has assimilated the material world, said Jibra'il. *Every being, every atom, every speck of dust is now a part of him. But he isn't complete. Not yet whole. He's come searching to see why the rest of existence has not become a part of him.*

What do you mean? whispered Susan. She sounded so small, like a faint echo from a distant corner of Jenny's head. *There's no world anymore?*

This is what they promised, said Miriam. *That we would be safe with them.*

"But who the fuck are you to promise that?" hissed Jenny through gritted teeth.

Adonai's face, her father's face, twisted into a shining snarl. Then there was another flash of light, and he turned into a little girl with two golden braids. "I am *EVERYTHING*," she screamed, twisting her foot and smashing Azra'il's whimpering face into the ground.

Defeated Angel (Stage VI - Level 332)

Jibra'il's sadness panged like an echo at the loss of his brother while Adonai took a menacing step forward, changing again, light melting through the little girl's body as she turned into an older woman. "Curious world we have come to. All my missing pieces gathering to wage war over my Trumpet."

"**You will *not* touch Rafa'el**," snapped Jibra'il through Jenny.

"What do you mean by 'world we've come to'?" asked Jenny. All she'd done was sever the world of souls. Shouldn't they still be there?

Adonai, still in the form of a woman, waved her arm, fingers seemingly grabbing something in the air before yanking into a fist. Chunks of the palace came crumbling away, crashing toward Jenny to reveal the sky beyond, the world beyond. With a cold, sick feeling, Jenny realized they'd brought the palace to Eve's world, where the angels had stopped fighting and hovered in the air; where all the souls rained down like a slow-moving meteor shower.

If Adonai got his hands on Rafa'el . . . what's gonna happen? she screamed silently at Jibra'il. Susan and Miriam whisked about, unable to tolerate Jibra'il's distress.

The angel shook. *Everything would end. The seven worlds would collapse*, he said. *They'd collapse, and there'd be nothing other than him. He would be all the worlds and everything that exists thereof.*

Adonai, light melting, turning into someone else, walked over to the edge of the palace, staring down at the world below. He'd become a young man.

He didn't seem concerned at all by Jenny; she wasn't a threat to him. Azra'il's corpse had evaporated away; he'd been nothing at all.

But beyond the boy in a tunic, she could see the dark sky of Eve's world, could see all the angels who'd risen up in worship.

He means to make them all a part of him. The angels. The souls. The remaining humans; all the powerful ones collected by the Antithesis. And of course, the Antithesis itself.

But then what? asked Susan. *After he takes all that, and he's everything. Then what?*

Then we are all at eternal peace, said Jibra'il with a note of resignation.

Golden light flashed. There was a visage of pink and red, and Eve appeared hovering in front of the palace, brandishing two new swords of light. Susan gasped as the knowledge of Eve's birth spread between them.

"Ah, yes," said Adonai in a deep, booming voice. He melted again into a woman, her voice changing to a sweet, melodic tone. "The one who swore to defy my plan."

Eve didn't speak. She didn't hesitate. With a scream, she flapped her golden wings and rocketed into Adonai, the two of them clashing in an explosion of light and debris.

Before Jenny or the others could think, the palace shook and crumbled. Light burst all around her, and she flew upward, crashing through the ceiling. The palace was falling out of the sky.

Flapping her wings and destroying rubble overhead with her swirling tentacles, Jenny rose higher and higher, struggling to breathe. Her mind was spinning with everyone's thoughts and fears, especially Jibra'il's. Below her, inside the crumbling palace plummeting toward the ground, she could see Adonai and Eve fighting, throwing themselves from one corner of the disintegrating palace to the other.

The Antithesis isn't powerful enough, said Jibra'il, panic in his voice.

Rafa'el is the one he's looking for, right? asked Susan. *So we can't let him get to her.*

All around her shimmered more angels in every color of the rainbow. They weren't moving. Their weapons were gone; their arms had dropped to their sides. They hung in the air as though they'd been placed there. And between them were the souls, falling out of the sky, screaming silently, leaving a trail of light as they hurtled to the ground.

"He's not just after Rafa'el, is he? He wants everyone who's in this world," said Jenny. "And what about . . ." The world of death, the world of demons, flashed through her thoughts, and she felt the others worrying as well. Sat'en and Leviathan and all the angel children and eggs. The demons . . .

"We need the demons on our side," whispered Jenny. "I can convince them to fight with us."

They will have to, agreed Jibra'il. *If Adonai finds Rafa'el, their world is forfeit as well.*

And the deaths? whispered Susan. There was a strange tremor in her thoughts, and Jenny recognized it as her own fear from when she'd seen the pillars that first time.

Adonai means to consume them all, said Jibra'il. *There will be no more deaths once he is complete.*

Red lightning ignited far below as the palace crashed into the ground. The world that had stood still, frozen almost, roared back to life, the angels flying rapidly through the air like a swarm of insects on a hot summer evening. And the people below, all the warriors that Eve had collected, threw themselves back into the fray.

Through her new eyes, Jenny could see Adonai and Eve going at it. Adonai was now in the form of a young child, swiping away Eve's swords with his fingers. Yeshua had appeared, bleeding all over. His fists crackled with red lightning as he jumped in to attack.

But each impact only rippled Adonai's form, making him transform. Sparks gathered around him as he stretched out his arms. Then, all at once, he launched both Eve and Yeshua away and melted again, shooting upward. He'd become a beam of liquid light, shooting all the way up into the sky to stop right in front of Jenny. Bricks appeared all throughout the light, and then something extended forward, a glowing tendril leaning to come up to Jenny's face.

She flapped her wings and flew back and away, but the light stretched and elongated to follow her. It was cooling down, taking the shape of a little girl. "Aw . . . don't run away. I only want to ask you a question."

Behind the girl was a tower, beaming up into the sky, more enormous than Azra'il's palace had been, larger than all the skyscrapers in New York put together.

A hand wrapped around Jenny's ankle despite her speed, despite her desperate flapping. The tower burst open, and enormous chunks of stone rained down on the world as Adonai's weight increased a thousandfold.

Jenny found herself plummeting with the debris, with the world screaming around her, as Adonai dragged her down.

CHAPTER FORTY-THREE

ERUPTION

She slammed into the ground with a thwack, feeling the exoskeleton covering her face and arms and chest *crack*. Her head struck a chunk of rubble that might've come from the castle, from the enormous pillar Adonai had turned into, or from the battle that had been waging.

"*Where is my Trumpet?*" hissed Adonai, leaping onto Jenny's back and grabbing her wings. He was a little boy again, face red with rage, straining as he tore out her feathers one fistful at a time, as his fingers scraped through her exoskeleton and dug away flesh.

All the eyes that covered her shoulders and back were crying. Several ruptured and leaked as he dug them out, but everything was still spinning from the hurtle from the sky, from the impact with the ground. Her mind was all over the place, the pain clouding every thought. She almost forgot who she was, who owned the body, and if it weren't for Miriam seizing control, for green light erupting from her mouth and blasting her away from the ground, she didn't know what might've happened.

Adonai released his grip on her wings as smoke and flame enveloped the two of them, and Jenny whirled away, tears streaming from each of her eyes as her exoskeleton struggled to recover. She almost wished she had Azra'il's egg inside her again—something to keep her alive; anything that might help against this unstoppable force.

Trying to catch her breath, she drew on Jibra'il's storm power again, letting the winds curl around her as Adonai emerged from the explosion. Green smoke whisked around him; he was a man again, large and tall, but instead of flesh, his body seemed to be made of dark melted rocks.

Golden eyes gleaming, golden hair flowing, the top of his body glowed red hot, and it was Susan who recognized what he was turning into: a *volcano.*

From the corner of her eyes, she saw Eve flying toward them, so Jenny turned midair. With a blast of air, she collided with Eve, knocking her away, ignoring the look of shock and aghast on Eve's face as the two of them rocketed away from Adonai, who *erupted.*

Lava plumed out of his head as his body expanded. Jenny held on to Eve and flew, her wings flapping vigorously as she tried to put as much distance as possible between them and Adonai.

But suddenly, behind her, ballooning faster than Jenny could fly, another enormous structure swallowed up the landscape: an actual massive volcano. Its summit seemed to stick out of the world, and rocks crashed into Jenny and Eve, sending them tumbling down the still-expanding side before they saw the lava shooting out of the top. The sound was like a million explosions all at once, the cloud of ash and darkness spreading to cover the world. Molten chunks seared through the air and exploded where they landed around them.

How do we stop him? screamed Jenny silently as she choked on the fumes and smoke.

Jibra'il took control of her body, grabbing Eve. "**Help me with this.**" Before Jenny or Eve or anyone could question what was happening, Jenny's arms had grabbed the wind, channeling the power of the silver angel, and yanked hard on the sky.

A storm broke out, and it began to rain. Eve seemed to understand what to do. She flew into the sky, her golden swords flashing every which way as she spun in figure eights, destroying the cooled-down chunks of lava still hurtling toward the ground.

Angels fluttered through the chaos, and humans rose up to meet them. They dodged the small chunks, rocks bouncing off their armor as they faced the angels. Light ignited. Screams echoed all over, and as Jenny looked around for Oliver, for her mother, for Yeshua, for anyone, the volcano shimmered brightly with golden light and collapsed onto itself.

Smoke and steam swirling all around, Adonai appeared again, hovering midair. Rain hissed as it struck his new form: an angel with countless wings fluttering out of his back, a shining halo over his head, and muscles bulging against his tunic. Golden hair swayed in the wind, and he was glowering. Jenny, as well as all the other minds inside her body, could feel the rage reverberating through the air, almost as though his anger was a physical thing.

Fire erupted from her wings, orange flickering before catching and turning blue with heat. Green light blossomed in her left hand, and electricity crackled through her right arm she summoned her hatchet back, golden light flashing. Then, with Jibra'il's storm powers bolstering her speed, she kicked off the ground, flapped her wings once, and activated Instant Acceleration, jetting toward the hovering, golden Adonai. She was going to hit him with everything they had.

They collided with explosive force, almost as though the volcano had erupted again. Her hatchet cut through one of his wings. Golden light evaporated away. Adonai threw a punch, but Jenny wrapped her tentacles around his arm and diverted the attack, slamming Miriam's glowing green orb into his chest.

But even with that explosion, even as it destroyed his tunic and burned away a section of his chest, Adonai didn't flinch. Golden light stretched like string through his wound, and he was healed before Jenny could strike again.

Her hatchet nicked him on the side of his face. There was no flash of light; he must not have felt any pain at all. But Adonai stared back, a bored expression in his golden eyes as the hatchet's sharp edge cut deep into his skull.

"Do you not tire of this, Jenny Huang?" he asked. He shut his eyes for a moment, light shifting through him, and when he opened them, he was her father again. The father she'd never met, whose face she'd never seen but couldn't help but recognize. Her jaw. Her nose. Even the distance between the eyes was the same as hers. "You've longed to be whole your entire life, have you not? To have a normal family. To be loved by two parents. To feel safe?"

Jenny tried to yank the hatchet out of her father's face, but it was no use. Even with her tentacles wrapped around one of Adonai's arms, *she* was the one who felt trapped in his vise grip. Where was Eve? Yeshua?

"And you," continued Adonai, changing again. This time, he appeared with long brown hair, a certain sternness on a freckled face, and a sharp nose. It was Susan's mom. "Didn't you, Susan Brown, want me to stay? Want me to hold you in the evenings for longer than a moment? Want me to read you bedtime stories? I could give you everything and more."

Susan shriveled inside Jenny. The memories of waiting in bed, blanket put aside, hoping someone would come and tuck her in. But it was always a meeting in the morning, or something important had come up, or another excuse. There was never enough time for her.

A tear slipped past one of Jenny's eyes somewhere on her back.

"And ah, my dear, dear Miriam," he said. His face changed again, brown hair sprouting from his cheeks as his eyes turned dark. His stomach rounded out, and it was Miriam's father staring forlorn. "Why don't you come home to Baba? They miss you so much. You can be whomever you want. You don't have to do what they want anymore. They will accept you now."

Every single one of her eyes were blurring with tears. She was shaking. Susan and Miriam's minds couldn't help but respond to Adonai's words, his promises. It was just a lure, they knew it, but they couldn't help but wish for those things.

Jenny tried again to break away from his grip, to pull away, but he transformed again, turning into golden-and-white light, formless but with his multiple wings still beating in turn behind him. An eye appeared in the midst of the light, the pupil made from darkness—the same darkness the angels had fallen through, that Jenny had fallen through—and Adonai leaned in so close she felt the moistness of his darkness against the tip of her nose.

"Jibra'il . . ." said a dripping, ugly voice. "Your beloved has accepted her place in existence. She is ready to finish the work dutifully. Why do you resist now after having worked so diligently? What do you hope to achieve?"

Silver light shone brightly, but he didn't have an answer. She could feel the turmoil. Could feel his pain. How a part of him wanted to bow and let all this end. He could take Adonai to Rafa'el right away—he'd seen Jenny's memories; he had the egg. What more could he hope to do?

Sorrow and regret and uncertainty expanded through her like storm clouds; her breath grew heavy. She wanted to fall away. She wanted to lie down. She wanted to go to sleep. What use was there in fighting?

Why not give in? Why not succumb? If she joined Adonai, everything would be whole. They'd all have what they'd always wanted: To never hurt again. To never feel alone again. No more misery. No more pain. All the love they ever needed.

Why not?

"Why do you choose suffering? Why must the violence wage on? The material world is mine.

"I am ascending.

"Join me.

"Join me in eternal perfection."

What would that look like? All of them wondered the same thing in unison. Would they still have their bodies? Would they still go to school and grow old and fall in love and have children?

Or would there be no point to any of that. There'd be no point in trying anything new. There'd never be any reason to be sad.

They might as well not exist.

I'd rather exist, she thought, and the rest of them agreed.

I want to exist with everyone else, said Susan. *I want to make mistakes. I want to be heartbroken. I want to be loved.*

I want to have more ice cream, whispered Miriam.

Adonai's dark eye blinked. His wings expanded all around him, and he raised his voice. "WELL?"

Jenny's hand shot out and touched the darkness. The iris rippled like she'd thrown a stone into a dark lake, and before she herself knew what she was doing, before any of the minds inside her could catch up, she used Valescent Light.

CHAPTER FORTY-FOUR

HOW DOES ONE HEAL PERFECTION?

The darkness rippled, Adonai's body convulsing and morphing into a sphere made out of jelly. Everything glistened and shone as the darkness turned golden, as lights and colors ignited throughout, and all his wings folded.

You did it! shouted Susan.

Is it over? asked Miriam.

But then, Jenny's fingers crumpled inward, each bone snapping apart, the flesh curling toward her palm as her hand melted away. She didn't get a moment to scream.

Countless arms, pasty white like the ghouls' had been, reached out of the light and grasped onto Jenny. Slender fingers with strength that she couldn't even comprehend cracked her exoskeleton wherever they grabbed her: her shoulders, her elbows, her hips, her knees, her ankles, her wings, her hair.

An ugly laugh bubbled from the eye. "How does one heal perfection?"

Another hand clamped around her mouth and squeezed so hard she felt teeth dislodge from her gums and cut into her tongue. Then every arm withdrew into the light, still squeezing her tight. He was trying to pull her inside.

Her tentacles lashed out, trying to squirm free of the hands that grasped them. Her wings tried to beat, but they cracked and shattered from the force of his grip.

And then, Jenny realized each hand, each arm, belonged to a person. People stared back at her from inside the light, their eyes wide with terror, their lips opening and moving. Not a sound escaped their throats. Their arms were no longer white and smooth like the ghouls', details appearing across them: Skin tones. Hairs. Bruises and cuts. And each face was pleading, begging; Jenny couldn't decipher whether they wanted her to save them or join them.

Muffled screams lodged inside her bleeding mouth. Jenny used Ignite, blue flames streaming out of her skin to singe all these arms, but all that did was make the people cry out and scream in pain.

She didn't stop. They were a part of him, weren't they? It had to be a trick. And even if it was real, what other choice did she have?

But even as she scorched their skin and burned their arms down to bones, the hands didn't falter—they only gripped her tighter, and now she could feel fingernails digging into her insides as they pulled her in even deeper. She was nearly completely submerged in Adonai's light; he'd taken her Valescent Light and transformed it into something else; he was . . .

And then, her exoskeleton snapped off, stretching forward like thick dough, coming off her as Jenny hurled backward, connected to Adonai's light by a stretchy, silvery goo. Jibra'il's mind emptied from her head like water through a drain, and she screamed, still feeling enough of the angel to feel his pain as Adonai clutched him.

Her wings disintegrating, her power flickering away, she didn't know what to do. She no longer had wings, but she held on, refusing to let go of the angel. Adonai would kill him. Obliterate him.

Endless hands clenched the angel's body, half light and half flesh from being shared with Jenny. She could see Jibra'il's thoughts rushing past: thoughts of regret, thoughts of hope, endless memories of flying through the human world, observing, jealous of their emotions and love, of their homes, jealous of how everyone simply lived their lives as they wanted to, a jealousy that Jenny knew all too well despite having been human her entire life.

"You can't have anyone else!" screamed Jenny, using Valescent Light again, trying to create a counterpull to Adonai's.

Red lightning flickered up from the ground, and Yeshua flew into the light, his hair and beard and purple robe billowing in the wind, his face dark with rage. With a glowing red-hot fist, he struck the spherical, melting mess of light and limbs that Adonai had become.

The sky blew apart.

The shock wave snapped Jibra'il back into Jenny, and they fell away, plummeting again, struggling to hold on to consciousness as a searing bright light expanded across the sky. It was a supernova.

She fell for what felt like ages but must've only been a few seconds, because a moment later, she crashed into the ground below, so hard that the impact threw rock and debris and corpses into the air, only for it to all rain back down on her.

Groaning, Jenny's mind whirled with everyone else's thoughts, with Jibra'il regaining composure. Valescent Light shone up and down her body, putting her broken bones and torn flesh back together, and resealing Jibra'il's exoskeleton to her skin. As she sat up, coughing up blood, her wings sprouted back into place, and her tentacles shivered back out, stretching into their elongated, thick shape.

Around her, the war still raged. Angels clashed with angels. Humans clashed with tarnished and wretched and desecrated angels. She could feel every drop of blood in the air, taste every scream and cry for help, hear every last shudder.

She saw golden wings shining as Eve flew up to the supernova in the sky where Yeshua and Adonai exchanged powerful blows, with bolts of red lightning and darkness splintering the air around them.

They are not powerful enough to stop him, said Jibra'il, his voice faint and weak.

Neither are we, added Susan. She kept picturing her mother. She was sure that she'd glimpsed her parents in the mess of people pulling on Jenny's body.

Jenny put her face in her hands, trying to steady herself, trying to get her heartbeat to slow down. She couldn't even tell why her heart was pounding so hard. Adrenaline? Shock? Fear? And if so, whose adrenaline? Whose shock? Whose fear? All of them were terrified, even Jibra'il.

Could they even run?

He has all the might of the material world itself, continued the angel. *Every being that existed. Every atom. Every star. Every planet. There is no returning to it, nothing left of it beyond him.*

"But he wants to blow the horn, right? Whatever Rafa'el has?"

What Rafa'el is, corrected Jibra'il. *The horn is held within her, is a part of her.*

So then . . . do we just go and . . . kill her? came Miriam's voice, quietly. Nervously.

Jibra'il's anguish at the thought made Jenny's body clench, tears streaming down one side of her face. Susan tried to comfort him, but nobody could completely reject the idea.

What happens if he gets Rafa'el? asked Susan. *What's she going to do?*

He brings forth the horn that destroys all of existence, he explained. *The catalyst that completes Adonai's transformation. He may be the entirety of the material world, but that's all right now. Raw material. But all that power, all that existence bundled up inside him will release once the horn blows. Nonmatter and matter will collide, leaving Adonai free to rebuild it all in whatever way he wants.*

"And he's angry that he couldn't have the three worlds I separated?" asked Jenny. An angel flicked toward her, but it must've sensed Jibra'il's presence because it looked away immediately and flew as fast as it could. She wondered if Oliver was all right. If he'd found their parents. If that even mattered in this hell.

He will have to take them one by one, consuming each world, cannibalizing them until they are a part of him. But he will begin with this one by eliminating the Antithesis.

And what does Rafa'el want? came Susan's voice.

For a long moment, there was silence. They could feel Jibra'il's memories, the hopelessness as his relationship with the other angel crumbled away, as Rafa'el chose duty over love. As Rafa'el submitted herself in complete subservience to Adonai, whom all the other angels were barred from seeing after the Failed One's birth. He'd lost her. Even though they'd spent endless time together, the time apart felt even longer. She'd chosen destiny over their love.

"I don't know," said Jibra'il, speaking through Jenny's throat as the eyes on her chest and shoulders wept.

What if we asked her? suggested Susan. She was trying to be kind. Trying to be understanding.

Why are you trying to stop this? asked Miriam, green energy flickering around Jenny. Her question was aimed at the angel. *I get that you changed your mind, but why?*

I . . .

Again, they could feel his emotions, his hurt and anguish and confusion. *I've always acted in benefit to existence. To ensure all beings would be happy.*

You call this happy? hissed Miriam. Her emotions flared to life, and they saw everything in the high school, everything with the angels trying to eat her and the others, everything Miriam had done as she gave into the horror. She'd betrayed her classmates and eaten kids who'd shown kindness to her. She'd torn apart the people who'd once mocked and teased her. And still, she showed the hurt of her life, how she'd never fit in anywhere, how sickly she'd always been. And how the survival challenge had transformed her from a little girl into a monster. *He is the ultimate monster, isn't he? God is the one who wants to devour everyone else. How is that "happy"?*

Shame emanated from the angel. *It was promised that His birth would bring an end to all suffering. To all questioning. I did not want to think anymore. I do not believe any creature wanted to truly think anymore. But I know now. What he wanted wasn't simply to house every being and give them shelter but to control. To shape in his image. To completely overwhelm so that there is no individuality left.*

So you have a kid and now you care? asked Miriam bitterly.

It was Susan who quieted things down. "**What does it matter why Jibra'il stands against him now?**" she said, speaking out loud through Jenny. "**We all get stuck thinking we're doing the right thing. Or too afraid to do what we think is right.**"

Jenny swallowed the lump in her throat. "And sometimes, we just don't act at all, despite . . ." Her cheeks turned red, as she knew all three of them could feel her feelings for Susan, the shame of her life, how badly she'd wanted to get away from everything. "What matters is that we're here now. Let's go find Rafa'el."

"That was precisely what I was going to say, brother," came a voice like an ugly bruise, and Mika'el shimmered into view in front of Jenny, webbed wings outstretched. Her hand came down as quick as a blur, but unlike last time, Jenny saw it coming.

Rage ignited in her chest as she remembered how the angel had split her down the middle. She stepped aside to dodge the slap. Her hatchet flashed into her hand and, fueled by the power of storms, crackling with electricity and green light, she slammed it straight into the larger angel's side.

Golden light flashed, and Jenny got a notification that was almost as delicious as the cry of pain on Mika'el's lips.

+6000 Energy

She could hurt the angel this time.

CHAPTER FORTY-FIVE

CONVERGING LIGHT

Jenny's satisfaction faded as quickly as it'd arrived. Mika'el's body flickered, blue-and-purple blood streaming out of the gash opened in her side, and the angel's other arm swung out from below, striking Jenny on the chin.

Pain rang through her skull as she was knocked back, but with a flap of her wings, Jenny stabilized before slamming all six of her exoskeleton-fortified tentacles into Mika'el's body, aiming for where her hatchet had hurt the angel.

Her tentacles struck Mika'el with enough force to send her rolling across the ground. Her long, slender form bumped and bounced before she did a flip, dark blue light shimmering, and landed on her feet with a spin. Her eyes narrowed with rage.

She won't be happy about that, said Miriam as green light flared to life in Jenny's throat. She dug her tentacles into the dirt around her, stabilizing as her body trembled with raw power. She remembered how she'd had to face these attacks in the high school when Miriam had tried to kill her. When Miriam had tried to kill everyone else.

Green light shot out of her mouth, a beam of raw energy crackling with silver light and electricity that struck Mika'el just as she leaped into the air.

My sister lives for battle, warned Jibra'il. *She is the strongest of all archangels, second only to Adonai. This won't be enough.*

Thanks for the vote of confidence, said Jenny, straightening up and wiping her lips. Smoke curled away from her nose, and as the cloud of dust and smoke cleared, she saw Mika'el hovering midair, her glowing blue silhouette missing an enormous chunk of her side, her arm, and a leg.

Did we hurt her? asked Susan.

No, replied Jibra'il. And before he could even explain, before they fully understood the memories of a much younger Jibra'il training with Mika'el more than a million years ago, the other angel was in Jenny's face again, furious and emanating a horrible aura. Her missing limbs spurted out of her bruise-colored form, and fists struck Jenny's face in quick succession, blows that cracked the exoskeleton covering her chest.

Every time Jenny tried to counter, the angel darted from side to side until it felt like Jenny was trying to parry off four assailants. Mika'el was too experienced. Too strong. And now that the angel wasn't underestimating Jenny, she couldn't land a single blow.

"Do you remember why I don't use weapons, brother?" came the angel's voice as fingers smashed into Jenny's neck, who dropped to her knees, clutching her throat, choking. An elbow struck her head from above, and Jenny tasted the ground before she felt the pain of her face burrowing into the dirt. Mika'el knelt and grabbed Jenny's hair, lifting her up. "Because I like seeing the pain. Feeling it right up against myself. It is the greatest pleasure there is."

Jenny groaned, but Jibra'il's voice spoke through her throat, rasping, "**What will you do once He's finished, sister? You will never have this pleasure again.**"

"I will have everlasting peace," replied Mika'el. "I will never have to *fight* again. It will all be over."

"**But you will cease—**" Jibra'il didn't get to finish as Mika'el threw Jenny into the air. She floated for a moment, her wings struggling to beat, her tentacles swishing, and then, a fist buried itself into Jenny's back. It ruptured through her exoskeleton, through her stomach, and burst out of her front. She spat out blood and what felt like all her intestines.

"I will be *whole*," said Mika'el. "I and everything else will be united, and there will be no need for battle. No need for conflict. Why do you falter now, when we are so close to achieving perfection?" With a flick of her arm, she sent Jenny flying, blood and silver light billowing from the hole in her stomach.

Jenny landed in a pile, coughing and aching. How was she supposed to defeat this angel? Blinking away tears, and as she clutched Valescent Light to her gaping wound, she could see that Mika'el's injuries hadn't completely healed. Blue-and-purple light crackled around the wound in her side. Her new limbs were a softer shade of blue.

Was that it, then? Just keep landing blows and hope for the best? Or . . .

"Mika'el," whispered Jenny, making the angel stop midkick.

"You dare say my name, mortal?"

"Mika'el," repeated Jenny, raising her voice as she stood shakily to her feet. Valescent Light continued working throughout her body, putting her back together, but she could feel the drain now. Even with Jibra'il's boosted powers and having two other souls alongside her, the pain was getting difficult to keep up with.

She inhaled deeply through her nose, looking up at the tall, slender angel who, all things considered, was rather beautiful. Her light was the color of sunset. Her slender body was graceful, like one of those birds with long legs. Even her webbed wings were different from that of the other angels. No feathers. It seemed like she'd taken notes from a nature documentary.

Maybe she was envious of material life. Like Adonai seemed to be. But she'd made it her own somehow. She could sense that Jibra'il agreed with her.

Jenny tried to smile, the angel blurring in and out of focus as her head throbbed with pain. "I think you would've liked living on Earth."

"What?" Mika'el faltered. The eye on her chest opened as if she was affronted by Jenny's suggestion.

"We have lots of creatures with webbed wings. Some squirrels that can glide from tree to tree." Susan seemed to grasp what Jenny was going for, as she added, "**We also have bats. So many kinds of them, and they are nocturnal.**"

"I think lizards too," continued Jenny.

Mika'el blinked, her light waning. "Why are you telling me this?"

"I don't know," said Jenny. "I just think you might've liked knowing about them, since you have webbed wings too."

Mika'el stretched out her arms and stared at her wings. "I only thought . . . they were interesting. How life evolved in the material world . . ." Her voice trailed off. Jenny recognized that trail—it was the way she'd start trying to hide her interest whenever her mother was around, whenever something wasn't "productive enough" or profitable.

Jenny swallowed the lump in her throat. Susan and Miriam had had the same experiences—feeling as though they had to hide their curiosity, their love for things—and Jibra'il's thoughts completed it for Jenny. This was what Adonai wanted: for nobody to be interested in anything other than him. That's what every self-obsessed creature wanted. They were envious of all that was around them.

And that was why he wanted to *be* everything. That was why Jibra'il rebelled; there was more to existence than just him.

And that was what he explained through Jenny's lips to Mika'el. "**You can be more than what He deems fit, sister.**"

But the other angel's face warped with anger, brows furrowing. "What does all that matter now? He already has subjugated the material world. All the beautiful creatures you speak of have become a part of him. Why should I care now? Once I join him, I will be a part of everything else, and they will be a part of me."

"**Sister,**" whispered Jibra'il. "**He never let you care. Please allow yourself to care. See what it *means* to care.**"

Mika'el shook her head violently, and then she was in front of Jenny again, towering over her. Fists struck Jenny on the face, knocking her down, only to strike her again in the chest. Fingers grabbed Jenny's hair and swung her around, everything swirling, lights and sounds and pain. But there was hesitation in her attacks now; they were slower, so Jenny reached out and grabbed the angel, wrapping her arms around Mika'el to stop the spinning.

The angel was shaking. Jenny's tentacles slammed into Mika'el, bashing the blue-and-purple angel over and over.

"**At least let me try!**" shouted Jenny. But it was Jibra'il speaking through her. "**If I fail, what do you have to lose? The result will be the same.**"

"No . . ." said Mika'el. She stood motionless as Jenny struck her repeatedly, and then she flew up into the sky. "He . . ." But before she could finish her words, light ignited overhead—another supernova. Except, this time, all the angels around them—the ones made of light, the ones that had been tarnished—shot up into the sky.

Mika'el turned to stare. Jenny felt her heart clench with horror as a *pull* tugged on Jibra'il.

"**He means to absorb the remaining creatures of light**," said Jibra'il.

Angels, screaming, flew upward into the blossoming explosion.

"**Sister,**" pleaded Jibra'il. "**Please . . .**"

It took Jenny a second to realize what he meant, but as she turned, she saw Mika'el floating, arms outstretched, going into the light. There were tears on her face. Was that acceptance? Or was it just cowardice?

Jibra'il wanted to save her, so Jenny reached out, her tentacles snaking toward the floating angel, but before she could reach Mika'el, the blue-and-purple light disintegrated and flew upward.

The shining light above grew brighter and brighter, so intense that Jenny had to cover her eyes. She could sense the other humans doing the same, along with the dread that Adonai would come for them all next. Helplessness and exhaustion filled the air as a voice filled her head. It filled all their heads.

Worship me, for I have risen.

Something landed beside her, and Jenny squinted to see golden wings and blood.

"He has him," gasped Eve as she struggled to grab Jenny, her body broken, her rose-petal armor burned and ashen. "He has the Failed One now. He's going to—"

But the light snapped shut, and the world was darkness again except for a concentrated little star. It shot down and hovered over Jenny, and she blinked to find it was Adonai. He looked exactly like Yeshua, except his hair and beard were golden and white, and in his hands was the actual Yeshua, hanging like a broken toy. They dropped to the ground, and a tremor shook the entire world.

"Thank you for returning my son back to me," said Adonai. He raised the unconscious man to his lips and sank his teeth into Yeshua's shoulder.

CHAPTER FORTY-SIX

TO THE VEIL

Oliver zipped around the battle, his heart pumping so hard there was no room for any thoughts other than to kill whatever got in his way, don't let Mackenzie get hurt, and find his parents. He never really understood what was going on, or why any of this was happening. No one had explained it. And if anyone could, they probably wouldn't take the time to explain it to him in all of this mess.

There were two Jennys. Except, the really powerful one wasn't really his sister, and the other one, his sister, barely looked like her. She might've been one of the tarnished angels, her eyes completely white. She'd always looked like she was struggling with something the entire time Oliver had known her, but now, she looked like someone had ripped out her soul.

But then, she'd healed him. She'd even hugged him, holding him tightly. Sadness?

He threw his knife at an attacking angel, a shimmering being of white light brandishing a spear. Mackenzie leaped over Oliver's head and landed behind the creature, and the two of them finished it off with another blow. The angels seemed to evaporate when they died, leaving behind a glistening orblike thing. Either Oliver or Mackenzie caught it, smushed or slashed it, and then, the notification would appear. Otherwise, the angels would just regenerate.

The normal angels were powerful on their own, but strewn amongst them, fighting, were the wretched and desecrated—powerful, enormous things that caused explosions and sent beams of energy shooting past, destroying everything around them recklessly. Oliver had estimated there were several thousand people collected by Eve, but was this why she'd collected them? For this war?

A war they couldn't possibly hope to win?

Not when an angel so powerful, its level seven hundred and forty-one, could snap his neck with an easy backhanded slap. Could dart all over the place killing everything it wanted to.

If Jenny hadn't been there, he would've died. Mackenzie would've died. Just like Mrs. Monique, who hadn't stood a chance.

And then, there was that guy who looked like Jesus. Was that actually Jesus? He couldn't tell. All he saw was that that person's notification had *Null* in it. He didn't bother trying to make sense of that.

He lost track of the number of angels they killed before finding his mother, running toward him, eyes frantic and wide. Mackenzie slashed down a tarnished angel as he spotted his dad shooting down a few more. Angels flashed over their heads.

What was he supposed to do now? Where could they go to get away from this? They were already in another world.

To the Veil, he realized. That space where they kept the imprisoned angel. If that's where they were keeping it safe from the war, then it would be safe for the rest of them. They could survive there. At least, he hoped they could. He shivered, remembering how it'd looked when the high school had been in there, surrounded by emptiness.

"Come on," he signed quickly at Mackenzie before he rushed over and grabbed his mother's arm. "Get everyone and follow us. We'll take you somewhere safe."

The look on his mother's face was so frightened it hurt to look at. She'd always been sweet to him, caring and kind; she always made him feel like he was home. His biological mother, on the other hand . . . Somehow, he was never good enough; he wasn't what she'd wanted. She picked at details: his hair, his face, his eyes, his skin. "*Why aren't you big and strong like your father?*"

But Nancy never made him feel like that. She welcomed him, curly haired and pimple faced and all. When she hugged him, it felt like a proper Mom hug; it felt like safety, and that's all he wanted to do for her and his dad right now.

"Please trust me," he said, looking at his father, who was holding his rifle. He nodded, and they both told the others who couldn't fight; it frustrated Oliver that they couldn't really fight, couldn't really use the system, but also made complete sense to him. Maybe some people just couldn't *see* and use it properly. Not everyone could daydream; not everyone cared to.

He went out running. The others who wore armor, who could fight, joined him. He didn't mind them too much, but one grabbed his arm—another boy, maybe a little bit older than Oliver, dressed in black armor and carrying a golden mace.

"We can't go in there," he barked. "The angel is imprisoned there."

"Do you wanna stay here and die?" asked Oliver, pulling away and shouting for everyone else to follow. Overhead, intense light filled the entire sky, a fight he had no hope to compete in. But at least, this way, if he could save a few people, maybe he could've mattered, him and all these random people who just happened to be here because they were related or connected to others who could fight.

Mackenzie cut down tarnished and wretched angels left and right. The other armored humans joined the fight, slashing angels and—A huge wave of light rippled across the sky, the ground shaking violently, everything coming to a stop.

Oliver's heart sank into his stomach for a second as screams echoed all around him, but it was the angels, both the ones made of light and the ones who looked like zombies. All of them were swinging their limbs, floating mid-air, struggling and gurgling as they were pulled toward the light in the sky.

But the fighting stopped; the humans could catch their breaths, heal. Now wasn't the time to stare at whatever crazy shit was happening—now was the time to run. He shouted again for everyone to follow; all he knew was the entrance to the Veil was near the lake. He remembered the others talking about it with the thing that looked like Jenny. Remembered that it was a gap between worlds, whatever that meant. He'd followed Jenny and the others when they'd left, and he'd watched them disappear into thin air—he hadn't followed. But now, he was glad he'd watched; glad he'd paid attention.

The lake was boiling, bubbles rising to the top and popping, steam emanating from it. In the water's reflection, he saw the light overhead, what looked like countless arms and wings and eyes, and it made him sick to his gut. His mother swore and cried behind him. Mackenzie ran ahead, and as he wondered how they'd find the entrance, how long they had until whatever was happening with the light would end and the angels would come back, Mackenzie vanished in midair. For a second, his heart faltered, fearing that he had lost her, but reality caught up, and he realized that had to be it. The entrance to the Veil.

"There!" he shouted, turning slightly to where Mackenzie had stood a moment ago. Barreling forward, channeling everything he could into his metal legs, he rushed across the singed grass. And then, like coming home from the rain, the suffocating pressure of the world suddenly vanished, and he emerged into a gray emptiness to find Mackenzie waiting there for him. He rushed right to her, wrapping his arms around her and holding her close. They were safe.

Behind him emerged his parents. Then, a handful at a time, the others came until a small crowd stood on what seemed to be glass tiles.

They were all safe, he thought, sinking to his knees. Mackenzie dropped with him. They were both covered in dirt and ash, looking ragged. But now what? They were in the Veil, where it'd all started, but . . . did they just wait? Go through the entrance every once in a while, check on the other world, see what's happening?

And what about Jenny? He'd just left her there. But she was with that other Jenny and that guy, Jesus. Maybe this was their fight, and he was supposed to just keep his promise: protect their parents and the others.

"You have done well, human," came a voice, chiming like a soft bell. Oliver turned.

"Did you hear that?" he blurted out without thinking.

Mackenzie had read his lips. She shook her head and signed, *What?*

He shuddered. And then the voice came again.

"You fight for what you believe in, even when you are unsure. Even though you are so young."

"Who's there?" he shouted, standing up and drawing his knife. The others looked at him like he'd lost his mind. His mother approached carefully.

"What's wrong? Oliver? Are you okay?"

He shook his head, looking around in every direction. Everything seemed the same. Empty. But there were things floating in the distance; they looked like chunks of buildings, rocks. And then, somewhere above him, he saw a green light—a shining green light.

"You can move freely through the Veil," said the soft voice. "My name is Rafa'el. I have watched over you your entire life, and I know what it is you want so desperately in this moment."

"You don't know anything!" he shouted, hyperaware of everyone around him staring. He looked at them with desperation. "You guys can't hear any of this?"

"You want to help your sister," said the voice. "There is only one way to help your sister."

Green lights flickered around him, and he knew everyone else could see them too. He wasn't losing his mind. The lights took shape, turning into words—How he knew they were words, he didn't know. They weren't in any language he recognized, but they formed, and as they formed, images filled his mind, and he saw Jenny, struggling, bleeding, falling apart as someone tore off her arms, tore off her wings.

"Jenny!" sobbed his mother, and her voice cut through Oliver's heart.

"You can stop this right now," said the soft voice. More letters appeared, and as they shimmered in front of him, he saw another image of a green angel, larger than the others, beautiful and sad, with golden swords sticking out of her body. She was pinned to a rock, imprisoned, and . . . all he had to do was go up there and release her.

"How will you help Jenny?"

"I will end all suffering," promised the voice, and Oliver, exhausted and tired, wondering if it was all over, believed her. At the very least, Jenny's suffering would end.

CHAPTER FORTY-SEVEN

ALL THAT WAS KEPT FROM ME

Your flesh is my bread," said Adonai with a deep, content sigh after swallowing a mouthful of Yeshua. "Your blood is my wine." He kept switching with each bite, with each loud *slurp*, changing from man to woman, young to old and back, and the more he ate and drank, the more erratic his changes became.

For an instance, he was a bird, blue feathered, its beak buried in Yeshua's chest through the shoulder. In another, he was a great lizard, scales across his face, a forked tongue flicking over the wound. And still again, he had the head of a rodent, whiskers twitching, beady eyes shifting, tiny now, with Yeshua on the ground while he nibbled on the exposed flesh. When Adonai turned into a mound of ants, Jenny leaped into him, stamping her exoskeleton-covered feet, trying to crush every little one.

Only for him to turn into a mass of vines, wrapping around Jenny's leg as a gargantuan, ugly flower emerged from the mess. A smaller flower, its petals folded, jutted out of the large one, and when it opened like an umbrella, Adonai was standing there, a little girl, clutching her belly and laughing as her pigtails swung every which way.

Eyes sprouted all over Adonai's limbs, her golden hair coming to life like the vines, before she erupted into a river of mud that crashed over Jenny in a thick, mucky wave and swept her away.

She cried out as the thick mud trapped her arms and legs, gummed up her wings. But with a burst of Ignite, with blue flames roaring from every inch of her body, the mud went dry and hard, and then Miriam's green light bloomed beneath her, exploding all the caked mud away.

She used Jibra'il's winds to sail back into the air, looking down with dread as Adonai, now having taken the form of a young man, sat ripping what was left of Yeshua apart and chewing. Blood dripped into the hardening mud around them. Red lightning crackled around Yeshua, growing back limbs, the mess of his torso on full display. How much longer could he last? How was she supposed to save him? She spotted Eve further away, lying face down.

"Where are all the other humans?" called Adonai as he rose from the bloody mess and mud. Blood dribbled down his chin and stained his shiny tunic. In another flash of light, he was a woman. Except, glistening fish scales covered his skin, and the webbed wings of a bat expanded between her arms and sides. "I have to finish feeding. Why won't you join me? I know you hunger just as I do."

Jenny's tentacles swiveled all around, searching, but there was no sign of anyone else, no matter which direction she turned her attention to. All the angels had been absorbed by him—the normal ones, the tarnished ones. And all the humans . . . Where was Oliver? Her mother? Father? What about all the other people fighting in Eve's army?

Had they all been absorbed by Adonai?

No. Then he wouldn't be asking for them.

Below, on the mud, Yeshua was healing, enormous bolts of red lightning crackling around him. Adonai transformed again, light melting, and he emerged as a man. But this time, fur covered his entire body, and Jenny almost thought he was a monkey for a second, but a horn stuck out of his forehead, and his ears were big and wide, fanning out like that of an elephant's.

He's struggling to contain everything. Jibra'il wondered if Adonai couldn't contain everything because of Jenny's actions, the severed worlds. It left Adonai unbalanced, and it might be the only chance to defeat him before he blew the horn.

But was that really a weakness?

With a cry and using Instant Acceleration, Jenny flapped her wings and flew at Adonai. Her tentacles zipped around and struck him one after the other as he crossed his arms in defense.

His face twisted with glee. "Are you offering yourself to me?"

She swore and slashed at his wrist with her hatchet, the edge cutting clean through and leaving a deep gash on his chin. Golden light sizzled, and when he lowered his head, he was a little girl again. She licked the blood off her lips, her hand sprouting back as a crab claw. With a series of cracks, her neck elongated. Her head reared forward, like the head of a giraffe, and teeth snapped in front of Jenny as she darted out of reach.

But she hadn't been fast enough. A hand grasped one of her tentacles and yanked, snapping her back like a yo-yo, and suddenly, the girl's teeth found Jenny's ear and pulled.

The scream tore out of Jenny's throat before she even realized what had happened. And when she slipped away, her wings trembling, she realized Adonai had pulled her ear off in such a way that he'd ripped the exoskeleton and skin off her body straight down to her hip. A long strap of skin hung as she flew, her ear dangling from the end of it.

Susan and Miriam grimaced inside as pain burned all down Jenny's body. Jibra'il scooped the ear up with a tentacle and held it against her head, other tentacles holding her skin back into position. Jenny tried to ignore the pain.

Adonai grew larger and larger, brown fur spreading all over until he was a towering beast with antlers, fully covered in brown fur.

"I will feast on your flesh, Jenny Huang. I will feast on the Failed One. I will feast on the Antithesis. I will have all that was kept from me."

"Haven't you had enough?" hissed Jenny as her ear healed into place. She cupped it with her hand and shuddered as the rest of her skin was restored.

Yeshua tried to stand below, but he fumbled, red lightning snapping around his body. His eyes rolled back, and he collapsed back onto the mud. Eve still hadn't stirred.

"You kept the world of souls from me," spat the furry creature, raising a hoof. Talons jutted out of its lower limbs. Dark feathered and enormous, the wings of a great eagle jutted out of his furry back. "But I have had them. Taken them for myself. You have stolen the world of death from me, but I will have them too. And you have stolen the demon's world as well. I know what you've done, Interloper. I will have you and everything else, and—"

Jenny threw her hatchet without thinking using Savage Throw, boosting it with electricity and storm power. The hatchet spun through the air and struck Adonai on his oversized chin with a hefty thwack.

But the hatchet melted, and to Jenny's horror, it sunk into his face as golden light shimmered and Adonai turned into a little boy again.

Her arm twitched. She tried to summon the hatchet back, but no matter how hard she willed it to return, her fingers closed around nothing. Her hatchet was gone.

"Thank you for the delicious meal," said Adonai, licking his lips. "Your weapon, born of all your suffering, forged in the pain of countless angels . . ."

He streaked forward, a blur of golden light. Before Jenny could think, before she could try making a new weapon, he struck her with an open hand.

She shot straight down into the mud, *bouncing* against the surface of the world, cratering everything around her. Yeshua's and Eve's limp bodies tumbled down to her, and Jenny lay there, wheezing for breath, unable to feel a single thing. The minds inside her whirred and spun. Nothing made sense, and she almost didn't understand as Adonai floated down.

"The three enemies of destiny, all in one place," he said. "I will end your misery. I will accept your subjugation. I will make you a part of me, and you will always remember. Always bear witness to my greatness." He raised his fist again, transforming into a woman. Golden lightning gathered around her hand.

Jenny groaned, trying to stand, but she faltered, nearly collapsing. Eve and Yeshua were still unconscious; maybe they were dead—she couldn't think clearly enough to tell. Clutching her chest, her tentacles struggling to rise, she tried to glare at Adonai, tried to stand, even if it was the last stand. Even if there was nothing left that she could do. Jibra'il and Susan and Miriam agreed with her.

Fuck Adonai.

"Perhaps it would be wiser to spare them, oh Merciful One," whispered a familiar soft voice that carried all throughout the world like a gentle breeze.

Adonai paused, her head cocking. Her lips twitched into a mad smile as she lowered her hand, the intense light fading away. "My dearest Rafa'el. Is that you?"

Green light blanketed the world, and Rafa'el appeared, gigantic, towering over everything. The top of her silver locks seemed to be coming down from the sky like graceful waterfalls. A radiant emerald dress fluttered around her body; she stood larger than any mountain, larger than anything else left in existence.

"I am prepared," she said.

And appearing all around the crater, standing at the top, were the humans. Jenny saw her brother with their parents. Mackenzie was with them. The other humans—the fighters and the noncombatants, some dressed in armor, most covered in blood—stood as well. All of them had a strange green glow about them, and in unison, they echoed what Rafa'el had said. "We are prepared."

"No!" shouted Jenny or Jibra'il or Susan or Miriam. She'd lost track of who, but she nearly collapsed from the effort of shouting, her legs shaking with pain. Her exoskeleton was cracked all over, and her wings were wilted. "Oliver! Mother! Father! What are you guys doing?"

"We know what we have to do," her mother called from above. "This is for you."

"No!" she shouted again. "Stop!" She took a step, trying to move, trying to rush up the crater and grab them, but her legs buckled completely, and she collapsed. She turned to Yeshua and Eve, both lying unmoving beside her. She shook them hard. "Come on. Get up. Please, get up."

Adonai was a bright star rushing up toward the planet-size Rafa'el. The green angel was crying, and Jibra'il was crying inside of Jenny.

"**There is nothing we can do now**," he said through Jenny. "**She has chosen her stance.**"

"*But then why did she give you the egg?*" screamed Jenny. She raised her head to the green giant. "Why did you give him your child?"

Rafa'el didn't answer. She didn't even seem to acknowledge Jenny or Jibra'il. But as Adonai reached her, the world shuddered. Green light shone brighter and brighter until Jenny had to raise her arm and cover her eyes.

"Finally," came Adonai's booming voice, rising in pitch, rising in volume till it sounded like he was speaking with a million voices. "**Finally, I am everything.**"

Squinting, straining, trying to feel and see with her tentacles, Jenny watched as the green light became the entire sky, covering everything.

Something shimmered in Adonai's hand. It was a horn, curving upward, the color of bone. Darkness swirled around it, and it seemed to radiate a horrid aura of its own. Adonai was once again in the form of the little boy she'd seen stepping on Azra'il's head. He was laughing, giggling and sputtering as he held the little horn like a prized toy.

Then, he pressed it to his lips and blew.

CHAPTER FORTY- EIGHT

DISINTEGRATE

There was no sound like it. It was every sound in the universe, every scream, every crash, every cry, every moan, every musical instrument or storm or accident. Every voice, every whisper, every slap. Every sound that ever could be, coming together in one great blow.

One by one, the humans gathered around the crater ascended, and Jenny cried out as her mother floated away toward the source of the great sound, at the look on her face, crying as her body disintegrated into dust, as she was absorbed into Adonai. Oliver. Their father. Mackenzie. Everyone else. She saw Eve and Yeshua floating as well, rising up like corpses floating to the surface of a lake they'd drowned in. The land around them crumbled and broke, streaking upward toward Adonai, ready to become a part of him.

Jibra'il was struggling too, ready to fall apart, ready to be absorbed into Adonai. Susan and Miriam were shimmering in and out of being, their minds going blank and empty before returning to scream and resist. The struggle was too much, the sound of the horn too much. And Jenny was . . . She was so tired. So exhausted.

But she threw everything she had into Severed Spirit, tearing open a gash through the crumbling world. Color sprang to life in her hand, and she plunged Valescent Light into the darkness. Jenny sank inside without a second glance at what was happening in the sky, as the world fell apart around them.

When the passageway snapped shut behind her, she floated, adrift. There were so few colors now. No more rivers of red and blue. No more enormous circles of green and orange. The light itself seemed less vivid, less bright, and it didn't heal her the way it used to. Everything ached and hurt, and none of the other minds in her body would respond. They were all battered. Broken.

She wondered what it would be like to just float here for the rest of time. Until she passed out. Until her body should die . . . At least, she wouldn't be a part of him.

"**Jenny,**" whispered Susan, using Jenny's lips, her voice small, as though she had just woken up.

"Yeah?"

"**He said he was gonna take the deaths and demons too, right?**"

"Yeah."

"**That means . . .**" Her voice faltered, fading before coming back. "**That means, those worlds are still there. He hasn't gotten to them yet.**"

Shuddering, Jenny opened her eyes and swam, trying to feel for those worlds, trying to navigate. But without the immense pull of the material world, she felt lost.

The center of it all no longer existed. The other worlds, the remaining worlds, seemed to float freely through the light. And so many directions were missing. Or rather . . . they'd been condensed, absorbed by Adonai. And he wouldn't stop till he had the rest.

He had all the angels. All the humans. What was left?

The demons. The answer came from somewhere in her subconscious, and even the other three seemed surprised at the little voice surfacing from the depths of her thoughts. A little boy. Her death. She knew he was right.

But would they be able to fight? Could they do anything? Sat'en was there. So was the Leviathan. At the very least, Jenny could entrust the eggs of the angels—the ones that Jibra'il had gathered—to Sat'en. And then . . . And then, they could wait it out for the worlds to end. Maybe it would take an hour. Maybe a year. But she could finally just rest until it was over.

Groaning, Jenny found the pull she was looking for, and she kicked, swimming through the light till her head emerged into fresh air. Right away, she was greeted with the heavy, wet scent of rain. All around her towered enormous trees, and as she emerged from the passageway, the light shivering shut below her, Jenny found herself in a rainforest so dense she couldn't see the sky.

"Is this the right place?" she whispered. She dropped to her hands and knees, her head spinning with pain. Her body felt wrong, shattered. She just wanted to lie down, but she was afraid of falling asleep. Afraid of never waking up. Of never wanting to.

Plants shook nearby, and Jenny swerved her head, trying to summon her hatchet. But nothing appeared in her hand, and the exertion of trying was enough to set off another dizzy spell.

Desecrated Angel (Possessed)

"Sat'en?" she whispered, stumbling forward. For a second, she thought it was her mother. She wasn't sure why. Long hair. A woman. But then, the angel's grim face appeared, eyes burning with multiple flames, and Jenny's eyes closed shut. She gave into the darkness.

When she awoke, someone was caressing her face. Again, as her eyes shifted into focus and the world blurred and brightened, she thought it was her mother. But instead, it was the sunken face of a desecrated angel, eyes burning with various colored flames, staring down at her.

"Sat'en?" she whispered.

"Yes," responded the angel. "And I am also Iblis."

Jenny bolted upright, blinking away the exhaustion, staring at the angel. The flames were orange. Sometimes red. Here and there, there was a wisp of blue. "What do you mean?"

Sat'en's lips curled upward. It was a sad smile on a frightening face. "I found every bit of him that I could, tracing him to the far edges of this world. It's not truly him, as he is no longer with us, but from the fumes of a star, a new one is born, and . . ."

Jenny stared for a long moment, guilt and sadness building in her throat, remembering Iblis's last moments, ripped out of Jenny's body and crushed by Azra'il. "So, is that like . . . your child, then?"

"In a way," replied Sat'en. "Or perhaps I am just mourning. And when I am ready, I will set these flames free to become whatever they might."

Children, thought Jenny, thinking back to the angel babies following her around, looking to her for guidance. She thought back to the younger deaths, who seemed completely lost. The souls of children sent away. The angel eggs, made of light, and the young angels guarded by Sat'en.

"Where's Leviathan?" asked Jenny.

"Swimming," she said, gesturing upward.

Jenny looked up, focusing through the green leaves and branches that covered the canopy to see stars in the distance.

"He and the children prefer being closer to the heavens," explained the angel. "But as I understand it, the heavens are falling. The horn has been blown. And one by one, the stars go out."

"Yeah," whispered Jenny.

"And you were at the epicenter of the end?"

She nodded. The other minds in her body were waking. Susan. Miriam. Jibra'il, who was catatonic. Empty. Like a marionette swinging from its strings, stuck inside Jenny's body.

Is he . . . dead? asked Miriam.

I don't know, said Susan. *I think maybe he's asleep.*

Maybe he's just sad.

"Are we safe here?" asked Jenny, even though she knew the answer.

Sat'en shook her head. "No. From the blowing of the horn, everything stops. Matter. Time. Energy. Everything will be sucked into him and become him, and soon enough, there will be nothing left *but* him. There's a chance it might not reach this world, but the imbalance of existence will take its price."

"What do you mean?"

Sat'en drew a circle in the mud, then two separate, smaller circles orbiting the bigger one. "If this large one is Adonai, who now has almost every world, and these two are—"

"The world of demons and the world of death?" asked Jenny. "I also severed the world of souls."

"Ah," said Sat'en. "Then you have separated three worlds. He cannot access them, cannot claim what's inside, but without them . . ." She drew several more circles inside Adonai. "Without the balance that the worlds had, the harmony, these three, isolated like a lost limb, will wither away and die. It might take years, generations, but . . ."

"So shouldn't we just stay here and wait it out?"

"We can," noted Sat'en. "That is always an option."

But Jenny got the sense the angel still wanted to fight. "Well, what else, then? How? He's too powerful. He's blown the horn. Isn't it game over?"

"I believe survival challenges only have one game-ending condition," said the angel.

Jenny shuddered. She hugged her knees. Susan and Miriam were quiet as well, feeling empty and hollow. "What do you mean? The survival challenge? Does that really matter now?"

"Every world got the same message," explained Sat'en. "About the final challenge. Adonai means to be the sole victor, but you have ensured he cannot win as immediately as he would like to."

CHAPTER FORTY-NINE

EMPTINESS

So, are you saying there's a chance to stop him?" asked Jenny, who was finding it more and more difficult to raise her head. A steady rain began to fall, drizzling down from above. The water was warm and soothing, and fog began to swirl around the two of them, blurring the trees and thickening the air. She wanted to use energy to make an umbrella, but then she remembered where all that energy had come from, and she stopped herself. What was a little bit of wetness, anyway? It felt nice dribbling into her cracked exoskeleton, soaking into her skin.

Sat'en didn't respond for a while. She too seemed to be enjoying the weather. "Did you know it had not rained in this world in quite some time? The demons welcome it, and it's all thanks to you."

"I thought they wouldn't like getting wet."

"Extreme cold is what stifles their being. But the water and temperature go hand in hand." Sat'en took a deep breath. "But there is another thing that goes hand in hand."

Jenny had a feeling she knew what Sat'en was going to say. "Are you talking about the horn?"

"Sculpted from essence from beyond anything of these worlds," explained Sat'en. "The emptiness that goes hand in hand with material existence. With light and energy, with matter."

"So it's not of these worlds?" Jenny thought about the sound it had made when Adonai blew it. The way everything had reverberated and disintegrated and floated up into him. He'd done it without the horn, hadn't he? When he'd absorbed all the angels? But he'd needed the horn for something else.

"What do you believe the Veil to be?" asked Sat'en after a long silence.

Jenny shook her head. "The space between worlds?"

"And where do you go when you move between worlds? Is it the Veil?"

She shook her head again, frowning even more. Were they both spaces between worlds?

"The Veil is a buffer zone between these worlds and the Emptiness," said Sat'en.

A chill ran down Jenny's back. Water trickled through her hair. She shuddered. Jibra'il had stirred at Sat'en's words, but he remained silent.

"What's in the Emptiness?" whispered Jenny, afraid of the answer.

"That I do not have the answer to," she replied. "All I know is that the worlds had been growing, pushing the Veil farther and farther, and that is something Adonai does not want."

"And he used a piece of that Emptiness? To destroy everything?"

"No," said the angel. "To change the constitution of everything. To drain everything inside of *him* rather than into the Emptiness."

"I . . . I don't get it."

"Where does anything come from? From the light? From the flame? But then, where do those things come from?" Sat'en stood, the flames in her eyes burning brightly despite the thick fog. "A big explosion? But then, what lit that first spark? What was there to burn?"

"The Emptiness?" asked Jenny. It might've been Susan; she wasn't sure. But they were listening intently. It was as though Sat'en was sharing the secrets of the universe.

"Is it truly empty?" asked the angel. "I do not know. There is no one in these worlds who can know, only claim to know. The only thing we can be certain of is that there is *something* beyond these worlds."

"And some people are afraid of that," whispered Jenny.

"Always. It has always been the case of the power hungry to isolate. To rule with fear and rage."

"So Adonai wants to take everything for himself 'cause he thinks everything will be empty eventually?"

"Something like that," said Sat'en. "Though I am sure someone contained within you right now can answer this question."

Silver light brightened slightly around Jenny, and Jibra'il spoke through her lips. "**He means to rebuild it all—every atom, every sentient thought— in his image. Of him. In subservience to him.**"

"Hello, brother," greeted Sat'en, and memories erupted through Jenny's mind of there being another angel standing beside Jibra'il and the other archangels in serving Adonai. An angel who turned away from the

Great Plan. An angel who wanted differently and was disgraced for her disobedience.

"**You were right,**" whispered Jibra'il, and Jenny's body shook as he cried, as his tears trailed down her face. "**I believed in his world. Believed it would be a better one. With no more suffering.**"

They were quiet for a long time as it continued to rain. Jenny thought about what that meant, a world without suffering, and whether it would be better to just submit to Adonai and let all of this be over. No more need to think, right? No more trying to survive; no more hoping for things to get better.

But then . . . there'd be no point in dreaming, and wasn't dreaming nice? There'd be no point in making things. There'd be no point to anything.

Susan agreed. Miriam too, even though she'd succumbed to Azra'il's whims before. They all talked about happiness and freedom and being whole, but what did that mean?

"Maybe," said Jenny. "Maybe it's not about just being 'happy' but fighting for and protecting that happiness."

"**But how much do we have to fight for that?**" asked Susan through Jenny.

Jenny was surprised by Susan asking that question. She was always the one trying to make things better for the people around her. Trying to help.

"**I feel like we're always just trying, you know? Just fighting. And every day, all the time, we have to fight for things to be okay. And then, they're just alright.**"

"**So do you want to join Adonai, then?**" asked Miriam, who was now also speaking through Jenny. Sat'en only watched, seemingly amused, the flames in her eyes brightening.

"**No,**" said Susan. "**I just . . . I feel like . . .**"

"We never really get the chance to be happy," completed Jenny, realizing what Susan was talking about. "We'll fight and beg and pray to be happy, but when it comes to being happy, somehow, it feels like we have to fight every damn time."

"**Yeah.**"

"But I think what Adonai wants isn't happiness," continued Jenny. "More like . . . dullness? Like, we won't be sad or angry or whatever, but we won't ever get to try anything or do anything that matters. We'll just be him."

With a shudder, she realized that's what it'd felt like living with her mother all those years. No matter what she accomplished in school or tried to do, it wasn't enough. Because her mother was hurt or whatever by her own life. Because they'd both struggled through so much. There was always a question of, can this be real? Can we be happy now?

And she felt Susan and Miriam share in similar realizations with their parents and families. How to some people, some things were never good enough because there was too much struggle to go around, too much pain. And not everyone was equipped to face that struggle, to grow from it.

They took it out on others. And they only did that because they were afraid.

"So, isn't Adonai just afraid?" whispered Jenny.

"**He's just a pussy,**" replied Miriam. And Jenny laughed.

"I guess we don't have to hurt people or want to control everything just because we're afraid."

"**So then, what do we do?**" asked Susan. "**There are always people who hurt others because of their own struggles, right? Do we just . . . ?**"

"**Eat them?**" asked Miriam.

"**Help them?**" asked Susan. "**But when do we get to live? Why do we have to deal with them at all?**"

"Does it really matter now?" Jenny rubbed her face. "Isn't everyone . . . gone? Dead? Stuck inside Adonai? He blew the horn."

"Possibly," said Sat'en. "What do you think, brother?"

Jibra'il shuddered inside Jenny. "**It was something Rafa'el said to me once. That blowing the horn the first time, sending Emptiness rippling through the worlds, would destroy everything.**"

"First time?" asked Jenny.

"**And blowing it a second time would send a second wave to restore everything, to begin the universe anew.**"

Jenny swallowed hard and stared at Sat'en's burning eyes. "What do you mean 'begin the universe anew'? What about all the people who lived in it? Died in it? What about us?"

"**That I do not know,**" said Jibra'il, and suddenly, he stood up, using Jenny's body. "**But I do wonder . . .**"

And Jenny understood just as he did. She asked the question for him. "Why did she give you the egg at that moment in time?"

"Egg?" asked Sat'en.

Jenny glanced down at the desecrated angel, smiling genuinely for the first time in what felt like a lifetime. She wasn't even sure if it was her smile or if the plan formulating in her head made any sense, but she was smiling. Jibra'il's memories intertwined with Susan and Miriam's thoughts, and Jenny was brimming with them.

If Rafa'el had been transcribing destiny, if she could see all of space and time and the possible outcomes of every action, every decision, then the only reason she'd do this, the only reason she'd send an egg to Jibra'il, was to end

Adonai's bullshit once and for all. Which meant she *saw* a way to win. Which meant she wasn't as subservient to Adonai as everyone had thought.

All they had to do was grab the horn.

"**But how?**" asked Jibra'il. "**How would we ever get close enough to do that?**"

"**Can we even use it?**" wondered Susan.

"I don't know," said Jenny, her breath deepening. Her wings spread, water dripping off her feathers. Her tentacles lifted off the mud. Then, she turned away from Susan and posed a question inward to the others inside her head, thinking about Severed Spirit and Valescent Light and how Adonai contained the entirety of the material world, the angels, the souls. She thought about the demons; she thought about the deaths. She thought about how these worlds were out of his reach for now, at least. *How many more people do you think we can fit in here?*

What do you mean to do? asked Jibra'il, but the thoughts were already reaching him, and he seemed to approve.

She turned around and explained her plan to Sat'en. "What if I were to let every demon in this world possess me?"

CHAPTER FIFTY

A NEW HATCHET

Sat'en didn't answer for a long moment. Jenny could sense Susan's hesitation and Miriam's glee. They both wanted to see what would happen, remembering Jenny's experience of carrying Iblis and using his flame to fuel her own, how strong she'd become. Could she handle taking on the force of more than one demon? Was there even enough room in her body? Jibra'il seemed positive that she could take it. Susan was hopeful. Miriam wanted to find out.

"Will it be enough?" asked Sat'en, echoing Jenny's thoughts.

It was Jibra'il who spoke, surprising them. "**The demons were the first beings, were they not?**"

"I thought the angels were the first?" asked Jenny.

"The source comes before the light," answered Sat'en with a smile. "What Adonai propagated was a great lie—one of the greatest lies—to give himself more power and to convince trillions of a false worth. There is much power in false worth."

"**One will do anything to protect that false worth,**" said Jibra'il solemnly. But he pressed on. "**The demons have more substance than the angels. But even with every single one of them agreeing to side with us, will it be enough to stand up to Adonai?**"

"**We don't need to defeat him,**" noted Susan. "**We just need to grab the horn and blow it.**"

"**Right in his stupid face,**" added Miriam.

"**What of the deaths?**" asked Jibra'il.

And another memory bubbled up to the surface of their thoughts. Something Jenny had completely forgotten in the chaos of everything. She'd found a pillar that housed something different from the other deaths; something that had caused her ability to rebound, just as it did when she used Valescent Light on Adonai himself.

It was *his* death, they realized together. She swallowed hard. If they added all the deaths, all the deaths that had ever been, to all the demons . . . and if they added Adonai's own death . . .

Could she even hold on to that much power?

"**Perhaps it is your usage of Severed Spirit—something forbidden, something that should not be acceptable by the guidance system—that enables you to do this.**" Jibra'il was wondering; he didn't know for sure. And she could feel that he didn't know. But it was something.

Memories of Existential Error crept through her thoughts.

"**Isn't that ability . . . wrong?**" whispered Susan. Through her, Jenny saw herself wriggling on the high school floor, torn to shreds, manic with blood-lust and hunger.

Miriam shuddered as well, and Jenny saw the creature she'd become, a monstrous form covered in a red exoskeleton, tearing into the poor girl as she screamed and begged for mercy.

"We won't know till we try," she told them, silently begging for their forgiveness. Though they could feel her thoughts, and though they forgave her, she promised them and herself that she would apologize once all of this was over. If it ended as hopefully as they were hoping for. "And besides, this time, I have you guys to keep me in check."

"**It's worth a shot,**" agreed Susan, determination emanating from her.

Sat'en raised her face, rainwater dripping off her exoskeleton-covered chin. "You have my aid, as well as what remains of my Iblis. And I shall ask every demon across this world to join us."

She asked for a moment of quiet. The rain continued drumming along, the sound comforting and encasing. Sat'en stood so still she looked like a statue, water dribbling down her gray face and shoulders. And then, a rustling shuddered through all the plants around them.

The rustling shuddered through Jenny as well, and everyone inside her could feel it: the fluctuations in temperature, the gradations in heat that coursed through her, as though she'd been running and running on a hot summer's day, the sun bearing down on her.

"They have accepted," whispered Sat'en, her flames burning even more brightly now. Rain hissed into steam above her eyes. "They are most grateful for what you've done for them."

"Can you tell them I'm sorry?" asked Jenny, shutting her eyes and feeling all the heat and warmth flowing around her. "For Iblis? For failing before?"

"You may tell them yourself," said Sat'en. "When you are ready."

"I . . ." She was about to ask how. How does she do this? Open herself up and let so many beings inside her?

It was Susan who gave her the answer. Gently, kindly, Susan emerged, separating from Jenny to look back at her. She was glowing in the rain, the water droplets going through her as though she were a ghost. She was a separate soul again.

"You can do this," whispered Susan, wrapping her arms around Jenny.

Jenny stood still, shaking, almost frozen. Despite everything, despite having had Susan inside her all this time, sharing their thoughts and feelings and memories, she felt shy. She felt sad. She felt happy. She could sense Miriam and Jibra'il looking on, sharing in her emotions, and she understood what Susan was trying to do.

Open herself to feel those emotions. Open herself up to the world. To take a chance. With a deep breath, Jenny raised her arms and pulled Susan in for a tight hug, burying her face in Susan's hair, trembling, still trying to hold back her tears.

"Let it out," said Susan softly. "It's okay. You . . . We can do this. We can do this. Together."

And then, like a star exploding, remembering how Iblis had blown apart, Jenny felt light surging through her. Light burst out of her skin, from her wings, from her tentacles, so bright that it outshone everything else around her, blinding her completely.

The demons swept into her, one at a time at first, but as she stood, the light moved with her. More and more demons added their flames to her own. She felt their presences—not as strong as Iblis's had been but plentiful. Susan stepped back inside Jenny as well, and then, she felt someone taking her hands, squeezing her fingers.

Sat'en's voice flickered through her ears. "From everything we are, matter. From everything we love, existence. Entrusted to you." And then, Jenny felt Sat'en's immense presence as well, a mind larger than any she'd felt before, larger even than Jibra'il's, and a cry of anguish filled her throat.

She clutched her face, stepping forward and back as the demons continued to flow into her, like a rushing flood filling up a small bowl. She couldn't handle this. She was overflowing. It was too much.

It was not enough.

Another scream tore through her. If Susan was saying anything, Jenny could no longer hear her in the mangled mess of thoughts and wants and dreams and fears that writhed through her head.

And through all that, she felt yet another presence snaking its way down from the sky, carrying with it countless more.

"But they're just kids!" she cried out.

Children who wish to offer their strength, said Sat'en, now speaking inside Jenny. *Children who will never see the light of adulthood without this fight.*

Colors streamed through the searing light, and Jenny convulsed, taking on the weight of countless young angels. Each one sprouted inside her head like a flower, radiating light and hope, each one a different color, too many to keep track of. And then, just as she thought it was over, something even more immense flew through her.

It was the Leviathan itself. Before Jenny could protest, could question, clarity rang through her as though someone had chimed a bell, bringing order to the chaos of thoughts and emotions.

And when Jenny opened her eyes, she found herself floating in . . . nothing. All around her, a glowing translucent emptiness. The plants were gone. The rain had vanished. The world itself seemed to have disappeared.

You have all the power of this world coursing through your veins, said Jibra'il.

The power of the Emptiness as well, gifted to you by the Leviathan, came Sat'en's voice.

Energy crackled through Jenny's arms as she stared at her hands. Her exoskeleton had changed. It was silver still, but through it shimmered all the colors of the rainbow, as though she was perpetually using Valescent Light. And her wings!

She curved them around her to see countless colors billowing away, flames of every shade of the rainbow sprouting from her feathers, and a feeling—something she'd never truly felt in all her life; something that made her want to cry and scream and sob with happiness—filled her lungs with such intensity that she did in fact let it out.

She screamed. Into the world she'd become.

Hope. She had all the hope of this world. And using it, she pulled open a strand of darkness, igniting it into golden light. The passageway glittered in front of her, moving gently, like a ribbon of shining cloth.

What would she find waiting on the other side? Rainbow light bloomed around her hand, and she looked down to find a new hatchet.

You might need this, came Susan's voice, flickering somewhere through Jenny's being. Rainbow light glittered along the curved sharp edge of her hatchet, its dark handle fitting perfectly in her grip.

Taking a deep breath and preparing herself for whatever might be lying in wait, Jenny climbed through the passageway.

CHAPTER FIFTY-ONE

INFINITE MOUTHS

The light between worlds had changed. Jenny floated through the golden light around her. It was still swirling colors that interacted with the rainbow flames emanating from her wings, but everywhere else, everything beyond her immediate vicinity, had turned to darkness. And not just any darkness but an oily, slick, disgusting kind that oozed and bubbled. She was alone in a little bubble of golden light, like a star lost in a silent universe.

"What is going on?" she whispered, her words shimmering away in little bubbles of various colors, bursting when they reached the darkness around.

As if in answer to her question, an eye opened in front of her. It was reddened, like the eye of someone who hadn't slept in forever, like the eye of someone who was furious. And around it, in different orientations—some horizontal, some vertical—countless more eyes opened till she was surrounded by them. Infinite eyes glared at her, all around her, no matter which way she turned. Left or right. Up or down. From the darkness came all the eyes of everyone who'd ever lived, it seemed like.

"You have taken the power of the demons, I see," came a voice, rolling off like drums. "And you want the world of the dead too, do you? The worlds you kept from me. The worlds you stole from me."

"I *freed* them," answered Jenny, red and blue light rippling away from her mouth. "I got rid of your bullshit from their worlds and—"

"WHAT DO YOU HOPE TO DO AGAINST DESTINY?" Adonai's voice crashed around her like thunder, but Jenny didn't wince. She floated as still as she could, gripping her hatchet, ready for whatever he might try to pull.

"I *am* Destiny," he said, dropping his voice.

"But you need the rest of these worlds to finish what you started, right?" Jenny smiled, her tentacles swishing around her, eyes opening all over them as well—her wings, her body—trying to show him she wasn't frightened; her eyes even had flames burning in them. Flames sprouted from the eyes across her torso, on her arms and legs.

"I do not have them as of *yet*," he said, some of his eyes shutting like stars blinking out in the night sky. "But do you know what I do have?"

"Narcissism?"

"Infinite mouths," he growled as something shot out of the darkness, a humanoid figure, a shadow come to life.

Jenny swung without thinking as teeth gnashed right beside one of her tentacles. Rainbow sparks burst where the edge of her hatchet slashed through the figure before it dissipated and faded away, dissolving in the golden light around her like smoke in water.

More shadows jumped toward her, reaching with ghostly hands, mouths open. They had no eyes, no other features, just silhouettes with teeth, and Jenny slashed and struck and whipped them into oblivion.

They were frightfully weak. She could outmaneuver them with ease, so what was he trying to do? Why wasn't he attacking her with all his might?

"I will consume death one by one if I have to," came his voice, and Jenny realized what he was doing: He was keeping her busy.

But how will we get there? asked Susan.

Through the darkness, said Jibra'il. *He has obscured the world of death. Engulfed it.*

Jenny flapped her wings, colors swishing and swirling, but no matter how hard she tried to move, the golden light bounced off the darkness and she was thrown back. "Fuck," she swore.

Laughter echoed around her. "Your power is inconsequential. The demons were a failed race from the beginning. And you, human, a waste of the gift of material."

"The only one who's a waste is *you*," she spat back. Then, she had an idea.

Will that work? Susan wondered.

It's worth a shot, came Sat'en's voice. *And it is rather fitting.*

Valescent Light flowed through Jenny's arm and into the hatchet. Colors swirled to life around it, shooting off the weapon like solar flares. Every bit glowed with bright light, bright enough that the darkness was pushed back, her little sphere growing in size as more and more of the silhouette creatures came screaming from the dark, trying to get to her. Trying to stop her.

"What do you hope to achieve? Submit. Give in. Do not—"

Jenny raised her hatchet back, taking aim in no particular direction, and launched her Valescent Light–infused weapon with Savage Throw, fueling it with the power of storms, the power of all the young angels, all the burning demons. Flames of every color trailed from the spinning hatchet as it burst away from her, and a horrible, cruel roar enveloped her light as the weapon spun through the darkness.

It cut a trail of golden light, the darkness swirling away from it as though it couldn't stand being touched. Black tendrils rippled with more silhouettes, but Jenny felt that *pull*—that push away from the world she'd left, the world she'd become, and the pull to what she was hoping to find.

She flapped her wings as hard as she could, jetting through the light, tentacles swishing all about her to knock away the silhouettes. *Adonai had no actual power here, did he?* she asked internally. *It was just the pretense of power.*

We don't have much power here either, noted Jibra'il. *We must get to the world of death.*

But seeing through the pretenses of power is often power enough, said Sat'en, and with a gush of light, with everything bursting, Jenny jumped out the passageway like a dolphin leaping from the water, light splashing. But instead of falling back down, her wings spread.

Burning clouds of rainbow light billowed away from her, and Jenny once again found herself in the world of the dead. Except, this time, it was crawling with dark silhouettes. They looked exactly the same as they had in the passageway: made of darkness; a standing shadow. No features other than their grotesque oversized mouths. And they were feasting, chasing down deaths, pinning them to the ground kicking and screaming, chewing through flesh and blood.

Several deaths saw her, reaching out with desperate hands even as the shadowy creatures chewed off their fingers, their pleas for help ringing in Jenny's ear.

"*Where are you?*" she shouted, her voice echoing throughout the world. Raising her hatchet up, she pictured an enormous bolt of lightning before thunder clattered across the sky, clouds billowing from the tip of her weapon to fill the world with a storm.

Light sparkled across the underbelly of newly grown thick clouds. Thick bolts of lightning in all the colors of the rainbow came raining down and blasted everything on the ground.

The shadowy creatures nearby screeched and melted away, vanishing into vapor. The remaining deaths crawled across the dirt, covering their faces even as the lightning healed their wounds. She didn't know how many had been eaten, how many Adonai had devoured, but there were still plenty left.

"WHY MUST YOU ALWAYS INTERFERE?" boomed a voice. Dark vapors gathered in front of her, like billions of mosquitos and little flies buzzing and collapsing into a new silhouette. Except this one had a face with several eyes, each one opening across its head. A mouth came next as muscular arms and legs formed, but nothing seemed affixed. Everything swished and sloshed, like the body was made from that oily, liquid darkness she'd seen between worlds.

She wondered if that was due to the trumpet. If everything had become this gooey darkness, waiting for him to be complete, waiting for him to reshape existence.

Rubbing his face and roaring, he shuddered and cracked open. The black shell fell away, and a naked, muscular man rose from it. A man with the face of Yeshua—the beard and hair and everything. "This will do for now," he said, eyes glazed red with anger. Golden armor oozed out of his skin and hardened across his body. "I will kill you with the hands of the Failed One."

Jenny twirled her hatchet, inhaling sharply through her nose. She was still very much outpowered, outmatched. His level must've been infinity, and hers had no number at all. The only thing she had on her side was his instability.

Light shining across her hatchet, she flapped her wings and flew at him, a scream bursting from her lips. She swung hard as she landed, but Adonai blocked with his elbow, knocking her forearm away. Turning to the side, she lashed out with her foot, making contact with his hip, the sound of his bones caving in ringing almost as loudly as the horn he'd blown. Her tentacles swooped right in, smashing into his bearded face, but he didn't react one bit.

With a chopping motion, he slashed through four of her tentacles then took a step forward. Golden light rippled around his fist, and when he punched her, the entire world seemed to fold inward as Jenny rocketed across the salty black ground. Before she'd even come to a stop, Adonai was above her, moving as fast as she was. With his hand replicating into six fists, he struck her again and again and again, every blow striking at the same exact time.

Jenny went crashing through the layers of hardened salt and rock of the ground below, burrowing so deeply the light of her thunderstorm faded away and dirt clogged her throat.

By the time she came to a stop, she couldn't even see the surface. She lay there, groaning in pain as her cracked armor regenerated. Pain rang through her in waves, but she pulled herself up, grabbing onto jagged bits of rock as blood trickled down her face, her arms, her legs.

She couldn't beat him in a head-on fight.

"You cannot defeat me," his voice boomed from above. Golden light shone so brightly there she almost thought the sun had been pulled in after her. And then, with her heart thudding into her throat, she realized it might as well have been.

An enormous ball of flame—swirling with yellow and orange and white, so hot that it melted the rock and salt and dirt around it—rushed toward her, barreling through everything, widening the space she'd fallen through. Liquid rained down around her, splattering on her exoskeleton and wings.

She gritted her teeth as the flames came closer, but then, the demons' voices flickered to life in her head; they knew heat. They knew what it meant to burn. And she shut her eyes and lowered her hatchet, and just as the flames reached her, just as they singed her hair and scorched her skin and melted her armor, Jenny did as the demons would.

She inhaled.

CHAPTER FIFTY-TWO

DISOBEY

Flames filled her mouth, swirled down her throat, expanded into her lungs. Heat ballooned inside her, and for a moment, she thought she would melt. She thought she would burst. But the demons assured her she'd be all right, and she trusted them. And once she couldn't inhale anymore, once there was nothing left to suck in, she opened her eyes to see the tunnel now darkened while her entire body brimmed with energy.

Grinning, she flapped her wings and rocketed up through the tunnel to see Adonai hovering midair, his jaw set. He might be all-powerful; he might be so much stronger than her, but she had just enough to make do. She could take all his hits. All his attacks. She'd just keep coming back.

Light thrummed through her hands and into her fists, into the tips of her tentacles. She didn't really have a plan; she'd wanted to absorb the world of death, absorb all the deaths, and use them to fight him, possibly become stronger than him, but this was the final battleground. This was where she either defeated him and found the horn and fixed everything—or he won.

Adonai kicked off the ground, ascending with his fists by his side as he glared at Jenny. Black lightning crackled and flickered around his form. "So you still choose to disobey me, child?"

"Disobey you?" asked Jenny. She licked the taste of energy off her lips. "I've been disobeying you all my life. No, I'm going to fucking *kill* you."

"Pathetic little mortal," he sneered, his voice low and rolling like thunder. More lightning rained down from the sky around them, igniting in multicolor sparks, killing off more and more of his shadowy silhouettes. "I have all your lives *writhing* within me. Disgusting wastes of material form."

"Yeah?" she said. "Then why did you want us so bad?"

"To solve the problem," replied Adonai, tapping his forehead. "To free you from the suffering. Look how you waste your lives, so much of it spent on foolishness. The aching. The longing. Fighting between one another."

"And what do you call all this?!" she shouted, unsure if she was speaking or if Sat'en or Susan or someone else had spoken through her. It didn't matter. They were in agreement.

"Necessity," he said. Black lightning crackling around him, trails of darkness swirling from his every movement, Adonai rushed toward her. She met him head-on again, her glowing fists striking him every chance she got. With the boost in her speed, the tremendous power surging through her muscles, her every tentacle smashed into him, his armor cracking with each strike, his body splattering like liquid. But it always reformed.

And each of his attacks—his punches and kicks, his shadowy blasts of energy—rattled through Jenny as though she'd been hit by a freight train. Rainbow light and flame flickered out of her wounds and healed her, but Adonai would just twist midair, his heel striking her chest or her face, and she'd be sent crashing back down into the dirt.

"Stop this madness," he hissed. His face shifted, darkness burning through his skin as Yeshua's bearded features melted away and Jenny's own eyes blinked back at her. It took her a second to realize it was Eve now. Adonai clutched her head, writhing midair, body changing, turning from one person to another. Eve's face vanished. It was another man next. Then a boy—A series of people ranging in age, ethnicity, gender. She even thought she saw animals again; lizards and birds and mammals and fish.

She coughed up blood. As much as she was healing, her new body was taking damage repeatedly. *All I'm doing is trying to slow him down*, she wheezed. Around her, she could sense more and more deaths being attacked, chewed up, and absorbed. Adonai was growing stronger with every death he caught.

But then, her tentacles twitched, and all of them swerved to point in one direction. Clutching her side, Jenny turned, using her new eyes—the eyes of trillions of demons—to see, and found a death she'd met before: The old woman, standing beside a pillar. The shadowy silhouettes were avoiding it, wouldn't go near it, and Jenny gasped. That was it, wasn't it? Adonai's death? He'd made himself material, and now he had a death.

She didn't know what she would do with his death, but something about it kept his silhouettes away. Something about it he didn't like. Maybe he was afraid.

Colors crackling, she healed the rest of herself then flapped her wings and flew, zipping through the creatures. She couldn't save any more deaths. She had to stop him—no matter what it took.

But Adonai must've realized what she was up to. He rocketed from the sky, roaring with rage, his unstable form expanding into dozens of people stuck together by that sticky wet darkness of his before collapsing into one singular form.

He was too powerful for his own good.

Jenny took the chance to keep going. The old woman's eyebrows went up, reaching out for Jenny as she flew nearer and nearer. But just before she could reach the woman and the last pillar, something struck Jenny on the back, right between her wings and tentacles, and she plummeted with a cry.

When she hit the dirt, sending up a plume of dust and salt, cratering the ground beneath her, she saw Adonai standing above her. He was still shifting, but his face melted again until it formed the face of her mother. It was Nancy glaring down at her now. Nancy's foot on her back. Nancy's voice screaming at her. "I know everything about you! I know everything you are ashamed of. Afraid of. Why don't you just do as you're told? You pathetic excuse for a human being." She leaned closely and grabbed a fistful of Jenny's hair, lifting her off the dirt. "You were a failure of a daughter. A failure of a child. Why don't you just—*Argh!*"

Electricity shot out of her tentacles where they wrapped around Adonai, and Nancy's face melted away as enormous bolts of lightning struck him over and over. Jenny screamed as she squeezed Adonai with her tentacles, trying to make him burst, trying to wring out all the souls and angels and people he'd absorbed. The darkness gushed like jelly, and Jenny stood back to face him. Lightning flashed, her hatchet appeared in her hand, and then she was hacking away, mindlessly slashing every which way, trying to cut him into a million little pieces.

But no matter how many chunks fell away, no matter how hard she squeezed his ribs and his arms and his head, he kept assembling back together. With an explosion of black lightning, her tentacles sizzled away into ashes, and Adonai's fist found her face. His knuckles dug into her skull, crushing and squashing everything. She felt his hand inside her *brain*, but this time, she refused to let him knock her away. New tentacles had burst out of her back, snapping around him just as he struck, pinning him to her. And the force of his attack sent them both crashing through the world, bursting through silhouettes and deaths and coming to a reckless stop with Adonai breathing hard on top of her.

"WHY—"

He punched her in the face again.

"WON'T—"

In the throat, his nails scraping her collarbone.

"YOU—"

He bound his hands together and struck again, and what was left of her skull broke inward, her head flattened against the ground.

"SUBMIT?"

He kept hitting her, over and over, all the while shouting, screaming, salivating.

"Isn't it better if humans don't have to think? You are happiest without thought! Partying. Dancing. Drugs. Prayer, even. Being told what to do! You live for this shit. So let me. Please. Just let me have everything, and I will see to a perfect world. A beautiful world. Where all can have everything, and no one will be left hurting and alone. There will be no jealousy. No heartache.

"NO PAIN!

"ISN'T THAT WHAT YOU WANT, JENNY HUANG?

"WHY MUST YOU PEOPLE ALWAYS DISOBEY MY COMMANDS?"

Am I dead? she thought. And millions of voices answered back. Light ignited inside her crushed skull, and her head reinflated, her eyes expanding back into shape. Adonai's face was a distorted mess of countless faces, each one fighting to be seen. He raised his arms to strike her again, but an arm shot out of Jenny's chest and grabbed his.

Adonai stared down in disbelief, his face flickering and melting and reforming.

The hand sticking out of Jenny was covered in a gray exoskeleton, and Sat'en emerged from inside Jenny.

"You!" spat Adonai.

"Salutations," she said. With a savage cry, she sank her teeth into Adonai's neck, the darkness of his body melting, and Jenny flew away as they both erupted into light and color and flame.

What is she doing?! she screamed internally, flapping midair. *Is she sacrificing herself?*

Don't let it go to waste! cried Susan.

Jibra'il flickered throughout her. *I must go as well. I must do my part alongside her.*

"No! I . . . I need you guys with me," Jenny said, frantically searching for the last pillar. For the old woman death.

What you need is time. Before Jenny could say anything else, Jibra'il evaporated off her skin, and again, her power dropped substantially as the angel, still riddled with holes, flew toward the battling Adonai and Sat'en. There was only a lingering thought of him left. *Please take care of my child and all the children of the angels.*

Screaming and gnashing her teeth, Jenny scanned the deaths around her. The shadowy silhouettes were still attacking them, but each one of them seemed to be struggling now. Some melted as they ran. Some splashed into nonexistence as they ate, the death beneath them scrambling away. And then, sparkling in the distance, she saw the pillar and the group of deaths huddling around it for safety. She tucked her wings—now red instead of silver, but the colorful flames still emanating from her back—and dove toward the pillar before landing with a crash.

The old woman greeted her. She was weeping, bleeding all over. And she seemed so familiar, the tug on Jenny's heart almost too much to bear, but the woman didn't say a word. She stumbled into Jenny and *dissolved* into her, a thought rising to the surface as more and more deaths reached for her.

I feel safe with you.

Tears flowed down Jenny's cheeks as they came, rushing away from the dark silhouettes, from the explosions of Adonai's fight, reaching for her, filling her once again with power.

"*NOOOO!*" bellowed Adonai from across the world.

Lightning shivered through the air. Jenny could sense Jibra'il and Sat'en struggling to hold him down, and as more deaths flowed into Jenny, she felt Jibra'il waver. Adonai ripped through the silver angel, pulling him apart and absorbing his light.

A cry of frustration filled Jenny's throat, but she placed her hands on the pillar in front of her, deaths still flooding into her, bolstering her with each passing moment, with each passing heartbeat. She felt Sat'en be ripped apart, splattering into a mess of blood and flesh.

Adonai tore across the world. The ground split open. The sky burst inward. The entire world shook apart and came together as a furious wind swept across the surface, carrying every last one of the remaining deaths into Jenny.

She channeled all the light she could muster through the final pillar and tore it open, unleashing the death inside.

CHAPTER FIFTY-THREE

WHAT IT MEANS TO DIE

The pillar melted away, dissolving into glowing light. Silence rang through the world, as all the screaming and crying had emptied into Jenny. All that was left was the child with no face sitting in the ground.

Death (Level 0)

The death of Adonai.

It didn't speak. All it did was shake. Its mouth opened and shut as though it was trying and failing to communicate.

Adonai stumbled to a stop behind her. "I . . . have a death?" he whispered. "I can die? But I am . . . everything. I am all. I am the creator . . ."

Every few moments, his entire body separated again, turning into several partial bodies connected by that thick black goo before converging again into a random human form. Stars kept rising to the surface of his skin and collapsing, falling back and away. Planets whirled around his face.

Jenny picked up the death, carrying it in her arms so that its arms and legs swung loose, its head nestled against her chest, then stood, turning to face Adonai.

He stared back, the rage gone. All that was left was fear. All he had left was shame. And wasn't that the source of all his desires? Wasn't that the source of her own suffering? Her mother's? Everyone's? A fear of the unknown. Shame for what they've done, for what they should've done and failed to. Fear and shame intertwined through all the worlds, allowing people to be gathered and collected, herded to follow the will of the creature with the most shame and fear in all of existence.

"You're pathetic, aren't you?" whispered Jenny, holding out her arms, offering Adonai's death to him.

Adonai shuddered. Darkness shot away from his body, strands dripping with ooze before collapsing back into himself. "I am the universe," he whimpered. "I am everything and everyone. I am . . ."

"You're just like my mother," she said as Adonai accepted his death and stumbled back, clutching the little creature and stroking its hair. "You're just like all those shitty rulers and corrupt losers and angry people. You always want too much. You want everything to go your way. And when things don't, you take it out on everyone else."

Adonai dropped to his knees, the world crumbling around all of them. In the distance, Jenny could see Sat'en's lifeless body—torn to bits—floating in the shifting salt as the world dissolved. Something shifted and bubbled on Adonai's back, and Eve's face, pinched up and red, sprouted from his flesh. She opened her mouth, gasping a lungful of air, eyes turning to find Jenny before the darkness washed over and buried her again.

Other faces emerged. Some from his arms. Some from his sides. Even on his scalp. People. Animals. Angels. Souls. Their notifications flickered through her head, and she stood witness, time coming to a stop, as all of existence was split between the two of them.

The world was gone. The *worlds* were gone. They weren't in the gooey darkness that Adonai had turned the warm light between worlds into. They weren't in the light either. It was just . . . emptiness. This was the Emptiness, wasn't it?

"So, what now?" asked Jenny. She was brimming with so much power she thought she could fight forever. Without stop. Without fail. They were balanced in a strange way; neither of them would lose. But neither of them could win. With all the deaths and demons, with the Leviathan, Jenny could never be defeated, even if she couldn't kill him.

Adonai quivered. "I don't know what to do now . . ."

Something inside Jenny snapped, twisted with rage and sorrow. "THAT'S THE WHOLE POINT, ISN'T IT?"

"What?"

"*That's* what we all struggle with. We all are born not having a *fucking clue* what to do. We just try. We try to do what's right. We try to be happy. We try to help others be happy. ISN'T THAT THE ENTIRE POINT? FIGURING IT THE FUCK OUT?"

She saw him clench his teeth. Saw the tears streaming down every face that rose and drowned from within his grotesque body. He was shaking, and the death he was holding—his death—was shaking.

"I do not accept," he growled. Then, he leaned down, the gooey darkness of his head separating like the jaws of an enormous lizard, and snapped his death up, swallowing it whole. Adonai turned—his face melting, all the faces melting—and burst outward like the Big Bang. Except, instead of light, it was nothing but complete and utter darkness.

"No!" shouted Jenny, lunging forward, radiating all the light—all the flame—she carried inside, swimming against the current of darkness. She held her arm up, aching and struggling, every step feeling as though she was carrying the weight of the entire universe. She kept thinking about her mother. She kept thinking about Susan. She kept thinking about Jibra'il and Sat'en and their loved ones. She felt the love of every being contained within her. The demons. The deaths. The young angels. The Leviathan, who was born out here in the nothingness; the nothingness that was now flooding with Adonai.

And then, her hand bumped into something, her fingers curled into a fist, and she yanked.

From the darkness, a silhouette came loose, knocking into her. She pulled it into her arms, a melting mass of darkness so heavy that she thought she would collapse just trying to contain it. And then, she did the only thing she could think to do. She pressed her lips against it and sucked it into her mouth with a powerful *Slurp!*

She began to chew and chew and chew, swallowing greedily, feeling everything become a part of her too. And something changed. Something became everything, and everything became nothing, and—

I learned how to be okay.

In the beginning, I am the gaping void itself.

Light escapes my lips, followed quickly by dust and energy. Gravity shudders through me, and I projectile vomit the universe across the abyss.

I splatter onto the nothingness. I drift apart, infusing my essence into every little atom struggling for uniqueness. There is a strong desire to coalesce, but an even stronger yearning for chaos. For escape.

Gravity guides me, binds me. It assembles me into planets, plucking stars and moons from my shape. I cough up asteroids. I touch myself and stir solar storms. I moan. I laugh. I scream. I die.

Emptiness folds and contracts around my spinning forms. When I reach out, it does not reach back, and I am left with an eternal longing. Billions of years slip now. I separate the heavens into various worlds, populating them with flame, with light, with love, with fear. I watch existence expand and contract. I watch nothing come to pass.

But no matter how many systems blossom and collapse, I do not understand what I long for. I only know that the act of seeking causes density, and I descend into a planet, into myself, and crash.

At first, all I see is blurry darkness. Shadows moving through water. There are others, but they, like me, are senseless. My insides take shape after countless years in these dark, turbulent depths. I start to feel with my skin. Direction begins to take shape, and this gives me reason.

When I am ready, I swim to the surface and take my first breath.

On the shore, I feel the agony of the sun. I am exposed. I sink into dirt and take root to gather my bearings. I cling to minerals and suckle on rainwater and reach for the sun. I steal its energy. I spread myself as far as I can. I come to understand the land and all that inhabits it. The roots, the fur, the teeth. Lust and hunger become my closest companions, and I change further still.

Life rises and falls. The planet changes. I stand on two legs and wonder if I am beautiful. This is the form I settle on; a familiar form that gives my thoughts more shape than ever before. I remember to call myself human.

I build civilizations. I hunt to satisfy my needs. I fuck to satisfy my wants. I give birth. I plunder and torture. I chew bones to dust.

I hurt. I love and hate my way around entire continents, wrapping myself around the world. Bliss and power tug me in every direction, and I surrender to humanity.

I make bribes and plunder and assassinate. I sleep in the dirt when my house is burned down. I take wives from conquered people. I give sons away to be wed. Foreigners claim my body against my will. I write books and paint the night sky and hang from nooses.

It becomes a game of cat and mouse. I chase myself; I find myself. I become too many. I see too many. And they are all me.

Me, always me.

Yet, I hurt them (me) still.

I love them (me).

I feel that it is strange to love myself with all my being yet still hurt myself. I forget that lesson time after time. I worship someone else. I idolize ideas written by another person, only to realize that I am the idea; I am the author, the creator. I am the person praying to myself, begging myself for salvation.

I ricochet across history. Sometimes, I am five years old and snatched off a busy street and thrown into a cargo shipment. Then, I am the decrepit creature purchasing the child. Then, I am the officer drinking herself to unconsciousness after discovering the child's body.

I bury my infant daughters in unmarked dunes. I am placed naked on sacred stones, my throat slit so that my virgin blood may spill from the altar. I am told the sun will not rise without my offering. I am the sun.

I collapse from heart failure. I revive patients after hours of surgery. I eat my fellow passengers after a plane crash strands us on an uncharted island.

Some things are happy. I die peacefully in my sleep with loved ones at my bedside. Other times, I am cut to pieces in the dark. Always, I am born, I forget, then I die and remember, only for the void to regurgitate me and renew the process. I tell stories. I invent new ways to capture light. I explore the unknown. I drown in my bathtub.

I am alive. Vibrant. I am most alive when I forget. When I am not one of you. You are real, with thoughts of your own, aren't you? Real living beings. Individuals to fall in love with and hate and learn from. Please tell me I'm not alone.

Life is addicting. It is a new adventure every single time I grow frustrated with where I am. I simply turn the page.

The change of pace leaves behind the pace of change. I meet myself when I am not myself. Over and over. I encounter new thoughts and wants and fears, and yet, it is all more of the same. Comforting. Disorienting. Heartbreaking.

What happens when I run out? When there are no more bodies to become? When I have no more patience or willpower or desire? When I am done?

I have seen matter crumble. I have seen stars fold. I know I am not only human but angel and demon and all else in between.

I know I am finite.

I know that I can never know forever.

And I know how I end.

I know my final life.

She walks the streets of New York City in the 21st century. Her mind is swollen with grand dreams and stubborn naivety. Anxiety builds nests up and down her spine, yet she still dreams of exploring worlds beyond her fingertips.

She wants to see the planet from afar, if only to prove it exists, drifting through the quiet. She wants to be safe. She is fragile, even though she hates to admit it. To make up for her shortcomings, she tries to love as hard as she can, and feels sick when infiltrated by ugly feelings of bitterness and anger. She hates everyone, she says, but I know her. I am her. She believes there is good in every being, no matter how deep it is buried. She knows something I refused to admit: that we are all made of the same star stuff I spit up in the beginning.

She struggles. The world is cruel and breaks her. It (I) drag her by her ankles into bed and pummel her till she is bruised and sobbing. Till she can't utter a coherent syllable. Till I make her mine in the worst possible way, knowing that I will cling to her (myself) for the rest of her life.

Sometimes, she convinces herself it has only made her stronger. That she can see the cracks in reality because she herself is cracked. So, she tries to fill herself with light, with warmth and fantasies. She says it is similar to the art of repairing broken pottery with gold. I began that tradition. I littered history with the art she loves; I destroyed history. So why do I falter now?

This life, her life, should be simple. There are many worse lives to live. She should have been simple. I am burgeoning with life. I have so much life to give. So why?

This life is the same as countless others. I have already lived through these troubles. I know this life.

But I struggle to access her. She grounds me, and I am stuck between lives. Hundreds of trillions of lives I have lived!

Every caveman, every martyr. Every concubine, every ruler. I am the French bourgeoisie waiting on the guillotine to fall. I am the blind girl on the village road holding a tin canister and begging for coin. I am every angel gracing the night sky. I am the demons building shelter inside forests. I am the fish. I am the ants. I am the spiders and the fungi and the viral infections.

I build the pyramids with my bare hands. I tear down cities with fire and ash. I fall from the skies like rain. I am the rain.

I take lovers from the stars. I grow to monstrous sizes. I slaughter trillions. I give birth to trillions more.

I keep finding myself becoming human. More and more human. I topple civilizations. I crown new kings. I make sacrifices to goddesses. I grow addicted to substances. I attack strangers. I fall in love.

I fly to distant galaxies and back. I suffocate in coal mines. I bite off my tongue and drown in my blood on slave ships. I starve to death.

I sail across a storm to plunder. I miscarry children. I raise money to help the impoverished. I force a desperate woman into carrying my seed. I convince men to kill one another. I lie and cheat and steal. I dig every single grave there ever is.

I lose control. I am lost. Over and over. And yet, this life. Her life.

I lose certainty. I lose the flow of time. I want to return to how I existed before the universe spat me out. She is all that remains. There is no more time left. I finally understand fear.

This is the fear that controls all beings, all living things, all matter. Death. The end. It comes for us all.

I am sinking.

I am falling.

What am I? Who am I?

Why?

Why is any of this? I didn't want this. If I stay here, I will . . . die?

I won't die. I can't die. I've already died so many times.

But where am I?

How many more lives must I live?

Why am I stuck inside *this* life of all lives?

I want to scream. I want to die. I want to be born again. Get me out of here!

This girl . . . Jenny Huang. A crush on her friend. I should ask her to prom. Why can't I ask her to prom? It would be so easy. I like her so much. But what if . . . What if she doesn't like me back?

I can't hold on to this. The uncertainty is gutting me. She feels these things too strongly. They all do. How am I meant to continue? I see her mother; angry, ferocious, driven mad with fear and shame and rage—and I am her. I can see through her eyes. I can see through too many eyes; I am so tired.

Why? Why am I here?

I don't want to be alone.

Please. Won't you . . . just love me?

And then I remember. And I shudder. I inhale for what feels like the first time in forever, and I do what I know I had to do since this all started. Since I became this, all of this.

I just have to let go.

I wasn't meant to hang on. None of these lives can hold on to their lives, can they? I just have to live them to the best of my ability. I just have to accept whatever happens will happen. And I just have to do my best.

With a shudder, I snap back to the start. I ignite and I burst open, waiting for when I'll be born. When she'll be born. And I know it'll hurt. It'll hurt so much, won't it? But I . . .

Not me.

I won't be *I* anymore.

She will have the strength to go on.

CHAPTER FIFTY-FOUR

JOY

When Jenny opened her eyes, she found herself standing alone. The ground beneath her felt fluffy and cold, and it took her a second to realize she was barefoot. She was naked. The armor was gone. Her wings. The flames. Everything was gone. There were no more voices in her head. No angels, no demons. Not even Susan. It was just her now. Alone. Naked. Standing atop of what must be a cloud.

Above her was the night sky—and it looked properly like the night sky, twinkling little lights scattered across the dark. It wasn't exploding with colors and light or anything like that. It was calm. Gentle and serene. She sucked in a deep, cool breath, filling her lungs with the pleasant air.

Memories stirred behind her eyes when she shut her eyelids. Horrible things. Beautiful things. Too many things. And then, a voice came to her, drifting through her like a gentle, pleasant breeze.

Green light shimmered into view, and standing before her was an angel. There was no notification in her head. No message. Nothing. But Jenny knew the creature was an angel by the name of Rafa'el. She couldn't help but smile; she wasn't sure why.

"Hello," greeted Jenny.

Rafa'el bowed her head. She wasn't as gigantic as she'd been before, but she was still twice Jenny's height. "Hello."

"I think I killed God."

"I would not worry about that," said Rafa'el. "There will be plenty more gods to come."

"So, what happens now?" Jenny looked around, seeing nothing but the empty surface of the cloud. "Is it . . . over? Am I dead?"

"I believe you have restored the worlds to their proper order," answered the angel, lifting an arm, her dress flowing around her. She placed it on Jenny's head. "Who should have thought the answer would come from a human?"

"The answer?"

"You are still alive, Jenny Huang. The tablet sings your praise."

"But I don't know what I did," she said, frowning.

The angel only smiled, silver light flashing around her. "The worlds can grow again. Can you not feel it? The excitement? The wonder? You have restored a certain magic back to existence. You have brought light to the darkness."

"I . . ." Jenny swallowed hard, not following at all what the angel was saying. "I'm really tired of you guys and your riddles."

Rafa'el laughed, then she wiped away a tear. "Look to the stars, Jenny Huang. What do you see?"

"Stars," she replied.

"Look closer."

Jenny squinted. She realized she no longer had the vision she once did. She didn't have the physical strength nor the abilities. Her fists clenched, but there was no hatchet to summon. No exoskeleton to burst out of her belly button. No tentacles. But she did as the angel asked and squinted hard, straining to see.

And as she did so, the stars seemed to move closer, drifting down toward her. She realized what they were.

Angel eggs, hovering right above them. They weren't stars at all.

One of them in particular drifted lower and lower, till Rafa'el could reach up and pluck it with her glowing green fingers. Cupping the egg, she stepped closer to Jenny and lowered her hands. "See?"

Tears ran down Jenny's cheeks as she stared at the silvery green egg. And she remembered. She remembered so much that it hurt. She remembered Jibra'il, who'd stood by her. Sat'en. Iblis. She remembered Susan and Miriam inside her, boosting her power, keeping her company through so much. She remembered fighting and fighting and fighting . . .

She covered her face with her hands and shook. She remembered Yeshua. Eve. Her mother and Oliver and everyone else.

She remembered Adonai.

She remembered eating him.

Her hand flitted to her stomach, and she looked up at Rafa'el. "What happened to everyone?"

"Well," started the angel, raising the egg back into the air and letting it drift away with the others. Back to being stars in the sky. "The one you called

God is no longer among us, scattered across the cosmos. The others . . . I am sorry to say that Death is an aspect of existence that cannot be undone."

"So . . . Susan?" whispered Jenny. "She's still . . . ?"

Rafa'el nodded.

Jenny's lips quivered, and she buried her fingernails in her palms.

"Everyone awaits in the material world. In stasis."

"What do you mean?"

"You reignited the Big Bang. You separated everything into the worlds again. Once you return to your world, all will return to being."

"But how are you here, then?" asked Jenny.

Rafa'el raised her hand. Light shone briefly before flickering with black lightning, and the horn appeared on her palm. She held it out for Jenny, as though offering it to her, and when Jenny shook her head no, the angel smiled again. She turned her hand, letting the horn fall through the cloud.

"The demons are awake. And after the flame comes the light. And from the light and the flame . . . comes matter. Slowly but surely, energy is returning to the worlds, no longer kept captive to fuel one being's desires."

"So . . . it's all over, then?"

"It appears to be," said the angel. "I unfortunately do not know the answer to what is next. I am only here to write, to transcribe it all. And to thank you."

The angel moved closer, and suddenly, Jenny was enveloped in the green glow, a pleasant feeling of warmth. The scent of flowers surrounded her. She shut her eyes and relaxed. She welcomed the angel's embrace. Then, she felt her feet slip through the cloud. Before she could say goodbye, before she could ask if she would ever see the angels again, Jenny slipped away and fell.

Light trailed behind her as she dropped away from the cloud. The world was bright and full of colors swimming every which way through the air. She turned, tears blurring her vision. They were angels. All of them were angels. And there was no more darkness tearing a hole through the world. But something else was waiting—a sliver of golden light, colors of every shade swirling through it. A passageway waiting for her.

Jenny fell toward it, letting her arms trail, letting the wind batter her hair and face, and she laughed with joy—pure, unfiltered joy—as she splashed into the inviting light.

CHAPTER FIFTY-FIVE

SUSAN'S DEATH

When Jenny emerged from the light, she found herself standing inside the ruins of her high school cafeteria. She shuddered as the light closed shut beneath her feet, leaving her in near complete darkness. There were holes in the ceiling. All the windows were shattered along the opposite wall, brightness from outside leaking through the dark space. But it looked like a section of the school had collapsed, blocking most of the light. Jenny hugged herself.

She was naked.

Trying to create armor, or maybe some clothes, she reached for the guidance system. But there was no response. There were no notifications in her head. No headache. No strange presence. Nothing. She didn't know whether to laugh or cry, and she rubbed her arms, feeling a chill on the breeze.

A moment later, she saw a glow coming from the center of the cafeteria. A source of light, as though someone had turned on a phone. It was past the upturned cafeteria tables and the burned sections of the broken pillars, and then, she knew what the light was coming from. A silhouette. A person, glowing in the dark. Susan.

With her arms folded behind her back, Susan was standing over something, and she turned as Jenny approached. She smiled at Jenny; a shy smile.

And as much as Jenny wanted to return that smile, there was a lump struggling up her throat. She didn't bother covering her chest or trying to hide the fact that she wasn't wearing anything. She figured they'd shared so much, been through so much, that it didn't matter at all at this point. But a part of her still felt so nervous, so shy.

She crossed the cleared cafeteria floor, eyeing the destruction, remembering all the fighting that had taken place here. Dead bodies littered the space around her. Burned-out husks of chrysalises lay stuck against rubble. There were even dead tarnished and wretched angels, their grotesque forms limp and lifeless.

She also spotted the desecrated angel—the first one that Jenny had fought—lying on the floor beneath a collapsed section of the ceiling. Its enormous arms were stuck to the floor with dried blood.

"You know I killed that thing, right?" said Susan.

Jenny stopped in front of her, looking at the enormous creature. "Really?"

She almost wanted to laugh, feeling awkward and shy. She somewhat folded her hands over her navel, unable to look Susan in the eye. So, she glanced down and almost flinched, realizing that Susan was standing next to her own body.

She was still dressed in that bloodstained blue armor she'd made, her blue hair covered in dust, her dried-out eyes staring up at the ceiling. A chunk of her throat missing.

Jenny couldn't help but cry, remembering the first few moments of the survival challenge, when she'd saved Susan from that first tarnished angel, killing it with a hole puncher. When the two of them were too afraid to leave their English classroom. When she'd sworn she'd protect Susan.

"I felt everything you did, by the way," spoke Susan, her voice low and quiet. She stepped over her own body and walked over till they were face-to-face. She took Jenny's face in her hands and lifted her head. "I was inside you, remember?"

Jenny bit her bottom lip, trying and failing to stop crying as she looked into Susan's brown eyes. As she stared at Susan's brown hair. As she wanted so badly to press her lips against Susan's and beg for forgiveness. Susan was so cold to the touch, her skin the temperature of ice, and Jenny flashed back to when she'd marched through the world of souls, when she'd seen the nightmare of Azra'il's afterlife. "So, what happens now?"

"I don't really know," she whispered. "I guess I'm dead?"

Jenny squeezed her eyes shut tight. "I'm sorry."

"I know," said Susan. "I know." She leaned forward till their foreheads touched, and they stayed like that for a long while.

Everything was quiet and calm. They moved closer, and Jenny wrapped her arms around her. Susan's fingers trailed down Jenny's back, and they pressed their bodies together. Susan felt so cold; Jenny was shivering, her shoulders shaking. She hoped her warmth wasn't bothering Susan. She hoped they could stay like this forever, a body and a soul.

But then, they heard voices. Other sources of light appeared, and Jenny and Susan looked around to find several more glowing forms. Just like Susan, they were all souls, wandering the cafeteria in confusion. Staring at the bodies. At the dead angels. Blinking at Jenny, as she was the only one who wasn't dead.

She recognized most of their faces. They were all people from her school: students and teachers and aides. She even saw Miriam slinking back in one corner near the janitor's closet—where the adjacent wall was completely demolished—hugging herself.

"So, you had a crush on me, huh?" said Susan, drawing Jenny's attention back to her.

Jenny's hand trailed down the length of Susan's arm, and she looked away, not able to hold her gaze. "Yeah."

"Yeah," repeated Susan with a soft laugh. "I kinda thought you did, too."

"I know," said Jenny. "I was inside your head too, remember?"

Susan's face reddened. Her entire form shimmered for a second, flickering like a screen struggling to stay on. She looked frightened for a second. She looked sad. But then, she smiled. "You know, I forgot how much I used to like my brown hair."

Jenny blinked away tears. Susan only smiled because she'd seen the look on Jenny's face. Jenny knew they were both thinking it: How much time did they have left? "I liked the blue," said Jenny with a sob.

Susan opened her mouth to respond, but then, she clenched her entire body. Tears spilled from the corners of her eyes.

"And," continued Jenny, reaching up to touch Susan's hair. To tuck a strand behind Susan's ear. "I liked you too. I liked you a lot. I wanted to ask you out to prom."

"Really?" whispered Susan, biting her bottom lip. She laughed and shook her head. "You know I was dating Kevin, right?"

"Oh, who cares about Kevin."

"Fuck Kevin," she agreed with a laugh. She pressed her forehead against Jenny's again. "Would've said yes. I would've totally said yes."

"You're just saying that," said Jenny, crying openly now as she pulled Susan into a tight hug again. She refused to let go. She couldn't tell which one of them was shaking that hard.

After a while, as Susan stroked Jenny's hair, she asked, "Do you think we would've made it as a couple? Like, if we tried it out and . . ."

"I think we'd just try," said Jenny, burying her face in the crook of Susan's shoulder. "And I think we would've had so much fun figuring it out because that's the best thing about loving someone."

"When did you get so wise?"

"When I killed God," replied Jenny.

Susan leaned back, breaking away from their hug, eyes wide with wonder. And then, they both burst out laughing. They laughed so hard they almost didn't hear the footsteps approaching, but Susan went quiet all of a sudden and looked past Jenny.

Jenny turned to see a familiar face—the old woman from the world of deaths. The one who had guided Jenny to the last pillar of salt. The one who had seemed so familiar, so kind. She was walking toward them, her wrinkled face smiling warmly. She was garbed in a purple robe—the robe Yeshua had fitted so many deaths with—and something about her seemed regal. There were other deaths, too, each one wearing the same purple robe, and she wondered if Yeshua was out there in the world of death, feeding and clothing them.

The woman didn't say a word, but she walked over to Susan and placed her hand on Susan's shoulder. She beamed at Jenny.

And Jenny knew who she was. She knew by the way Susan looked at the woman with such love. Such longing. She knew by the way they fit together so perfectly.

The old woman was Susan's death.

Jenny wiped her face. She couldn't breathe. Her heart was pounding so hard in her chest she was sure her entire body shuddered with each beat. She looked at Susan, who was smiling at the old woman.

"So you're my death?" she whispered.

The old woman nodded, her kind smile never wavering.

"No," said Jenny. "No. Can't you stay? Can't you just stick around a bit longer?" She reached forward and grabbed the old woman's arm. "Please? Please, let her stay?"

The death shook her head and gently removed Jenny's hand from her arm. And Susan reached out to wipe Jenny's face. "I think it's time, Jenny."

"No," sobbed Jenny. "No. Just possess me again. You can stay inside me for the rest of my life too."

Susan chuckled, smiling even as tears streamed down her cheeks. "It's alright, you know? It's been alright. We did so much."

Jenny grabbed Susan's hand and held it against her cheek. "We finally . . . I just . . ."

"I'm glad I got to meet you. Know you. I'm glad we spent all those late nights gaming. Thank you for being my friend."

"No," sputtered Jenny. "No. No. Not after all that. Not after everything. We did so much. It's not fair."

"I know," exhaled Susan. "I know. It's not fair." Jenny could tell she was trying to be strong, trying to be brave, but Jenny wanted everything right then. All of it. The tears. The laughs. The love. Every single thing. She wanted everything from this life with Susan.

"Please don't go."

"I . . ." Susan started, like she was going to say something else. But she fell forward into Jenny's arms, crying and sobbing loudly. "I don't want to go just yet. I always thought . . . you know. We'd grow old and still hang out and do stuff. And maybe . . . Maybe we could've been an *us*, right? Just . . ."

Jenny couldn't respond. She was choking. Every breath felt like she was stealing a moment from Susan's life. This was all her fault. It was her fault that Susan was dying. Her fault.

And then, in her arms, Susan began to fade, her light dimming. The old woman nodded toward Jenny and began to fade, too.

Susan looked back at her death, eyes wide with shock. Her breaths came shallow and quick, and she grabbed Jenny's hand. "I . . . I'm . . ."

"I'll find you," said Jenny, squeezing her hand back. "It'll be okay. I promise. Whatever happens, I'll find you. I'll . . ."

"You have to, okay?" said Susan. She looked down at her body as she faded again before coming back. She spoke quickly, hurriedly. "But not anytime soon. Once you've lived your life. Once you've done all the things you always told me you wanted to do."

"I will. I promise."

"You gotta tell me everything. Every last detail. Okay? I want to know everything about your life."

"Susan, I . . ."

"I'll see you in the other world, Jenny," whispered Susan. Her light faded again, and for a second, she was completely gone. But then she came back. Her death was shining brighter and brighter. "I'm . . ."

"I love you," blurted out Jenny, pressing her lips against Susan's.

For a moment, Susan didn't kiss her back. Jenny wasn't even sure if she was kissing correctly. All she'd done was press her lips against Susan's. She could feel Susan's surprise, her shock. And then, she felt a pressure against her lips too, a warmth rising to her cheeks. And when they broke away, her heart pounded in her chest, and despite the coldness of Susan's soul, everything felt flushed with heat.

"Jenny?" whispered Susan softly, their noses still touching. She came in for another kiss, holding it for a long time. "I love—"

And then, she was gone, the coldness gone with her. The old woman had vanished, and Jenny waited for a minute, several minutes, hoping Susan would fade back into her arms. Tears dripped off her chin as she stared around at the other souls. They all were crying too, holding on to their deaths as their lights faded and blurred. She caught a glimpse of Miriam, who was sitting on the floor now, hugging her knees. Next to her was a young girl with braided hair, beaming with joy and patting Miriam's head. They faded away together, as did all the other souls and deaths, and Jenny was left completely alone in the dark, shivering.

Jenny knelt and pressed her lips to Susan's corpse. She stroked the dirty blue hair and shut her eyes. She ran her fingers over the horrible wound in her throat, shuddering as she remembered biting her. Remembered the burst of flavor. How delicious it was. She remembered her death, cowering in front of her cross, apologizing.

"It was my fault," she told herself, hoping her death could hear her. What would happen when she died? Would her death come to pick her up, too? But she'd eaten her death, hadn't she?

Or had everything been reset? Her memory was hazy after Adonai's collapse.

She sat next to Susan's corpse for a long time, just trying to remember everything, wondering what she would do next. She couldn't move. She couldn't bring herself to leave. She could've stayed there forever, alone in the dark. But then, a cry broke through the silence—a baby's wail, shrieking at the top of its lungs.

Wiping away tears, Jenny squeezed Susan's cold, dead hands one more time before standing. She looked around, trying to find the source of the crying, and made her way through the debris, stepping over the other corpses. She wondered if it was an angel baby. Were they still around? Or was it some other monster?

She found it tucked in a corner beside a collapsed vending machine. It was lying on top of what looked like scraps of her red exoskeleton. A baby, naked, its pudgy arms and legs kicking as it cried.

And even though it looked like all newborn babies, wrinkled and tiny and strange, Jenny knew right away who it was.

"Eve?" she whispered, laughing incredulously as she knelt and scooped the baby up. Was this the baby she'd given birth to? Before it grew rapidly with light and turned into a fully grown adult?

The baby squirmed and struggled, but stopped shrieking when Jenny nestled her against her chest. Its crying settled down to a gentle murmuring, blowing bubbles from its lips. It smushed its face against Jenny's skin before looking up at her with bright black eyes. Her eyes.

For a second, Jenny saw her death, the little boy, staring up at her again, begging her to love him. She could see herself raising the baby, raising Eve, and she wondered if Eve's consciousness was still in there. The being she'd once thought was some supernatural force beyond this world; a godly entity that had appeared to her in the form of a three-headed figure.

But as she looked into its eyes, she felt something else. Something strange. A pressure that started in the back of her mind and pushed its way to the front, gathering right between her eyes. With a soft cry, she felt a notification surface between her thoughts, a thought that wasn't her own thought, and she almost dropped the baby.

The Guidance System has been initiated.
Jenny Huang
Human (Level 1)

The streets of the city were flooded with too many people, way more than usual, and Jenny wished so badly that Susan were with her. They could complain about tourists. They could be rude to the gaggle of obnoxious students who'd stop to take selfies and make too much noise. But of course, nobody was being rude; nobody was in the way. Most of them were naked. Most of them were deaths wearing purple robes and guiding glowing souls to the next life.

Souls crowded around Jenny as she walked down the street away from her ruined high school. She was carrying the baby. Someone kind had draped a towel over her shoulders. Trucks had rolled up with supplies, and people were trying to help. But most people were weeping. Some for joy. Some for loss. Jenny didn't care. Couldn't care.

As far as she could tell, nobody else had the system in their heads. She got plenty of notifications: Souls. Deaths. And everyone else registered only as Humans. There were no levels. No stages. Nothing.

Did this mean what she thought it meant? She looked down at Eve, wondering if something had remained with her when she'd been turned into a baby. When the universe had been reset. When she'd brought existence back into being.

Or was it because Eve had taken something from Jenny so long ago? And now that it had been returned to her, she could access the system again?

Her heart was beating. And then, it skipped a beat when she heard her name shouted. She turned to see her mother pushing past people and deaths, tears streaming down her face. She was a human. She was alive.

Nancy ran up to Jenny and stopped, red in the face and out of breath. Then, she caught sight of the baby in Jenny's arms.

Jenny smiled. After everything, it was nice to see her mother. And she realized she was finally ready to accept her mother's love. That she could accept the efforts her mother had made in trying to be a better parent after remarrying.

She just didn't know if she could forgive yet. Maybe with time. Maybe with space.

She handed Eve, the little baby kicking and crying, over to her mother. "Here," said Jenny. "She is my daughter. Probably. But she'll grow up to look just like me. You can try again, alright?"

"What?" whispered her mother, gently rocking the baby in her arms, staring at Jenny. "What do you mean? Where are you going?"

Jenny was already turning away. "I'm not really sure, Mom. But it's going to be alright. Take care of her."

"Jenny?" called her mother, her voice rising in pitch. The crowd around her shimmered with light as souls and deaths coupled together and rose into the sky.

"Her name's Eve!" shouted Jenny. "Love you." Then she stepped into the crowd, wrapping the blanket tightly around her. Her heart thudded with excitement. For the first time in her entire life, she felt absolutely and completely free. She even had the system still in her head. She could do so much. Could grow strong again.

Maybe she could find a way to the world of souls? Or whatever the world had become. Maybe she could find Rafa'el. She didn't know. She didn't have any of her old abilities. She didn't have her boosted stats anymore. She was starting again from square one.

But she knew what she was going to do with this second chance. This new lease on her life.

She was going to live the hell out of it.

About the Author

Tess C. Foxes has haunted New York City all of her life. She loves beaches on rainy days, reading stories until four in the morning, and munching on too many hazelnut snacks. She dreams of living in a cabin on a seaside cliff one day, but for now, she jots down all of her anxieties and wishful thoughts as best she can.

RESPAWN YOUR CURIOSITY

follow us on our socials

 podiumentertainment.com

 @podiumentertainment

 /podiumentertainment

 @podium_ent

 @podiumentertainment